The Academy
of Smoke and Mirrors

A BOARDING SCHOOL
ON THE BRINK

A NOVEL BY ALEXANDER TROY
AND JIM PARRY

ISBN 979-8-98823580-4 (Paperback)
ISBN 979-8-98823581-1 (eBook)
Library of Congress Control Number: 2023916616

Lion of Judah Press
16767 Cabreo Drive
Naples, FL 34110

AUTHORS' NOTE

This novel is, in all respects, a work of fiction. All of its characters, the Hampton Acres Hebrew Academy, and the city of Bradleyville are imaginary. Any resemblance to actual people, living or dead, events, schools, or locales is entirely coincidental. Any references to historical events, real people, or real places are used fictitiously.

PART ONE

"I put this school where nobody thought this school should be. Everybody said this is crazy—you're pissing away a fortune. But I know better than those nobodies. This school will be in Bradleyville for f**king forever."

—Manny Kleinman,
Founder, Hampton Acres Hebrew Academy

"We're supposed to call it 'The Academy.' Most people call it 'HAHA.' But among the faculty, it's known as the last stop on a streetcar named Galut (exile)."

—Rachel Fish,
Dean of Academics, Hampton Acres Hebrew Academy

ONE

THE BOMB AND THE BEAST

Right up until he learned about the second bomb threat, Jeff Taylor had been feeling pretty good.

He had just gotten off the phone with the loan officer in charge of the school's mortgage and had managed, with half-truths, flattery, and some let-me-explain-what-maybe-you-don't-quite-understand, to put the man off. Jeff didn't feel good about doing this. He had done this—had *had* to do this—every three months. What he *did* feel good about was that he wouldn't have to do this ever again. For he had, mentally, just penned a final revision to his letter of resignation—inserting the word "great" in front of the word "privilege" in "a privilege and honor to have served as Head of School these past two years." Jeff was about to retype the letter, call his boss, give her the news, put the letter in an envelope, seal it, and then walk down the hall and set it on his boss's desk.

The subtext of Jeff Taylor's letter:

It might have been a good idea to put this school—Hampton Acres Hebrew Academy, America's only Jewish boarding school—on one hundred acres on the outer edge of the city of Bradleyville in central Georgia. But, turns out, this place, HAHA for short, is as screwy as Chelm, in Jewish folklore the imaginary city of wise fools. HAHA is surreal. Pieces of it break loose and float in the sky like the subjects in a Marc Chagall painting. HAHA is dysfunctional. Organizationally, psychologically, and every other which way. Especially financially.

Especially financially—that's what the loan officer suspected, and that's what Jeff had more or less convincingly denied.

It was 10:10 a.m., Monday, March 7. Six days ago, Hugh Pettiver, the loan officer at M&F National Bank in Bradleyville, had received HAHA's financial statements for the preceding three months. Given how bad they were, Jeff was surprised Hugh hadn't phoned him immediately. Maybe it had taken Hugh six days to get over the shock? In any event, this was how, starting just before ten a.m., the conversation had gone:

"Jeff, I'm looking at these numbers and I'm getting nervous. They're looking worse. You've got this balloon payment due July fifteenth."

Meaning the entire loan: Fifty million dollars.

"Right," said Jeff, "and we're going to make it."

"Yes, but last time we talked, when I talked with Sammy, she said you guys were going to get another five million in, from two big donors. I don't see it here."

Meaning Samantha Kleinman, HAHA's CEO and daughter of HAHA's founder. Sammy Kleinman, huckster and hustler in high heels. Sammy Kleinman, boss lady, Jeff's boss, who cheerfully told Jeff (but certainly not M&F Bank) that "I'm doing it with smoke and mirrors."

"Right, Hugh," said Jeff, "and you're a smart guy. You know that when a donor says he's going to give, it's not like he's signed a loan. It's not like we can sue him. We have to romance him. Trust me, these two donors will come across."

"Look, I much prefer talking to you than to Sammy. You come from real finance, I *do* trust you."

Meaning, Jeff, until two years ago you were the number two man at a Wall Street hedge fund.

"Thanks," said Jeff, "and look—for my part—I feel for you. You didn't make this loan, you inherited it. Hey"—Jeff laughed, a *we're-in-this-together* laugh—"and *I* inherited this school's financial condition."

Meaning, come July 15, with a fifty-million-dollar mortgage going tapioca, HAHA declares bankruptcy. Even if we got the fifty, we need another twenty million to give us a runway to succeed. Ain't gonna happen—we're never going to get seventy million dollars. The last day of school is June 21. And June 21 to July 15, as doom approaches, will be a horror. I am *not* going to be caught up in it. So, effective June 21, three and a half months from now, I am out of here. That's what my letter—ready for Sammy—says. And I tell her and the Board of Directors today.

"Yeah, I would never have made a fifty-million-dollar loan to a Jewish boarding school." Hugh Pettiver gave a small laugh. "Well, I guess when Manny started it . . . " He trailed off.

Manny Kleinman, Sammy's father, had founded the school with one hundred and fifty million of his own money, proudly saw it open in 2004, and dropped dead in 2011. By then, his home-building empire had collapsed, and the school was struggling. Manny had wanted sons; he had only a daughter. So he had raised Sammy as a son, raised her to take over his empire. In 2011 there was no empire to take over. But there was the school, and Sammy was determined to make *it* survive, honoring a dead but—in the very air of HAHA—a still-demanding father.

"Manny Kleinman," said Jeff. "One of a kind. I never met him but, hey, the stories."

"Yeah," agreed Hugh.

After some small talk, the phone call had ended. It was 10:06 a.m., four minutes before the second bomb threat.

Jeff had stared at the phone. He thought, The things I have to say to people. This is a shit show. I came from Wall Street with credibility. Now, as Head of this dysfunctional school, my credibility is being parceled out among Hugh Pettiver and the teachers and staff of this school, and the parents of the students of this school, and even . . .

He had looked at a framed photo on his desk: His wife, Michelle, who, come May 12th, would be dead three years. And their daughter, Jordan, seventeen, a junior at HAHA.

Even losing credibility in their eyes, thought Jeff.

He missed Michelle terribly. And he still heard her voice in his head. She had been telling him, *No, hon, you're still aces with me.* He loved the old lingo "aces with me," but he didn't believe her.

Damn.

Okay, so, come July 15, HAHA is bankrupt. Note to self: Find out how Wall Street is pricing the school's bank debt. If it's, say, ninety-five cents, the Street knows—or thinks it knows—more than I do. The Street is saying the debt will be repaid, and the school saved. But I'm guessing it's trading more like seventy cents on the dollar, and the school foreclosed.

But can HAHA even make it till the last day of school, June 21? No, it cannot.

By aspiration, Jeff had become an educator. By training, Jeff knew numbers.

The numbers:

A month ago, Jeff had started projecting, based on the school's burn rate, when the school would be out of cash. His first projection was June 15—hence the school's drop-dead date. Back then, he had created a password so he could access the school's bank balance. The password was arewebrokeyet615. 615 stood for June 15, which would get the school through graduation on May 30 but not to the end of the school year.

Since then, about once a week, Jeff had done a new projection. Each new projection showed that the burn rate was going up, and thus the drop-dead date was moving up. From June 15 to June 11, to June 5, to May 30.

A week ago, last Monday, the last time Jeff looked, the school had $3.47 million in cash. Not in M&F Bank—which is where Hugh Pettiver and M&F *wanted* the cash, so M&F could *see* what cash HAHA had—but across town in First Bradleyville Federal. This was Sammy's doing; she was no fool. Last Monday, Jeff calculated the school's burn rate was $1.24 million per month. At this rate,

HAHA would burn through its cash on May 26—before graduation. What a mess.

Now, sitting at his desktop, Jeff typed in arewebrokeyet615. He looked at the balance: $3.02 million in cash. He did a swift calculation. Yes, the burn rate was still going up; now it was $1.36 million per month. So the drop-dead date was still moving up. Now the school would run out of money on May 22.

Jeff sighed.

David Ben-Gurion, Israel's first prime minister, famously said, "In Israel, in order to be a realist you must believe in miracles." Trained by Wall Street to be a realist, Jeff believed only in realism.

Jeff couldn't do much about HAHA's numbers—Sammy (cunningly) raised money for the school, and Sammy (profligately) spent money on the school. But Jeff had tried so hard to do everything else for HAHA: to fix it organizationally, educationally, psychologically.

All this effort. I came here knowing this place needed help. I came here in part because of that. *Tikkun olam:* a Jew's obligation to repair the world, or this small part of it. My father taught European history at Rutgers; I grew up surrounded by books; learning and teaching were sacred. I made money on Wall Street, I felt I should give back—not money but myself. I think I have. I've been here nearly two full years, I've given this dysfunctional place 110 percent, and all I've accomplished is to prevent it from becoming *more* dysfunctional. So even if Sammy's smoke and mirrors somehow conjure up a couple of million soon, even if Sammy keeps this place going to June 21, I'm outta here with a clear conscience. I'm outta here June 21, outta here six days before I turn fifty, outta here with gray hairs that are only metaphorical.

And if the fifty million magically appears, and Sammy pays M&F in full July 15? This *mishegas*—craziness—is my successor's problem.

Jeff started to retype his letter of resignation effective June 21. He also started composing what his exact words would be on the phone to Sammy. Sammy was somewhere in one of the Stans (Kazakhstan?

Tajikistan? Uzbekistan?). Thus Sammy was ten hours ahead. What time is it here? 10:09 a.m., so 8:09 p.m. there.

Hey, Sammy, how's it going there? Did you have a good dinner? Listen, Sammy, I don't want to upset your honed-flat-by-many-crunches stomach but . . . *I've got an announcement for you.*

At 10:10 a.m., as Jeff was typing and composing, Clarice Dawkins walked in.

Clarice was a laid-back Black woman, a "church lady," the school receptionist, and Jeff's assistant. She announced:

"Jeff, another bomb threat. I just got off the phone with someone. I tried to keep them talking, tried to get them to say where the bomb is. If there really *is* a bomb. They—I couldn't tell if it was a man or a woman—they just kept saying, 'I'm no way fooling / You getting schooling / By a bomb.' Then they hung up."

"The same hip-hop bomber?" said Jeff.

"I think it's a hoax just like the last one. Except this was a live person. Not a robocall."

"Clarice, please, until I can get Jerome on this, keep it to yourself."

"'Course. And, Jeff, *I'm* no way fooling. When they catch this person, I'm going to wash out their mouth with lye soap. The nerve! Disturbing this fine place. A bad habit."

And she returned to her desk.

On his smartphone, Jeff called Jerome McKool, head of security.

Waiting for McKool to answer, Jeff sighed and looked out his windows. His office was in a prime spot in the Admin building and he had a fine view. Across the quad, in the morning sun, the buildings' white Jerusalem stone glowed coppery. The dogwood trees were in full bloom. The campus was, as usual, gorgeous. There was the land's natural beauty. And there were one hundred and fifty million dollars in buildings designed by a protege of I.M. Pei—Manny Kleinman had had taste.

There was much about the school that was not smoke and mirrors, much that was solid. And not just its trees and its buildings. The school took Jewish values seriously. Jeff taught these values in a class titled Jewish Thought and Culture. Kids could get a great education here. The campus felt like it was home to an extended, eccentric family. Like Anatevka, Tevye's tightknit shtetl. Anatevka hadn't made sense, living there had been as precarious as fiddling on the roof. But Tevye hadn't wanted to leave.

It was a lovely and seemingly peaceful kingdom.

Yes, one mile away was a giant pig farm, with a giant manure lagoon. But as there were thick woods between here and there, it was out of sight. And as it was to the northeast, it was downwind. No smell intruded on the kingdom.

The pigs were not a problem, but The Beast was.

Jeff thought, With this bomb threat, The Beast will be riled. The Beast will be up again, chewing at the kingdom.

TWO

BASICALLY FRIENDLY, BASICALLY NEUROTIC

The Beast was Jeff's metaphor for HAHA.

The Beast had a short temper and a short memory, a small brain and huge energy. Usually, it would be lying half-sleep, fretful, on guard, nostrils twitching, one eye open, one ear erect. Then—red alert!—something would happen to make it jump up, hyper-awake. And bolt! And slam against the furthest extent of its chain. Engaged but confused, it would lunge back and forth against its chain, roaring. Then the *something*, whatever had aroused it, would vanish. Then The Beast—which was basically friendly, which never meant and rarely did any harm—would stop, chase its own tail in a nervous circle three times, and collapse back into half-sleep. And if The Beast could talk, it would say it couldn't remember what the *something* had ever been.

But of course The Beast had people who could and did talk for it.

The Beast had one hundred and forty-five students, Jewish kids from all over the country and the world, Mexico to Malaysia. The Beast had sixty teachers, almost all of them Jewish, and a staff of fifty, a third of them Jewish. The Beast had many Jewish mothers, led by the irrepressible Rhoda Friedlander, who were ferocious advocates for their children. In the minds of its teachers, staff, students, and their mothers, HAHA was a special, precious place. A place about which they cared very, very much. So much that, when the least thing happened, the thing would instantly rile everyone, would possess the school, would generate a tizzy of texts, emails, phone calls, and intense in-person conversations. *"What do you think?!" "What do we do?!"*

The Beast was *up*, and lunging back and forth. Often, like a big, friendly St. Bernard in a small room, it was knocking down furniture.

Then somebody, usually Jeff, would do something. Take care of the *mishegas*. Or, often as not, there was nothing *to* do; the thing that triggered the tizzy would resolve itself. In either case, The Beast returned to its half-sleep.

Nice Beastie, *stay* there.

To try to get it to nod off faster, Jeff would talk to The Beast. Send reassuring emails and texts, make reassuring phone calls. In person, sweet-talk the school's seven deans and whoever else might influence The Beast. If need be, Tuesday morning, at the school-wide meeting called Project Ruach, address the students and faculty. Whenever this worked, Jeff congratulated himself.

I am The Beast Whisperer.

January second, The Beast had gotten really riled. That's when one hundred Jewish institutions across the U.S—secondary schools, colleges, major synagogues, JCCs (Jewish community centers)—received a robocall with a bomb threat: "Hey, all you Jews / Be in the news / Yeah, here is why / You're blown sky-high / By a bomb."

HAHA was one of the one hundred. Jeff's response? With Jerome McKool, he had reviewed HAHA's security measures. Finding them more than adequate, he had conveyed that well-founded (he thought) confidence to all of HAHA its teachers, staff, students, and their parents.

Then what happened? Nothing. Nothing at HAHA, nothing at any of the other Jewish institutions. Within three days, the FBI pronounced the threat a hoax. On the seventh day, having worn itself out lunging against its chain, The Beast collapsed and went back to what

Jeff thought the Pentagon would call DEFCON 5: normal readiness. Except, with The Beast, it was normal *neurotic* readiness.

So this time, Jeff looked at his letter of resignation on his laptop. Damn. With The Beast about to be up and roaring, I've got to postpone this. There is no way I can call Sammy today, no way I can *tender* this today. That would be bad optics. But certainly seven days from now. This school will be relaxed by the seventh day . . .

C'mon, Jerome, answer your phone. Let's you and me *deal* with this bomb threat. So the seven-day clock can start.

Age sixty-four, big and tall, an imposing Black man, Jerome McKool was a former Bradleyville cop. Whether sitting in his security command center at the school's entrance or patrolling the campus in a golf cart or deploying the half-dozen guys who worked for him, McKool was fazed by nothing. McKool kept a wooden matchstick in his mouth, with deliberation moved it back and forth, up and down as he worked. The man would be on the case.

Jerome answered.

Jeff told Jerome about the bomb threat. Jerome said he would call the police and let the FBI know. Jerome said, "The feds will tell us if everybody else got this call like on January second, and the cops will come with bomb-sniffing dogs like on January second. But it's probably just like January second: nothing. Still, I understand the need for good optics—we'll start searching the campus where people can see us."

Jeff agreed, and added: "Executive committee meeting at four p.m." They clicked off.

THREE

A VOICE FROM
THE GREAT BEYOND WITHIN

As soon as Jeff clicked off with Jerome, Jeff texted the school's other six deans—the other members of the school's executive committee—and told them, meeting at four p.m.

Between now and then, would the news of the bomb threat get out? Jeff answered his own question: Of course it would. At HAHA, everything leaked. So Jeff knew he should pre-empt the leak. He composed an email to all students, teachers, staff, and parents. The gist of it: There has been a bomb threat . . . yes, the police will soon be here to investigate . . . no, there appears to be no immediate danger . . . and yes, of course if you're here at the school and you see something, say something. Otherwise, continue with your usual activities.

Meaning, if you're a student cheating on a test, continue. If you're a teacher sneaking a scotch before noon, continue. If you're a janitor stealing cleaning supplies, continue. If you're a parent texting outrage over HAHA's continued failure to be included in *US News & World Report's Top 100 Boarding Schools in America*, continue.

If we interrupt our dysfunctional patterns, the terrorists have won.

Jeff's right index finger hovered over "Send."

He didn't yet press "Send."

Leaning back in his chair, he surveyed his office. He admired the view. Not for the first time, he thought:

I have this fine mahogany-paneled office whose walls display my diplomas (Yale BA, Yale JD), and plaques and framed letters of thanks from local organizations (Rotary, Hadassah, etc.), and beautiful photos of this school. Its floor is partly covered by a huge forty-thousand-dollar rug that Sammy secured from one of the Stans. I sit in a four-thousand-dollar "executive work chair" at a five-thousand-dollar cherry desk made by one of Georgia's most eminent craftsmen.

It is an office of a man in command. And I've tried to command, contrive, and convince this school to be less dysfunctional. I've failed.

Two years ago, for *tikkun olam*, I left Wall Street and a sane life in Greenwich, Connecticut. But two years ago, when I told the *Yale Alumni News* that I was taking this job, I never imagined how *much* HAHA needs repair.

While, collectively, the school was a nervous, anxious Beast, the vast majority of its students, teachers, and staff were good-hearted, even idealistic. They *cared*. Not just about the school. They cared about learning, about community, about *tikkun olam*. (And I still care.) So they deserve a great school. My heart goes out to them. Come July 15, the teachers and staff will suddenly be out of work, job-hunting at the worst possible time—after all the jobs have been filled. Except for the seniors who have graduated, the students and their parents will suddenly be school-hunting at the worst possible time—long after schools have set their rosters. But for me, it became caring about a big beautiful house for which you no sooner fix the plumbing than the electricity goes, and you no sooner fix the electricity than the furnace goes, and you no sooner fix the furnace than . . .

Still, should I reconsider? Should I stick it out all the way through July 15? Is that part of my obligation?

Jeff, hon . . .

Again, he heard Michelle's voice. He looked at the framed photo of her and Jordan. Both were lovely, both were smiling with a wry intelligence. At odd times during the day, Jeff half-summoned, half-was-hit-by, Michelle's intelligence.

Jeff, it's not just the house's plumbing, electricity, and furnace. You know the house is gonna be foreclosed. And it's not your house, it's Sammy's. When the repo men come and roll up the rugs, let them roll up Sammy inside them. Her and whatever twenty-grand Birkin bag she's carrying that day. You should be gone. And, you didn't put in 110 percent. I've done the math, you put in 120.

"Yes, ma'am," said Jeff. "Thank you, ma'am."

Now send that email.

Jeff had left their big house in Greenwich, had put miles between it and him, had come here, because the house was full of Michelle's absence. But of course she remained present in his mind.

Bracing himself for The Beast, Jeff pressed "Send."

FOUR

UPON ME, THE DELUGE

Less than a minute after Jeff pressed "Send," the deluge hit his smartphone: dozens and dozens of texts and emails and phone calls from students, teachers, staff, and parents. *Bomb threat?! Bomb?! What's happening?! What?! What?!* The first email to reach his inbox was—predictably—the steamrolling Rhoda Friedlander's: *What's your plan to protect my Ashley? My Thayer? TELL ME!*

One out of ten emails came to Jeff on parochet@haha.com. Parochet is the curtain that covers the Torah Ark. Thus parochet@ haha.com provided a curtain of anonymity. Thus here, this morning, some student or teacher was anonymously telling Jeff that the bomb threat probably came from such-and-such redneck whom *I've seen driving around in a pickup with a gunrack and an incendiary bumper sticker* . . .

Jeff answered only one missive. He texted Jordan: *Almost certainly a hoax. Don't worry.*

The Beast kept barraging him. He could hear, outside his office, The Beast was making Clarice's phone ring and ring, and Clarice was trying to cope.

Turning off his phone's ringer, Jeff put his letter of resignation in an inside pocket of his blazer. Walking out, he gave Clarice (on the phone, patient in the storm) a thumb's up, told her "Sorry about this," and headed down the hallway, toward the door.

His plan: Spare Clarice the tsunami of people about to roar in—people for whom a call, text, or email was not enough. For he had learned that a Head's calendar was written in disappearing ink. At any moment, someone would appear at his office with a request, demand, or complaint that you, Head, must know about and act upon right *now*. And this wasn't just any moment. In the view of The Beast, this was a dire moment. Dozens and dozens of students, teachers, and staff were about to appear, swamp him.

Therefore, don't be trapped behind a desk. Instead, walk the campus and, one lone man, with stride firm and head high, do what a Head does: Convey calm and confidence. With that calm and confidence, speak to the alarmed and agitated. Be The Beast Whisperer.

Halfway down the hallway, he paused at the doorway to Sammy Kleinman's office.

At the moment, unoccupied.

Sammy, age fifty and with the energy of a thirty-year-old, was roaming the world, including some of the most unlikely places, snagging Jewish students. Right now she was in one of the Stans hunting for any warm adolescent Jewish body whose parents would pay for their kid to attend HAHA. Yes, there were some rich Jews in the Stans, and some wanted their progeny—especially their sons—to get a Western and Jewish education. Tuition, room, and board were forty-eight thousand a year, but that was only a fraction of what was needed to fend off HAHA's impending doom.

Yet even halfway around the world, in the former Soviet Union, Sammy managed to keep HAHA going. A tough, smart (Columbia BA cum laude 1996), good-looking, brassy Jewish woman, she was working on tough, new-money, Jewish oligarchs. She was extracting money and children from extractive-industry kings. *Could* Sammy somehow pull off a miracle, find the fifty million to save the school?

Two springs ago, William Schwartz, Jeff's predecessor as Head of School, a pleasant, quiet man who had tried his best for five years and now was calling quits, had warned Jeff.

"Sammy's smoke and mirrors will only work for so long. Sammy needs a big benefactor. And she thinks she has one in Vegas. You know what casinos call the guys who drop millions at their tables? Whales, right? Well, Seymour Gutfreund, with his casinos, Vegas to Macau, he's worth twenty billion. So Sammy sees Gutfreund as her whale. And Sammy keeps trying to get in front of him. In person. In Vegas. Jeff, if a meeting with Moby Dick ever does get scheduled, Ms. Ahab is going to drag you out there with her. Part of your job description: harpooner."

What William Schwartz *hadn't* told Jeff: "Part of your job description is being second-guessed by Sammy."

Second-guessed in a split second. For even halfway around the world, Sammy almost immediately knew everything that went on at HAHA.

Moving on, heading for the front door, to start his Nothing-To-Worry-About Tour of the campus, Jeff thought, I've got enough trouble waiting for me outside. Sammy—leave me alone.

When Sammy was on campus, Jeff dreaded the *click-click-click* of the heels of her Christian Louboutins behind him, closing on him. And when Sammy was supposedly far away, like in the Stans, Jeff dreaded the *squeak-squeak-squeak* of her rolling suitcase behind him, closing on him, announcing *I'm b-a-a-a-ck!*

Several yentas in Bradleyville's small Jewish community were certain that Jeff and Sammy were *bashert*, destined to marry. Jeff was certain that was unthinkable. True, Sammy was a smart, good-looking, single woman. But she was also a slick, hustling sharpie, the kind of operator he hated trading with when he had worked on Wall Street. Jeff was neither sexually nor romantically attracted to her. And besides, there was someone Jeff loved.

Now he heard quick footsteps behind him, closing on him. He turned to face Clarice, who was waving her smartphone.

"Jeff, it's Sammy."

FIVE

TAJIKISTAN CALLING

"Here I am halfway around the world, capital of Tajikistan, and I hear about this bomb threat not from you, who ought to be telling me, but instead from others. I know things, Jeff—but why didn't *you* tell me?"

Samantha Kleinman was in Dushanbe, Tajikistan with her smartphone in her hand and her voice in Clarice's smartphone against Jeff's ear. Jeff knew Shakespeare said a low voice was "an excellent thing in a woman." Sammy's low voice could be an excellent weapon of rebuke.

"Well, I—" began Jeff.

"None of it surprises me—not the threat and not your silence. For years I've foreseen the need for security. That's why I've made us one of the most secure Jewish institutions in the world. The fence, the cameras, the security force led by Jerome McKool—all my doing. Now, with this threat, here's what *you* should do. You should . . . "

And Sammy proceeded to tell Jeff to do what Jeff had already done.

After insulting Jeff by telling Jeff to call McKool and call an executive committee meeting and email all students, teachers, staff, and parents, Sammy said, "And of course if you want me to call in to the executive committee meeting, reassure everyone, I'm free for the next three hours . . . "

"Gosh, Sammy, the meeting is six hours from now. Two a.m. where you are."

"And of course if you want me to reassure the students, teachers, parents . . . "

"Not necessary, Sammy. I'll handle it."

"And of course, I have a good relationship with the mayor so I'll call him . . . "

"Fine, Sammy."

"Fine? Listen Jeff, I have to tell you, you're taking this pretty *casually*, but that's not *my* modus operandi. I've been working for the Academy the last twenty-four hours straight. On planes, in and out of airports, taxis, meetings—meetings with parents, students, working my *tuchus* off, bringing in more revenue. I don't know what *you're* doing but I've just about landed the heir to the greatest fortune in Tajikistan. But I can top that."

"That's great."

"Here's the big one. I just got off the phone with Rabbi Menachem Perl in Chicago. The rabbi is sending you his thirty-year-old daughter. Tzipora. Hire her. The rabbi will thank us. You know who Rabbi Perl is, right? *Only* Seymour Gutfreund's Rebbe. *Only* the only man he listens to. It's how to finally get Gutfreund to open his wallet for us."

"Fine."

"He'll open his wallet. I know how to do this. Hit the open man."

Jeff sighed. Her junior and senior years at Columbia, Sammy had been starting point guard, women's varsity. She never tired of telling him she had great court vision, could thread a pass in anywhere, find the open teammate. Now, find millions more dollars.

Sammy told him, "Get that fifty million from Gutfreund."

"*Anything* is appreciated," said Jeff. "Even the Tajik kid's tuition. We're going to need money for the fence, for more cameras, maybe—"

"Jeff honey, hold on. I planned and oversaw all that. Do you think it's insufficient?"

"Not at all. Just that we may need to—"

"I think we need you to call Ritchie & Ravenel. In light of this bomb threat, our viability is going to be under even greater scrutiny. So schmooze 'em, soft-soap 'em, you reassure Ritchie & Ravenel that . . . "

And Sammy continued, and Jeff moved Clarice's phone further from his ear.

Ritchie & Ravenel, HAHA's accounting firm. Ritchie & Ravenel, occupying all of 900 square feet in the nearby Hungry Hollow strip mall. Ritchie & Ravenel, paid by Sammy to conceal the fragility of HAHA's finances.

Listening to Sammy, Jeff silently vowed, I am not going to further wreck my credibility by stroking those sketchy CPAs.

"Tell the accountants we're closer than ever to a big gift . . . "

As Sammy blew smoke, Jeff thought of mirrors, the funhouse kind that play tricks. I'm tall, six-two—she's short, five-four. I'm an ex-hedge fund guy dressed like a headmaster: Navy-blue blazer, repp ties. Sammy, the school's CEO, dresses like a hedge fund queen: two-thousand-dollar Michael Kors pantsuits and a gold Cartier tank watch, its gold matching her salon blow-dried-out hair. A business guy who wants to be a school leader, and a school leader who thinks she's a wheeler-dealer. What a pair.

Sammy said, "I've told the Board we're good, and the Board says they're behind us one hundred percent. Let's not disappoint them."

Ah, yes, thought Jeff, HAHA's blue-chip Board of Directors. A Board, meeting only in Manhattan, which I think is one hundred percent in one of Sammy's many Birkin bags. Sammy says, "Here's what the Board says . . . " and, for all anyone knows, she's making it up.

"And Jeff," said Sammy, "next time do *not* turn off your cellphone, do *not* force me to call Clarice to get you. Are we on the same page?"

"You bet."

"Because it is your responsibility . . . "

"So good to talk with you," said Jeff. "Now I gotta run."

Come June 21, run and not return.

Clicking off, Jeff handed the smartphone back to Clarice.

He continued on, reached the front door, looked outside, onto Emmanuel Kleinman Quad.

On most days, this was a peaceable kingdom. Beautifully manicured, the quad was bracketed by four handsome buildings. Besides the Admin building were the huge Zelda Kleinman Center for Enlightenment (the dining hall and two big meeting rooms, the Moadon and the Beit Am), Stuart Kleinman Hall (classrooms for the humanities and social sciences), and Harold Kleinman Hall (STEM classrooms: science, technology, and mathematics). Just off the quad but visible from within it was one of the few things at HAHA not named for a Kleinman: Leopold Hirszfeld Hall, honoring the eminent Holocaust survivor and scholar who, until his recent death, had often come to HAHA as guest lecturer.

Right outside the Admin building, four handsome flags flew high: those of the USA, Israel, Georgia, and Hampton Acres Hebrew Academy. The HAHA flag—blue, white, and gold—featured a burning bush and the motto, "Burning for Jewish Achievement."

Today, Jeff sensed that what people wanted to achieve—what The Beast wanted to achieve—was *Lemme at Mr. Taylor.*

Summoning the calm and confidence necessary to be HAHA's Head, he opened the door and stepped out onto the quad.

SIX

THE KEEP-CALM-AND-CARRY-ON TOUR

One step out onto the quad, Jeff had two dozen people coming at him. Another few steps and he was in the middle of a mob.

From a pack of pupils: "Mr. Taylor, have they found anything?"

From a troop of teachers: "Close the place down for the day!"

From a stampede of staffers: "Where are the cops? Where are the feds?"

From the head of the school's geothermal plant: "My cousin works for a security firm in Atlanta—they could have professionals here STAT!"

From one especially unhinged student: "Where is the IDF?"

Giving reassuring, noncommittal answers, Jeff kept moving. He wanted to cover the entire campus, which meant doing the "Kleinman walk," visiting every building named for a member of Sammy's family.

"Mr. Taylor, has any part of the school been searched and declared safe?"

"Mr. Taylor, should we shelter in place?"

"Mr. Taylor, what should we *do*?"

As anxiety mounted, the foreign students reverted to their native languages. Jeff was barraged in Spanish, Russian, Hebrew. Keep calm, he kept telling the small mob.

But he knew this was just the mob's leading edge. And now, as third period ended, students and teachers poured out of class, converged, and overwhelmed him.

First was Ella Bronstein, editor-in-chief of the student newspaper, *The Lamp*.

"Mr. Taylor, what's *not* in your email?"

Ella, smart and ambitious, was a senior intent on going to Brown this September. She wore a Brown sweatshirt, jeans with machine-ripped holes at the knees, and round eyeglasses. Slightly nerdy, she looked relatively harmless. Looks can be deceiving. Jeff thought of her as "Ella Woodstein," as in Woodward and Bernstein. In just this school year, she had unearthed two scandals at HAHA, and was always sniffing for more.

She was destined to bring down an administration. Jeff didn't want it to be his.

Luckily, thought Jeff, there's no new scandal. "Ella," he said, "my email says it all. All we know."

Ella persisted: "Is it the hip-hop bomber? The rapper?"

Whoa! Where did Ella get that? From Clarice? From Jerome?

"Ella," said Jeff, "if you'll excuse me . . . " He nodded at the crush of people hurling *their* questions at him. "I've got all these constituents. Gotta answer to them."

Pulling out her smartphone and thrusting it at him, Ella said, "On the record? Video and audio?"

"Be my guest."

Gently pushing through the crowd, answering people, Jeff—with Ella at his side, recording—continued to walk the campus. He continued to project calm and confidence to people who were masters of stress and dread. As people complained they hadn't been able to reach him, he reluctantly turned his smartphone ringer back on. As Jerome McKool and his men searched the campus, people tracked them. Students protested: *Mr. Taylor, they're only searching the obvious places!* Teachers and staff buttonholed Jeff with everything from *There's this tweet about a theft of ammonium nitrate, that's bomb-making material!* to *I've heard half of our security cameras don't work!* At a quarter to twelve, six Bradleyville cops arrived with two bomb-sniffing dogs—and Jeff could see students with their eyes and fingers on their smartphones, trading rumors. *Did you see, in front of Hirszfeld Hall, how that German shepherd suddenly went crazy?!*

HAHA's students were usually possessed by *shpilkes*—nervous energy. Today they were possessed by manic energy. And they made The Beast manic.

Jeff cursed the makers of Apple's iPhone. Because of them, the massive, many-tongued Beast fit in the phone, and the phone fit in the inside pocket of Jeff's blazer. And everywhere he went, The Beast was with him.

Keep calm, Jeff kept telling The Beast. Keep calm and carry on.

At a quarter past twelve, as almost everyone else had just gone into the dining hall and as Jeff was walking through the doors . . .

Ella jumped in front of him. "Mr. Taylor!" She waved her phone. "Mr. Taylor, my staff has just learned! Something else you didn't tell us. Today's bomb threat. It wasn't a robocall. Not like all the calls back on January second. Not a robocall—a live call. What do you think *that* means?"

"Um," said Jeff. "I really don't—"

He was drowned out by . . .

. . . a huge ROAR! low overhead. A Boeing 747-200B. One of the two planes outfitted and designated as Air Force One. The Secret Service kept this plane at the Bradleyville Airport and two, three, times a month it flew over like this. So HAHA's kids should be—thought Jeff—used to it.

But today's roar prompted several kids around him to shout, *"Mr. Taylor, that sounded just like a BOMB!"*

SEVEN
FOOD FOR
DISTURBING THOUGHT

HAHA's dining hall, named for Manny's wife, was meant to evoke a great tent, its high and arched ceiling converging at a single point. Facing Emmanuel Kleinman Quad, tall windows let in, on a day like this, abundant sunlight. Sunlight bathed fifty circular tables, each accommodating twelve people. The room had been designed to glorify Manny's envisioned enrollment of four hundred served by a faculty of one hundred and twenty.

As two-thirds of these tables were—except for graduation—always empty, Jeff often saw the room as a sad commentary on that vision. But as HAHA's one hundred and forty-five kids were loud and, as the graceful ceiling made for terrible acoustics, at mealtime the room rocked with noisy life.

And from the ceiling proudly and colorfully hung the flags of the twenty-five countries these kids came from: The flags of the United States (seventy-one kids), Mexico (forty-seven kids), Israel (four kids), and Canada (two kids). The flags of (one kid each) the UK, France, and Germany . . . Panama and Brazil . . . Malaysia, China (Hong Kong), and Australia . . . Morocco, Tunisia, and South Africa . . . and seven former Soviet republics. And the flags of (one kid each) countries that Jeff associated with very private bank accounts: Switzerland, Lichtenstein, and Monaco.

On ordinary days, looking at those tax-haven flags, Jeff often remembered Sammy complaining that she couldn't pry more money out of the parents of those three kids.

And on ordinary days, walking into the dining hall, Jeff was barraged with ordinary complaints from students and teachers. Today, Jeff knew he wasn't getting off easy.

Walking into the dining hall on this extraordinary day, walking in after almost everyone else had gone down the food line and was now seated, Jeff knew: I am about to be barraged by stuff that will make me *wish* for the ordinary complaints.

And he was. Barraged.

Getting up from tables, students and teachers who somehow hadn't cornered him this morning—or who *had* cornered him and needed to corner him *again*—were at him. Several dozen people gathered around him, asking him about the bomb. The big room's bad acoustics kept the assault bouncing back on him. Jeff tried to answer and reassure. Finally these several dozen people were—if not reassured—at least answered. So they sat back down.

Helping himself to spaghetti, salad, and tomato soup, Jeff now surveyed the fifteen-or-so occupied tables. Where to sit?

A strategic decision. At which table were the students and/or teachers with the most clout? The students and/or teachers who—if they chose to try to calm fears of the bomb—would be listened to? And thus calm The Beast?

Each table was occupied by a clique.

The lacrosse team training table: male jocks presided over by Coach Bill Davidoff.

A table of boys and girls fresh from chemistry class, all still—as a mark of pride—wearing their lab coats, chattering with their chem teacher, Preston Tom.

A table of seven boys and girls from seven former Soviet republics (including several Stans), all the kids talking in Russian.

A table of very earnest Orthodox boys. From it came a familiar melody from Saturday morning services. This was the "synagogue skills" table; Rabbi Benjamin Baum was mentoring the boys in some of the Shacharit prayers.

A table of American girls, effortlessly multi-tasking: eating and talking . . . and consulting, and their fingers flying on, their smartphones. One of the girls was Jordan; she avoided acknowledging her father as he passed.

A table to avoid: the sophomore outcasts, presided over by Eli Margulies. Eli was called "Shark Boy" because he went nowhere without, on his head, a plastic shark hat with a gaping mouth right above his own goofy grin. Jeff hated to admit it, but he wasn't sure of the names of the three kids with Shark Boy. He recognized them though, because whenever he visited school therapist Celine Johnson at the Health Care Center, they were there, waiting for their sessions.

As for the other tables . . .

Jeff's eyes went to four tables of Mexican kids, two tables of boys, two of girls.

He thought, Of course.

HAHA's forty-seven Mexican kids. After the American kids, they were the biggest group here. And while the American kids were a diverse lot, the Mexicans had a strong group identity. Which made them powerful. Other HAHA kids were impressed with the swagger of the Mexican kids. If other kids sensed something—Yikes! The *Mexicans* are afraid?—other kids would be more afraid. If the Mexican kids' parents sensed their kids were afraid, the parents would pull them. Since they were the biggest concentration of fully-paid students—and since more parents would follow—the school's already weak finances would be wrecked. The school wouldn't make it to this weekend.

Hence, if Jeff wanted to influence anyone, it was the Mexican kids. Especially the table of Mexican boys that included HAHA's alpha male, Jose Rivera, a senior from Mexico City. Smart, handsome, charismatic, first-born son of almost-billionaire Moises Rivera, Jose assumed he was bound for Harvard. When the occasion called for a sports jacket, he wore a crimson one. Jose was also, Jeff knew, sleeping with Jordan.

Continuing through the tumult of the dining hall, Jeff finally reached the table of twelve boys at which Jose was first among equals. Six of the boys were Jose's posse, the others were wannabes.

As Jeff stood there, the twelve immediately fell silent.

"Guys . . . " said Jeff. "Lots of other kids here"—Jeff waved at the dining hall—"are worried about the bomb threat. They're acting like it's for real. But you guys—I can tell you're cool about it. You know it's a hoax." Jeff smiled. "So I sure wish other kids could . . . ah . . . take a cue from you. Of course, some of you guys"—Jeff eyed brothers Miguel and Rafael Goldblatt and their wingman, Antonio Mendes—"do have *real* reason to be worried. The Sanhedrin, right? A week from today."

Miguel, Rafael, and Antonio tried to maintain their cool, but only partly succeeded.

Jeff saw that Jose was carefully studying him. The kid, who intended to be a powerful man, was taking notes on Jeff's use of power, Jeff invoking the Sanhedrin.

The Sanhedrin—the same name as the ancient Jewish Supreme Court—was HAHA's honor council. Meeting on Monday afternoon if needed, it could impose strict penalties—for instance on Miguel, Rafael, and Antonio who, on Saturday night, were found drunk on the quad, surrounded by cans of Dos Equis. While the judgments of the Sanhedrin had to be approved by Jeff, Jeff regularly approved them. Otherwise, what was the point of having the institution?

But if Jeff sensed a judgment was about to go against his judgment, he was *not* reluctant to gently lobby the five judges to see things his way.

This table of Mexican boys knew this.

"But," said Jeff, "I know the Sanhedrin takes into account public-spirited actions. Actions that boost school morale, actions that make going to school here a more positive experience. A more worry-*free* experience. Right?"

The twelve boys nodded.

"Right," said Jeff. "So if, a week from today, when the Sanhedrin meets, it's clear that all twelve of you and"—Jeff indicated the three other tables of Mexican kids—"your compadres have been *active* . . . have been doing your utmost to calm the fears of kids who aren't as cool as you . . . convince them that the bomb threat is, of course, a hoax . . . well, I'm sure the Sanhedrin would judge that it far outweighs three of you getting sloshed on the quad. Right?"

The boys smiled, nodded.

"And, Jose" said Jeff, "I'm sure *you* can take the lead in this."

"Right, Mr. Taylor," said the flattered kid, the future Presidente of Mexico. Turning to his posse and the wannabes, he repeated, "Right."

"Great," said the Head of School.

CRASH*!*

More than one hundred heads turned.

A student had dropped his tray with the remains of spaghetti in red sauce. On an ordinary day a dropped tray triggered applause. Not today. Several kids screamed. One wailed, *"It looks like BLOOD!"*

EIGHT

THE FOUNDING FATHER

Returning to the Admin building, walking down the hall toward his office, Jeff was about to pass the open doorway of the conference room. There, at the back of the room, at the end of the long conference table, set on a plinth, was a bronze bust of Sammy's father.

Emmanuel Kleinman, founder of HAHA.

Jeff stopped.

Ah, Manny.

The bust's sharp eyes demanded, What are you *doing* with what my millions created?

Jeff provided a silent answer: Floundering.

Manny Kleinman, Bradleyville native, had made his fortune in real estate. Kleinman Homes Inc. And Jeff knew what Manny should have done with these one hundred acres: built luxury homes. *That* would have made sense—if Manny had bought out the nearby pig farm. But a Jewish boarding school? Well, maybe near New York City—say, Great Neck. Or in a suburb of Boston or Chicago. A place near a big Jewish population. But here, in central Georgia? Made as much sense as Jerry Falwell's Liberty University on the Upper West Side.

Manny, what were you thinking?

Jeff knew what Manny had been thinking. Meeting Jeff last year, the sculptor of the bust described her conversation with the man who had sat for her back in 2005. This was when HAHA—the product of Manny's chutzpah—had been open for one year and when its founder was sixty-eight.

"Don't make me look nice," demanded Manny. "Or friendly. Or jovial. You understand?"

"Well . . . " said the sculptor, "how do you want to look?"

"Tough. A *macher*. Moses whacking the worshippers of the golden calf."

"All right." Working in clay, the sculptor tried to capture the *macher* before her.

"My bust will go in the conference room. I want anybody who comes after me, anybody making decisions in the conference room, to be terrified of screwing up my school."

"All right."

"I want them to think that Manny Kleinman had the vision and the money and the *drive* to create this school and we are not going to mess it up."

"Understood."

"I put this school here where nobody thought this school should be. But I know better than those nobodies. You've heard of 'Build it and they will come'?"

"Yes."

"Students will come. I've built it for four hundred students. I'm making it free until it *has* four hundred. Which it *will*. That will attract donors. My school will have an endowment of five hundred million. I will have built a school that nobody who comes after me will *dare* screw with. Understood?"

"Yes."

"You know how the European Jews almost ended up in central Africa?"

"No."

"In the early 1900s, Theodor Herzl was trying to find *some* place for Europe's Jews. The Brits offered five thousand square miles in Uganda.

Which of course didn't happen. And there's a punchline: The Brits were confused. The land wasn't even in Uganda—it was in modern Kenya. But you know what?"

"What?"

"It wouldn't have mattered. *Whatever* land they had been given, the Jews would have made it work. *Whatever* land Moses or Herzl led them to. The same with me. This land here—I'm making it work. I'm making a school here."

"Okay."

Manny Kleinman laughed. "*Here.* In the middle of Georgia. And it will be a *great* Jewish college-prep boarding school—here for f**king forever. Understood?"

"Yes."

"Make my bust *tell* people that. For f**king forever."

"Yes," said the sculptor, back in 2005.

Eyeing the bust, Jeff commiserated with Manny's shade.

The other wealthy Jews whom Manny thought would share his belief, his vision, and their millions . . . hadn't. Then, in 2008-2009, the housing bubble burst and splattered Kleinman Homes Inc. With only Kleinman money behind it, HAHA plunged into dysfunction.

Meeting the gaze of the bust's sharp eyes, Jeff asked it, Manny, on your deathbed in 2011, did you think your daughter the basketball star would somehow save this place?

Manny, lemme break it to you . . .

NINE

COS-LOOT PROBLEM

"Cos-loot," said Preston Tom, chemistry teacher and head of the science department. He sat across from Jeff in Jeff's office. "Cos-loot problem with the air. My gauges detect it."

"Cos-loot?" said Jeff.

"Cos-loot. Cos-loot."

"Ah yes, *kashrut*. How can there be a *kashrut* problem with the air, Preston?"

Kashrut. The laws that determine what is kosher and what is not. Jeff had no idea of how there could be a "*kashrut* problem with the air"—but after five hours of having people barrage him with worries about a bomb, what a relief to have a different problem. And a relief to have it—whatever it was—presented to him by earnest Preston Tom. Born in southeastern China, Tom hadn't totally mastered English and he struggled to pronounce any Hebrew but, unlike most of the HAHA community, he was a master of his emotions.

At three p.m., Jeff had returned to his outer office, to find—a miracle!—no one waiting to harangue him about the bomb. Instead, Preston Tom. Unlike so many of his peers, Preston Tom never bothered Jeff with requests, demands, or complaints. So Jeff had said, "Come in."

And got, "Cos-loot problem with the air."

Preston handed Jeff a sheaf of colorful graphs. The graphs had lines that moved left to right, forming gently sloping hills—and then, at the end of the last page, leaped into towering mountains.

"Cos-loot," said Preston. "Pork."

"Pork?"

"Molecules, biologic. Animal-based. Pig. Zhu. My readings supposed to keep us a green school. Now they show this. Cos-loot. Not good for Jewish people."

Now Jeff understood. The giant pig farm. Emmitt Bailey's Premier Porcine Facility. A CAFO: concentrated animal feeding operation. It seemed every time Jeff drove outside HAHA, a tractor-trailer was delivering more pigs. Jeff told Preston, "Well . . . pork. We aren't supposed to eat it, but I don't think there's any rule against breathing it in."

"Is that right? Good." A look of relief, which quickly vanished. "But maybe we should check with Rabbi Baum? Should I share these test results with him?"

No no no! thought Jeff. I'm already going to weather one hundred and three more days of *mishegas*—I don't need Baum adding to it.

Now age fifty-two, Baum's life's work was to make Hampton Acres Hebrew Academy even more "authentically" Jewish. If he could, Baum would find a hundred Jewish holidays per year on which HAHA should close. At nine this morning, Baum had emailed, "Last year we failed to celebrate Shushan Purim. As I told you, this is unacceptable. To celebrate it, we must suspend all normal school activities."

Shushan Purim was the day after Purim—two weeks from now. Jeff's mental reply to Baum: "Same answer as last year: Sushan Purim is celebrated only in Jerusalem and walled cities. That's not us."

But HAHA's one-hundred-acre campus was surrounded by a six-foot-high steel picket fence, painted green as if to make it eco-friendly. Jeff could hear Baum, in his signature singsong: "The Mishna says a high fence is a wall to all those who live behind it." The Mishna was the first part of the Talmud, and Baum used it as both a defensive wall and an offensive weapon.

Now Jeff knew: If Preston tells Baum, Baum will demand a real wall. A wall guaranteed pork-molecule-proof. Plus Baum will tell the whole school. And everyone will freak out.

Of course at HAHA, everything leaked—but Jeff needed to delay this leak as long as possible.

"Yes," said Preston. "I think Rabbi Baum would be interested. I take readings three times a day. Three times for the three daily prayer services, that's what Rabbi Baum insists. At twelve different sites on campus. Twelve for the Twelve Tribes, that's what Rabbi Baum insists. Twelve very sensitive readings."

"Right," said Jeff. "Who helps you take them?"

"Students too busy. I do it myself."

"And the data. Who else has access?"

"Just me. Very sensitive."

"Good. You're discreet. Devoted to the school."

"And to the chemistry department."

"And to the chemistry department. In fact, you've been very patient waiting for that, uh . . . "

"High-capacity refrigerated centrifuge." Preston Tom smiled.

"Yes," said Jeff. "And it turns out that one of our new parents runs a med tech company. He gave me a pledge that will cover that centrifuge which, I remember, is expensive."

Preston Tom smiled. Across the desk, Jeff and he shook hands. A deal that neither man would have to acknowledge. Jeff's respect for the chemistry teacher had risen considerably.

He played me like a pro, and I never saw it coming.

Jeff touched his sports jacket over the pocket that held his letter of resignation. *So now HAHA is breathing pork molecules. Great.*

"Thanks for calling this to my attention," he told Preston Tom.

With the promise of a centrifuge, the chemistry teacher left.

Jeff gazed out the window. In the quad, a stand of elms swayed in the breeze. They looked like they were davening in Rabbi Baum's minyan. Fanning pork molecules in this direction.

He checked the time. 3:28. The executive committee meeting was in thirty-two minutes. Jeff could already feel the school's seven deans headed this direction.

Wackiness being fanned in this direction.

TEN
THE EXECUTIVE COMMITTEE MEETS

The purpose of the meeting was not to decide what to do; Jeff already knew what he was going to do. The purpose of the meeting was to make HAHA's seven deans *feel* they were being consulted on what to do. Individually, three or four of the deans were more or less sane; the other three or four were not. When all seven got together, the whole—the insanity—was much greater than the sum of its parts. Hence Jeff had these meetings on Thursdays at five p.m. when everyone was worn out from the week and looking forward to getting a little rest before Shabbat, when the kids got *really* demanding. Too worn out to quarrel *too* much. Only in extreme circumstances would he hold an executive committee meeting on Monday, when everyone was more or less fresh and alert.

Yeah, thought Jeff, I guess a bomb threat qualifies as an extreme circumstance.

At 3:45 p.m.—people couldn't wait to vent—the boardroom was packed with the seven deans.

In order of arrival: Rabbi Benjamin Baum, Dean of Jewish Life. Rachel Fish, Dean of Academics and Chair of the English Department. Stevie Blau, Dean of Information Technology. Bill Davidoff, Dean of

Athletics and lacrosse coach. Clara Glatt, Dean of Healthcare, a fancy name for school nurse. Madison Angel, Dean of Student Life. Jerome McKool, Dean of Security.

And, uninvited, but walking in like she belonged, Celine Johnson, the school psychotherapist. Jeff sighed—the insanity quotient had just spiked—but he knew he couldn't throw her out.

Around the conference table, all eight faced Jeff. From the back of the room, the bronze bust of founder Manny Kleinman faced Jeff.

Jeff mentally told Manny, I know, I know. If you had it your way, you'd fire half of them.

Jeff told the eight, "I have no news beyond what you already know." He nodded to Jerome McKool. "Jerome has called the FBI. They'll be here within the hour. Jerome believes that, like the January bomb threats, this is a hoax. Assuming—"

Rachel Fish interrupted. "Assuming you can keep feeding us this line, Jeff? No news? How about the news that we're the only one to get a second bomb threat? You've kept that from us, haven't you?"

Age forty-five, Rachel was tough, skinny, wiry, intense, brilliant, politically to the left of Leon Trotsky, aggressively and proudly lesbian, so "woke" Jeff doubted she, metaphorically, ever slept. And so argumentative he was always surprised she didn't actually wear combat boots. Merely work boots. Jeans, work shirt. Iron-gray hair cut almost like a Marine's. Large eyeglasses with thick purple frames, almost like VR goggles. Certainly she saw and made her own reality. Politically and culturally, Rachel was a perfect fit for the six elite prep schools she had taught at. Six in fourteen years. Because she always kept her knives out, she kept being tossed out. If she weren't such a fabulous teacher, Jeff, too, might have fired her.

She demanded, "What else have you kept from us?"

Jeff said, "Kept from you? Nothing."

Rachel persisted, "And you think it's a hoax. Why? *Think*, Jeff! Of all the Jewish institutions who got a threat last month, we're the most isolated. In the middle of redneck nowhere. Near damn few other

Jews. But very near, I bet, the Klan. We're the perfect candidate for the second threat, the threat that turns out to be *real*."

Jeff knew better than to engage Rachel. He drew himself up inside his armor of casual but Ivy authority, straightened his repp tie. Turning to everyone else, he said, "*Assuming* the police find nothing, assuming there is no bomb, we still should tighten security. I have some ideas. But I'd like yours."

Ideas from the deans. Oh, be ready for a flood. For why did someone become a dean? Except for Coach Bill and Jerome McKool, here's why: As a kid, they loved school. They always had the answer, they always spoke up in class, they loved being patted on the head. They thought they had the answer now, and Jeff had damn well better pat them on the head.

And, except for Coach Bill, Madison Angel, and Jerome McKool, the four other deans—and Celine, the psychotherapist—were like most of the faculty and students: High-strung, anxious. *Pat me on my head, or I will hold my breath and roll on the floor.*

And except for Jerome—who had retired with honor from the Bradleyville police after twenty-five years to join HAHA fourteen years ago—all the deans and Celine had, like Rachel Fish, checkered pasts. They had been forced to leave other prep schools. They could be hired only at a school like HAHA—"last stop on a streetcar named *Galut*" (exile). If they had to leave HAHA, where could they possibly go?

"Who first?" asked Jeff.

Rabbi Baum said, "It always starts with Torah. As Pirkei Avot says of the Torah, 'Turn it and turn it again, for every answer is in it.' But are we a school of Torah values?"

Around the room, people shifted in their seats. Familiar with Baum's rabbinic fondness for questions, no one answered.

Baum appeared not to notice. Leaning back in his chair, he rested his brawny hands on his large belly. Baum wore the uniform of his Hasidic sect: black jacket and dark tie, white shirt, and black *kipa* atop graying curls. His gray beard reached down to his impressive pecs. He looked like a sumo wrestler trying to go native in Crown Heights.

Baum said, "These threats are the stick God beats us with because we have strayed. We are failing in our mission: to be a *baal teshuva*."

Jeff knew *baal teshuva*. Literally "a master of repentance," this is a secular Jew who has returned to Orthodox practice. Baum was himself a *baal teshuva*. He had told Jeff he had grown up secular, and illiterate in Hebrew. He had been a party animal in high school and his first two years in college and then—age twenty—a revelation! He became Hasidic, he studied the Torah. But for all of his fervor, his Torah knowledge and his Hebrew pronunciation were spotty.

"*How* have we strayed?" said Baum. "Most recently, we did not observe the fast of Esther. So here"—he pulled out a sheet of paper— "are all the fasts and festivals that we have shamelessly desecrated that from now on we *must* observe. Jeff, as I already told you, next up is Shushan Purim."

Jeff did not nod his head. Around the room, people rolled their eyes.

Baum said, "And we must, at once, have all our students chant *tehillim* every morning.

Someone coughed. Chairs creaked. Some deans dug out their smartphones, becoming very interested in almost everything else.

Baum said, "We must use the protective power of *mitzvot*. Just as thousands of Israelis donned *tefillin* before the Six-Day War started, many for the first time. It worked, right?"

Rachel Fish drummed her fingers on the conference table.

Baum said, "But to be safe, we must close the school today and check every mezuzah. Open up each one and make sure the parchment isn't damaged."

Coach Bill exploded. "Every mezuzah? On every doorway? We must have a thousand doorways."

Baum said, "Yes, but while we start opening the mezuzahs, there is way to speed up the process. My cousin in Gush Etzion has a startup. He makes a hand-held scanner, lets you inspect the parchment from outside the mezuzah."

Jeff said, "Uh, great. Sure, contact him."

Now Rachel exploded. "No! Jeff, we are not going to use settlement products at this school."

Baum said, "Yes. And I will write a letter to my Rebbe. I know he will answer with more good advice."

Baum's Rebbe had been dead more than two decades. But Baum said the man always did answer him: "In my dreams."

Jeff said, "Uh, great. Sure, write your Rebbe." Looking around the room, he asked, "Any more suggestions?"

Celine Johnson, the psychotherapist, jumped in. Passionate about everything, overwrought, she proclaimed, "We are overlooking the most basic need. This event has psychologically impacted each of our students, and perhaps traumatized many. We are talking PTSD— post-traumatic stress disorder. Immediately, within the next three days, each student needs a three-hour one-on-one in-depth evaluation by a trained therapist such as myself."

Around the room, at "trained therapist," people rolled their eyes.

Celine, age fifty, with a degree in social work from Chenango Valley Community College in central New York, was built like an opera singer. She was good at folding a needy student into her huge fleshy body and providing weepy sympathy. "Tell me your troubles, honey." But providing real therapy? Forget it. Her office had a huge jar of individually-wrapped chocolates to lure kids—chocolates that Celine ate. In fact, she was needier than many of the kids she counseled. And whatever a student told Celine? No guarantee Celine would keep it to herself. She leaked tears and secrets.

But Jeff was impressed with Celine's chutzpah. She saw the bomb threat as a chance to assert herself, get out from under reporting to Nurse Glatt. Nurse Glatt, who knew what her subordinate was up to, was bristling. She looked ready to pounce.

Celine appeared not to notice her boss's anger or the skepticism in the room. She plunged on.

"Yes. On a crash basis, I can do three students per day. Nine a.m.

to noon. One p.m. to four p.m. Five p.m. to eight p.m. Three days, nine students. That means we need . . . let's see, one hundred and forty-five students divided by nine equals . . . " She frowned. "Math was never my strength."

"Sixteen," snapped Rachel.

"Yes, sixteen. Myself and fifteen more therapists. If we reach out to Emory, Georgia Tech and UGA, we may be able to get them."

Around the room, almost everyone went back to his or her smartphone.

Jeff thought to ask, At what cost? but stopped himself.

Celine apparently read his mind. "The cost is insignificant compared to the cost of *not* evaluating them. Then"—Celine waved an *Aha!* index finger—"my opinion is that at least twenty percent will have PTSD and will need intense therapy for the rest of the school year!"

From around the room, titters and groans.

"Celine," said Nurse Glatt, a Teutonic control freak, "instead of your three-hour evaluations, I'm sure we could administer a standard psychological test."

"Standardized testing!" said Celine. "Yes! But not as a *substitute* for the one-on-one three-hour evaluations. As an immediate *preliminary* to them. All these tests are available for purchase online." Pulling out and consulting a three-by-five card, Celine said, "The Minnesota Multiphasic Personality Inventory. The Millon Clinical Multiaxial Inventory. The Rorschach Inkblot Test. Then I will score the results."

"You . . . ?" sputtered Nurse Glatt. Her bulldog jowls quivered.

While not an Orthodox woman, Glatt dressed like one; she covered every inch, wouldn't shake hands. It was said that the HAHA interviewers had thought she was Orthodox—and she had thought she was taking a job at an evangelical Christian school (whoever heard of a Jewish boarding school in Bible Belt Georgia?). She brought to this job the austere authority and judgment of the Torah or, as she called it, the Old Testament.

"I am more than qualified," Celine told Glatt. "I wouldn't tell you how to wrap a sprained ankle. Our students will take the tests on their cellphones, and the results will come to me."

Glatt stared at her in fury.

Jeff admired Celine's power play. Especially because he bet Celine's familiarity with these tests probably came only from googling them today.

And talk about anxiety and trauma? Jeff imagined all one hundred and forty-five HAHA students staring at their smartphones as each new question came up and their sweaty thumbs twitched over the screen: *What's the right answer? Gotta get it right. If I answer too many wrong, I'll get identified as a headcase—and have to spend hours with Celine.*

"And," said Celine triumphantly, "if one of our students is the perpetrator, the tests and evaluations will identify him."

ELEVEN

SHARK BOY'S DREAM

"**C**atch it, Rebecca! C'mon, you can—! Okay, Rebecca, that's okay. Except if you didn't flinch every time when it gets close, if you didn't close your eyes—hey, I'm not shaming you, I'm trying to be helpful. I'm—okay, I'll shut up. Just pick it up and throw it to Gilbert, okay?"

Frisbee.

Outside the Admin building, on Emmanuel Kleinman Quad, as the executive committee was meeting, four sophomores—two boys and two girls—were throwing a Frisbee around. The activity had been organized by the sort-of leader of the quartet, Eli Margulies. Eli wasn't—he'd be the first to admit—all that well-coordinated himself, no great hand-eye, nothing that would ever catch Coach Bill's eye. But he was a *little* better than Rebecca, and he felt maybe he could help her . . .

"Rebecca, now when you throw to Gilbert, it's as simple as . . . "

He shut up.

Who am I kidding, Eli told himself. She's hopeless. All four of us are pretty hopeless.

But I sort-of make up for it by being Shark Boy.

Wherever he went—to classes, to meals, to free time—Eli Margulies relied on his plastic shark hat. His shark was his protection and his power. It said, Oh, no, I am not *that* hopeless. I'm a Great White.

Of course, Eli knew that all the other kids at HAHA—except the three kids out here playing Frisbee—thought he *was* hopeless. They saw him as a loser. Eli knew that if Jose Rivera was at the top of HAHA's coolness ladder, he was at the bottom. He knew that being Shark Boy meant the only HAHA kids he could hang out with were these three. And who were they? One bedwetter girl (Rebecca), one nose-picker boy (Gilbert), one nail-biter girl (Ariana).

This was semi-okay by Eli. The three were semi-good company. They laughed at his jokes, although Eli knew the jokes were really at the level of an eight-year-old, not sixteen-year-old sophomores. Or at least they groaned, which was some acknowledgement that he existed.

Today, as they (shakily) threw the Frisbee around, Eli—aka Shark Boy—called out a new joke.

"What do you get when you cross a shark with a snowman? Frostbite."

In return, he got some laughter.

But what I want, thought Eli Margulies, is much more. What I want is acknowledgment of my *real* power here at HAHA.

Someday I will get it. Someday soon.

TWELVE

THE EXECUTIVE COMMITTEE MEETING ENDS IN—SURPRISE—DISAGREEMENT

"**I** think we can rule out our students as suspects, Celine," Madison Angel said. "Yes, we have some troubled kids, but no one who would do that."

Jeff trusted Madison—mostly. A Wellesley graduate now closing in on forty, she dressed preppy in plaid skirts, sweaters, and pearls. A former field hockey and squash star, she was trim, athletic, strong. She would take on anyone, especially in defense of her students. But, as Dean of Students, maybe she couldn't be open-minded to the idea of a student being the culprit. Jeff didn't have that luxury. Memo to self: pay more attention to the student emails on Parochet.

Jeff looked around the room. "Any more suggestions?"

Stevie Blau, Dean of Information Technology, said, "Let's get practical. We must upgrade our physical security. We need high-end intrusion detection. We need smart security, including remote arm/disarm. We need more video surveillance: cameras and storage. We need face-recognition tech. We need—" He eyed Jeff. "I'll give you a list."

While Stevie's affect was peace-love-and-granola, he really knew cybersecurity, and now it seemed he also knew "hard" security.

Yet Stevie was the opposite of hard. A roly-poly, junk-food-gorging guy, he was, along with his wife Meadow, a houseparent. The kids loved the Blaus because they served chocolate-chip pancakes for breakfast.

Jeff asked, "Um, all this physical security. How much will it cost?'

"Only a million dollars."

If jaws dropping made a sound, from around the room came that sound.

"And," said Stevie, "we must immediately upgrade our cybersecurity. Management to identify and remediate vulnerabilities. For routers, switches, load balancers, and firewalls. And especially the servers. Provision, deploy, and patch servers."

Jeff asked, "And how much will this cost?" He figured a *bit* more than the recording device he planned to have Stevie install on the school's main number, the phone Clarice answered. Better to arrange that in private, and avoid Rachel's privacy protests.

"Only another million."

More jawdropping.

Stevie added, "But well worth it. If we are hacked, just imagine. Our students are online, studying Jewish history and suddenly Hitler's face appears, screaming they should be sent to the ovens." Stevie turned to Celine. "Imagine *that* trauma."

Celine choked. "Stop it, Stevie, you're traumatizing *me*."

Celine's eyes were tearing up. Madison Angel handed her a box of tissues.

"Um," said Jeff, "any more suggestions?"

"Look," said Madison, "we're getting much too worked up. Jeff's right; this almost certainly is a hoax. That's what the police will confirm. Let's listen to the steps that Jeff has in mind to tighten security, and just implement them."

"Madison's right," said Coach Bill Davidoff. "Let's just keep our heads down, keep quiet and bull through this. Hit the line. Three yards and a cloud of dust."

Jeff smiled. Davidoff was a small, wiry man with the crew cut of a sixties jock. He talked like a sixties coach. *When the going gets tough, the tough get going.* Today, as usual, he wore a blue HAHA tracksuit and a baseball cap. The jacket of his suit had "Coach Bill" in cursive script over his heart. Around his neck was a lanyard that held a whistle. Coach Bill knew his fellow deans didn't respect anyone dressed like this, but he didn't give a damn.

And he was building his own empire. HAHA's multi-million-dollar lacrosse stadium was brand new. (And the millions came from where? Jeff was in awe of Sammy's smoke and mirrors.) Two months from now the stadium would host the first Hampton Acres Invitational, a tournament that Coach Bill planned to win.

Coach Bill elaborated: "Keep quiet and tomorrow the headline will be about somebody else. It's hard enough recruiting good athletes. They all have to be circumcised. They all have to be willing to go to school in the middle of nowhere. Bradleyville! Nowheresville! The more extreme measures we take, the harder it becomes. The word will get out, kids and their parents will be scared." He sighed. "Do you know how few Jewish lacrosse players there are? Jewish mothers don't like their boys swinging sticks at each other."

"Why aren't you recruiting girls? Why isn't there a female lacrosse team? It's not right that only boys play in that gold-plated stadium of yours," Rachel said.

Bill shot Jeff a look that was an appeal for help. Jeff felt for him. A generation ago, his jock self would have, culturally, been on top and Rachel's lesbian self would have been way down the ladder. Now things were reversed, but Bill hadn't reconciled himself to the new order.

"Okay," said Jeff. "I thank everybody for their input. Taking it all into account, this is our response. We will install more cameras on the fence, but, because real cameras are expensive, these will be dummy cameras. And—"

"Dummy ones!' spat Rachel. "Great. Let's put up lots of 'Beware of Dog' signs, but of course we won't get any dogs. Jeff, the Klan isn't *that* stupid."

"Rach is right," said Stevie, "I'm concerned that—"

"We don't have the money," said Jeff. "But we do have the money for protective film for our windows. And, what will cost us nothing or close to nothing . . . "

He explained:

"We'll reinspect every foot of the fence. There are spots some of our students know about: places where the metal bars are loose and can be bent, so a person can squeeze through. We'll find those places and tighten them. We'll require that every school that brings a team here emails us, ahead of time, a list of everybody on their bus—and we'll check everybody on that bus against the list. And of course, based on anything we learn from the police and the FBI, possibly more measures."

He *didn't* mention the recording device that would soon be attached to Clarice's phone.

Jeff concluded with, "So I thank you and . . . "

To make clear this meeting was over, he stood, as several deans began to argue.

Manny Kleinman's bronze bust grinned fiercely at Jeff. *Look what I have created: In the boondocks of central Georgia, a sanctuary as disputatious as the Knesset.*

THIRTEEN

SHTOYYOT! NONSENSE!

*J*eff, ma shlomcha? Ha kol beseder?

Noga Weinstein, chair of HAHA's Hebrew Department, texted her usual greeting. Every conversation they had, whatever the topic or medium, started with the same elementary Hebrew phrases: How are you? Everything okay?

Sitting in his office, Jeff texted back a lie: *Ha kol beseder. Gam at?* (Everything's fine. And you?)

Noga: *Baruch Hashem. I could have helped you at the meeting. Even though it was the EC and I'm still not a dean . . .*

Jeff: *Noga I'm sorry. Things moved so fast.*

Noga: *Not so fast.*

Jeff: *You're right. You should have been there. My bad.*

Noga: *Next time then.*

Jeff: *For sure.*

Noga: *About the new security measures . . . people are already talking.*

Jeff sighed. The meeting had broken up ten minutes ago. He no longer expected anyone to keep things confidential. That wasn't going to happen at HAHA. But ten minutes? That wasn't enough time for the deans to get back to their offices and classrooms. Was someone secretly livestreaming the meeting? President Nixon had his plumbers to stop the leaks. HAHA needed a dam builder.

Noga: *These measures. Can I be honest?*

Jeff: *Of course.*

Noga: *Shtoyyot!!! It's all nonsense.*

Noga was usually the center of energy at mealtime when the Israeli teachers gathered at one table to speak rapid-fire Hebrew. Jeff could see her flashing black eyes. He could see her smiling white teeth, her lips pulled back contemptuously. An Israeli from a kibbutz on the Syrian border, she looked like Bizet's Carmen, without the flower in her hair. A more fitting image: a knife in her teeth. Noga was a Sabra, descended from Kurdish Jews. One day, tired of the persecution, her grandparents left their mud hut in Iraq and started walking, like latter-day followers of Moses, to Israel. Seven hundred eighty miles.

As an Israeli Jew, Noga viewed American Jews as the equivalent of Bud *Lite*, Coors *Lite*, Miller *Lite*.

Noga: *Dummy cameras! Lists of visitors! Jerome looking under every bus! It's a big nothing. A fiasco.*

Jeff could hear her voice when he read her texts, hear her saying, the way Israelis speaking English always do, "Eh . . . eh . . . eh." An Israeli says "eh" when an American says "uhm"—but while "uhm" says I hear you, an Israeli's "eh" says I hear you *and you're wrong.* And Jeff could feel Noga's frustration that her English, which was strong, could not express her emotions, which were stronger.

Noga: *It's no better than the schlubs who do the active shooter drills. Training our kids to throw toilet paper at the terrorists! Truly full of shit!*

Noga had served in an IDF intelligence unit. And lived on the Golan, always in the shadow of enemies. Armed and ready. Terrorism wasn't academic for her.

Noga: *This school needs REAL security measures.*

Jeff: *What do you recommend?*

Noga: *Every teacher gets an Uzi. And training. Like in Israel.*

Jeff imagined Rachel and Coach Bill at the EC meeting, each toting a loaded Uzi. He heard Celine's quavering voice, "Jeff, I'm very uncomfortable with this."

For once he agreed with the therapist.

Noga: *Class is starting. Got to go. Lehitraot!*
Jeff: *Lehitraot. Goodbye.*

Jeff stared out his windows. Ah, so beautiful out there.

But he had to catch up on the less-than-beautiful. Going to parochet@haha.com, he started reading the roughly two hundred anonymous emails that had poured in over the last seven hours—students, teachers, staff, and parents all bomb-threat-blitzed. Missives from a wedge of worriers, a drove of dreaders, a posse of panickers.

The further Jeff read, the further he felt the price of the school's debt drop, reflecting the market's decreasing confidence the debt would be repaid.

I wonder what it's actually trading at.

FOURTEEN

DISTRESSED DEBT, DISTRESSED MAN

I t was the end of a long day in the Kingdom of Judah, and Jeff was grateful to finally be able to leave it.

He was out of his office, heading for the bridge.

The campus of Hampton Acres Hebrew Academy was divided in two. The acreage called the Kingdom of Judah held the residential and academic buildings, the dining hall, the Admin building, and the student activities center. Across a small ravine lay what was called the Kingdom of Israel. Here were the athletic center, the performing arts center and, among smaller structures and a bit removed from them, his house. Called the "Head's house," Manny had unaccountably failed to slap a relative's name on it.

Jeff spent most of his waking hours in the Kingdom of Judah. At the end of most days, especially stressful ones like today, when he stepped onto the small, graceful footbridge that arched the ravine to head home, he breathed a sigh of relief.

Today, at the exact center of the bridge, he stopped and surveyed the gorgeous landscape and the buildings on it.

Then he took out his phone and called a number in New York. A man from his hedge fund days. Bobby C., a trader in distressed debt.

"Bobby."

"Jeff! Long time! What is it—two years? I heard this crazy thing about you. You're running some school in West Virginia."

"Georgia. Hey, Bobby, strangely enough, this place has a lot of bank debt. I'm curious—where is it trading? Hampton Acres Hebrew Academy. And the lender—M&F National Bank Bradleyville."

"Now *that's* an obscure piece of paper. Hang on."

As Bobby put him on hold, Jeff felt the hedge fund reflex he had retired two years ago come to life. Surveying the school, he added up its gross square footage. The dining hall and the two assembly halls (the Zelda Kleinman Center) forty thousand, the two academic centers (Stuart Kleinman Hall and Harold Kleinman Hall) one hundred and fifty thousand, the Admin building twenty thousand, ten residential houses at ten thousand each, the athletic center thirty thousand, the performing arts center, various other structures, all but one named Kleinman . . . cuff the total at three hundred fifty thousand square feet.

It was quality space, featuring Jerusalem stone and landscaped like a Robert Trent Jones golf course. At one hundred dollars a square foot, what buyer could resist that valuation? Half the replacement cost. The buildings alone were worth thirty-five million. Value everything else—the land, fixtures, golf carts, the geothermal power plant, Sammy's fancy rugs—at zero, and divide by the fifty million of bank debt: seventy cents on the dollar. At seventy, the debt was rock solid.

And perfect for a University of Georgia extension campus.

Manny Kleinman would turn over in his grave.

Waiting for an answer from Bobby C., Jeff heard—imagined— the voice of his former boss and colleague, Evan Rose of Rose & Company. While Evan spent much of his time prowling his trading floor, watching everyone and everything, kibbitzing, complimenting, and criticizing, he would always return to his desk on the floor, to the left of Jeff's desk. And there give Jeff a piece of his mind. In Jeff's ear, he now heard Evan say, *Hey, Jeff, even Bobby thinks you made a crazy decision, leaving us to go down to that place. You're wasting your time and your talent. Your calculations—you haven't lost a step. Come back here and put it to real use. Your desk is—*

Bobby C. came back on the line. "As luck would have it, one of my colleagues makes a market. You could buy as much as you want for sixty cents."

Sixty cents on the dollar. Jeff was surprised. He'd figured seventy. So *The Street knows—or thinks—we're even shakier.*

"So," said Bobby, "it's great you're back. What do you want to do?"

"I'm not ready to do anything yet."

"So you're just sniffing around. Okay. But when you're ready, I expect I'll get the call."

"Just like the old days. And, if you're ever down this way, the town has a great sports bar. Every craft beer you ever heard of. And the best burger ever. I'm buying."

With a few more seconds of small talk, Jeff clicked off.

And immediately heard Evan again in his ear: *Yeah, good calculation, Jeff. Except you thought it was seventy. And I knew it wasn't higher than sixty-two.*

Evan Rose, who was always right, and always told you he was right.

Jeff shook his head. *Evan is making hundreds of millions, and I made the mistake of coming here.*

But it is so beautiful. And I do so love it.

Turning his eyes away, he headed for what, for another few months, was his home.

But not to stay long. Just to get out of these slacks, dress shirt, and sports jacket and into jeans and a pullover, and drive to a great home-cooked meal at a good woman's home.

FIFTEEN
MISCHIEF-MAKERS

Jeff had to get out of HAHA. Yes, he had to really, *permanently*, get out by June 21. But right now, tonight, he would get out *temporarily*.

Getting in his three-year-old Lexus SUV, he headed to Barbara Travis's house.

HAHA was on the western edge of Bradleyville, three miles from the city center. Barbara lived on the city's eastern edge. It was a twenty-minute drive to her house. Halfway there, stopped at a red light, Jeff was confronted by a Bible Belt billboard

"Draw me not away with the wicked, and the workers of iniquity, which speak peace to their neighbors, but mischief is in their hearts." Psalm 28:3

The billboard had been up for a month; he had never paid attention to it. Now he did.

Mischief.

When the bomb threat came in this morning, Jeff had thought, This'll upset The Beast for seven days max, and once The Beast goes back to somnolence I can tell Sammy that on June 21 I'm *gone*. All I have to do is project calm and confidence—that's enough to help The Beast along. But I've seen that Rabbi Baum and Celine Johnson and maybe even Stevie Blau are not going to easily let go of worrying about a bomber. And Noga is at me saying every teacher should be toting an Uzi . . .

Given all the people at HAHA whom these four people inter-act with, what fears can they stoke and spread? What mischief can they make?

Jeff thought: Keep an eye on them. Be prepared to stage an intervention.

And what about any students? Mischief-makers tying tin cans to The Beast's tail . . .

The light turned green, and he drove on.

Jeff, hon, said Michelle's voice, *let it go and enjoy the evening. I bet Barbara has some comfort food for you.*

She does, thought Jeff.

So there, said Michelle. *She's a good woman, let her be good to you.*

Ten minutes later he pulled into the driveway of Barbara Travis's small, neat house. From here he could see her backyard full of her pas-sion: the huge sculptures she made from scrap metal. The kitschy stuff she loved, which Jeff tried to overlook because he felt, yeah, I love her.

And now his love was opening the front door and smiling at him. Kind, good-looking, wicked smart. Age thirty-seven. Native Georgian. Niece of an evangelical pastor, the Reverend Pat Travis. Reverend Travis' faith was a bit "attenuated" in Barbara, as she liked to say. Paralegal in a Bradleyville law firm, which she cleverly concealed that she basically ran. Maker not just of bad sculpture but of good exec-utive decisions. And fabulous meat loaf, which she had promised for this evening.

As he got out of his car, she called, "Jeff! You look like you need a drink. To go with the meat loaf I have a nice Malbec, and maybe three fingers of scotch?"

SIXTEEN

THE BEAST WHISPERER

arfufket, fartoost, fermisht: befuddled, bewildered, anxious.

For a people who highly value clear-thinking, we Jews—thought Jeff—have a wealth of Yiddish words for the opposite. And it was clear to him that HAHA's students and teachers were *farfufket, fartoost,* and *fermisht* about the bomb threat. His reassuring email of yesterday and his walking the campus yesterday hadn't done the job. What had followed—the executive committee meeting—hadn't helped either. And the two hundred messages to Parochet were alarming.

What would help?

Perhaps words from The Beast Whisperer at Project Ruach?

Ruach is Hebrew for wind, breath, or spirit. Project Ruach was intended to build school spirit. It brought the whole school together every Tuesday right after breakfast, from 8:15 to 8:40 in the Beit Am, an assembly room right next to the dining hall. According to the ethos of HAHA, it was student-led. And it was live-streamed to all parents. This morning, the morning after the bomb threat, Jeff intended to use Ruach to build confidence that *no bomb is coming.*

As Dean of Academics, Rachel Fish ran Ruach. This morning, before it started, Jeff told her he was going to speak briefly at the end. "Two minutes."

"Jeff, you'll eat into first period."

"Only two minutes. And I'd like if you can have Isaac emcee it."

"Why?"

Why? Because Isaac Greene was the student body president and a level-headed kid. Jeff wanted an emcee who would not set a crazy tone.

Rachel Fish's default tone was *machloket*: argument. Before Jeff could answer her *Why*, she lit into him: "Isaac? Again, a male emcee? What are you saying, Jeff? That females are too emotional? No menstrual angst flowing from Isaac—is that it? Jeff, I guarantee you, when we catch this bomb-calling terrorist, he'll be a man. A white man, Jeff. Like Isaac—and you."

Jeff let Rachel talk herself out. She ended by saying, "Sure, *have* your Isaac."

All one hundred and forty-five students sat. As did all sixty teachers. Up on stage, Isaac, mic in hand, confident on his feet, started with a joke: "Why should you always carry a bomb onto a plane? Because the chances of there being *two* bombs on a plane are infinitesimally small."

The audience laughed, nervously.

Jeff stood in back between Rabbi Baum and Stevie Blau, who was videoing this and putting it online. Listening to Isaac, Jeff's heart sank. Far from being quieted, The Beast will be growling. Parents will be barraging me. I should have listened to Rachel, should have put a girl up there.

Isaac went on to say that the chances of there ever being a bomb at HAHA were infinitesimally small, and Jeff debated with himself whether Isaac was an idiot or genius for starting this way.

After a few more upbeat words, Isaac handed the mic to Amy Lovitz, captain of the girls' softball team. She told everyone to *come out this afternoon and see us play—and beat!—Christian Academy.* Kids cheered and applauded.

Amy handed the mic to Beth Katzendorf and Daniel Golub. Beth and Daniel, HAHA's leading student activists, were propelled from one cause to another by whatever happened to be trending on Twitter. The cause du jour was food deserts. Beth and Daniel asked everyone to sign their petition to the Bradleyville City Council. "There is a Whole Foods at the Margaret Mitchell Mall but no affordable place to shop for downtown residents!"

As Jeff expected, HAHA students responded. Not all of them on-topic.

"Why are we not allowed to go to the Margaret Mitchell Mall on the weekends? That's unfair!"

"Do we have to get up for Ruach? What if we don't care about this stuff?"

"How can you not care about people going hungry?"

"How can you not care about us being sleep-deprived?"

Not for the first time, Jeff marveled at what Project Rauch often dissolved into: All the digressions and fine points of Talmudic argument minus Talmudic seriousness. The Beit Am, which means "House of the People," had become House of the Off-the-Point Students.

And now Jeff's phone came alive with commentary from HAHA parents. A Red Sea deluge of texts.

Is it worth getting them up early for this? Research shows . . .

How can you let this food desert persist? What kind of Jews are you training?

I don't see my Brittany! Is she OK?

Rabbi Baum leaned over and whispered in Jeff's ear. "I need a minute to tell the kids why this is happening to us. We must become a Torah school! Just one minute!"

Jeff showed his open palms, as if to say, I can't do anything now. Then he whispered, "Let's talk, after Ruach, Rabbi."

At 8:38—Jeff saw it exactly on his phone—Rachel thanked everyone and said, "And now Mr. Taylor has a few words."

Jeff went up on stage and took the mic from Rachel.

Sweeping his eyes across the audience, he said, "I know what's on all our minds: Why are we the only Jewish institution to get this bomb threat? Well, consider it a tribute to how special we are. Hampton Acres Hebrew Academy is the world's finest co-ed international pluralistic college-prep Jewish boarding school. Yes, the finest!" Jeff paused, smiled. "Of course we are also the world's *only* co-ed international pluralistic college-prep Jewish boarding school."

From the audience: relaxed laughter.

Jeff gave two minutes of fatherly reassurance, which was well received. He was confident he had made HAHA less *farfufket* (befuddled), less *fartoost* (bewildered), and less *bazorgt* (anxious).

Except for Baum. The Rabbi was primed to undo Jeff's calming words. Jeff had to stage an intervention, quickly.

SEVENTEEN

VISITING A RABBI WHO TALKS TO A DEAD RABBI

Rabbi Baum told Jeff, "I believe our most serious offense—what is most likely to have provoked God to rebuke us with this bomb threat—lies in our mezuzahs."

Baum said this from an armchair in the living room of his family's residence within Beit Gibborim, House of the Mighty. The room was lined with thousands of religious books in Hebrew and Yiddish. And while Jeff sat in an armchair facing Baum, Jeff noted that Baum was actually looking a bit to Jeff's right—at, on a bookshelf, a photograph of Baum's Rebbe.

The dead Rebbe who talks to Baum in Baum's dreams, Jeff thought. I sure wish the dead Rebbe *would* talk to this stubborn man—spare me the trouble. It was 9:15 a.m., early in first period. Since Baum didn't have a class Tuesday first period, and Jeff's own class, Jewish Thought and Culture, met after lunch, he had come here straight from Project Ruach. He needed to persuade Baum to stop spreading post-bomb-threat anxiety. He doubted words would do any good. Besides, right now, Jeff's mouth was full of honey cake that Baum's wife, Chava, had just baked. Well, it was very good honey cake. And Jeff suspected that if it were ten or eleven a.m., Baum would be offering schnapps to help the cake along. Instead, there was coffee and tea. And, from Baum, just before Chava returned to the kitchen, the reminder: "Wonderful food, eh, Jeff? And there are a few wonderful women who would like to meet you. Chava and I would like to invite you and one of them to dinner soon."

Meaning, Jeff knew, What are you doing with that shiksa Barbara, that niece of Pastor Travis? Jeff, you need a Jewish wife.

The cake tasted great. The room smelled great. Upstairs were the rooms of eighteen HAHA students, all boys. In the other three residence houses for HAHA boys, the smell of old pizza and old sweat and stale laundry permeated everywhere. Not here. Here Chava's baking held sway.

Baum was saying, "Yes, the fault lies in our mezuzahs. As you know, the klafs must be checked for defects at least twice every seven years. As far as I can tell, they were last checked eight years ago."

Jeff refrained from pointing out that since Baum had been at HAHA nine years, this was Baum's fault.

"And Jeff," said Baum, "only true repentance will appease Hashem, which means fixing every defective mezuzah."

Jeff thought, Well, here goes. "Um, Rabbi . . . I understand your concerns. I do. But Job teaches we can never be certain why God lets someone suffer. Job's three comforters tell Job that he must have done something wrong—but what happens? God rebukes *them* for their presumption. So I suggest that we can't really know why—"

"Why God has singled us out!" said Baum. "Out of one hundred Jewish organizations, why only *we* were threatened again? We *can't* really know. But it must be something. The defective mezuzahs! The fasts and festivals that we have desecrated! Six fast days a year and we grudgingly observe only one! In one or the other of those the fault must lie. So we must—"

"Have three men praying for us at the Kotel for the next seventy-two hours, seeking forgiveness of Hashem in the name of"—Jeff nodded to the photograph—"your Rebbe."

"What?" said Baum. But he began to look pleased.

The Kotel was the Western Wall. This was a usual practice: pay people to pray for you. Three men for seventy-two hours would cost about eighteen hundred dollars.

"And of course," said Jeff, "all three will be strictly Chabad." Meaning Baum's sect of Hasidim. Jeff made it clear: "No Belzer Chasid, no Gerer Chasid, no Bobov Chasid." Meaning no one in the three other sects of Hasidim—the sects that Baum and all other Chabad considered imposters. Any other imposter sects? Jeff, who wasn't feeling very patient with Rabbi Baum, was tempted to add No Dasher, No Dancer, No Prancer, No Vixen, No Comet, No Cupid, No Donner, No Blitzen. He restrained himself.

Baum's smile grew.

"And," continued Jeff, with a grand wave to encompass this living room and the kitchen beyond, "since everyone flocks here on Friday night, for your and your wife's excellent, generous hospitality . . . why don't we increase your household budget? I'm sure you and the Rebbetzin"—meaning the rabbi's wife—"can use it well."

Meaning, if not all that money goes into the hospitality, if some of it goes into your own pocket, Rabbi, *I don't care.*

Baum's smile covered his whole broad face.

"In return for which," said Jeff, "I would hope you will back off from your requests about mezuzahs and feasts and festivals and prayers . . . yes?"

Baum didn't answer immediately.

"How *much* of an increase in the household budget?" he asked.

Which Jeff and he worked out, and shook hands on.

After which Jeff ate the last crumbs of the very good honey cake and reflected that being Head of HAHA required, among other things, having the soul of a soulless Chicago ward boss. He also remembered the definition: An honest politician is one who, when bought, stays bought.

Jeff wondered, Will Baum stay bought?

EIGHTEEN
VISITING A POSSIBLY PSYCHO PSYCHOTHERAPIST

Fresh from—he hoped—buying off Rabbi Benjamin Baum, Jeff went to see if he could buy off Number 2 on the Spreading Bomb-Threat Anxiety Throughout HAHA Hit Parade.

Celine Johnson.

Crossing the Myron Kleinman Quad, he approached the Dr. Walter Kleinman Center for Health. This was the only building named for a Kleinman who was neither a hustler (Sammy) nor a hustler's deadbeat relative (Harold, Stuart, etc., etc.). Yes, Dr. Walter Kleinman, many degrees after his name, had an actual practice as a radiologist in Cleveland.

Degrees were on Jeff's mind because a degree is what he planned to buy off Celine with.

Confidently tapping the letter of resignation in his breast pocket, he opened the door to the Kleinman Center, stepped into the entry . . .

. . . and immediately got a frown from the bulldog on guard. Bulldog-faced Nurse Clara Glatt. Without a "Hello," the school nurse rose from behind her hallway desk and blasted him with a disinfecting aerosol spray.

Choking, Jeff managed, "What was that for?"

"Kids are coming in here afraid of the bomb," said Nurse Glatt.

"Super anxious. I'm discouraging them from going any further."

"Well, you just about discouraged me," said Jeff. "Now if you'll excuse me . . ."

He walked past Glatt and into Celine's outer office.

Here all six chairs were filled with anxious students. Jeff knew three by reputation: A bedwetter, a sleepwalker, and a nail-biter. The other three stymied Jeff; he had not thought they were medically-challenged. Damn! Are they bomb-threat-blitzed?

On the walls were saccharine posters. HUGS SAY LOVE WITHOUT A WORD and I AM A SHOULDER TO LEAN ON.

Jeff thought, Yeah, I know that one should never interrupt a therapy session, but given Celine's brand of "therapy," I'm probably doing the child in there a favor. Nodding to the six students, he knocked on the door to Celine's inner office.

She opened it. Behind her, in a comfy chair—facing another comfy chair from which Celine had risen—sat Hannah Newins.

Hannah, HAHA's poster child for anxiety. But not, Jeff knew, free-floating anxiety. Rather, the targeted kind, coolly *used* by clever, manipulative Hannah. Hannah's face was tear-stained. Real tears, thought Jeff. Real ammo. Hannah Newins could twist you around her little tear duct.

"Celine!" said Jeff. "Could I have a word with you? Hannah! Sorry to interrupt."

Hannah wailed. "Mr. Taylor! We are almost done . . . you can't do this to me!"

Hannah got up and threw herself into Celine's outstretched arms.

Pulling Hannah to her and stroking her head, Celine said, "Hannah, dear . . . if you could give us a minute . . . ?"

"The school doesn't care about me. The Head doesn't care about me," Hannah sobbed, firing live ammo as she left the room.

Celine called out to her, "Hannah, wait in the hallway for me. I will get you excused from afternoon classes so we can get back to work."

Closing the door, and turning to Jeff, Celine said, "You really set her back. We were on the verge of a breakthrough."

Sure you were, thought Jeff.

He said, "Sorry. I'll keep this short. Look! Celine, you're the only person standing between our kids"—he waved toward her outer office—"and the demons that plague them, that make them anxious. So, Celine, we don't want *you* to be anxious."

Which of course she was.

Jeff continued laying it on her. "We want you to feel secure. I know you feel you are not sufficiently appreciated here. But you *are* appreciated. And you deserve, to go with your name, a degree that speaks to the esteem in which you are held. So I am here to tell you that I will get you into a PhD program, which of course the school will pay for."

Note to self: There must be somewhere, somewhere on the web, a site that grants PhDs to people who can't even get into the University of Phoenix. Find it!

Celine's eyes watered. Wrapping her large fleshy arms around Jeff, pressing her large fleshy body to him, she sobbed her thanks.

"Jeff . . . Jeff . . . what can I say?"

Gently extricating himself, Jeff thought, You could say, *I'm going to stop pumping up HAHA kids' bomb-threat anxiety.* You could say *that.*

But what Celine Johnson said was, "Oh, Jeff! A PhD program. How wonderful. But a challenge! It makes me anxious!"

Damn! thought Jeff. It's backfired!

He tried to undo the damage. "Uh, listen, Celine. Anxiety. Any kid's anxiety about the bomb. As you think about embarking on this PhD program, think how *Doctor* Celine Johnson—as a good *doctor*—will be dialing a kid's anxiety *down*, will be *appreciated* for doing that."

Celine nodded vigorously, yes, yes, of course. But Jeff wondered—did he just make a deal? A principle from Contract Law 101 came back to him: to have a deal, there must be a meeting of the minds.

If their minds had to meet, could he please bring a chaperone?

NINETEEN
MOLECULES AND MANURE, VENTILATION AND VANITY

It was a rare day when the odor of Emmitt Bailey's pig farm reached HAHA. But this late afternoon was hot, heavy, and humid. Walking toward the Admin building, Jeff's nose twitched in annoyance. *Damn it, I may be smelling it only now, but we're breathing the stuff every day.*

Jeff eyed his office windows. There, Preston Tom had installed, disguised as a thermometer, a gauge that measured the extent to which HAHA was inhaling pork. Preston had shown Jeff how to read the gauge. Today, Jeff didn't dare read it. Jeff needed to *act.*

I can't save the school. But I can fix this.

Jeff phoned Emmitt and asked if he could come over and get a tour. Emmitt sounded surprised—it seemed no Head of HAHA had ever contacted him—but said, "Sure."

So Jeff drove the three minutes to get there.

His first sight of the farm was its bubble-gum-pink manure lagoon. Emmitt's six thousand hogs had produced that lagoon and who knows how many zillion pork molecules? Jeff did know it wouldn't be pretty when The Beast finds out it has been breathing those molecules.

Gotta fix this before that happens. Stop those pork molecules from being inhaled by the children of Israel.

Jeff pulled up in front of Emmitt's neat, white, nineteenth-century farmhouse.

Emmitt, seventy-two, tall, heavy-set, and friendly, stepped down off his front porch, shook hands, said, "Mr. Taylor, I'm pleased to meet my neighbor." Like the speech of many big men, his was soft and measured. Jeff had become familiar with the slow talk of people around here—they'd say one word in the time that most New Yorkers would say three—but Emmitt deserved a record for slowness.

"Y'all want to see my little operation here?" asked Emmitt.

"Yes, please."

Emmitt walked Jeff over to and inside one of his six buildings, Number 4. Football-field-long, it was nearly wall-to-wall with one thousand pigs, each pig—about the size of an NFL running back—crammed in a pen too tight to turn around in. The heat and the stench were unbearable. As thick and hot as the air was outside, it was far worse in here.

Jeff stared at the animals whose life consisted of eating, excreting, and growing. On their way to becoming ham, bacon, sausage. All the while broadcasting pork molecules.

"Can't you ventilate this place?" Jeff asked. He thought, Vent the air *away* from HAHA?

"What I'm doing," said Emmitt Bailey.

He pointed to some impressive-looking equipment. He said, "The latest industrial air pollution control. That precipitator recirculates seventy-five to one hundred percent of the treated air. And achieves good particle control. Costs me another dollar per pig, and I'm about to spend more. I've ordered some gas-fired heaters—they'll bring CO_2 concentrations down near two thousand ppm, that's parts per million." He looked at Jeff. "I'm trying to be a good neighbor."

"Uh-huh," said Jeff. He had done some reading about raising pigs, but he had no idea if he could ask Emmitt to do more.

But from his former life, hedge funds, he knew a bluff could work. He said, "I appreciate that, Mr. Bailey—"

"Please. Call me Emmitt."

"Thanks, Emmitt. And if your nearest neighbor were, say, an Amazon warehouse, maybe two thousand ppm would be fine. All those workers *in*side. But we're a school, with kids and teachers walking around the campus, in the open air, *out*side. So I think your target ought to be five hundred ppm."

Emmitt looked flustered.

Jeff had zero—zero!—idea if Emmitt could hit five hundred, but what the hell. Four years ago, at Rose & Company, working with Bobby C., he had been negotiating with a bank that wanted to sell the debt of a plumbing supply company that had produced defective pipe. The bank said it would sell at thirty cents on the dollar. According to a study done by the bank's law firm, the pipe was in a half-million homes with a liability of one thousand dollars per home, total liability five hundred million dollars. Lying through his teeth, Jeff told Bobby to say, "We've done *our* research and that pipe is in at least a million homes, so the liability is at least a billion dollars." He told Bobby that Rose & Company would pay no more than eighteen cents.

A deal was done at nineteen cents—and Rose & Company made an excellent profit.

"Five hundred ppm?" said Emmitt to Jeff. "I don't know if *any* number of heaters can do that."

"But you'll look into it," said Jeff.

"I'll look into it."

"Appreciate it."

Emmitt recovered, reassumed his confidence. He said, "And over here . . . "

He walked Jeff to a corner of the building. Here, in a larger enclosure, was a single humungous pig, a pig four times bigger than any of the others, a pig the size of a Harley-Davidson. A true hog, thought, Jeff. And with, it seemed, the coiled energy of a Harley.

"Big Bob," said Emmitt, proudly. "A landrace boar. Not raising him for the market. Raising him to see how big I can get him. The record is nine hundred and sixty-two pounds. Right now, Bob is eight-twelve."

"Impressive."

Bob thanked Jeff with a grunt that sounded like an industrial vacuum cleaner.

"Now, how about some iced tea?" said Emmitt.

They sat on Emmitt's front porch and sipped. Jeff tried not to gag on the overdose of sugar. Trying not to gag on the smell from the lagoon, he wondered how Emmitt could live with it. Well, maybe Emmitt has gone noseblind, or the money smells sweeter.

At which Jeff heard Michelle in his ear: *Hey, hon, and backcountry Greenwich doesn't have its odors? What about the stench from our neighbor the payday lending king?*

Point taken, Jeff granted.

"You know," Emmitt said, "that your boss will be sharing the cost of those new heaters."

"Sammy Kleinman?"

"Yes, sir. Miss Samantha. The Kleinmans own almost twenty percent of the farm. You knew that, right?" Emmitt looked uncomfortable, but Jeff, back in bluff mode, reassured him.

"Sure, I knew. It's just, well, you know . . . "

"They don't like saying they're in the pork business? I read the Old Testament—I understand. Wouldn't look good for Bradleyville's most important Jewish family. Besides it wasn't like they planned it. Fact is, Manny, the daddy, was going to buy me out. He had an option on the whole spread. Then when things went haywire back in '08, we worked out a new deal. They got near about twenty percent, and I never hear from them."

Jeff nodded as if he had heard this all before and made himself finish the tea. After a bit more small talk, he pointed to the darkening sky. "Looks like a storm's coming. I'd better get going."

Emmitt agreed. He said, "Gonna be a real gully-washer."

"Uh-huh."

As they shook hands, Emmitt said, "Don't be a stranger."

Jeff thought, When I was helping run a hedge fund, did I ever imagine I'd be told not to be a stranger by the owner of a manure lagoon?

TWENTY

FAKE CAMERAS, REAL SURFACE-TO-AIR MISSILES

On Monday, Jeff had promised the executive committee that every foot of the fence surrounding the school would get reinspected.

Now, on Thursday, that's what he and Jerome were doing: walking the one point six miles of six-foot-tall, forest-green, close-set, sharp-pointed vertical steel bars.

Close-set. But, as Jeff had suspected and as he and Jerome were now discovering, in some places the bars were pried apart. So HAHA kids could sneak off campus and sneak back in. Jerome was noting all the places to be fixed.

And Jerome was noting all the places—about every two hundred feet—to install what Jeff had also promised: dummy cameras. There would be forty of them.

With Jeff and Jerome, here came—huffing and puffing in an effort to keep his plump body up with theirs—Stevie Blau. Stevie kept voicing what he thought of dummy cameras: "We need *real* ones, one hundred and thirty degree field, each with four LEDs for fifty feet of night vision. With Wi-Fi. Plus motion-sensing and audio." He pointed to the woods that bordered this stretch of fence. "To sense and hear anything coming."

"Stevie," said Jeff, "there's no money for any more real cameras."

The only real cameras were at the school's only entrance, its front gate.

"What happens," said Stevie, "when word gets out that all the cameras you're going to put here"—he pointed to the fence stretching to the horizon—"are fake?"

Stevie had a point. HAHA leaked information.

Before Jeff could answer, another voice was in his ear. "Eh, Jeff, what good are even real ones? Eh?" The voice came from, out of nowhere, suddenly at his side: Noga Weinstein. She had appeared as stealthily as an undercover Mossad operative. She continued: "Real cameras that scan at ground level, scan for someone walking toward this fence? What if someone is not walking."

"Not walking?" said Jeff.

"Not," said Noga.

She pointed overhead. With perfect timing, out from above the woods, came an ultralight. At the controls was HAHA's teacher of the Holocaust and Israel's Wars, former IDF commando Nadav Peretz. Expertly riding the wind, he flew over the fence, landed ten yards inside and, with the bearing of a commando, strode toward Jeff, Jerome, Stevie, and Noga.

Muscled and fit, with close-cropped hair, Nadav wore a three-pound watch that looked like it could remotely detonate Iran's nuclear facilities. He grinned like a man who would *do* it.

Noga was also grinning. Stevie was gaping. Jerome was slowly moving his wooden toothpick from one corner of his mouth to the other.

"Noga," said Jeff. "We can't protect against *every*thing. What are you suggesting? Surface-to-air missiles?"

"I have a cousin in Haifa," said Nadav. "He's got some Barak II's. Eh? Designed for shipboard. They'll do just fine."

"You're joking," Jeff said.

Noga's flashing black eyes told him Nadav was not.

TWENTY-ONE

A GOLDEN HOUR

Do I believe in God? Jeff asked himself.

Now, as at the start of each Shabbat dinner, he did. At least in the God whose Sabbath the Hampton Acres Hebrew Academy kept.

For now, at dusk, gathered in the Moadon, was a community. Here were all one hundred and forty-five students and two dozen teachers and staff members. Here, at the end of a week that started with The Beast roaring over a bomb threat, the mood was one of quiet, ease, and security. All the kids looked both tired from a long week and—recently scrubbed and polished—fresh. Even glowing. All were better dressed than during the week: the boys wore polo shirts and khakis, the girls were in skirts and dresses. No jeans. A sense of order and happy expectation. A golden hour.

Thinking of Greenwich, Connecticut's iconic animal, Jeff imagined a noble-looking Golden Retriever.

For a moment Jeff could almost believe that Manny Kleinman had not made a mistake creating HAHA. And that he, Jeff, had not made a mistake coming here. Of course, he knew this feeling—of enchanted contentment—was ephemeral. It would last through dinner, then vanish. But while it was present, he gave himself over to it.

Shabbat started with the seventy or so girls lighting the more than one hundred and forty candles. To the glow of faces was added the glow of flames.

Then, as for each Shabbat, Rabbi Baum had selected a student to give a *d'var Torah*—a brief talk—on this week's *parashah* (section) of the Torah. This week he had chosen Ella Bronstein. And this week the *parashah* was verses 1:1 to 5:26 in Leviticus. Ella was fairly secular. What, Jeff wondered, would she say about these passages specifying the rules of burnt offerings for priests?

To his surprise, Ella talked about how, while these rituals are foreign to us and while they can't be performed until the Temple is rebuilt, animal offerings are a way to express gratitude and reverence. "And we should be grateful and reverent every day."

Now it was Jeff's turn to give a *d'var Torah* on the same passages.

In case anybody here was still worried by the bomb threat—looking at you, Hannah Newins, and at you, Celine Johnson—Jeff talked about how these rituals connect us to God. "Even without these offerings, that connection remains strong, and it still protects us."

That was more pious than he actually felt, but part of the job of the Head of School was to reassure, was to appear to be a *Tzadik*, what gentiles call a saint. Which I'm not, thought Jeff. And, calm and contented, he felt a connection to something higher.

Then he joined everyone as Baum led them in singing *Ma Tovu*, the song that opens the Friday night service. *Ma Tovu* is usually sung with fresh energy. But Baum, being Baum, jumped, clapped, danced, and practically shouted the words. Baum was acting as young as the teenagers he would be leading out into the dusk—perhaps even younger, thought Jeff.

Then Ella announced where, tonight, the Orthodox, Conservative, and Reform services would be held, and the assembly dispersed to those three residential houses. Tonight, Jeff went to the Reform service; he tried, ecumenically, to spread his presence around.

Then, after services, everyone reassembled in the dining hall for the week's best meal.

After dinner but before dessert, there was a long prayer—by which time, Jeff could see, the kids wanted *out*. The mood was dissolving.

The kids wanted to get back to their residential houses for *Oneg* (dessert) and/or get to the serious Friday night treats of vaping, drugs, drinking, or hooking up.

Seeing Jordan and Jose rise from their tables, fall in step, and walk out together, Jeff felt the moment of contentment vanish. It was replaced by helplessness.

In his head, Michelle spoke reassurance. *Jordan says she's on the pill. We have to believe her.*

Sure wish you were here to make sure, thought Jeff.

Hon, said Michelle, *there is no such thing as sure.*

Jeff's darling daughter and a hundred and forty-four other teenagers bounded out the door. Jeff had the sudden image of happy, heedless Golden Retrievers wagging their big, bushy tails and knocking over furniture and everything else in their young lives.

TWENTY-TWO

THE HERO

OF THE HARDWOOD

Tomorrow's the day, thought Jeff.

It was nine a.m. Sunday, March 13. Jeff was at his kitchen table, making what he vowed were the last edits to his letter of resignation . . . *precious memories to be forever cherished . . .*

He put his pen down. At least, tomorrow was supposed to have been the day.

Six days ago, when the bomb threat came in, he had figured give The Beast seven days to calm down. He had figured seven days and then tell Sammy: come June 21, I'm gone. Okay, so it hadn't been that easy—he had had to buy off Baum and Celine. And a few phone calls and emails still came in from bomb-anxious parents. And last night, when he looked at Parochet, there were a few new messages from bomb-anxious kids.

The Beast was semi-riled.

Okay, so give The Beast another two, three, days.

Do I have to deal with anyone else? Buy off anyone else?

Well, from walking the fence, it's clear Stevie Blau is still upset. But Stevie's not going to *do* anything, right? Nothing that will upset *other* people, right?

And what about Noga—Noga and Nadav showing up at the fence

like IDF commandos mounting a special op in the mountains of Lebanon. And the other Israelis? Well, they aren't going to *do* anything, right? Not going to equip every teacher with an Uzi, right?

Before I give Sammy the news, I've gotta make sure.

Right.

Okay, so right now there was nothing to do but put this letter away and enjoy breakfast.

His phone rang.

"Jeff, go to our website!"

"Sure, Sammy, what's up?"

"Jeff, even here in Tashkent, I know what day it is. You think Columbia's all-time assist leader would forget Selection Sunday?"

"Right," said Jeff. The announcement of the sixty-eight teams selected for the NCAA Men's Division I basketball tournament. The beginning of March Madness, a sacred day on the calendar of, if not Georgia, all the surrounding states. But what was that to Sammy in Uzbekistan?

"Right!" said Sammy. "And right before your eyes—if you go to our website—you'll see it. A video I just posted, to tie in with March Madness."

"Okay . . . "

Jeff fetched his laptop.

There it was. A new video titled "On The Ball."

Jeff clicked, the video started. The scene: a basketball court, but not HAHA's. The star:

Having traded her Michael Kors pantsuits and her Louboutin heels for a HAHA basketball uniform and Nike sneakers, it was Sammy, holding a basketball and grinning.

The former starting point guard, Columbia women's varsity basketball, announced, "Hello, I'm Samantha 'Sammy' Kleinman, CEO of Hampton Acres Hebrew Academy. I'm here at the top of what, in basketball, is called the *key*—here to tell you about the *key* to success for your son or daughter. What is that *key*? It's a diploma from our great school. Yes, any student who comes here gets a *jump* . . ."

Sammy launched a jump shot with a fluid motion Jeff admired. It swished home.

" . . . a *jump* on the competition." Sammy pumped her fist. "Yes, if your son or daughter comes here, their success is . . . "

The video cut to Sammy driving to the basket. She launched herself and—through the magic of editing—elevated above the rim and drove the ball in.

" . . . a *slam dunk!*"

"So get your child to Hampton Acres Hebrew Academy and get on the ball!"

With those words, triumphant marching-band music played and the video ended.

Jeff blinked. Sammy's enterprising spirit never failed to amaze him. And now Sammy was back in Jeff's ear: "Don't you love that? I just love it. I haven't lost a step! And we are a basketball and academic powerhouse! In the South, it's UNC, Duke, and *us!* This video is going to bring us the next dominating power forward from Samarkand! The next dynamite point guard from Tel Aviv!"

"You bet, Sammy."

Sammy laughed triumphantly and hung up.

And what, Jeff wondered, will bring us the fifty million? He typed arewebrokeyet615 into his laptop. There was $2.77 million in cash, which meant the burn rate had risen again since he had checked a week ago, and the drop-dead date had moved up to May 19.

Fifty million! Where will we find two million—enough to get to June 21? Last June, when they had shaken hands on renewing Jeff's contract for this year, Sammy had said, "You focus on running the place. I'll take care of the rest."

Jeff considered that a soft promise not to close HAHA early. Sammy wouldn't do that, right? If she did, the staff and faculty would be out on the street after schools had finished hiring. And, except for the seniors, students would be scrambling to find a new school after admissions had been closed out.

He and Sammy would be sued in every country whose flag hung in the dining hall. Rhoda Friedlander was crazy enough to send hit men after them. The Beast would be *righteously* rabid.

No, that can't happen.

If Sammy can't find a donor, she will have to fill the hole herself. And she can do it—the Kleinmans were still rich. And still crafty. Jeff realized that if Sammy couldn't find anyone, she would lean on Jeff to pitch in. He could see Sammy, smiling and unctuous, putting the touch on him: *Jeff the kids love you. And you love them.*

No, I'm not gonna do that. HAHA is the Kleinman fiefdom. I just work there.

Jeff addressed the frozen image of Sammy the basketball player on his laptop. "It's on you, Ms. Hardwood Hero. You've got the ball and enough time for a buzzer beater. Don't blow it."

TWENTY-THREE
BUTTERFLY BONANZA

"Here!" said Barbara Travis, pointing, enthusiastic, and turning her battered Ford F-150 off the two-lane blacktop onto the dirt track. "Junkyard in here. Great stuff." She grinned across at Jeff. Sunday late morning, they were far out in the country, on back roads where farmland surrendered to scraggy second-growth woods. Jeff had been slumped in the seat, inattentive. Barbara said, "Might have something perfect for *Butterfly*."

"Great," said Jeff. "Great."

What do you do when you're in love with a woman and you can see yourself marrying her, spending the rest of your life with her, and she thinks she's a serious artist, but what she really makes is kitsch? What do you do when she's currently making a *huge* piece of kitsch, a collection of welded-together metal junk titled *Butterfly* that sometime soon will be installed right outside your office window where you'll have to look at it every day until you finally leave?

That was Jeff's dilemma with Barbara.

He and she mostly liked the same music, books, and movies. They mostly laughed at the same stuff. They more than mostly meshed in bed. The only disagreement they had was: where was a good place to live? Barbara said she couldn't imagine leaving Bradleyville. Jeff said he couldn't see himself—once HAHA went under—staying there.

That they could talk about. Jeff knew there was nothing he could say that even hinted at *Barbara, you're a horrible artist.*

God, was she a horrible artist.

Industrious, yes. Enterprising, yes. Energized, yes. For the scrap metal for her sculptures, she knew and scoured every dump and junkyard around, plus every woods and gully with a "NO DUMPING" sign that people had ignored.

All to make industrial-sized kitsch. *Butterfly* would have ten children, enough to make the work monumental in scale. "Why ten?" Jeff had asked.

"A minyan," said Barbara.

Barbara Travis was such an earnest, well-meaning WASP. Jeff didn't want to point out that a minyan was composed only of adults, and only for certain religious obligations. He feared Barbara would tell him that *Butterfly* fulfilled a religious obligation.

That was how creators of kitsch thought.

In a welder's mask and wielding a no-nonsense welder's torch, Barbara dared a strong man to stand his ground. *Butterfly*, nearly complete, made Jeff recoil.

C'mon, hon . . .

This was Michelle, in his head.

Did you like everything I liked? I gorged on triple-decker Victorian novels. Anthony Trollope. You said the plots were unworthy of daytime soaps.

True, replied Jeff. But you didn't write them. You weren't a bad artist.

And the thing was: As bad an artist as Barbara was . . . she could be a great lawyer.

She didn't want to be a paralegal forever, and she sometimes talked about going to law school part-time. She said she saw opportunities. "Half the world goes to sleep every night without a proper will."

Jeff encouraged her. She was wicked smart. But he didn't see her in Trusts and Estates. As she was indefatigable, he saw her as a tax whiz, digging through the IRS Code, using its obscure corners to save her clients millions and being rewarded for it. This would be a change from what she pulled in as an "artist"—which was no fees.

In fifteen years of making kitsch, she had sold exactly zero.

He told her, Yes, go part-time.

"But, dear," Barbara always said, "then I wouldn't have time for my sculptures."

"Right," said Jeff.

Now Barbara pulled her pickup into the junkyard, hopped out, and plunged in. Jeff watched her disappear in a sprawling pile of discarded household stuff. He got out of the pickup and stood, waiting.

"Success!" yelled Barbara.

She emerged, waving something. As she came closer, Jeff could see it was a trowel. "For Aaron's right hand!" cried Barbara.

Barbara had named the ten children in *Butterfly*—five boys and five girls—and Jeff had seen that Aaron already had two hands, both of them welded-on garden trowels. Did he need a replacement?

Barbara showed Jeff. "Look, five prongs. More realistic. Replace the four-prongs he's got now."

"An improvement," said Jeff.

She put Aaron's new right hand into Jeff's. "Here, hold onto it. I'm going back, see what else there is."

The trowel in Jeff's hand felt like a heavy weight. Barbara's *Butterfly* was inspired by *I Never Saw Another Butterfly*, the famous collection of art and poetry by Jewish children in the Theresienstadt concentration camp. Barbara said hers was an answer to that sad collection. Her piece was a semi-circle of ten life-sized children with hopeful smiles . . . each child reaching a hand up toward—and joining at—a point where a metal butterfly fluttered. With a letter in the hand of each child, the title of Barbara's work of art would be spelled out: I SAW ANOTHER BUTTERFLY.

Cringeworthy and saccharine.

"Jeff!" From deep in the sprawling pile of junk came the triumphant cry of his beloved: "Jeff! *More* success!"

TWENTY-FOUR
THINGS DON'T GO SWIMMINGLY

"**A**m I hearing you correctly?" asked Jeff. "You want to baptize twenty kids in a Jewish swimming pool?"

"And pay you for it," said the Reverend Pat Travis.

Late Sunday afternoon, inside the world-class natatorium of HAHA's athletic center, Jeff stood with the head of Bradleyville's largest evangelical Christian church. A man who—Jeff reminded himself—is Barbara's uncle.

Rent the pool to Reverend Travis? thought Jeff. *That* would make waves.

"I'd like to," said Jeff. He knew that Sammy, eager to scoop up any buck, would do it. "But . . . ah . . . many of my constituents would be . . . ah . . . unhappy." Rabbi Baum would have apoplexy. The Beast would be howling. "So, I'm afraid, no amount of money . . . "

"Too bad," sighed the Reverend Pat Travis.

He felt it was bad.

Reverend Pat suspected the school needed money. And he knew—because Barbara had told him—that Jeff planned to leave at the end of this school year.

For Barbara's sake, Reverend Pat wanted to keep Jeff here.

For humanity's sake, Reverend Pat wanted—needed!—to keep the school here.

He loved the Jews. The presence of HAHA in Bradleyville gave him hope, the presence of *two hundred Jews living by their Torah!* Reverend Pat knew the Tribulation and the Rapture were coming very soon. The resurrection of all the dead in Christ. Reverend Pat knew that being neighbors to all these Jews meant the Rapture would *not* pass Bradleyville by. For look at what has, miraculously, already come to pass. Just as God started gathering the Jews to their homeland (fulfilling verses in Isaiah and Ezekiel), so, starting in 2004, He gathered these two hundred Jews here.

But if HAHA failed, if it were closed . . .

If the HAHA Jews were dispersed as the Jews had been dispersed thousands of years ago . . .

Unthinkable!

The Reverend Pat knew that the thousand dollars he could pay to rent HAHA's natatorium for an afternoon was a mere drop in—well, not in a bucket . . . say, a mere drop in the pool. But as Ecclesiastes says, "Cast thy bread upon the waters" and who knows how the favor would be repaid. Perhaps, if God willed it, the thousand dollars would be multiplied a thousandfold?

The Reverend Pat knew that Samantha Kleinman was out there hustling. Perhaps the favor would be repaid by one of the rich people Samantha was courting . . . ?

Now the Reverend Pat said to Jeff, "You're sure you have to say 'no'? I bet Sammy would say 'yes.'"

"Well, Reverend, this cup isn't going to pass from me. *I'm* saying no. How about you baptize kids in the YMCA pool?"

"That's not the point. Jeff, I want to help you. I want to help this school."

Jeff was touched. He knew Barbara's uncle really did. "C'mon," said Jeff, "let's get out of here before the chlorine warps my brain and I say 'yes.'"

Walking out of the HAHA natatorium with Jeff Taylor, the Reverend Pat was disappointed. But hardly defeated. To hasten the

Rapture and ensure it would not pass Bradleyville by, he had a much bigger plan in mind.

TWENTY-FIVE
FORGING A SWORD

It was six days since the bomb threat and Noga Weinstein, frustrated by the *rachamim*—pitiful!—security measures Jeff was implementing, now took matters into her own hands. To form *Cherev*—Sword—she enlisted three other Israelis at the school. Two women: Shulamit Mouchly and Ilana Weiss, both Hebrew teachers. And Nadav Peretz. All had served in the IDF.

And because Noga knew Cherev needed IT help, she enlisted Stevie Blau.

Nadav, who had been studying the neighboring hillbilly and redneck culture as he had once studied the Arabs of the neighboring West Bank, was professionally engaged.

Stevie was *psyched*. He had spent eighteen of the last twenty-four hours making his house, Beit Rashi, secure. Now he was pumped to make the whole school secure.

Cherev met in Noga's apartment at HAHA.

Cherev's five members quickly agreed on the following:

1. All video feeds to Jerome McKool's security command center will also go to our computers.

2. In case of any intruder, we will quickly neutralize them.

3. To make sure we can neutralize any intruder, we will establish a nearby rifle range and practice with our Uzis.

4. All outsiders coming "legally" onto campus will be surveilled by

one or more of us. Any outsider who doesn't fit—anyone who looks nervous—will be politely stopped. If politeness doesn't work, we will drop it. "The Americans—eh!—are uncomfortable with profiling," said Noga Weinstein, "but you bet we will do it."

As if on cue, as Noga said "profiling," Rachel Fish—uninvited—walked in.

Rachel had heard of the meeting, heard of the five people who would be here. Rachel generally had no use for Israelis who supported the colonialist, apartheid state of Israel. Worse, for Israelis who had been in the IDF. But right now she *did* have a use.

Walking into Noga's apartment, Rachel told the five surprised members of Cherev, "Profiling. Anybody with a missing tooth, we stop. Anybody with a very red neck, we stop."

"Rachel," said Noga, "that's *Shtoyyot*." Nonsense.

"And," said Rachel, "we match all faces with a databank that includes personal histories. So anybody who's ever gone to a monster truck rally, we stop. Anybody who's ever gone to a wet T-shirt contest, we stop."

"Eh! Rachel," said Nadav Peretz. "Eh, that's not going far enough. Anybody who's ever mowed their front lawn and discovered three cars, two pickup trucks and one wringer-washing machine, we stop."

"Exactly!" said Rachel.

"That was a *joke*," said Nadav Peretz. "Eh—an *American* joke."

A joke at my expense! thought Rachel. But then the four Israelis started arguing with each other in Hebrew. Rapidfire. Emotional. Supplemented with hyperactive hand gestures. Rachel didn't understand it, and she saw that Stevie didn't either. But it was intense, and she felt at home.

TWENTY-SIX

HIGH SPIRITS

"**I**t's about Purim, Mr. Taylor. We want the whole school to celebrate it right."

This was from Sacha Reznick, a bullet-train of *wholeschooltocelebrateitright*. To himself, Jeff sighed. Sacha, a junior, was an outstanding student and a pain in the ass. Nine a.m. Monday, Sacha, Rabbi Baum, and Shlomo Goldstein sat across from Jeff at his desk. Shlomo, who had come from Miami Beach to HAHA in September as the very secular Stevie Goldstein, had turned into a mini-Baum: he wore a black hat, black suit, and white shirt. His furious parents blamed Jeff for their child's transformation into a Hasid.

"With *Kavanah*," added Shlomo, using the Hebrew word (pronounced *Ka-VON-ah*) for the right mindset when engaged in Jewish ritual. Baum nodded, affixing rabbinic approval to his disciple's pronouncement.

A bad sign, thought Jeff.

Pressing his fingertips together, Jeff looked past the trio, out his window. Keeping his face bland, he furiously tried to remember everything he knew about Purim, now eight days away. What were they after: animal sacrifice? Baum was crazy enough to want to make a burnt offering on campus—a whole ox on a pyre in front of the athletic center?—and crafty enough to get a student to ask.

"Uh-huh," said Jeff.

Baum placed his fingers on Jeff's desk—a man laying out his cards. He said, "The minhag—the custom—is quite clear. On Purim, a good Jew must drink so much that he cannot tell the difference between blessed Mordechai and cursed Haman."

That's what they want? "Rabbi, you can't mean you want one hundred and forty-five kids getting roaring drunk on campus."

Baum nodded rapidly, the brim of his black fedora going up and down as if he were praying. "Well, not the girls. They don't have the obligation."

"Not the girls," Jeff repeated mechanically.

"Mr. Taylor," said Sacha, "the mission statement"—Sacha pointed to outside Jeff's door, where it hung—"says the school is committed to helping every student make his or her Jewish practice more authentic." He started quoting the thing, going so fast the words were a jumble of slogans and clichés: *timelessvaluescontemporarychallengespersonalcommitmentcommunaleffort . . .*

Jeff thought, Read slowly and given careful thought, they sounded pretty much the same.

"Sacha, Shlomo, Rabbi," said Jeff, in the warm, chummy tone he often used to say *no,* "it's not possible. It's way off the reservation."

Careful! Jeff told himself. I said "reservation." Not Woke. Thank God Rachel isn't here.

Undeterred, Sacha whipped out a well-thumbed copy of *Derech Eretz, The Way of the World,* the school handbook. Flipping to a page marked with a Post-it, he read, "Section Five, Sub-Section Eight, Paragraph Three. 'Authentic observance of all holidays and festivals is of consuming importance.'" Sacha grinned, said, "Consuming!"

"I will watch them, Jeff," said Rabbi Baum. "We will shut the gates. No one leaves campus. It will stay under control."

"I will help make sure," said Shlomo.

Jeff thought, So I should relax and trust Baum, the eternal teenager.

"Jeff," said Baum with great gravity, "this bomb threat reminds us: we must be good Jews. If we had not strayed, we would not have been threatened."

Jeff sighed. He thought, Baum, we have a deal. I'm giving you prayers at the Kotel and more money in your household budget—in return you're supposed to act sane.

"The kids will grow spiritually," added Rabbi Baum.

"Rabbi, I leave it to you how to celebrate Purim. Just don't confuse spirituality and spirits," said Jeff. "And keep the spirits under a hundred proof."

TWENTY-SEVEN

MR. BLAU,
TEAR DOWN THIS WALL

"**S**tevie," yelled Jeff, "what is this?! What are you doing?!"
Jeff confronted Stevie Blau outside Beit Rashi. All
around the building, Stevie had unfurled—and had
anchored three feet apart—two eight-foot-high walls of chicken wire.
He had lined the chicken wire with heavy-duty fabric liner. Now, with
a front-end loader from Roger's U-Rent It, Stevie was filling the space
between the walls with dirt and gravel.

A huge crowd of students, teachers, and staff had gathered. Some
people were laughing, some were anxious. In the front of the crowd,
all eighteen Rashi boys—the kids for whom Stevie and Meadow were
houseparents—looked especially anxious. Off to one side, Meadow
just shook her head.

What was Stevie doing?

Clearly, protecting Beit Rashi. Jeff had heard that Stevie had bought
and installed two surv-cams on Rashi's outer walls.

Okay, Jeff had thought, I don't have a problem with that.

But now Jeff had heard that Stevie was putting up this . . . protective barrier? Which was freaking out The Beast. An email from a
mother in Mexico City: *Our children are going to live in bunkers?*

From the formidable Mrs. Friedlander: *Where's Ashley's bunker?*

Where's Thayer's?!!

Over the thunder of yet more crashing dirt and gravel, Jeff yelled, "Stevie, what *is* this?!"

Stevie looked down from the driver's seat of the front-end loader. Beaming, he said, "A Hesco barrier. Used by our troops in Iraq and Afghanistan. Protects against explosives. They're too expensive to buy, so I've made my own. Not bad, huh?"

"Stevie," said Jeff, "would you come down here so we can talk."

Reluctantly, Stevie maneuvered his plump body down off the machine. Jeff put an arm around Stevie's shoulders and walked him away from the crowd.

Jeff said, "Stevie, you can't do this. You're freaking out the kids, teachers, parents, *every*one."

"I'm houseparent to eighteen vulnerable boys. I'm protecting them."

"Stevie, you have to dismantle this. Now."

"I can't. Not in good conscience. Not with only dummy cameras going up on the fence. Not with intruders able to get in *undetected*."

Jeff was ready for this. "Take it down, and I'll find money for eight real cameras."

"Eight?! We need forty. One every two hundred feet."

"Eight real cameras," said Jeff.

"Thirty."

"Eight."

"Twenty."

"Eight."

"Jeff, don't do this to me."

"Eight."

Reluctantly, Stevie Blau agreed, and shook on it. Then he pointed back at his half-completed Hesco barrier. "But Jeff, what do I do with the materials?"

Jeff considered telling Stevie, "Use the chicken wire to confine yourself and every other HAHA whackadoo."

But Stevie Blau was a sweet, caring guy. He didn't deserve ridicule.

And he was a sweet, caring guy who loved sweet food.

Jeff said, "Stevie, you know Braddock's?"

That stopped Stevie. Of all people, Stevie especially knew this locally-famous Bradleyville bakery.

Jeff went on: "Their great chocolate cakes? How about I order six for Beit Rashi. Braddock's will deliver within the hour. Dismantle this by then, and the cakes are on me."

"How many cakes, Jeff?"

"Six."

"Eight."

They shook on eight. Stevie grinned in triumph.

TWENTY-EIGHT

METAPHOR MAN

Stuck thirty-five feet up the athletic center's forty-foot-high climbing wall, hanging in a harness attached to a rope jammed up in a belay—Jeff felt, Okay, I recognize this.

It was like the headline he had once seen in *The Onion*. Above a photo of the Titanic: "WORLD'S LARGEST METAPHOR HITS ICEBERG."

In my case, thought Jeff, I am a minor metaphor for being stuck.

A week ago, when the bomb threat came and The Beast roared, I told myself that in one week The Beast would be quiet and I could announce my resignation effective June 21.

Now, a week later, I realize I can't. I am still stuck.

But, metaphor aside, why am I stuck on this wall?

Because I needed a break.

Yes, he had.

A half hour ago, at 9:30 p.m., he had used his master key to let himself in. Looking to unclench the muscular and mental vise he had been in since the bomb threat, he harnessed and roped himself, and climbed.

Yes, he knew: Given HAHA's finances, it was ridiculous, a year ago, to put up this fifty-thousand-dollar climbing wall. But here it stood. Here, not far from the rope course and skateboard park that, like the wall, Sammy said "would pay for themselves" by attracting students.

But that glorious day, of enough new students to keep the school open, was like the top of this climbing wall. No matter how high Jeff climbed, it kept receding before him.

He would have called for help, but his smartphone was down there in his windbreaker. Smart phone on the floor, dumb man in the air, thought Jeff.

Another metaphor. Jeff feared he was out of touch. Yes, people were always coming into his office. And, yes, there was parochet@haha.com. But did he really know what was going on? His father, professor of European history, had a riff about clueless leaders: The Tsar is always the last to know. The Tsar finds out what's going on only after he's deposed, taken to a basement, and stood against the wall.

"Dad! What are you doing up there?"

Jeff looked down. There was Jordan, shouldering a bulging back-pack, her brown hair in a ponytail coming out the back of her Sages baseball hat.

What is she doing here? marveled Jeff. I can't keep track of her, but she has some ESP about me? How did she let herself in here?

He called down to her. "I'm stuck. I think, if you climb up next to me, you can unstick me. But keep your phone with you in case you get stuck too."

"Sure." Jordan shed her backpack, took down a harness, stepped through its leg loops. "I was walking to your house when Jerome drove by on his golf cart. He said he saw you heading here; he lent me a key." She pulled up the harness, tightened the waist belt and the leg loops. Taking a climbing rope, she made expert loops and knots, then fed the working end of the rope into the belay loop on her harness. "I was coming over to talk to you about Jose. I'm worried about him, he's under like unbelievable pressure. If he doesn't get into Harvard . . . "

"He'll get into *some* excellent place."

"Some place where all the kids claim they never wanted to go to Harvard."

"Jordan, most kids end up loving the college they go to."

Feeding the climbing rope through more loops on the harness and making more knots, Jordan told her father, "Says the man who went to Yale."

"Guilty as charged. Now can you get me down?"

"Can you help him, Dad? Help him now? Is there anything you can do before Harvard decides?"

Taking an ATC belay device, Jordan clipped it to the belay loop on her harness. Now she was ready to climb the wall.

Jeff told her, "Not now, sweetie. But maybe later. Maybe if he's stuck on the waiting list—if Harvard leaves him hanging. Bad place to be."

"Ha ha, Dad."

Watching the care Jordan had taken with the climbing equipment, Jeff had been trying to spot what he had failed to do, what had gotten him stuck. He couldn't spot it. *Lined up to be shot, the Tsar asks himself, "Where did I go wrong?"*

"Now," said Jeff, "can you get me down?"

"Coming at you."

Jordan—HAHA soccer star—climbed the wall, swung next to Jeff, and unstuck him.

The metaphor and his daughter let themselves down to terra firma.

TWENTY-NINE

INTERVIEWING
A SCIENCE TEACHER?

Eight days ago, calling from Tajikistan, Sammy Kleinman told Jeff that Tzipora Perl was coming to HAHA. Now, late Tuesday afternoon, here she was. Rabbi Baum, who feared Tzipora's father, had nothing against her but also wanted nothing to do with her. Chava, Baum's wife, the Rebbetzin, brought her to Jeff's office and, because an unmarried Hasidic woman is not to be alone with a man, stayed.

While both Hasidic women were dressed conservatively, Chava wore a stylish blouse and some jewelry. But Tzipora . . . ? Age thirty, Tzipora was dressed like a *very* conservative Hasidic woman of age sixty, seventy, eighty . . . Skirt down to her ankles, blouse buttoned at her wrists and her neck, her hair under a tight scarf, "sensible" shoes. She had a pleasant if plain face. With a shy smile, she told Jeff how happy she was at the prospect of working at Hampton Acres Hebrew Academy.

Hmm, right. But at what job?

Tzipora was the eldest daughter of Menachem Perl, big-deal Chicago Hasidic rabbi who was the trusted spiritual advisor to Seymour Gutfreund, hard-nosed Las Vegas billionaire. Growing up in a Hasidic household, Tzipora had been allowed only the education necessary for her role in life: wife to a Hasidic scholar. But for some reason—don't ask!—Tzipora was unmarriageable. Now her continued presence, unmarried, in her father's house, was an embarrassment to the big-deal rabbi. And it would be a double embarrassment if she were working in Chicago *outside* her father's house. Which was a golden opportunity for Sammy Kleinman. Sammy's latest scheme: Give her a job at HAHA. Overwhelmed with gratitude, Rabbi Perl would sing HAHA's praises to Gutfreund. Softened up, Gutfreund would yield to Sammy's request for a significant gift to the school. Of, say, seventy-five-million dollars.

Fifty million would wipe out the school's debt. Another twenty million would allow the school to stay open for a few more years, long enough, hopefully, for another of Sammy's schemes to kick in. And the remaining five million? Hmmm. Jeff suspected that at least some of it would find its way into one of Sammy's Birkin bags.

So! What could Tzipora Perl do at HAHA? Sammy had told Rabbi Perl, "The school has two openings: security guard and freshman science teacher."

"Science," Rabbi Perl had said. "My Tzipora knows science."

Now, sitting across from Jeff, responding to Jeff's gentle questioning, Tzipora assured Jeff that she indeed knew science.

"Great," he said.

But did she? For example, dinosaurs.

As HAHA's freshman science teacher, Tzipora would be teaching about them. Some Orthodox scholars found no contradiction between dinosaurs and the Torah, but most Hasidim said no way. Did Tzipora accept the existence of dinosaurs?

"Oh, Mr. Taylor, they existed. They don't contradict the Torah. And"—Tzipora smiled a small, pleased-with-herself smile—"I fooled my parents. Secretly, I watched *Jurassic Park*. So I made the connection. Adam and Eve were driven out of the Garden of Eden by velociraptors."

"Ah," said Jeff. "And your other scientific knowledge? For example, what do you know about atoms?"

Tzipora looked puzzled. "Atoms? Like the *The Addams Family?*"

Jeff despaired.

But he noted that Chava Baum was trying to hide a smile of satisfaction. Why? Ah, of course. For the sake of her husband. If Tzipora were living and working at HAHA, her big-deal rabbi father would be all over small-time Baum, questioning Baum's rabbinic qualifications, Baum's scholarship, Baum's Yiddishkeit. Chava knew her husband couldn't measure up.

But I have to hire Tzipora, thought Jeff.

"Well," said Jeff. He stood up. "So nice to meet you, Tzipora. So nice to have you here at HAHA. Let me think about how best to use your talents."

Tzipora smiled and, about to rise, lifted her skirt an inch, revealing an inch of her left ankle. And Jeff could swear that as she did, she made eye contact with him and then directed her eyes—and his—down there. As if to say See? Attractive, yes?

My God, thought Jeff, are you *flirting* with me?

You don't just want a job? You also want me?

Yikes.

Escorting Tzipora and Chava out of his office, Jeff turned Tzipora over to Clarice, to get her settled at HAHA.

But what in the world is she going to *do* here? wondered Jeff. I can't make her a science teacher, I can't make her a security guard. Therefore . . . what?

Returning to his office, sitting down at his desk, Jeff looked out his windows. So peaceful. A balm for his worries.

Out there, on Emmanuel Kleinman Quad, students sat, laughed, and talked; students threw Frisbees; dogs romped.

Jeff figured, A fine moment for me to catch up on Parochet.

What un-peaceful news awaits me here?

Whoa!

Jeff read emails about Noga Weinstein:

Gunshots! Gunshots are coming from the Whitneys' place—right past the dorms.

It's Cherev.
They've set up a rifle range. They're firing Uzis.
Are we going to be attacked? Are they going to try to defend us?
I can't deal with gunshots!

THIRTY

HOME ON THE RANGE

"**N**oga!" Jeff yelled. "NOGA!"

Uzi in her hands, high-tech muffs over her ears, Noga Weinstein stood in the middle of the firing line. Shulamit Mouchly and Nadav Peretz were on her left; Ilana Weiss and Stevie Blau were on her right. All five were blasting away at distant targets: silhouettes of men.

Approaching carefully from behind her, Jeff tried to get her attention.

"NOGA!"

Finally she sensed him, stopped firing, and took off her high-tech ear muffs.

"Hi, Jeff. Sorry. I couldn't hear you. Eh, what's up?"

"My point exactly, Noga. It's the noise you guys are making. Bullets flying. At the school"—Jeff waved to the east, beyond the Whitneys' land—"everybody can hear you. Gunfire! It's making the kids nervous. Teachers, too."

"Eh, they shouldn't be nervous. It should be making them secure. Knowing that Cherev is out here, practicing, so we can protect them."

"An Uzi is not going to protect against a bomber. If there is a bomber—which I seriously doubt—he is going to quietly get in, quietly plant the bomb, and quietly leave. You'll never notice him, never have a chance to shoot him."

"Not true. Cherev is also installing an extensive profiling system. We *will* be able to spot a bomber." She lovingly patted her Uzi. "And eliminate the threat."

"All we've had is a phone call," said Jeff. "From someone chanting mediocre rap."

"Eh . . . someone can chant mediocre rap and still make a good bomb."

"You've got to stop this *RAT-A-TAT-TAT!*"

"Eh! As you Americans say, we're going to give the bomber *tit for tat.*"

The mid-afternoon sun shone on the Whitneys' rolling green land. It gleamed on the shell casings flying out of Shulamit's, Nadav's, Ilana's, and Stevie's Uzis. Stopping to reload, Stevie caught Jeff's eye. Stevie smiled, a smile that said *You got me to stop putting protection around my house, but I don't think you can get Noga to stop.*

Jeff wondered, Is he right?

When Jeff had handled Baum, Celine, and Stevie, he'd come prepared. He had bought off Baum with a bigger household budget, Celine with a PhD program, and, at Beit Rashi, Stevie with chocolate cakes.

Now, he wondered if he could buy off Cherev.

On Wall Street, it was an axiom that every person has their price. But, famously, it was axiomatic that Israelis don't.

"Eh," Jeff said to Noga, and started back to HAHA.

THIRTY-ONE
PURIM SPIEL

"**M**r. Blau! Mrs. Blau!" cried Isaac Greene. "It's been weeks since you made chocolate-chip pancakes for breakfast! Please! Tell me you've got pancake batter and chocolate chips in there! Please!"

Up on the stage of the Beit Am, student body president Isaac wore a baseball cap sideways and tortoiseshell glasses with rims the size of salad plates. Dangling from his neck, a placard read BEIT RASHI FRESHMAN. Stuffed under his T-shirt, a pillow gave him a huge belly. His "Please!" was directed at two HAHA students coming at him, each pushing a wheelbarrow with a tarp covering a high heap of *some*thing.

"Sorry, kid." Mimicking the voice of Stevie Blau, Jorge Goldblatt kept pushing his wheelbarrow. Dangling from his neck, a placard read STEVIE BLAU.

Right behind Jorge, Amy Lovitz kept pushing her wheelbarrow. Dangling from her neck, a placard read MEADOW BLAU. Mimicking Meadow's voice, Amy told Isaac-Beit Rashi Freshman, "Sweetie, chocolate chip pancakes will just have to wait. We must keep bringing in more dirt and sand." At this, she and Jorge pulled the tarps off their wheelbarrows, revealing—of course—dirt and sand.

"Yeah," said Jorge, "Gotta keep filling the bomb-proof barriers. You can't enjoy pancakes if you're blown to pieces."

Packing the Beit Am, the rest of HAHA's students laughed. Standing in back, Jeff nodded.

Isaac-Beit Rashi Freshman sank to his knees in front of "Stevie and Meadow Blau." He begged them, "Please!" Pointing to his belly, he cried, "See my belly, swollen from hunger? Long before this school explodes, *it's* gonna explode!"

The students hooted.

This, first thing Tuesday morning, was Purim Spiel. Traditionally, it was a comic dramatization of the Book of Esther. At enlightened Jewish schools, it was skewering teachers and staff. Skewering *lovingly*, Jeff hoped.

The two "Blaus" kept pushing their wheelbarrows past "Beit Rashi Freshman," heading off stage. Just before she disappeared, "Meadow Blau" turned back and said, "Hang in there, sweetheart. You'll love eating pancakes in the Beit Rashi Bunker."

To raucous shouts and applause, the "Blaus" exited.

Isaac-Beit Rashi Freshman yelled after them, "Stevie! Meadow! I'm going to call Ms. Kleinman about this. She owns the place."

Jordan came on stage wearing a placard that read CLARICE DAWKINS. She had a pillow stuffed under her blouse. *No blackface*, thought Jeff. *That's a relief.*

Isaac-Beit Rashi Freshman mimed phoning Clarice.

"Miz Kleinman's office," drawled Jordan.

"This is Ivan Schmendrick, the new student," said Isaac. "I need to talk to Ms. Kleinman about getting my pancakes."

"You can't talk to Miz Kleinman today. She's in Kissit."

"She's where?"

"Kiss it."

The audience roared. Isaac-Beit Rashi Freshman smiled, as if his luck had changed.

"Clean up your mind, young man," said Jordan-Clarice Dawkins. "It's a city in Southern India. Five Jews live there. One of them is a kid."

"How about tomorrow?" asked Isaac.

"No go. She'll be in Screwu."

Jeff cringed.

"She'll be where?"

"Screwu. Don't they teach y'all geography anymore? It's a mid-sized city in Sri Lanka. Two Jews there. They don't talk to each other. Miz Kleinman is going to get one to come to HAHA to get away from the other."

"Well, when will Ms. Kleinman be back?"

"Not for six weeks, honey. Can I help you with anything else?"

"Six weeks!" said Clueless. "That's outrageous. Let me speak to Mr. Taylor then."

"Oh, I wouldn't waste my time with him. Take it from me—it won't get you anywhere."

Having dropped the Southern accent, Jordan-Clarice winked at the students, who rose to their feet, clapping madly. Then she walked off.

Jeff smiled. *Yeah, Jordan, play it up. The rest of the time here, being my daughter has got to be a drag.*

Isaac-Beit Rashi Freshman wailed, "The only good thing in my life is chocolate! I may not have chocolate-chip pancakes, but at least I have *this!*"

Producing a spoon and a container of chocolate ice cream, he started to eat.

At this, Sacha Reznick rushed on stage. He wore a long white beard, a tallis, and phylacteries. His placard read RABBI BAUM. Running to Beit Rashi Freshman, Sacha-Baum wrestled the spoon away.

"No!" he cried. "You can't eat! Don't you know today is the Fast of the Lost Pumpernickel Roll?"

"The what? Rabbi, I've never heard of that fast." Beit Rashi Freshman looked like he was about to cry.

I know the feeling, thought Jeff.

"The fast was established," chanted Sacha-Rabbi Baum, "to mourn the day the fifth Rebbe was making himself a herring and hummus sandwich and dropped the bread."

"So let him get another slice." Grabbing back the spoon, Isaac-Beit Rashi Freshman dipped it in the ice cream—but Baum again wrestled it away.

"It was Shabbat, see. He couldn't go out and buy another one."

"Not my problem!" exploded Beit Rashi Freshman. He jerked back the dessert-laden spoon—and the ice cream splattered his face.

The audience roared and began chanting, "NO MORE FAST DAYS! NO MORE FAST DAYS!"

Jeff wanted to join the chant. He thought, Baum and his "authentic" Jewish observances! Tonight how many students is Baum going to get drunk? I have had it with Baum. I have had it with Sammy. I have had it with The Beast.

As the chant continued, the authentic Stevie Blau turned up the lights and closed the stage curtain. With HAHA's students deposited on the last safe peak of exuberance, Purim Spiel was over.

My last HAHA Purim, thought Jeff. Now it's on Baum to keep tonight's celebration safe. Hopefully his Rebbe will help him.

THIRTY-TWO
CHEREV CAN'T BE BUDGED?

Jeff asked, "You're sure it's not a zoning violation?"

From behind his impressive desk, Gregg Sutcliffe, managing partner of Ellis, Lynch, Hay, and Prioleau, shook his head. "Afraid not."

Ellis, Lynch, Hay, and Prioleau was Bradleyville's top law firm. It was where Barbara worked as a paralegal, it was the law firm that—behind the scenes—Barbara basically ran. Yesterday, right after confronting Noga, Jeff had called Sutcliffe, who promised they'd get right on it. "Our associates will burn the midnight oil." This morning, right after Purim Spiel, Jeff had called Sutcliffe again. Sutcliffe had said, "Sorry, we dug and dug. But there's no legal prohibition against the Whitneys letting that land be used as a shooting range."

Jeff couldn't accept this. He had said, "This afternoon, I'd like to come over, talk to you."

Sutcliffe had said okay, but there's nothing, no prohibition.

Now, face to face with Sutcliffe, Jeff said, "All right, not a zoning violation. How about an attractive nuisance?"

"You mean," said Sutcliffe, "the gunfire will attract kids, and kids will get shot?"

"Something like that."

"Sorry," said Sutcliffe. "Too much of a reach."

Jeff said, "How about an environmental hazard? Lead bullets. Lead leaches into the soil."

"A hazard to whom? The aquifer is a thousand feet down. That's even more of a reach."

"How about the sound of the gunshots? Could they be violating a noise ordinance?"

"Okay," said Sutcliffe. "On your campus, let's say right up against the Whitney land, how loud are they?"

"They sound like POP! POP! POP!"

"But not"—Sutcliffe yelled—"*POP! POP! POP!*"

"Afraid not," admitted Jeff.

"Well, there you have it," said Sutcliffe. "Sorry, no case."

"But they're still upsetting my people."

"Sorry."

From behind Jeff, at the doorway to Sutcliffe's office, a woman's voice. Barbara's:

"But they're upsetting the grouse."

Jeff turned. Barbara was standing there. She said, "Sorry, Gregg, but I was walking by and I heard . . . "

"The grouse?" asked Jeff and Sutcliffe simultaneously.

"The lesser ruffed sage grouse," said Barbara. "It's on the endangered species list. And the Whitney land is part of its habitat. A habitat the grouse are legally entitled to. The gunshots have got to be driving them off." She smiled. "Jeff, Gregg, there's your case." Then she thought of something else. "And what about the bullets? Lead, right? So even if people started shooting with silencers, the lead is going into the soil, and then into ferns and clover, and the grouse eat those ferns and that clover . . . and the grouse get sick and die."

Jeff stared at his beloved in amazement. Thirty of his law school classmates were law professors. One was a US Supreme Court Justice. None were as sharp as Barbara Travis.

Behind him, Gregg Sutcliffe said, "I'll call the lady who runs the local chapter of the Sierra Club. And the editor of the *Gazette*. And the Bradleyville police. We'll have Cherev off the Whitney land by end of business today."

Jeff touched his jacket right over the pocket that held his letter of resignation. Getting closer.

Except . . . except . . .

Jeff knew Israelis. Israelis don't get discouraged, Israelis don't quit.

Okay, so Cherev will get tossed off the Whitney land. So what? The Jews have been handling expulsions since the year 72. Where will Cherev pop up next?

THIRTY-THREE
PARTY PARTY PARTY!

t was around 11 p.m. on Purim. Walking past Beit Gibborim, House of the Mighty, the residence of Rabbi Benjamin Baum, Jeff felt he was hearing a UGA frat house on a night that Georgia had defeated Alabama to win the FBS national championship. From inside came raucous, drunken shouts. These voices were *supposed* to be only of Baum and nine HAHA boys. This morning Baum had assured Jeff, "I'm just inviting nine older Orthodox boys, they can be trusted." Baum had grinned. "My Purim minyan, Jeff. No less, no more." But it sounded like Beit Gibborim had at least two dozen celebrants. Including some girls. Jeff paused in wonderment. And now, rushing past him in the night, giggling and shrieking, came six, eight, ten, twelve more HAHA students, boys and girls, some merely freshmen, merely age fifteen, heading for Baum's door. Party time!

They pretended not to see the Head.

Jeff did them the courtesy of pretending not to see them.

Jeff thought, If I were staying past June 21, if this school were going to be in operation past July 15, I'd fire Baum on the spot. But I'm not, and it's not. Besides, where else in late March could HAHA find an Orthodox rabbi who can teach six courses, hold services, and oversee Jewish life on campus?

Besides, I let Baum do this. I should be fired. I want out, but not that way.

Sure hope our Chasid can hold his liquor and prevent any of the thirty underage drinkers from smashing their foreheads on toilet bowls as they kneel to puke.

Jeff reflected that *that* was one of the most fervent prayers he had ever mentally uttered.

In the vast rabbinic literature of devotion, is there a prayer wishing drunken teens a safe Purim?

Yeah, probably, but the only man within fifty miles who knows it is inside that house, pouring liquor for children. Using the money I gave him for extra "household expenses," the money to buy him off, to make him stop radiating bomb-threat anxiety.

Nothing to see here, Jeff, he told himself. Walk away.

Which he started to—but *wham!* was stopped by a punch in his gut: Is *Jordan* in there?!

Jeff heard Michelle tell him, *No, she's probably off somewhere having sex with Jose.*

Oh, thanks, thought Jeff. That's reassuring.

THIRTY-FOUR

THE SAGE ON THE STAGE RECEIVES RESTRAINED RAGE

Five minutes after Christina Rountree finished teaching her third-period class, she got a call from Mrs. Rhoda Friedlander: "Perhaps, Ms. Rountree, you are not familiar with current advances in pedagogy. You are not aware that the teacher should no longer be 'the sage on the stage.'"

"The what?"

"'The sage on the stage.' That's the transmittal model. The student sits passively before the teacher. It is based on an out-of-date assumption, a hierarchical assumption. Don't you know this?"

Christina, age thirty, native of Bradleyville, had a new PhD in European History from UGA-Bradleyville. In August, when her husband had been laid off, she had been lucky to get this, her first teaching job, European history at HAHA. She felt she knew her stuff. She felt she had been doing pretty well with her students, who included Mrs. Friedlander's daughter, Ashley, a bright senior.

Christina knew Ashley was *intent* on getting into Princeton. She sensed Mrs. Friedlander was INTENT on getting Ashley into Princeton. Mrs. Friedlander believed her daughter was America's next great cinematographer, and she expected the Princeton admissions office to recognize that too. Christina's colleagues had warned her that Ashley's mother was difficult. Thus far, she had been spared any calls from Mrs. Friedlander.

Now, this call: Mrs. Rhoda Friedlander holding forth and, listening in, her husband Arnie. Arnie made the money to send Ashley to HAHA; Rhoda dispensed the educational theory by which Ashley was to be well-served by HAHA.

Christina didn't know educational theory.

She told Mrs. Friedlander, "Um, enlighten me."

"The sage on the stage assumes that the student's brain is an empty container into which the teacher pours knowledge."

Christina thought, But my students' brains aren't empty. They're full of knowledge about everything from Adele to Drake to Taylor Swift. From scrunchies to the nomadic preppy look. True, this morning, some of them looked full of alcohol, hungover from last night, from Purim—in Christina's view, a very weird rite. (Just as she struggled to understand Mrs. Friedlander, she struggled to understand Judaism.)

Mrs. Friedlander continued: "Ms. Rountree, instead of 'the sage on the stage,' today's teacher is 'the guide on the side.' Today's teacher is a facilitator. She helps students think for themselves. Gives them a problem, divides them into small groups, and students produce knowledge rather than *re*produce it."

Christina thought, My students are supposed to produce knowledge about the Franco-Prussian War of 1870-1871?

This is what she had been teaching them today.

Christina had to object. "But none of my students had even *heard* of the Franco-Prussian War. Much less its causes and consequences. Someone had to tell them. I told them."

"Ms. Rountree—"

Christiana said, "And I doubt any of them know anything about the condition of Jews in nineteenth-century Europe. For example, next week, I'll tell them how, in 1894, came the Dreyfus affair which—"

"Julia Louis-Dreyfus?" said Arnie Friedlander, the first thing he had said since "Hello." Now Arnie needed to enlighten Christina: "You mean *nineteen* ninety-four. That's about the middle of her run on *Seinfeld*. Gosh, she was good then and she's gotten even better. Didn't you watch *Veep*?"

Christina Rountree stared at the phone in her hands.

THIRTY-FIVE

CUCUMBER

NIGHT WATCHMAN

t was Thursday at five p.m., forty-eight hours since Gregg Sutcliffe, true to his word, had gotten the Bradleyville police to throw Cherev off their shooting range. Since then, Jeff had received zero texts from Noga. Why hadn't she barraged him on his phone or in person, complaining, arguing? From Cherev: only quiet. Like they say in Hollywood war movies set on the front lines, *too* quiet. What was Cherev planning? What was Cherev doing? In the executive committee meeting that Jeff had just run, had just returned from, he had raised the question, and none of the deans had an answer.

Stevie Blau, a member of Cherev and the executive committee, was conveniently absent. Stevie had sent Jeff a last-minute email complaining of back pain.

Parochet also had nothing to say, not one rumor.

Which forced Jeff back to consider one of his other pressing problems: What to do with Tzipora Perl? He stared at his walls and found no answer there.

His phone rang.

Ah, Barbara.

Ellis, Lynch, Hay, and Prioleau was almost done for the day. Jeff and Barbara talked about the day each had had. Jeff explained his Tzipora Perl dilemma. He told Barbara, "I can't have her teach science, I can't make her a security guard. So I'm thinking—ha!—cucumber night watchman."

"What?" said Barbara.

"In ancient Israel, it was a real job," Jeff said. "Guarding a cucumber field from thieves and wild animals. In Talmudic commentary, 'cucumber night watchman' was a joking way to refer to a really easy job. The kind I need for Tzipora."

"One that doesn't require the school planting a cucumber field?"

"Right."

"Well," said Barbara, "I've never known a school whose food couldn't be improved. Put Tzipora in the kitchen."

"In the kitchen?"

"Jeff, you say she's a thirty-year-old woman who's barely been out of the house. A thirty-year-old housebound woman who's been raised to be a housewife—what has she learned to do? Cook."

Jeff thought, Of course.

I have a BA and a JD from Yale. And I have a rabbi (Benjamin Baum) who says every answer is in the Torah. And a student (Sacha Reznick) who says every answer is in *Derech Eretz*, the school handbook. I have all these (supposedly) brilliant Jewish minds. But where does the answer come from?

From the same person who answered "How can we get Cherev off the Whitney land?"

This smart person now asked Jeff, "You want to come over for dinner? I have some cucumbers that the thieves failed to get. How about Thai chicken with herbs, lime, and cucumbers?"

"Sold," said Jeff. "On my way." He was about to click off. Then something hit him. He said, "Wait. Smart person. I got another problem for you. It seems the pig farm down the road is . . . "

Swearing Barbara to secrecy, Jeff told her that HAHA was breathing pork molecules and asked if she had a solution.

Barbara laughed sympathetically. "Nope. You still gonna come here and breathe Thai chicken molecules?"

"You bet," said Jeff.

THIRTY-SIX

A PERL BEYOND PRICE

On Monday morning, Rachel strode into Baum's classroom just after his last student had left. Baum was gathering his notes. "What dirt can we find on Menachem Perl?"

"Excuse me?" said Baum.

"This school has hired his daughter."

"We've hired her?" said Baum, his heart sinking. "I know Sammy wanted to. But I heard she failed Jeff's evaluation. I assumed—"

"Jeff hired her to work in the kitchen. Maybe Tzipora can cook. That's not the point. The point is it's a scheme to get to Seymour Gutfreund's money."

"We don't want his money?" Baum didn't care about Seymour Gutfreund. Baum cared about Rabbi Menachem Perl. Baum's heart was now a leaden lump because he feared Perl as much as, apparently, Rachel hated Gutfreund.

"Goddamn Seymour Gutfreund," said Rachel. "To the right of anybody ever said to be to the right of Attila the Hun. Rather than have HAHA take a nickel from that blood-sucking bastard, I'd see the school go under."

Baum, taken aback, pulled away from her.

Gritting her teeth, she said, "His money is tainted. So, to repeat: What can we get on Perl? Something to show Jeff, make Jeff undo this."

Baum nodded. He knew that, with Tzipora here, Rabbi Perl would be always looking over his shoulder, judging him. Perl would complain about ignoring all the fast days. Nor did Baum relish Perl, who would be on the mailing list, reading his D'varot Torah. Baum knew his scholarship was shoddy, and Perl would call him on it.

Baum asked, "But *dirt?* How would I know how to find any dirt on Menachem Perl?"

"You're Orthodox! He's Orthodox! All you people—you take in each other's laundry! You've got to know the stains on the laundry! The grease spots on each other's bekishes."

"I don't!"

"You do!"

"I don't!"

"Then write your dead Rebbe. Tonight, in your dreams, he'll tell you."

"I don't think he knows *that*," said Baum. "Not how to get dirt on Menachem Perl."

"Then what good is your dead Rebbe?!"

Crazy woman, thought Baum. Menachem Perl is so far above me. Asking me to get dirt on him is . . . it's impossible. Baum tried to stay calm. He told Rachel, "I agree we've got to get rid of Tzipora but—"

"Don't tell me you agree with me . . . " sputtered Rachel, "when you really don't!"

"I do!"

"You don't!" Numbskull man, thought Rachel Fish. She screamed, "You don't! If you agreed, you'd do something!"

"Do what?!" screamed Baum, losing it. "*What?!*"

They were still screaming five minutes later when Jerome put his head into the classroom. "Rabbi? Ms. Fish? Everything okay? I got about a dozen texts from kids saying there was some drama here."

THIRTY-SEVEN

"WOODSTEIN" STRIKES!

"**M**ind if I record this conversation," said Ella Bronstein, taking out her smartphone.

Jeff winced. When Ella comes to your office, sits down across from you, puts her backpack on the floor, and starts a meeting this way, nothing good can follow.

"Whoa, Ella," said Jeff. "Slow down, please. And"—a fake laugh, feigning he was at ease—"what are we talking about? The bomb threat?"

"A different story, Mr. Taylor. Breaking news. We'd like a statement about a story *The Lamp* is about to run."

About to run? Today was Wednesday, *The Lamp* came out every Friday. If Ella had unearthed something new, something whose publication would embarrass the school, Jeff knew he had very little time to stop her.

He said, "Breaking news. Sounds ominous." His tone was light, but he was on his back foot. Yes, "Woodstein" was on the case.

From Watergate, from Woodward and Bernstein, came the investigative reporter's mantra: "Follow the money." What if Ella has been following HAHA's *lack* of it?

Ella smiled. "Ominous? You tell me." Reaching into her backpack, she said, "Mr. Tom has installed these thingamajigs all around campus."

"Thingamajigs?" *How the hell did she know?*

Ella pulled one out. "Turned up on the ground. Must have been blown down by that big wind last week. It monitors air quality."

"Uh-huh."

"And I found the company in Atlanta that services it and took it there. Gave it to a technician. You know what he said?"

"No idea."

"He fiddled around with it, took a reading and laughed. I asked him what was so funny. 'Y'all ain't supposed to eat pork. But you sure are breathing it in.'"

"Pork," said Jeff, as if he had never heard the word before.

"Has to be from Emmitt Bailey's place. These last few months, he's brought in a ginormous number of pigs."

"Emmitt Bailey," said Jeff, his tone indicating that *maybe* he had heard of the man.

"Mr. Taylor, as Head of School, what do you think of the fact that a Jewish boarding school is breathing in massive quantities of pork molecules?"

Jeff hesitated. He was not surprised by Ella's enterprising journalism. But now, in retrospect, he *was* surprised that fact of the pork molecules hadn't leaked weeks ago.

He envisaged *The Lamp*'s front-page headline day after tomorrow:

HAMPTON ACRES BREATHING PORK

He said, "Ella, can we talk off the record?"

Woodstein eyed him. "Sure," said Ella, pressing a button on her smartphone that Jeff *hoped* turned off audio.

"Look, Ella . . . " began Jeff.

But he didn't know where to go. His mind was working fast, like it used to on the trading desk when a trade went bad and his team scrambled to limit the damage. *Yes, I'm going fast, but I'm going in circles, going nowhere. How do I quash this scandal?*

"Look, Ella . . . " He was stalling. "Look. Give us time to correct the situation. Reduce the number of pork molecules." *Ha! "Reduce"? How are we going to do that? Introduce swine flu across the road?* Jeff faked confidence: "And as we reduce them, I'll give you exclusive briefings. Your eyes only. So once we *have* reduced them, *The Lamp* can run a complete, in-depth story."

"How are you reducing them?"

"Well, I can't tell you yet."

"Why not?"

Right, thought Jeff, why not?

"Because . . . " Again, he was stalling.

Then it hit him.

Just as he had bluffed Emmitt Bailey . . . he could bluff Ella.

"Because," said Jeff, "we are engaged in delicate negotiations with Mr. Bailey. Negotiations which would be . . . ah . . . jeopardized by the premature publication of your story."

Ella regarded him with mature-beyond-her-years journalistic skepticism. She said, "Really?"

"Really."

"Let's say . . . " said Ella. "Just for argument sake, *let's say* that *The Lamp* holds off on this story and *let's say* you give us the exclusive briefings . . . *The Lamp* still needs a story for this Friday. We need a front-page story to run where this one *would* have run. Do you have *that* story for me?"

"Um . . . "

Jeff hesitated. Speaking of negotiations, Ella was no slouch.

He said, "Yes, Ella, I'll give you a bigger pork story."

"Bigger?" Woodstein looked both skeptical and eager.

"Yes, literally bigger," said Jeff. "But in return for it—and for the in-depth exclusive—I need something else."

"Something else?" demanded Ella.

You bet, thought Jeff. You may be no slouch at negotiations, but neither am I.

"Yes," said Jeff.

"What?"

"Cherev," Jeff told Ella. "Yesterday afternoon, I saw them, locked and loaded, heading out on Route 16. Do you know where?"

"Sure," said Woodstein. "The State Police Barracks. The state's shooting range. Now they're training there."

Jeff marveled at Woodstein's abilities. He said, "Thank you, Ella, for telling me."

Thank you, and let's see if we can stretch this deal a little more. Ella was a very good negotiator, but, for all her precocity, she was still at the age where the impulse to please adults was hard to resist.

Jeff asked, "Do you think a student could have made the last bomb threat?"

"Do you?" Ella leaned forward, radiating intensity.

"No, it's unlikely, but I've got to consider all the possibilities. I just hope I can count on you—if you suspected something . . . for the good of the school." Jeff didn't say "you'd tell me" for fear of getting the same reaction Jordan always gave. *I'm not going to be your narc!*

"You bet, Mr. Taylor. Now, what's the *bigger* pork story?"

"You didn't hear this from me," Jeff said. "You did your own excellent digging."

"Of course," said Woodstein. "Like everything I just told you, you didn't hear it from me. Now what is this?"

"Well," said Jeff, "it turns out our pig farm neighbor has had a long-time secret partner. Someone who would be very embarrassed if their interest in pork production were, ah, public knowledge."

"And who would that be? And why would it be embarrassing?"

Jeff smiled. He envisioned *The Lamp's* front page headline the day after tomorrow:

KLEINMANS' SLICE OF BACON
FAMILY OWNS 20 PERCENT OF PIG FARM

THIRTY-EIGHT

HEPHAESTUS SPEAKS

"I 'm sure something will happen to solve this for you. Something will convince people they're safe."

Barbara's voice came from within her iron welder's mask. Watching her at work in her back yard, her torch blazing, Jeff thought it was like seeing a god—Hephaestus, the Greek god of the forge. Like seeing a god if you ignored what the god was doing. Having removed the four-prong garden trowel that made the right hand of a boy in her *Butterfly* sculpture, Barbara was now welding the five-prong trowel she'd found in her latest scavenge.

Jeff doubted the gods made kitsch. And he doubted the gods ever told mortals to just chill—as HAHA students said. As he recalled, the gods usually told mortals that they were doomed.

He asked Barbara, "Something will happen? What?"

It was five in the afternoon on Wednesday. He was thrilled to have been able to get away from HAHA for a while. Get away physically. But of course he couldn't get away from HAHA's problems. He had just told Barbara what he had learned from Ella: Noga and Cherev were blasting away at the State Police rifle range. "I've got to somehow convince the kids they're safe. If I don't, I can't tell Sammy I'm outta here June twenty-first."

He knew Barbara didn't want him to resign; she wanted him to stay here. But she also cared about him. So, from within her mask, an actor in ancient Greece wearing the mask of Hephaestus, she voiced faith in fate.

She said, "I don't know. But something will. You've tried so hard to save the school."

This continued over dinner.

For dinner, Barbara had made a pot roast as delicious as one from any Jewish mother. Studying a piece of meat on her fork, Barbara—as if a seer contemplating an offering—again said, "I'm sure something will happen to solve this for you."

This time, Jeff knew enough not to ask, "What?"

Three hours later, lying in bed together, après-sex, both knowing Jeff soon had to leave and go back to HAHA, Barbara again said, "Something will happen to solve this for you. You're due."

This time Jeff spoke: "Honey, you'd make a terrible hedge fund manager. 'We're going under, but we've tried so hard, something will save us.'"

"It will," said Barbara, kissing him goodbye.

Driving back to HAHA, Jeff despaired: As long as Noga and Cherev are acting out, and spreading anxiety to others, I cannot leave HAHA.

At which, he got a cellphone call from Jerome.

"Jeff, I've just had a phone call from the Secret Service people running security over at the Bradleyville airport for Air Force One."

"Yes . . . ?" said Jeff.

Which is how Jeff was able to call a school-wide assembly for the next day, Thursday afternoon.

THIRTY-NINE

DEUS EX MACHINA

Five p.m. Thursday, March 24.

Standing on stage in the Beit Am, flanked by Jerome McKool, Jeff said, "I'm pleased to introduce Agent Grant Spisak, who will . . . "

Agent Spisak informed the school that the Secret Service was enlarging the security perimeter around Air Force One and the Bradleyville Airport to a seven-mile radius. This included Emmitt Bailey's Premier Porcine Facility and Hampton Acres Hebrew Academy. "So thanks to your government, everyone here should now feel secure that . . . "

Scanning the audience, Jeff's eyes fell upon Noga and the rest of Cherev. They were smiling in relief.

Baum moved his lips in silent prayer, no doubt thanking God for this deliverance and assuring Him that HAHA would never miss another fast day.

Even Hannah Newins smiled in relief.

True, Jeff knew that Hannah would soon find something else to frighten her, something else to manipulate teachers and staff—but Jeff didn't care.

It was over.

Now he could email the HAHA community and tell everyone—especially parents—that the bomb threat (which was never real anyway) was done.

Now The Beast will go back to its state of semi-somnolence.

And now, today, right now today, *I can tender my letter of resignation effective June 21! I can call Sammy!*

Tell Sammy now, and then, tomorrow, at Shabbat dinner, announce it to everyone else.

Tajikistan is ten hours ahead. So, 5:15 p.m. here, it's now 3:15 a.m. there. Sammy is going to be pissed enough at this news—I don't need to wake her to tell her But Sammy is usually up by seven a.m. So, nine p.m. here, Sammy, I'm giving you the news.

Lost in this ecstatic reverie, Jeff got through dinner and early evening. Back at his house, at nine p.m. he called Sammy. And got voicemail, that low voice, somewhere between a purr and a growl: "Hello, this is Samantha Kleinman, CEO of the Hampton Acres Hebrew Academy. I'm out somewhere making the Academy even greater. Please leave a message, and I'll get back to you—and tell you how we can make your son or daughter even greater."

Jeff didn't leave a message.

He called at ten p.m. Got voicemail. Didn't leave a message.

He called at eleven p.m. Same result.

Damn it! Jeff swore. She's always able to reach me. Now why can't I reach her?

FORTY

SAMMY KLEINMAN, LIKE BACON, IS FRIED

Five-thirty a.m. Friday, Jeff's phone woke him.

"What the f**k, Jeff! What the f**k!"

Groggy, Jeff tried to cope. He managed, "Uh, I don't know, Sammy. What?"

"*The Lamp*. Today's *Lamp*. It just came online. So as I'm about to go into a meeting with the precious metals king of Tajikistan to try to get him to send us both of his precious sons, what do I read? What do I hope the king *doesn't* read?"

"What?"

Sammy shrieked: "'Kleinmans' Slice of Bacon! Family Owns 20 Percent of Pig Farm!'"

"Uh, Sammy, what can I tell you? The editor—Ella Bronstein—she's pretty enterprising."

"Enterprising! How about *you* being enterprising and shut her up!"

Jeff was about to say, Well, the horse is already out of the barn. Or, more precisely, the porker is out of its stall. Instead, somehow, mysteriously, Sacha Reznick spoke through him: "Uh, *Derech Eretz*, Section Three, Sub-Section something promises 'wide latitude' to student journalists—"

Jeff found himself talking to a dial tone.

135

Jeff thought, Hmm, perhaps this *isn't* the right day to tell Sammy that come June 21 I'm gone.

FORTY-ONE

"WE REGRET TO INFORM YOU . . . "

Saturday April 2. All day Jeff had been wishing he could call Sammy back and announce, *Come June 21, I'm gone.* Until Shabbat was over, he couldn't. At 6:45 p.m., as he walked into Kleinman Dining Hall for dinner, he thought, Only two hours to go.

As Jeff headed towards the trays of food, a senior—Ari Black—bolted from his seat and ran to Jeff.

"Mr. Taylor!" Ari's face was contorted in anguish. "Mr. Taylor, I've been rejected by Vanderbilt! And wait-listed by Sewanee! The only place I got into is Mercer—that's one hundred and fifty-third down *US News's* list. I can't go to Mercer! I *can't!*"

"Uh, Ari, I'm sure . . . "

Sure of what? The only thing Jeff was sure of was, I'm an idiot! I was so wrapped up in how HAHA was bomb-threatened, I forgot that right now—early April—is when most colleges post their decisions online. Their acceptances. Their rejections. And their states of limbo called waiting lists. I forgot because Dina Strauss is gone; our one-time college counselor is now in the care of her parents, the Upper West Side psychiatrists. And without Dina, who was good at dealing with disappointed seniors (last year, of forty-one seniors, there were four or five who were disappointed, devastated, desolated), it will fall on me.

Is falling on me. Right now. In the person of Ari Black.

After Ari, there will be more.

"Uh, Ari, come around to my office tomorrow. We'll . . . "

We'll what? Well, I can make some phone calls. I know some people. Not people who can get Ari into Vanderbilt. Not even people who can move him up the waiting list and into Sewanee. But maybe people who can grease the wheels to get him into some place better than Mercer. Instead of one hundred and fifty-third down the list, maybe a mere one hundred?

Doubtful, fearful, Ari said, "Thank you, Mr. Taylor," and went back to his seat. Jeff watched the kids at Ari's table. Other seniors. A few looked embarrassed for Ari; Jeff figured they had gotten good news from colleges. Others looked worried; Jeff figured they saw in Ari what *they* might be when colleges gave *them* the news. Jeff scanned the room, landed on other seniors, kids he knew well. A dozen of them were talking too loud or too fast, covering their anxiety. Some were staring obsessively at their smartphones. It hit him: Come seven p.m., more colleges would be posting decisions, and students will be logging in to learn their fates.

Shabbat wouldn't end for another hour and half, which meant the kids were supposed to stay off their phones until then. Or at least be discreet about using them in public. Fat chance! This night was different from all the others.

Jeff went to the food service line. Helping himself to pasta, he heard a shriek. Not of joy.

He turned. It was Fanny Kolton, a senior who, he knew, wanted to be a fashion designer, wanted to get into FIT, New York's Fashion Institute of Technology. Fanny had her head buried in her hands. Regaining her composure, she resumed eating. No, *trying* to eat. Then she spotted Jeff. Rushing to him, she blurted, "Mr. Taylor, I've been wait-listed at FIT, accepted at the University of Rhode Island. But the FIT wait list is death—everybody accepted there goes there. And URI—they call it 'the high school after high school.' I don't want to keep going to *high school!*"

"Uh, Fanny, I'm sure . . . "

Jeff was going to say, Hold on, Fanny, wait till you hear from the other places you applied to. I'm sure there's an acceptance from some place better than URI.

But of course he wasn't sure of that.

In any case, before he could utter such a transparent lie . . .

Up from another table came Evgeni Stamgazi, a senior from Kazakhstan. Evgeni wanted to go to the University of Maryland, get a business degree, return to help run his family's oil and gas company. He had a bit more composure than Ari and Fanny. "Mr. Taylor, I've just learned I've been wait-listed at Maryland, accepted at Central Arkansas. But Central Arkansas is a joke. It's where *Borat* would go to college!"

"Uh, Evgeni . . . "

So Jeff told Evgeni and Fanny what he told Ari: come to my office tomorrow.

The next day, Sunday, April 3, they did. And even as Jeff talked with all three, one after the other, and got information to help him advocate for each . . .

. . . all three got more rejections.

And even as Jeff was telling them to wait and hope because there were a few colleges they *still* hadn't heard from . . .

. . . their parents weren't waiting. Jeff was fielding angry calls from the parents of Ari Black and Fanny Kolton and, not the least, from Evgeni Stamgazi's father in Kazakhstan. Indignant calls. "I pay you all this money and you promise to groom my kid for success, and *this* is what you call success?"

And even as Jeff was dealing with these cases, three more seniors came with verdicts that left them reeling:

Drew Lazar, wait-listed at Florida State, accepted at the University of Alabama-Birmingham. Terri Fernandez, waited-listed at BU and Syracuse, accepted at the University of Texas-El Paso. Guy Friedman, rejected at Wharton, wait-listed at the Kelley School in Indiana.

Now six seniors. This already beat last year's number of emergency cases.

The next day, Monday, April 4, three more:

Cooper Pressman, wait-listed at the University of Texas, accepted at Texas A&M. Lucy Greenberg, wait-listed at Davidson, accepted at LSU. Ashley Friedlander, rejected at Princeton, rejected at Colgate, rejected at Bucknell.

Nine kids! Can I possibly help all nine? Jeff was dazed.

I never saw this coming. *Should* I have seen it? As Evan Rose is so fond of saying, If you're playing poker for half an hour and you still don't know who the patsy is, it's you.

Jeff talked with Ari, Fanny, Evgeni, Drew, Terri, Guy, Cooper, Lucy, and Ashley. Said more encouraging things, drew up lists of more people to call on behalf of each.

And was hit with more parental wrath.

From Manhattan's Upper East Side, the call Jeff had been dreading the most—from Rhoda Friedlander: "Buck-f**king-nell? You are telling me that my Ashley also got rejected by her f**king *safety* school? You're kidding me. You cannot just tell me this and do nothing. Princeton gone, Colgate gone, Buck-f**king-nell gone. What are you going to *do*?"

Jeff held his phone at arm's length. The tirade continued: "What! What!"

"Well, there's Clemson. I think—"

"*Clemson?!* My Ashley is not going to Clemson!"

"I'm pretty sure she could get in. Their acceptance rate is fifty-one percent. Yes, technically, it's too late for this year, but—"

"Too late? I'll tell you what it's too late for. For you to be making any excuses about how you failed my Ashley. My Ashley is not going to Clemson—"

Jeff wanted to say, *I'm suggesting Clemson because they're the Tigers, their colors are orange and black, so if you bought any orange-and-black Princeton gear, it'll work for—*

He restrained himself.

Mrs. Friedlander yelled, "—not going to college with rednecks!"

"But—"

Mrs. Friedlander yelled, "But nothing! You get Ashley into Princeton like you said you would, or—"

"Mrs. Friedlander, I never said—"

"—or I am driving down there and I am taking Ashley and Thayer home with me, and that is the last you see of any Friedlander until you see me in court to answer criminal charges of fraud!"

"Mrs. Friedlander, I am about to make calls on Ashley's behalf. I am . . ."

About to do what? wondered Jeff. Drive Ashley up to Princeton— drive her myself?—for a second interview?

"Better do *something*," commanded Mrs. Rhoda Friedlander.

Click!

FORTY-TWO

MINYAN OF MISERY

Monday evening, with Mrs. Rhoda Friedlander's *Better do something* fading from his mind, Jeff watched the NCAA Division I men's basketball championship game. It was a great game between two teams in which he had no stake. He thought that while, yes, he *did* have a stake in the nine HAHA seniors who had been rejected by the universities and colleges of their choice, nine wasn't a critical mass.

So tomorrow is the day.

His resignation letter, with many handwritten edits, lay in front of him, on the coffee table. As he watched the March Madness winners cut down the net, he thought, And *my* madness is over. First thing in the morning, I'll print out a clean copy, sign it, take to Sammy's office, leave it on Sammy's desk, call Sammy wherever she is—Tajikistan? Uzbekistan?—and tell her. Then I'll send Sammy and the Board an email with the exact same wording.

Yes, DONE!

As he headed to the bedroom, to go to sleep, his smartphone rang.

"Mr. Taylor, this is Wyatt."

"Yes?"

Wyatt was one of Jerome's men. Jeff figured Wyatt was working the swing shift, four p.m. to midnight, roaming the campus in a golf cart.

"Mr. Taylor, I was just going past the Beit Am and I heard some music and I poked my head in . . ."

"Yes . . . ?"

"Uh . . . there are some musicians . . . uh . . . tuning up. A band. And there are some . . . uh . . . like . . . performers. Like a circus or something. Some kind of show . . . "

"A band?! A circus?! Wyatt, what the hell is going on?"

"Uh . . . Mr. Taylor, maybe you'd like to come over and see for yourself?"

Damn right, thought Jeff. He clicked off.

He was fast out of the house, across the bridge into the Kingdom of Judah, onto Emmanuel Kleinman Quad and into the Beit Am where, coming through the door, he *did* hear musicians tuning up, and then saw them: a ten-piece band seated in front of the stage on which three jugglers were practicing beneath a tightrope on which a tightrope walker was testing his footing . . .

This about-to-be-launched production supervised by an impresario who turned around to Jeff to reveal himself as . . .

Moises Rivera.

Direct from Mexico City, the almost-billionaire himself, Jose's father.

"Jeff!" cried Moises. "So glad you're here. In"—he looked at his watch—"one minute, midnight exactly, Jose will be here, Jordan is bringing him here, a surprise for him and for her but we are *not* surprised at what will happen at twelve-oh-one. No, we *aren't*. When Harvard posts its acceptances, the band will play to celebrate Jose's achievement and these other professionals—some of whom have been with Cirque de Soleil—Jeff, I spare no expense for my son—they will also . . . "

"But Moises . . . " said Jeff.

From behind him, Jeff heard . . .

"Dad?! Dad?! What the f**k?!"

Jeff turned. It was Jose, coming in with Jordan.

"Jose!" cried Moises. "Jose! Welcome! You are the man of the hour! The man of the minute! As soon as Harvard posts its—"

"Dad!" snapped Jose. "What are you thinking—"

"I'm thinking we need to celebrate! Go ahead, Jose, it's time—log in."

Taking out his smartphone, Jose's fingers danced over the keyboard. He read, exhaled, and handed the phone to Moises.

A hush fell over the Beit Am. Jeff, Jose, and Jordan turned to Moises, who stared in gaping disbelief at his son's phone. The musicians, sensing something, let their instruments fall silent. They also turned to Moises. Then, from Moises's mouth—the mouth of the almost-billionaire—came a soft, piteous, "No no no . . . "

"Rejected?" asked Jordan, her voice a whisper.

"Wait-listed," said Moises.

"Fucking great, Dad," said Jose.

"*NO!*" cried Moises. He turned on Jeff: "*You* did this. You failed my son!"

"Dad!" said Jordan. "He's right. It's your fault!"

"Mine?" asked Jeff. "How?"

"You were the one who—"

"Jordan!" said Jose. "Whatever it is—another time. Right now, let's go."

He turned on his heel and, with Jordan by his side, headed toward the door.

"*NO!*" cried Moises. "*NO!*" He ran after Jose and Jordan. "*NO! Jose!* I won't let this stand. I will do everything, spend everything, to undo this. Everything to get you off the wait list and into Harvard. I will . . . "

Jose and Jordan, with Moises in pursuit, went out the door.

Jeff sighed. He thought, Well, I feel for Jose, but I'm heading home, to sleep and—

Then it hit him: HAHA's nine rejected seniors had turned to ten. A minyan. A minyan of misery. And . . . that tipped things.

Yes, tonight I can go to sleep, but tomorrow I've got to go to work. Got to start working to get all ten seniors into college. If not the colleges of their choice, at least colleges that they and their parents aren't ashamed of.

And until I get all ten *in*, I can't send my letter, I can't inform Sammy and the Board that, come June 21, I'm outta here.

Jeff looked around. The musicians, the jugglers, and the tight-rope walker were packing up. Lucky them, thought Jeff. *They're* outta here now.

He headed to the door, to get some sleep before the tomorrow's trials.

And heard, from outside, heading this way, a certain *squeak-squeak-squeak.*

Sammy Kleinman's rolling suitcase?

And now, on top of the *squeak-squeak-squeak,* a certain *click-click-click.*

Sammy Kleinman's high heels?

Yes. The woman herself, slim and trim in black trousers and a dressy white shirt, came through the door and said, "Hey, Jeff! While I was gone, bomb threats, unhappy seniors, cranky moms, right? And Moises ran by—he was mad as a hornet—we can't have that. But I'm back and now the Academy is in capable hands. Right?"

"Right," Jeff managed.

Not tired from her long trip back from the Stans—instead, *energized*—Sammy tapped Jeff's shoulder. "I have great court vision, right?"

"Right."

With Sammy up-close as his buddy-buddy colleague, Jeff was enfolded in expensive perfume and the stale smell of having been on airplanes for twenty-four hours. HAHA's alpha-female CEO said, "So let me share my vision. I'll tell you what you and I are going to do to *save* the Academy."

PART TWO

"Thanks to my father's largesse, the school's substantial financial resources underwrite a rich education which allows our graduates to matriculate at some of America's most prestigious colleges and universities."

—Samantha Kleinman
CEO, Hampton Acres Hebrew Academy

"We're broke, and some of our seniors will be lucky to get into Northwest Nowhere State."

—Jeff Taylor
Head of School, Hampton Acres Hebrew Academy

FORTY-THREE
HOPE IS A THING
WITH FEATHERS . . .
THAT FLIES AWAY

Being Head of School under Samantha Kleinman was for the birds. *Literally*, thought Jeff as, on the phone Tuesday morning, he strained to hear the wealthy widow on the other end—strained to hear her over the inhabitants of her aviary.

Peeps, trills, hoots, squawks, screeches . . . their voices ruled.

Jeff was on the conference room phone. The widow and her birds were on speaker. Sammy was on her feet, clapping her hands at Jeff, conveying, *It's okay, we can do this.* To Sammy, Jeff mouthed, *Impossible.*

"No way!" said Sammy. "Every confidence!"

Every confidence, said Michelle in his head. Michelle, loyal wife.

"We can *do* this." Sammy Kleinman, relentless optimist. Sammy Kleinman, expert with smoke and mirrors—and, this morning, the ability to penetrate the cries of a hundred birds?

Last night, Sammy had assured Jeff that now that she, Sammy, was back from the Stans, together they would save HAHA.

Save it financially.

In the conference room and beneath her father's watchful

bronze-carved eyes, Sammy had told Jeff that, come morning, "We will call Mrs. Esther Zwerdling of Shaker Heights, Ohio. Her husband, Arthur, renal failure, in hospice, a week to live tops, he was going to give us a million bucks. Written into his will. A million bucks! Last week, night before he died, she got him to change his will. A million bucks to her beloved birds. Out behind their house, she's got an aviary with every bird mentioned in the Torah. But you, Jeff, you who can charm the birds out of the trees, you can charm that million out of the widow Zwerdling. Ten a.m. tomorrow. She's agreed to talk to us."

But not agree with us, thought Jeff as—over the squawks and screeches—she boasted of where every penny of Arthur's re-routed million was going:

"To the dove, eagle, raven, owl . . . I have two of each of them, Mr. Taylor—my son says I am the Noah of Torah ornithology—and they all need so much love. And that's not the end of it. As for the owl, I have the little owl, the great owl, the horned owl. As for the eagle, I have . . . "

And I have a headache, thought Jeff. As she reeled off the names of more birds, Sammy stage-whispered, "Speak, Jeff honey. Speak!" But Mrs. Zwerdling and the warbles were winning.

Jeff gave up, handed the receiver to Sammy. Who also failed.

The call over, the two HAHA honchos looked at each other.

"No problem, Jeff," Sammy said. "I've got a lot more possible pigeons lined up. *Geese* with golden eggs. And *you're* going to help me separate them from their gold. Be ready to clear your calendar."

On a decisive *click-click-click* of high heels, Sammy departed.

Jeff sighed. He touched the breast pocket of his blazer, which contained his letter of resignation.

When can I submit it?

Not when I've got the Traumatized Ten—the ten seniors I have to help get into better schools. Help even as tiger-mother Rhoda Friedlander shreds me online with her newly launched Facebook attack group called "Taylor-Made Disaster."

But, before I can submit my letter, do I also have to get enough money to keep the school alive until June 21?

June 21? Ha! It's enough of a challenge to keep it going until May 30. May 30, Memorial Day, is *supposed* to be commencement. The seniors say goodbye; the rest of the students labor for another three weeks.

May 30? Jeff typed in arewebrokeyet615. Now, at the new burn rate, the drop-dead date had moved up yet again, to May 16. Which means comes May 16, we declare the seniors have graduated (no final exams, they'll like that) and mail off their diplomas.

But say, somehow, we make it to commencement, our last one. There is the small matter of getting a commencement speaker. Not so small. Sammy is convinced that Seymour Gutfreund's bottomless pockets hold the medicine that will revive a nearly-dead HAHA. Gutfreund gives us millions, we give him the dais. Failing that, and that *will* fail, I need HAHA's constituents to agree on someone. I have some candidates. Soon I'll start polling teachers, staff, students, parents.

Ask two Jews, get three opinions.

What was I thinking when I took this job?

Clarice poked her head in the conference room and announced, "Mr. Pettiver is on the line."

Jeff took the call. Hugh said, "Please, give me something to tell my boss. Tell me how you're going to make the July balloon payment."

You mean lie to you? thought Jeff. He didn't want to do that.

"Brilliant timing, Hugh! We just got off the phone with a very interested donor." Jeff left out that the widow's interest was birds, not boarding schools.

"Did you get a pledge? Say you did."

"Almost. Don't sweat it, because we have a plan to pay you off, and it's working. This month Sammy and I will be crisscrossing the country, raising money. We kicked off the tour with that donor because we knew she'd be the toughest sell. From here on, it's only going to get easier."

Although Jeff had said nothing that, in the fine old phrase, *You could take to the bank*, Hugh got off the call grateful that he had *something* to report.

Jeff thought, This job is for the birds! I am Head of a cuckoo's nest and I—whoops! Can't say that anymore. *No* cuckoo's nest. No, HAHA is a "safe place for the mentally different."

Mentally, he asked Michelle, *How's that? Woke enough?*

Sweetie, according to you, it's true.

FORTY-FOUR

GOING TO BAT
FOR THE BATTERED

Ten-thirty Tuesday morning. Putting Mrs. Esther Zwerdling and her birds behind him, Jeff started working the phones for the Traumatized Ten.

He phoned a Bradleyville *macher* who had graduated from the University of Georgia: "Roger, I've got this great kid, Drew Lazar, wait-listed by Florida State. He's going to be a huge success—twenty years from now he'll give major bucks to UGA. His academics? Well, not so great but, as you know, lots of C students reach the C-suite. As I recall, you told me you got straight D's at Athens your freshman year because of . . . no, I haven't told anyone that story . . . yes, Roger, I realize you were drunk when you told me . . . no, I *don't* see you as a drunk, I apologize if . . . "

He phoned a HAHA parent who owed him a favor, a parent whose sister taught at New York's Fashion Institute of Technology: "Harriet, I've got this great kid, Fanny Kolton. She's been wait-listed by FIT and accepted by her safety school, the University of Rhode Island. Fanny is ready to shine at *college* and be a great designer. She loves Nicole Saint-Denis . . . Really? Nicole Saint-Denis has been accused of stealing designs from her cousin? Well, I don't see how that should stop you from asking your sister to help Fanny at FIT . . . It would? But Harriet . . . "

He phoned an assistant dean at SUNY-Purchase: "Tom, I've got this great kid, Ashley Friedlander. She's been rejected by Princeton, but she'd be a real catch for you guys . . . Now, come on, Tom, I know you have influence . . . Don't give me that old line. An assistant dean is *not* a mouse studying to be a rat. I think you have cunning rat-like power *today* . . . You don't? Well, okay, I'll try elsewhere . . . "

Every confidence, said Michelle in his head.

FORTY-FIVE
YOUR FUTURE LIES AHEAD OF YOU

"**A**nd so I tell you, with all confidence, that your future lies ahead of you . . . "

Really? What a revelation! Thank you, Mr. Commencement Speaker!

That's what Sammy had foisted on HAHA last year—the owner of a chain of Bradleyville drugstores. Sammy gave the role to this big *macher* because, in return, the man gave the school twenty thousand dollars. Facing the podium in Manny Kleinman Quad, for twenty minutes students, parents, teachers, and staff were showered with sentiments that you *might* say the big *macher* had gleaned from the Hallmark cards on the racks in his stores—except Hallmark would have found them too saccharine.

This year, Jeff was determined to get a better speaker.

So that afternoon, Jeff was in Sammy's office saying, "Hey, you know, last year's commencement speaker, there was blowback. A dozen parents told me the school deserved somebody more . . . ah . . . elevated. So this year, I'm hoping a criterion is *not* how much money a speaker will give us. Instead—"

Sammy cut him off. "Jeff, how much would we get from somebody? Maybe twenty grand, tops? I am one hundred percent confident that this month you and I—me with my connections, you with your silver tongue—will get the three million to keep this place going through commencement and the fifty million to save it permanently. So, twenty grand? Bupkes! Get any commencement speaker you want."

Stunned, Jeff almost said, *"Really . . . ?"*

"So," said Sammy, "who do you want?"

"Three possibilities. There's an archeologist at the University of Georgia. She and her team are excavating this really important site near the Dead Sea. Then there's this guy based in Atlanta who's an activist against food deserts. Since we sit in the middle of one, he'd be appropriate. Especially since our Beth Katzendorf and Daniel Golub are getting lots of signatures on their food-desert petition, getting really known as social activists. And there's the head of Legal Aid in Bradleyville, he—"

"No. Not him, not ever. Twenty years ago, he tried to unionize Kleinman Homes, all my father's carpenters, plumbers, electricians, every single—"

"Hmm. Didn't know that. Okay, well, there's also this local rabbi who's formed a gun-control group. He's liberal, but the group cuts across red-blue lines."

"Any one of them, Jeff, as long as it doesn't cost us anything."

"I'm pretty sure they'd all speak for free."

"But the food desert guy," said Sammy. "We'd have to feed him."

"Well, yes, I mean—"

"That's a joke," said Sammy. "We'd have to feed the food desert man. A joke, Jeff. Don't you get it?"

"Ha!" said Jeff.

"But," said Sammy, "whoever it is, you've got to get a consensus. Parents, teachers, staff, students."

"Right," said Jeff. "Thanks."

Before Sammy could change her mind, Jeff turned and started walking out.

But, on his way out, Jeff knew: Get a consensus!? Sammy expects me to fail. Maybe *wants* me to fail. At which point Sammy—*no* consensus—makes a deal with someone like last year's speaker.

Sammy called after him. "Keep your priorities straight. First is working with me to raise money."

Jeff said, "You bet."

"And second—what is going on with our senior class? I've got parents telling me you're personally responsible for some of our best seniors not getting into the college of their choice. This Facebook group called 'Taylor-Made Disaster' is a disaster for the school—"

"Sammy, that's—"

"That's your second priority. Get them in somewhere better."

"You bet."

"Remember," said Sammy, "their future lies ahead of them."

FORTY-SIX

THE HAMMERIN' HEBES

"**G**onna *knock you back to the Middle Ages! / Go, Sages!*"

That was the sometime chant from HAHA student spectators directed at opponents at, say, a basketball or soccer game. Jeff had heard it only a few times. HAHA students weren't all that passionate about sports. That even included many of HAHA's "student athletes."

"There's not enough school spirit," said Rick Kessler, lacrosse captain.

"There's not enough team spirit," said Amy Lovitz, softball captain.

"We want to change that," said Isaac Greene, student body president.

"By retiring the Sage," said Sacha Reznick, holding a fistful of notes and a copy of *Derech Eretz, The Way of the World*, the school handbook, bristling with Post-it notes. "Replacing the old, bearded guy with someone young and active."

"Who?" asked Jeff.

Wary, behind his desk early Wednesday afternoon, he eyed the four students massed in front of him. They wore their serious faces. Their we're-acting-like-adults-when-we-petition-the-Head faces. But, standing just behind them, Rachel Fish wore a smirk. Goddamn it, Rachel, thought Jeff, what are you about to hit me with?

"The Hammerin' Hebes," said Isaac. "This school's teams will be The Hammerin' Hebes."

Jeff figured he hadn't heard right.

He said, "The Hammerin' Hebes? H-E-B-E-S?"

"Yes," said Rachel, triumphantly.

"This is a joke, right?" Jeff eyed Rachel, then the four students. All four shook their heads no. Jeff told the four, "You *know* 'Hebe' is a slur. It's like 'Kike.' It's ugly. It's what bigots say. Anti-Semites."

"Yes," said Isaac, "it's like what 'queer' used to be. But look what the gay and lesbian community did. Took the enemy's word and flung it back in their face. Made the word a badge of pride. The LGBTQ movement. That Q is for Queer."

As if on cue, Rachel said, "Reclaiming Hebe, *nullifying* its derogatory meaning, aligns us with other oppressed groups. It's aggressive, it's transgressive. It says we won't be pushed around."

"Look at Kinky Friedman and the Texas Jewboys," said Rick Kessler.

"Unofficially," said Isaac, "we've been polling the students. There's overwhelming support for getting rid of the Sage, going with the Hebe."

"Support for being tough Jews," said Rachel, with a clenched fist.

"And support in here," said Sacha, flipping open *Derech Eretz* to one of the Post-it-marked pages. "Section Four, Sub-Section Two, Paragraph Seven." He recited, "'As each generation must make its own Jewish identity, students have the right to . . .'"

Jeff held up a hand.

"Okay, okay," said Jeff. He tried to get his bearings. "Look, if we want to say we're tough and Jewish, then . . ." He was going to say, "Why not call ourselves the Maccabees, like Yeshiva University? Or, if we want a tough *alliterative* name, why not, instead of Hebes, call ourselves the Hampton Acres Hawks? Or . . ."

Or what? Jeff knew it was useless.

"So," said Isaac, "what we want to do is conduct an *official* poll, online, of all Academy students. We can do it today. The results will be immediate. We expect ninety percent in favor. Then all that has to happen is—"

"Brace for impact," said Jeff.

He thought, Brace for screams from your parents, from Sammy, from the Board, from most teachers and staff and especially—Jeff's heart went out to him—from Coach Bill Davidoff. Bill was a traditionalist. Bill would hate to see The Sage replaced.

"Then all that has to happen," said Isaac, "is design the logo for the Hebe. Maybe a Zealot—first century AD—the Jewish Revolt. Against Roman rule. A zealot wielding a big hammer."

"Uh-huh," said Jeff, dazed.

"And raise money for the mascot's uniform," said Rick.

"Mascot?" said Jeff, dazed.

"With a big foam head," said Amy. "And a big foam hammer. To roam the sidelines. Whip up the crowd. Take on the mascots of all the teams we face. Bop 'em with the hammer."

Jeff tried to remember if any teams that HAHA played *had* mascots.

"Lead the crowd in a chant," said Isaac.

In unison, Rick, Amy, Isaac, and Sacha demonstrated: "Go Hebes! Go Hebes! Go Hebes!"

Rachel grinned. "Gotta go with it, Jeff."

Jeff tried to look on the bright side. He thought, It could be worse. The device outside his window was still registering pork molecules in the air. If Rachel had wanted to be *really* transgressive, she and her student acolytes could have demanded that HAHA's mascot be a pig. Yeah, the Hammerin' Hog.

A starring role for Emmitt Bailey's eight hundred-and-twelve-pound Big Bob.

FORTY-SEVEN

THE NEXT BECKHAM

Standing on the sidelines of the HAHA soccer field, Jeff Taylor, Madison Angel, and Coach Bill Davidoff watched the "highlight of the game" in various combinations of amazement, sorrow, and anger.

Coach Bill spat, "So Moises Rivera hasn't heard of Varsity Blues?"

He meant the 2019 federal investigation that snared dozens of wealthy parents for faking athletic prowess for their high-school-age children, fakery to get their kids into elite colleges.

Jeff said, "I bet he has. But those parents—their *crime* was paying money to the colleges. They were nailed for bribery. Moises isn't doing that. The only money he's laying out is to HAHA and to Global Strategy and to our students. Nothing illegal."

"Just goddamn unethical," said Madison Angel.

Global Strategy was an international corporate-image firm. If your company created a huge oil spill or sold lettuce laced with E. coli, you called Global Strategy. Or if you wanted your son off Harvard's waiting list and into Harvard.

Jeff, Madison, and Coach Bill watched as, out on the soccer field, Jose tried to maneuver the ball past two defenders. As the defenders— paid to make it look like Jose was a soccer wizard, a Beckham—let the ball go through their legs, two cameramen from Global Strategy shot the scene: Jose triumphant, the defenders bested, the ball in the net.

Another Global Strategy cameraman shot one hundred-plus HAHA students—paid to pack a section of the stands and cheer—cheering.

"Goddamn disgusting," spat Coach Bill.

And goddamn swift of Moises, thought Jeff. At 12:01 a.m. Tuesday, Jose learned Harvard put him on the waiting list. At 9:15 a.m. Tuesday, Moises was on the phone, a conference call with Sammy and Jeff. Moises said he was hiring Global Strategy Group. "For campaign messaging, they're the very best. And I'm launching a campaign. Tomorrow afternoon they're shooting a video. The message is, the video is, look how truly great my son is. It's a video that will make it impossible for Harvard *not* to admit him. Now, my only question for the two of you . . . "

The only question was: to facilitate this, how much money did the school want?

Jeff wanted to say the school wasn't for sale.

But since it was Sammy's school, of course it was for sale.

Jeff had seen the storyboard for the video. After this soccer scene, there would be a debate club scene: Jose clinching an argument by quoting, from memory, hunks of John Stuart Mill and Maimonides. Then a "community outreach" scene: Jose at the athletic center's climbing wall with low-income white and African-American Bradleyville grade school students, helping the kids into climbing harnesses.

At this point, the storyboard said ANNOUNCER VOICE-OVER: Jose Rivera knows that *none* of us rise unless we help *all* of us rise.

At that point, Jeff Taylor wanted to barf.

As Jose and his supporting cast went back to their starting positions to reshoot the soccer scene, Rachel Fish joined Jeff, Madison, and Coach Bill.

She snapped, "Goddamn Sammy sold out too cheap. Price for this should've included Global Strategy videos for our nine other seniors— our kids sweating out being wait-listed and rejected."

"Nine other videos full of lies?" snapped Coach Bill. "Sports isn't like theater, Ms. Fish. It's not make-believe. It's real."

"I didn't say videos full of lies," said Rachel. "Videos that are the truth *well told*."

"I'd buy that," said Coach Bill. "But too late for that, isn't it?"

Rachel nodded. Jeff nodded. He thought, This is the first time I've ever seen Rachel and Bill agreeing, and it will probably be the last.

Wait till Bill hears about the plan to turn The Sages into the Hammerin' Hebes. Wait till he hears it's Rachel who's pushing for it. Before Bill has a chance to go totally ballistic, I had better talk to him. But what can I do to soften the blow . . . ?

"Very impressive," said Jerome McKool, joining them and nodding at the soccer production. "But I just got a call from Agent Grant Spisak, the Secret Service guy at the Bradleyville airport. You know, protecting Air Force One . . . "

"Yes?" said Jeff.

"Hour ago, they spotted a drone flying awfully close. They think it's from"—Jerome pointed to the Global Strategy crew—"those guys. Big no-no getting so close."

"I'll tell them," said Jeff. "Keep the drone here."

He was surprised that, with all the money Moises Rivera was laying out, Moises had somehow failed to pay off the US Secret Service.

FORTY-EIGHT
YOUR CANDIDATES
AREN'T MINE

Thursday morning, Jeff started polling HAHA teachers: who should be this year's commencement speaker?

The UGA archeologist, the anti-food-desert activist, or the gun-control rabbi?

Jeff ran the candidates past Rabbi Baum, Rachel Fish, and Noga Weinstein. None of these teachers liked any of Jeff's candidates. The liberal Bradleyville gun-control rabbi especially drew ire.

Baum said the man wasn't a real rabbi. "We need someone who teaches Torah—not this watered-down Judeo-Christian stuff."

Rachel said the man was a Zionist.

Noga said gun control was for corpses.

Thus confirming Jeff's experience, which was: a Jew is often more passionate about what he or she *doesn't* like.

Of course, Baum, Rachel, and Noga *did* have candidates.

Baum wanted Rabbi Mendel Lifshitz. Lifshitz, a former study partner of Baum's Rebbe, was a ninety-seven-year-old Kabbalist who spoke only Yiddish and Hebrew.

Rachel wanted Iman Abdullah, the founder of the Bradleyville BDS movement.

Noga wanted the head of the Mossad. "My cousin knows his

wife's sister. Yes, the man's identity is secret. Eh—he'll go up to the podium, speak from behind a curtain and through a voice distorter. No problem."

Sure, thought Jeff, no problem.

Rachel said, "As long as we don't have a speaker like last year. That pharmacy guy. Cliché spouter. 'Life is not a destination, it's a journey.' Total crap!"

Every confidence, said Michelle in his head.

FORTY-NINE
"HEBE NO!"

Speaking of polls . . .

At 12:16 p.m. Thursday, Isaac Greene texted Jeff the result of the online poll of HAHA students: seventy-two percent favoring The Hammerin' Hebes.

At 12:17 p.m., Coach Bill was on the phone, screaming in Jeff's ear: "*Hebes?!* What the hell?! *Hebes?!*"

"Where are you?" asked Jeff.

"In hell. Being tortured. Where they hell do you think I am?"

"I mean literally."

"In my new stadium."

"I'm on my way," said Jeff. "See if we can make this any better for you."

"There is *no* way this can be made better!"

In the lacrosse stadium, Jeff walked with Coach Bill. Waving at the bleachers, Jeff said, "Going to be finished in time for the tournament, right?"

"Yeah." Bill tried to brighten, but failed.

"Showcase your team. In the very first Hampton Acres Invitational."

"Yeah." Bill was still mostly glum. Then angry: "And showcase a Hammerin' Hebe?! A kid in a mascot's costume!"

"What if I got ESPN to come?"

Bill tried to brighten, did a bit better. "You could do that?"

"I think so. They live-broadcast high school football. And that's declining. High school lacrosse—*this* is on the rise."

"But they'd—for what they call 'color'—ESPN would shoot the damn mascot."

"Yeah, probably . . . "

Bill pointed to where—up next to the press-and-PA booth—the giant steel cut-out of The Sage surveyed the stadium. Bill said, "He oughta come down and—okay, not *shoot* the mascot—but kick the goddamn mascot in the ass. Jeff, this is desecration! Isn't there something in the Torah, something against this?" Bill brightened. "Hey, Baum would know. And Baum would be against this. Does Baum know?"

At which, Jeff's phone rang, and Jeff said, "Hi, Rabbi," and had Baum screaming in his ear: "Jeff, this is desecration, this is—"

Jeff interrupted: "How would you like your household allowance expanded even further? . . . You would? Then perhaps you could set Coach Bill's mind at ease about the Hammerin' Hebes . . . "

Jeff handed his phone to Bill, who listened and continued brightening.

"You mean," Bill said, "Let the kids say 'Hebes,' and we'll say 'Hebrews' and eventually it will be 'Hebrews? Just like we got BC to change to BCE, 'before the common era'?"

Baum was getting somewhere with Bill, but then the Coach grimaced. "Lemme call you back, Rabbi," Bill said and tossed the phone to Jeff. "Sammy's calling."

Catching the phone, Jeff had Sammy screaming at him before it reached his ear: "You think it's *been* hard to raise money? Now's going to be f**king *impossible!* I've lined up six *machers* to see. This idiocy will be the perfect excuse for all six to cancel."

"Maybe not," Jeff said. "Take Evan Rose. You always say, how come I can't get Evan to give? Well, Evan always says, 'To a man with a hammer every problem is a nail, and since most every problem *is* a nail, the first thing to do is hammer it.' So I think Evan will love the Hammerin' Hebes."

"Thank God my father's not alive to see this . . . How could I explain this to him?"

"I'm sure Manny would understand if the name change came with a five-million-dollar gift. And while no one can say for sure, I know Evan better than anyone else, and I say he will love it."

Sammy paused and said, "You do?"

"I do."

Sammy exhaled a long breath. Her usual purr-growl became a sigh. She said, "Okay . . . why not? I've tried everything else. What the Hebe."

FIFTY

A BREAK FROM PUTTING OUT FIRES

At one-thirty, the start of sixth period, Jeff was in a classroom in Stuart Kleinman Hall, teaching the nine students taking his Jewish Thought and Culture class.

This was one of his favorite things at HAHA. I'm not just an administrator, thought Jeff. I'm not just putting out fires. I'm a teacher, lighting fires in young minds.

Jeff said, "Okay, we had readings on Gershom Scholem and Walter Benjamin, two German Jewish intellectuals who were contemporaries. And buddies. But we only have time to talk about one of them. So, first question: which one, and why him?"

The weather was warm and sunny, the school day was almost over, and prom night was getting close enough to be a distraction. Jeff knew the only way to keep them awake was to get them to talk. When no one volunteered, he caught Isaac Greene's eye.

"Well, the reading on Scholem was, like, twice as long—so him?"

"Shrewd, Isaac," said Jeff, which drew a few laughs. "You caught me. But why did I game it that way? Anyone?"

"Mr. Taylor," said Amy Lovitz, the softball captain, "Walter Benjamin's story is so sad. He kills himself. But Gershom Scholem escapes the Nazis and gets to Israel."

"Home run, Amy, a grand slam." Turning to the class, he said, "Remember, guys, when you're in college, that reading list didn't fall from the sky. Someone put it together with a plan in mind."

"And your plan was to have us focus on the Zionist who makes it to Israel, keeps Jewish life going," Sacha said, speaking uncharacteristically slowly.

"Yes, Sacha! Kudos to Isaac, Amy, Sacha for seeing the plan behind the reading. That's great. But what about the reading itself? What's Scholem's big point?"

Isaac said, "Myth and mysticism—the irrational—are as important to Judaism as the rational stuff, like the laws."

"Exactly," said Jeff. "Now let's bring it home—do you see the same thing here, at HAHA? The rational part and the not so rational, each playing a role in giving the school its character?"

That stumped them, so Jeff said, "Like can you think of a ritual involving dance, loud music, going a bit wild, but not too wild—"

"The prom," they shouted.

Jeff said, dryly, "Are you talking about a prom at *our* school? I can't imagine it."

The students chuckled.

Amy said, "But what's an example of rational stuff at HAHA?"

Jeff wanted to say *I've been wondering myself,* but Isaac answered her first: "Like the Sanhedrin judging a student. Or"—he turned and faced Jeff—"the stuff you do with the board to, like, keep the school running smoothly."

"That stuff is *definitely* more irrational," Jeff said, and the class laughed. The bell sounded, signaling the end of sixth period at 2:20 p.m. The nine darted out of the room as one, like a school of fish.

Jeff would have been happy to keep teaching, but it was time to put down the lesson plan and take up axe and helmet. There were fires burning all over campus.

FIFTY-ONE

GOING TO BAT
FOR THE BATTERED,
CONTINUED

Ignoring the attacks on him in social media, Jeff was working the phones. Working to get the Traumatized Ten into better schools.

He phoned a Bradleyville native, a woman who now was one of North Carolina's top trial lawyers, a graduate of Wake Forest: "Bethany, I've got this great kid, Terri Fernandez, fabulous writer. She's been wait-listed by BU and Syracuse, so imagine, thirty years from now, Wake Forest being able to claim her as its own. So I wonder if you . . . Really? I didn't know that. You were part of the legal team? . . . Yeah, the tobacco companies were culpable . . . RJ Reynolds . . . And you helped put RJR into bankruptcy . . . Right, a Wake Forest icon. But, it was more than thirty years ago, and you were a very junior member of that team—I wouldn't think Wake Forest Admissions still . . . But they do? . . . Right. Well, some grudges . . . "

He phoned Evan Rose, who was a generous donor to NYU: "Evan, I've got this great kid, Ari Black. He's going to be a wonderful public policy guy, great advocate for good causes. He's been wait-listed by Vanderbilt, and I wonder if you could advocate for him at NYU . . . ? Oh, really? You did that last year for her . . . ? A Choate grad? And

how did it work out? Oh, she . . . you're kidding! The NYPD . . . !
Did she get indicted? . . . Oh, just expelled. Lucky girl. So she misled
everyone, including . . . But Evan, the NYU Admissions people can't
blame you . . . They do.? . . . Uh-huh. So it's going to be a few years
before you can again advocate for . . . I totally . . . How's it going
here? Swimmingly."

Jeff wanted to hit Evan up for the three million, but he knew if he
tried over the phone, Evan would hang up. So Jeff kept saying things
like "swimmingly," but in a tone that said "not very swimmingly." He
was laying groundwork for when he'd have the chance to hit Evan
up in person. Jeff wasn't looking forward to that meeting because,
contrary to what he had told Sammy, he thought Evan might chuckle
about the Hammerin' Hebe, but he'd never fund the school.

For the next kid, no phone call was needed.

Jeff walked into Samantha Kleinman's office. "Sammy, I'm here
for Lena Navuluri."

"Right! " said Sammy. "A lovely girl. We're lucky to have her. I
still remember: Samarkand, two years ago. I meet her parents. The
Navuluris own the biggest gold mine in Uzbekistan. They wanted
their daughter to go to America. And here she is. Graduating this
June. Wants to be an architect, right?"

"Right," said Jeff. "But she's been wait-listed by Missouri. Accepted
by Central Nebraska—but she says, if she goes there, she will bring
shame on her family. So what about Stauffer?"

Stauffer University, fifty miles away, in Macon, was light on academics but growing like crazy because of all the amenities it offered
students: a steak house on campus, massage and facial treatments.
Tuition was a big ticket-item. The Navuluri family could easily afford
it. Jeff knew Sammy fawned on its president.

"Done!" proclaimed Sammy.

Jeff knew that while Sammy often bullshitted, this was one promise she would deliver on. "Thanks," said Jeff. He left his boss's office
having turned the Traumatized Ten into the Nervous Nine.

FIFTY-TWO

THE TWELVE TRIBES
HIGHLY HONORED

"I have a surprise for you," said Barbara Travis.

Taking Jeff's hand, she led him through her back yard, through the clutter of scrap metal that she collected. This was the clutter amid which, as he watched, she had been welding together her Holocaust sculpture, her *Butterfly*.

She led him past it, led him toward where he rarely went: behind her barn, to where there was, he knew, more scrap metal awaiting more of her inspirations.

As they rounded the barn, he wondered, What new kitsch awaits?

"There!" said Barbara. "The last three weeks! What I've been working on!"

Jeff stared at a dozen rusty bicycle wheels, each mounted on a rusty pillar, all in a row.

Yes, he now realized that, this last month, at junkyards around Bradleyville, he had seen Barbara walk off with old bicycles. Now a dozen of their wheels had come together. Why? What is this?

"I call it *Strong East Wind*," said Barbara. "Exodus 14:21. 'And the Lord caused the sea to go back by a strong east wind, and made the sea dry land.'"

"So the children of Israel could escape the Egyptians," said Jeff.

"Exactly! Twelve giant fans for the Twelve Tribes. It's not just symbolic. With twelve electric motors, it's also going to be functional. Beneficial. Emmitt Bailey's pigs? Up on the roof of Leopold Hirszfeld Hall, *Strong East Wind* will drive the pork molecules back!"

"On the roof of Hirszfeld Hall?" said Jeff.

"Yes!" said Barbara. "My surprise gift to you, and to the school. I got permission from Sammy. Aren't you happy?"

"Uh, I sure am," lied Jeff.

"Of course," said Barbara, beaming at her creation, "you can keep the pork molecules a secret. You don't have to tell anyone that's what *Strong East Wind* is doing. In fact, better to not let the kids near it. Just let them think it's a great work of art. Which it is."

"But it could be dangerous?" Jeff asked.

"Well, it will have twelve strong motors, which can be set from one to ten, set from low to full blast. Just don't run them anywhere near ten, because—"

"Because the world will end?" Jeff said.

"No, sweetie. It will just sound like the world is ending."

"And Sammy knows all this and still said 'yes'?"

"I showed a photo to Sammy and went over all the details. She said, 'Yes! Up on the Hirszfeld roof. I just love it!'" Barbara beamed at Jeff. "Your boss is a true connoisseur of art."

"She sure is."

Leaning into him, nodding at the assemblage, Barbara said, "Isn't it beautiful?"

"It sure is."

It is, insisted Michelle in his head. *Your beloved created it, so it is.*

Well, Jeff thought, it could be worse. I can't see the roof of Hirszfeld Hall from my office.

FIFTY-THREE
AN UNBLEMISHED EFFORT

"Emmitt," said Reverend Pat Travis, "do you believe in the End Times?"

"Enzymes?" asked Emmitt Bailey. His hearing aid wasn't working so good today. "Yes, I do. Supplemental xylanase. It improves nutrient digestibility. Results in bigger pigs."

"No," said Reverend Travis. "End Times. The Rapture. When Jesus returns to usher in a thousand years of peace and harmony."

"Oh, of course."

The two men were sitting on the front porch of Emmitt's house, fifty yards from the leading edge of Emmitt's CAFO. It was a killer hot day and, being hospitable, Emmitt had served his pastor iced tea. But Emmitt was worried. He figured his pastor was here to hit him up for more money for the church's building fund. For his part, Reverend Travis appreciated the cold drink; today's heat made the smell from Emmitt's six thousand pigs overwhelming. But, mopping his brow with a handkerchief, using the motion to surreptitiously pinch his nose shut, Reverend Travis wished his congregants would offer him a real drink.

"So," said Reverend Travis. "That's why I'm here. End Times. And today is the right day to talk about it. For tomorrow is . . ."

Reverend Travis paused to give Emmitt the chance to show he was a good Christian.

"Uh . . . Good Friday?"

"Exactly," said Reverend Travis. "Christ crucified. And this Sunday, Easter Sunday, Christ risen. And when will Christ come again? What is necessary? The Second Coming cannot occur until the Third Temple is built in Jerusalem. And the Third Temple cannot be built until it can be purified with the sacrifice of a very specific animal. Numbers 19:2: 'Speak unto the children of Israel, that they bring thee a red heifer without blemish.'"

"I've heard that," allowed Emmitt. He fiddled with his hearing aid. It was rude not to listen to the Word of God. If the preacher was going to cite more Scripture, this farmer would pay attention.

"And the red heifer must be born in Israel."

"I didn't know that."

"But the effort can start here."

"Really?"

"Yes. Over in Mississippi, for more than three decades now, a good man, a preacher who is also an expert cattle breeder, has been at work. He has been trying to breed red heifers to export to Israel, so a red heifer can be born there."

"Doing the work of the Lord," allowed Emmitt.

"Trying to," said Reverend Travis. "The heifer must not have more than three white or black hairs on its body. In Israel, the rabbis have stringent tests to make sure it is entirely red."

"Is that right?"

"Yes. Thus far, no heifer has passed this test."

"A shame."

"Why," asked Reverend Travis, "has this God-fearing cattle breeder not succeeded? I believe it is because he is breeding heifers far from any of the children of Israel."

"Ah."

"But you, Emmitt, you are blessed. With the presence of children of Israel. You have their Academy as your immediate neighbor. And you are an expert breeder of animals."

"Pigs. Not cows."

Emmitt didn't cotton to big animals like cows. Of course he did have Big Bob. Big Bob probably wouldn't reach a half-ton, but he wouldn't fall short by much.

Emmitt told Reverend Travis, "Breeding pigs is its own knack."

"A knack," said Reverend Travis, "and a gift that I am convinced is transferable. A gift you are called upon by Scripture to give to this effort."

"Reverend, among other things, it's gotta be expensive breeding heifers."

"I have a source of funding."

"Really?" Emmitt was impressed. *Instead of the preacher coming here to pick my pocket, he's come to fill it.*

"Truly. I'll email you all the details." Reverend Travis mopped his brow. "Come, let us pray." *A quick prayer,* thought Reverend Travis. *I can't take this smell a minute longer.*

"Alright."

The two men got off their seats, lowered themselves onto their knees.

"Oh, Lord," said Reverend Travis. "We call upon Thee to fill thine humble servant Emmitt Bailey's heart with wisdom, so that he may raise the red heifer as foretold to bring about the Second Coming. We ask this in the name of your son, Jesus Christ. Amen."

"Amen," said Emmitt.

Quickly, Reverend Travis was back up on his feet. Quickly, he shook hands with Emmitt. Striding away toward his car, he applied his handkerchief. Now, with his back to the pig farmer, he could keep his nose pinched and covered. *God! What a stench!*

But, ah, when the red heifer is sacrificed in Jerusalem! It will be a burnt offering, a food offering with—as Leviticus says—"a pleasing aroma to the Lord."

FIFTY-FOUR

BADMINTON AND GOOD MEMORIES

Sunday dawned pale but grew sunny. At his kitchen table, at breakfast, Jeff worked on the *New York Times* crossword, became stumped on the upper right-hand corner. To his pleased surprise, Jordan texted him: *Beat u at badminton?*

Back in Greenwich, Jordan and Michelle and he had played. He realized he missed it. And the Head's house had come with a net and racquets and birdies. He texted Jordan an emoji: thumbs-up. She came over and, true to her word, was quickly beating him. Before he knew it . . .

"Seventeen-nine," announced Jordan.

"I thought it was seventeen-ten."

"Nine. You have nine." She shook her head and her ponytail went side to side, saying *Wrong, Wrong.* "You have nine."

Not only am I losing, thought Jeff, but apparently I don't even know the score.

A fitting metaphor for me quite a lot these days. Me as Head of School. Me as Jordan's father.

As Jordan got ready to serve again, he heard Michelle tell him, *Jeff, play hard. If you don't play hard, if you let her win, she'll hate you for it.*

He told Michelle, I *am* playing hard.

Which he thought was true. He had been swinging hard, had been trying to whack the birdie back hard—but mainly, he felt, the birdie flew back softly.

Another metaphor, thought Jeff. These last two years, as Head, I've put so much into everything . . . with so little result.

Less self-pity! said Michelle. *More pluck!*

Yes, ma'am, replied Jeff.

He dug in, dug deep. Here came Jordan's next serve, a zinger, making him dive to his right. He managed to return it, a weak return which Jordan put away.

"Eighteen-nine," announced Jordan.

"Right," said Jeff, picking up the birdie and tapping it back to her.

"You know . . . " said his daughter, about to serve.

"Yes?"

"I feel like Mom is watching us."

"Really?"

"Yeah, like she used to in Greenwich."

"Watching you crush me," said Jeff.

"Yes."

"Well," said Jeff, "that's why, right now, I *don't* feel her watching us. I hated losing to you in front of her."

"Liar," said Jordan, with a wide grin.

She tossed up the birdie, served another zinger, this time making Jeff dive to his left. He reached it, whacked it back—into the net.

"Nineteen-nine," said Jordan, retrieving the birdie. "And you"—she grinned an even wider grin—"*are* a liar. Cuz I remember the first time I beat you and Mom saw it. I was only eleven. You were so proud. You told Mom, '*Michael* Jordan has nothing on our kid.' You loved losing to me in front of her."

"Maybe that first time. But not afterward. Not consistently."

"Yes, consistently. Well, maybe you didn't love it, but you *respected* it. Dad, you're attracted to strong women. You love them."

"Well . . . "

"Like Mom. Like Barbara."

"And like you," said Jeff.

"Exactly. Me. Who is gonna win the next two points and beat you."

"We'll see about that," said Jeff.

At which Jordan served, another zinger, a zinger just inside the line which Jeff dove for and which his racquet couldn't even reach.

"Twenty to nine," announced Jordan. "Game point." Jeff picked up the birdie and tapped it back to her.

"You ever play against Barbara?" asked Jordan.

"Uh, no."

"You don't dare?" said Jordan, grinning.

"Well . . . "

"Dad, I really like her. Happy you met her. She really cares about you. But she'd beat you bad as me."

"Probably. Now serve. Get this over with."

With a flip of the head, a flip that told Jeff *With pleasure*, Jordan flipped her ponytail, then served. It looked like it was going to be another zinger but she faked her father out. It was a high lob over his head which he turned and ran for and dove for . . . and missed.

"Twenty-one to nine," announced Jordan. "Game over."

"That's a relief," said Jeff, picking himself up.

Jordan ducked under the net, came toward him. "Dad . . . " She gestured toward the whole campus, the Kingdoms of Judah and of Israel, green and glowing in the noon sun. "I'm really glad we came down here."

"So you could beat me at badminton north *and* south."

"Yep," said Jordan. "Only for that. Dad, I gotta run. I've got a date with Jose."

"Another man who is attracted to a strong woman," said Jeff. "A woman who knows her own mind. And uses it." He grinned. "Sometimes uses it to diss her poor father."

Jordan grinned. "Yes." She tapped her father on the shoulder. "Thanks, Dad."

And she was gone.

Well done, big guy, said Michelle to Jeff. *Now go back to the cross-word. See if you can win there, too. I've got every confidence in you.*

FIFTY-FIVE
BONDING OVER BRISKET?

O h, damn. *That's* why I'm here tonight. Baum is playing match-maker. Trying to wed me to Tzipora Perl.

Sitting down at the Shabbat dinner in Baum's house, obeying Baum's friendly but commanding nod to sit right *there*, next to Tzipora, Jeff mentally sighed.

Hey, Baum, I *have* a significant other. Oh, Barbara, why does your uncle—Reverend Travis—and his wife have to have their thirty-fifth anniversary dinner tonight? Yes, I understand you have to be there. I don't understand how Baum learned that. Crafty, cunning Baum. Rude Baum. Hey, Baum, because you've been so blunt about fixing me up, I've been avoiding your house. But a Head can't keep that up. So here I am.

At the dining room table were the Rabbi and his wife Chava (eager to entertain their guests and—Jeff knew—to entrap me), their children, Stevie and Meadow Blau (eager to devour Chava's rich food), and Tzipora Perl (shy, but eager to snare me).

At many card tables set up and jammed into the living room were two dozen HAHA students, also eager for Chava's food.

Shabbat began.

Chava lit the candles and said the blessing. Covering her eyes with her hands, she then extended and waved them toward her face, as if guiding the candlelight to her closed eyes. Baum then poured the dark red wine into a silver cup until it overflowed onto a matching silver saucer, chanted the blessing, and drank.

Everybody rose, and went to the kitchen for the ritual hand-washing with a special washing cup.

Everyone returned, and Baum blessed a pair of challot.

As everyone dug into the appetizers—gefilte fish and, spread over the challah, hummus—Baum delivered a d'var torah based on the week's Torah portion. He held forth on Leviticus 21:13: "He shall take a wife in her virginity." What, asked Baum, do the Talmudists say this means beyond the plain words? Based on this verse, our rabbis teach that you must marry a woman who has never been betrothed to anyone else.

Since, a decade ago, Barbara had been briefly engaged to a guy and—since Baum had apparently somehow learned this—Jeff wanted to leap across the table and strangle him.

Having completed his hit on Barbara, Baum wrapped up with some sweet-sounding generalities. The students, to whom Baum's talks were usually directed, looked perplexed.

Now Baum asked, "Does anyone else at this table want to share a Shabbos thought?"

With Chava Baum at her side quietly urging her, Tzipora spoke in a soft voice: "I love the school. I'm grateful to the Head for giving me this chance, and to God for guiding me here."

Stevie and Meadow Blau then talked briefly about the evils of capitalism and the blessings of environmentalism. Next was Jeff. He couldn't ignore Tzipora's words or encourage her hopes—either would be cruel. He said, "The whole school is pleased you're here, Tzipora, and I am proud of the way the community has welcomed you."

Then came chicken soup with huge, floating globs of fat.

Then came fried potato pancakes and rich brisket.

Everyone dug in. The two dozen kids were rowdily happy. The adults were politely happy. Jeff observed Tzipora trying to eat sparingly—small bites, well-spaced—but not succeeding. Her body was covered in a long-sleeved blouse and a skirt to her ankles. Her hair was in a colorful kerchief. Jeff's heart sank to see that she was trying to be attractive to him; she wore nail polish, lipstick, a necklace, and rings. On the pale skin of her pleasant, plain face she wore makeup.

"You have such a big job," said Tzipora. "What's your favorite part?" She was blushing.

Jeff answered with bland clichés. He felt for her. Ah, Tzipora, you grew up in the shadow of your father, the big-deal rabbi. Your drive goes only into baking rich desserts and challot. You feel shame at being thirty years old and unmarried.

Meanwhile Baum was pressing the case. As dinner went on, he said, "Jeff, it's great when your spouse knows how to celebrate Shabbat." . . . "Jeff, you can't make latkes like these if you don't have a Jewish neshama." . . . "Jeff, for dessert, you must see what Tzipora has made for us."

Dinner concluded with Tzipora's chocolate cake and her honey nut baklava.

Taking small bites, Jeff politely praised both.

Then Baum took out the little prayer book with the *Birkat HaMazon*, the prayer after eating. Led by Baum, everyone sang the prayer with gusto.

Please, thought Jeff, let this evening be over.

Finally, it was officially over. Happily full, Stevie and Meadow left the dining table to go back to their house to supervise their students. Happily full, the two dozen HAHA students left the card tables, to find their friends and roam the peaceful campus. As Tzipora helped Chava clean up, Baum took Jeff aside. "Look at Chava and me," he said. "How well-suited we are to each other, how . . . "

Right, thought Jeff, and if I really wanted to save HAHA, I would marry Tzipora. Her father would be so thrilled—ecstatic!—he would praise the school to Gutfreund. And Gutfreund would give the school tens of millions. But Sammy, why is this my responsibility? You want to save HAHA, *you* find a match for Tzipora.

Chava and Tzipora came back from the kitchen. Now, clearly, Baum expected—and Tzipora hoped—that Jeff would walk Tzipora back to her small apartment on campus.

Sighing inwardly, Jeff suggested that he and Tzipora walk together because "it's on my way."

They followed the well-lit path that threaded its way through the student houses and towards the bridge that Jeff couldn't wait to cross. Walking a few feet behind them, as if she were a bodyguard, was Chava Baum. Jeff knew the Rebbetzin would never allow them to be alone, but trust me, Chava, you don't have to worry!

"So you like it here," Tzipora said, "in Bradleyville."

Jeff allowed that he did, and then asked Tzipora if she would like to start a student baking club.

"You mean for girls who want to bake?"

"Or the boys—HAHA doesn't always hold to traditional gender roles."

Tzipora, who had spent her life under the roof of her very traditional father, was flustered by the thought of boy bakers.

"Well—I—uh . . . "

"We've arrived at the bridge, ladies. Tzipora, think about the club—it would be a great way for you to meet more students. Shabbat Shalom to both of you."

They parted. Jeff entered the Kingdom of Israel and recited his last prayer of the evening, one of gratitude for having sidestepped the Baums' matchmaking mischief. At that moment, his phone rang.

Sammy.

"Jeff, honey, clear your calendar for next week. I've lined up a slate of meetings with the money guys."

Jeff sighed. He thought, if only you had been Samuel, not Samantha. Then you could have married Tzipora and been weighed down by babka, not bank debt.

FIFTY-SIX

WHAT MANDATE ARE WE TALKING ABOUT?

Five minutes after Cristina Rountree finished teaching her third-period class, she got a call from Mrs. Rhoda Friedlander: "Ms. Rountree, I had expected to hear from you by now. You've had Ashley's paper for a whole week."

Christina gritted her teeth. This was true. One week ago, Mrs. Friedlander had emailed her a scholarly paper, "Some Overlooked Factors in the Establishment of the State of Israel" by—it claimed—Ashley Friedlander. Along with the paper came Mrs. Friedlander's firm suggestion: Since Christina was on the advisory board of the *Piedmont Journal of International Affairs*, Christina should see to its immediate acceptance for publication there.

Christina knew three things.

One: This paper was very well written.

Two: Mrs. Friedlander wasn't giving up on Princeton. Mrs. Friedlander wanted to wave in Princeton's face this paper's acceptance by the *Piedmont Journal*.

Three: The chances that Ashley had written this paper were about the same as the chances that she, Christina—not Alexander Hamilton, James Madison, and John Jay—had written *The Federalist Papers*.

Christina Rountree was incredibly flattered that she, a newly-minted

PhD from a less than prestigious institution—UGA-Bradleyville—had been invited to serve on the *Piedmont's* advisory board. So she knew a fourth thing:

Four: I am *not* going to flack for this ghost-written paper.

For one week, Christina had put off telling Mrs. Friedlander, "Sorry, I won't." Now, confronted on the phone—Mrs. Friedlander jawing in her ear and Mrs. Friedlander's husband, Arnie, breathing in her ear—Christina knew she had to say something.

She said, "Well, yes, it's a really fine paper. For example, in its analysis of life under the British Mandate, it—"

"Wait a minute," said Arnie Friedlander. "Are you talking about Ashley's paper? It's about the founding of the State of Israel. It's not about Covid restrictions."

"Covid restrictions?" said Christina.

"Yes," said Arnie Friedlander. "You said 'The British Mandate.' Did you mean British mask mandates? Or testing mandates? Or vaccination mandates?"

Christina Rountree stared at the phone in her hands.

FIFTY-SEVEN
RITCHIE AND RAVENEL'S
RED LETTER DAY

"**W**ell now, Jefferson, we'd best get down to business. Do y'all have any reason to believe fraud is being committed in the financials?"

This from the mouth of Spencer Ritchie of the accounting firm of Ritchie & Ravenel, offices in Sabbathday, Georgia in the Hungry Hollow strip mall. This said in the HAHA conference room, Spencer Ritchie and Greer Ravenel across the table from Jeff.

Spencer's mouth being full of Tzipora Perl's excellent strawberry rugelach, "financials" came out as "fineshulls."

Jeff sighed—not wise in front of your accountants—and shook his head.

"Spencer, Greer—I don't have a single reason to think there's fraud." Eyeing Greer, Jeff pointed to the platters of Tzipora's rugelach and chocolate babka. "Eat up."

Greer Ravenel, tall and slender, shook his head. Spencer Ritchie, short and fat, dug in more.

Jeff thought of Don Quixote and Sancho Panza, on a quixotic quest for financial exactitude.

"That's good," said Ritchie, spraying rugelach flakes at Jeff.

Jeff didn't know if he meant the baking or HAHA's books. Early afternoon Monday, Ritchie & Ravenel had begun their annual review of HAHA's financials. Jeff was meeting them alone. Sammy was conveniently up in New York City, unreachable. But at the far end of the room, the fierce bust of Manny Kleinman glared.

"That's *really* good," said Spencer Ritchie. He turned to his partner. "Greer, you gotta help yourself right now to some of this rag-ah-ick. I guarantee you can't get anything like this in Sabbathday."

Greer Ravenel looked up from the pile of work papers in front of him and again shook his large, long, bald head. "Come on now, Spencer, you know I'm on a diet." Turning to Jeff, he said, "What about your systems and processes? Policies and procedures? Software, record-keeping, inventory-tracking? Any weaknesses detected since last year?"

Jeff shrugged and made a vague gesture. "Notta one."

Not a single reason, mocked Michelle. *Notta one. Hon, you don't have one reason—you have ten. Lucky for you, Barbara isn't asking the questions.*

Ritchie and Ravenel continued asking Jeff the same questions they put to him last year, the same they'd put to his predecessor, William Schwartz. Jeff continued giving the same ambiguous, Delphic-like responses as last year; words that sounded firm but were as squishy and unreliable as a leaky inner tube, or—more to the point—as a HAHA IOU.

As they'd done last year, the accountants pretended to press and probe for financial weaknesses, while Jeff maintained the pretense that all was well.

You and these two good ol' boys, said Michelle. *The trickeracious trio.*

Jeff hated this tap dance. He hated it even more than having to expel a floundering kid. This year he was going to wrap it up fast. And he meant to walk away with an extra benefit he figured he might need if the truth about HAHA's finances leaked. For this purpose, he had brought his laptop and had connected it to the conference room's printer.

"Fellas, I know you want me in here for hours going over these records with you, but my plate is full. I've got finals and graduation around the corner, and tonight I'm flying to New York, joining Sammy on a fundraising campaign that'll be a game-changer. So can I be excused? Tell you what—let me out now, and I'll sign a letter saying that this year is pretty much like last. Only now you'll have it in writing? Deal?"

Ritchie and Ravenel looked at each other.

They were as eager to finish as Jeff was. Their long-perfected art—delving into a company's books deep enough to make it seem a diligent review had been conducted but not so deep as to expose the financial corpse concealed therein—was exhausting. And the offer of a letter to hide behind, a letter signed by an ex-hedge fund guy who could be sued? *That* shouldn't be passed up. Each knew what the other was thinking: *Let's grab that letter and get back to Sabbathday.*

Jeff drafted the letter on his laptop with the two accountants standing behind him, looking over his shoulder. He could hear Ravenel wheezing and Ritchie chewing. Having finished the rugelach, Ritchie was on to the babka. When the letter was done, Jeff let his finger hover over the print key.

"You know, since I'm giving you a letter, I think I should get one back. Seems only fair. How about you give me a draft clean opinion, blessing our financial statements for this year?"

"But Jefferson . . . " said Ravenel. "We aren't close to finishing our work. We've got months before we can sign that letter, assuming we don't find anything."

"Not that we expect to find anything," said Ritchie.

Jeff said, "That's why I said 'draft.' Put 'draft' all over it, guys. In big type. Now, I think that swap is *more* than fair."

So Jeff and Greer switched places. In short order, Greer Ravenel produced the clean opinion. It had the sentences Jeff prized, sentences saying—surrounded by thickets (hedges!) of qualifications and evasions—that HAHA's financials were in order and its health was solid. Perfect! On every page in big type was DRAFT, but it was what Jeff needed.

Both documents were printed and, under the fierce gaze of Manny Kleinman, signed.

Their business concluded, Jeff showed the undynamic duo to the door.

FIFTY-EIGHT
HOLOCAUST COMPETITOR

Shulamit Klaczko's Park Avenue apartment was a shrine to her late husband.

The walls were covered with framed photographs of Benoit Klaczko with presidents, prime ministers, and popes. Also, mementos from his extraordinary life: a vicious-looking six-inch-long piece of barbed wire from Auschwitz, encased in Lucite, hung next to his Nobel Prize in Literature.

In the middle of the apartment, in a commanding armchair in the living room, sat the keeper of the shrine, Shulamit herself, age eighty-nine and as sharp—observed Jeff—as that piece of barbed wire.

Jeff knew that he and Sammy—sitting next to him, on a couch facing Shulamit—were not going to *easily* get anything out of Benoit Klaczko's widow.

What they were here to try to get—Sammy's whackadoo quest, thought Jeff—were Benoit Klaczko's papers.

Elie Wiesel, Primo Levi, and Benoit Klaczko. That was the Holocaust Big Three. Jeff wasn't sure where Wiesel's and Levi's papers were, but he knew where Klaczko's belonged: At a place like Harvard, Oxford, or the Sorbonne. Not at HAHA. No matter that Sammy had promised a fifteen-million-dollar Frank Gehry-designed building to house them. No matter that Sammy had told Shulamit that HAHA already had a commitment of that fifteen million to build it.

Good luck, Sammy.

Sammy had told Jeff this story: In March 1924, when Chicago's WGN radio first went on the air, an enterprising nobody told WGN's management he had exclusive rights from Chicago Cubs to broadcast their games—*and* he told the Cubs he had an exclusive agreement from WGN to broadcast their games. Neither statement was true. But instead of checking it out, both organizations said "Sure," and signed on the dotted line. The enterprising nobody became a rich somebody.

"My daddy loved that story," Sammy said. "That's turning smoke and mirrors into gold."

Sammy *wanted* to tell the National Endowment for the Arts she had an agreement from Shulamit. She *wanted* to tell Shulamit she had an agreement from the NEA. Unfortunately for Sammy, this was not 1924. Both the NEA and Shulamit would check. So Sammy had kept the source of that commitment of "fifteen million" vague.

But if they could get a commitment out of Shulamit . . . ?

Then, therefore, fifteen million out of the NEA . . . ?

Jeff knew that before any of that money went into the Benoit Klaczko Library, some would go to keep HAHA open through commencement. And he suspected some would go into Sammy's luxurious Birkin bag. Which Sammy would—with her version of a clear conscience—justify as payment for her efforts.

Well, good news-bad news: I think we're doomed to fail here. Just look at that look on Shulamit's face. Hawk-eyed. Lips set in a grim line. She had not been in the camps; she had got out of Poland in a 1938 Kindertransport. But she was as fierce as Benoit, who, as a teenager, had been in the camps, and had been fierce enough to survive them. She was bathed in late-afternoon light; it did not give her a *gentle* glow.

Shulamit opened her thin, hard lips. She told her guests:

"This morning, I did what I should have done before you educators got on a plane to come up here. I Googled more deeply into your school. You propose to house my Benoit's papers? Really? I discovered that for three years, up until his death three years ago, Leopold Hirszfeld often came to your school as a guest lecturer. And you have named a building after him. Hirszfeld Hall. Where kids play foosball."

"Yes," said Sammy, "we are very proud to have had such an eminent Holocaust survivor—not nearly as eminent of course as your late husband—grace our campus."

"Grace?!" snapped Shulamit Klaczko. "Let me tell you about that man. Whenever he and my Benoit crossed paths—at any gathering, any ceremony—he always needled my Benoit. 'Let me see your tattoo—*my* number is lower, *I* was in the camps first. And in your books, you say how long you had to go without food—*I* had to go longer.'"

"Well . . . " said Sammy.

"And then you know what that man, that Leopold Hirszfeld, had the nerve to do? Three years ago, when my Benoit, age ninety-eight, lay dying, that man had his people call here every day. Why? To find out if my Benoit was dead yet. And only *after* my Benoit died did that man, that Leopold Hirszfeld, die. He held out for two more days. Why? So—as he told the media—he could say he was the camp's oldest living survivor. Infuriating! Never again will I have to deal with him."

"Um . . . " said Sammy. "Um, we could certainly take Leopold Hirszfeld's name off that building of ours and—"

"What you can do," snapped Shulamit Klaczko, "is take your *tuchus* off my sofa and take yourself, both of you, out of my and Benoit's home."

Which Sammy and Jeff did.

Okay, Sammy, thought Jeff, any more bright ideas?

You still have every confidence in me? Jeff silently asked Michelle.

Every.

But before that answer, Jeff heard—or imagined—a significant pause.

FIFTY-NINE
CALLING UPON THE KING

When you have to ask people for money, you wear a suit.

Jeff was in New York to ask for money. Earlier this afternoon, on the tenth floor of the handsome pre-war apartment building on Park in the mid-70s, when, Sammy at his side, he asked Shulamit Klaczko for money, he wore a dark-blue suit and repp tie. Now, here, on the sixty-fifth floor of the gleaming, charmless 1990s office building on Park in the mid-50s, to ask Evan Rose for money, he wore the same.

When you're the person who has the money, you wear whatever the f**k you want.

Evan Rose had the money. Evan wore a very expensive black sweater, khakis, handmade shoes and no socks. He also, metaphorically, wore his surroundings. His company. The entire sixty-fifth floor. He sat with Jeff in his, Evan's, conference room, one side all glass overlooking his, Evan's, trading floor. Where money was being made and lost, but mainly made. Millions of dollars, in eyeblinks. Over the course of the year, several billion.

Despite what he had said to Sammy, Jeff felt the true odds of his being able to get any money—three million, to be precise—out of his former boss were about one in ten; maybe, to be honest, one in twenty. Jeff was here because he had sort-of promised Sammy he would try. And besides, since he was already in Manhattan, why the hell not come here and ask? The trick was to ask strongly enough so that afterward, he couldn't say, *Hey, Jeff, you sure did that pretty pro forma*—but not so strongly that afterward, he would say, *Hey, Jeff, you sure made a fool of yourself groveling.*

Ask with dignity. Leave with dignity.

At least Jeff was here alone. No Sammy. Had Sammy known about this meeting, she would have pulled rank and demanded to come. Her presence would have cut the probability of success in half. Evan would have thought, no way am I backing a slick Southern woman who sounds like a good old gal.

And Jeff was here in what had been, up until twenty-two months ago, his own accustomed habitat. Here, number two man in the firm, he had worked the phones, asking prospects for money for the firm to invest. Of course, then, he was backed by the firm's proven success.

Now he was about to ask for money to get a failing school through commencement. Here he was "backed"—if backed was the word—by the school's impending failure.

"I sure hope," said Evan Rose, "that you're here to ask for your old job back. In which case, the answer is of course yes. Because, A, you made this firm a lot of money. Because, B, once you left, the system you had put in place made us—when the black swan hit—a lot more money."

The black swan: the recent flash crash.

"And," said Evan, "Because, C—I told you that school was a losing proposition, told you don't leave here. You being back here would prove me right. And I'm always right."

Evan said *And I'm always right* with a grin that gave Evan an out. It said, *Hey, I'm kidding.* Except anyone who knew Evan knew he wasn't kidding. His grin was like his ready laugh: supposedly gregarious, in truth often cutting.

Evan Rose, age fifty but looking early forties, was tall, lean, and athletic—honed body and honed brain—with a full head of black hair, blue eyes, and unforgivingly white teeth. At Yale, Jeff had come across the work of the Persian poet, Rumi. Rumi said, "The tiger is most handsome when it is after food."

Rumi knew Evan Rose.

On the trading floor, a scrum of Evan-Rose-wannabes—a dozen alpha males and a half-dozen alpha females, from places like Harvard and Yale—worked with cool urgency. Around them were screens with talking heads and flashing numbers. In the middle of the trading floor Evan had placed a yacht's massive bell, the size of a Viking range. When a particularly profitable trade was made, the bell was rung. For quieter times, Evan had also installed, on the trading floor, a putting green. Evan was a scratch golfer. He had told Jeff, "I never get the yips." A golfer's yips are the nerves that causes him to blow shots. Evan was nerveless.

And Evan never doubted his judgment. On the non-glass walls of the conference room, where other wealthy men might have hung Pollocks, Warhols, and Basquiats, Evan had quirky pieces. Weird. Intimidating. Contrarian. Pieces that maybe someday might prove to be worth more than any Pollock, Warhol, or Basquiat. If none ever did, well f**k it, Evan had judged them pleasing.

Now Evan judged Jeff, and judged correctly: Barking a laugh, Evan said, "But I'm guessing you're not here for your old job. So why?"

Jeff told Evan that on July 15, the school would be forced to declare bankruptcy. He said that, to save it, seventy million was needed; he didn't say Sammy hoped to get that from Seymour Gutfreund. He said this in the hopes that, in comparison with what the school needed to get through June 21, him asking Evan for that three million would sound like a *small* ask.

"Three million," said Jeff. "It won't save the school. What it will save, what I feel obligated to try to help save, is the school year for one hundred and forty-five great kids. They've put in so much. If we're forced to close May 9—that's just ten days from now—which, absent the three million, is what will happen—the kids will lose the year. Come September, they'll be forced to start it all over again. That would be so unfair to them."

Evan eyed Jeff.

"A contribution of three million," said Evan. "That's"—he did the math in his head—"slightly less than twenty point seven thousand per kid."

"Yes."

"No. Not going to do it."

Jeff knew he shouldn't ask why not.

Evan told him why not. "Jeff, before you took that job, you did your due diligence, you discovered the school was shaky. But you figured that wasn't any risk to you. And you were right. Okay. But the parents of those one hundred and forty-five kids? They're smart people, they could have—should have—done *their* due diligence. They'd have learned the school was f**ked. Ton of debt, no cash flow, no business model, lousy location. You, Jeff, you're the only plus. The parents risked their money and their kids. I'm not going to bail them out."

"Evan, think of it as a hedge. Mostly, it costs. Like the black swan hedge. But—"

"But what? When does it pay off? And with what?"

"It keeps us going until we get what we need to be stable. So, ten, fifteen years out, you get to say there are five, six hundred kids out in the world, representing your school."

"How is that a hedge?"

"It's a hedge against . . . " Jeff hesitated for a split second. What he was about to say was borderline an insult. He said it anyway. " . . . dying with a pile of money and a thimbleful of impact. Call it the 'I mattered' trade.'"

Evan gave Jeff a look that was half *I'm insulted* and half *I admire your nerve.*

Evan said, "I already matter."

Jeff nodded.

I asked more strongly than pro forma. But I didn't grovel. Leave it at that.

He told Evan he understood, Evan grinned, and they made small talk for fifteen minutes or so.

Then Evan stood and started to show Jeff out. Pausing by one of the paintings on the wall, Evan said, "Another artist driven out of Williamsburg to Hoboken to Jersey City—and now being driven out of Jersey City."

"So where is the next place? Where are you looking next?"

"Not telling," said Evan, with that grin.

As they walked to the elevators, Evan asked, "So how's Jordan?"

Jeff was touched. Evan didn't care about the one hundred and forty-five kids he had never met. But he was mensch enough to care about his former partner's daughter.

SIXTY
WOODSTEIN
STRIKES AGAIN!

Wednesday, nine a.m. Jeff faced a busy day.

With money to raise and kids to help get into better schools, he had a long task list. And since he needed to find a commencement speaker . . .

He did *not* need Ella Bronstein talking her way past Clarice, walking into his office, sitting down across from him, taking out her smartphone, and saying, "Mind if I record this conversation?"

"Whoa," said Jeff. "What are we talking about?"

He feared it was a follow-up to the agreement they'd made weeks ago. Ever since she came in with the air-quality monitor with the pork molecule readings, Ella and he had honored their deal. In return for her sitting on the story—HAMPTON ACRES BREATHING PORK—he had been giving her "exclusive briefings" on the progress being made to reduce those molecules.

Of course those briefings were lies; there was no such progress. His intention was to string Ella along until either there was progress, the school shut down, or, come Memorial Day, she graduated.

Jeff feared, Is that what she's here for? She's learned I've been lying?

"By the way," said Jeff. "Congrats on getting into Brown."

As he said congrats, he realized what she was in here for: to grill the Head about his failure to help many of her fellow seniors get into the colleges *they* had aimed for.

"Thanks, Mr. Taylor," said Ella. "I'm here to talk about a story we're going with this week. The school's finances." She pointed to her phone. "So may I turn this on?"

Jeff's heart sank. He said, "Um . . . what about the school's finances?"

"I've learned the school's bank debt is trading at sixty cents on the dollar. I've asked around. That means the smart people know the debt isn't going to be repaid. Which means the school is in bad shape."

Jeff sincerely wished Ella were here to grill him about his failure to help the Nervous Nine. Instead, she had done what he had feared: followed HAHA's lack of money. He envisaged *The Lamp*'s front-page headline day after tomorrow that would set The Beast off:

HAMPTON ACRES IN ACRES OF DEBT
UNLIKELY EVER TO BE REPAID

"Bad shape," repeated Ella. With a very obvious finger-click, she turned on her phone. "*How* bad, Mr. Taylor?"

"Um . . . Ella, the school is actually in excellent shape."

"So why is the bank debt trading at sixty cents?"

"That reflects what the smart people learned a month and a half ago—we got that bomb threat."

"Really? But three weeks ago, the smart people should have learned that we're safe—we're within the security perimeter for Air Force One."

"Well, they *haven't* learned. Or if they have learned, they're being irrational. Ella, you've heard of 'irrational exuberance'—unfounded market optimism? Well, there is also irrational depression—unfounded market pessimism. That's what's going on here."

"Really, Mr. Taylor?"

"Really. And here"—Jeff opened a desk drawer, pulled out a document—"here is *well*-founded *realism*."

With that, Jeff handed Ella Bronstein the document, the clean opinion from Ritchie & Ravenel, the CPAs' findings that HAHA's financials were in order and its health solid.

As Ella started reading the doc, she said, "Thanks. When *The Lamp* runs the story on the school's bank debt trading at only sixty, we'll run excerpts from this for journalistic balance."

"You do that, Ella. But before you run any such story, if I were you, I'd dig a little more."

"Hmm," said Ella. "Maybe."

"Don't want to have to run a retraction."

"Hmm," said Ella. She held the doc uncertainly.

Jeff pointed to it. "You keep that copy. I've got others."

"Hmm." She stood to leave. "Thanks, Mr. Taylor."

SIXTY-ONE
CLEARING THE AIR

Nine a.m. Monday.

The flatbed truck with a crane pulled up at Leopold Hirszfeld Hall. The truck carried Barbara Travis's twelve rusty bicycle wheels each mounted on a rusty pillar—the components of her sculpture *Strong East Wind,* her sculpture that could function as fans. Taking the day off from the law firm, Barbara arrived right behind it. Jeff joined her. Some HAHA staffers—and some teachers and students (those without a first period class)—gathered to watch. Barbara supervised the truck's crane operator as he lifted the wheels-and-pillars onto Hirszfeld Hall's roof. With an electronic bullhorn, she started supervising the men who were positioning the first wheel-on-pillar to bolt it into place. "A foot to the right. No, too far. No . . . "

She turned to Jeff. "Damn it, it's still off. By at least six inches."

Jeff agreed. "'God is in the details.'"

Barbara knew the quote. She said, "Mies van der Rohe."

Jeff nodded. Mies van der Rohe, a pioneer of modernist architecture, held to the motto, "Less is more." Unfortunately, Barbara believed that more is more.

"I'm going up there," said Barbara. "You want to come?"

Jeff agreed and, once *Strong East Wind* was in place, Barbara showed him how to operate it. "This dial controls all twelve wheels. Set it at four, and watch Preston's pork readings shrink."

"How about five to really clear the air?"

"Anything above four will be way too noisy," she said.

"Got it! Set it and forget it."

Just then his phone rang. It was Clarice. "Jeff, you have a call from the American Jewish Association. National headquarters. A Mr. Irving Knipel. You want me to give him your mobile number?"

Jeff knew the AJA, but hadn't heard of a Mr. Irving Knipel. "No," he told Clarice. "No, I've got stuff at my desk I've got to review with his organization. I'll be right there."

Jeff squeezed Barbara's hand. Telling her, "You're going to be Rabbi Baum's hero for koshering the air," he left.

SIXTY-TWO
THE MAGNIFICENT
MR. KNIPEL

Wondering whether Barbara's *Strong East Wind* really could drive down the pork molecule count, a somewhat distracted Jeff took the call from AJA's national headquarters, from someone he had never heard of.

"Yes, this is Irving Knipel, I'm the Associate Vice President of Development. We were wondering if . . . "

Jeff tuned out the *words* but tuned in to the *tone*. To his ear, it was a perfect example of American TV announcer English, as if Mr. Knipel—although now in New York City—had grown up in, say, Peoria. Confident, low-key, level. And now, as Jeff tuned in to the words, he heard that Mr. Knipel was speaking in complete sentences. Noun, verb. Noun, verb. Here and there, a properly placed adjective. No malaprops. And no uhs, ahs, ums. Remarkable, thought Jeff. The man could be selling me storm windows—or reporting on a nuclear strike on Omaha.

Could Mr. Knipel be that rare individual bland enough that no HAHA constituency would find him objectionable? Years sitting on a trading desk had taught Jeff not to get excited too quickly at a promising idea.

"Excuse me, Mr. Knipel, but could we continue on Zoom?"

They switched to Zoom.

Jeff could see that Mr. Irving Knipel was maybe late-forties, regular and pleasant features, what people might call "Jewish" but maybe Midwestern, intelligent-looking but not nerdy. He wore a white shirt and repp tie under a Navy blazer.

Jeff suspected that Mr. Knipel might be amenable to having some-one write him a short, cliché-free speech. Someone else being Jeffrey Taylor, so Irving Knipel's address would not sound like the pharmacy guy from last year.

"Mr. Knipel," said Jeff, "have you ever been a commencement speaker? And if so or if not, at the end of this month, would you like to be?"

SIXTY-THREE
THE NERVOUS NINE
DROPS TO ONE

Thanks to Sammy's connection, Lena Navuluri was going to Stauffer University, which meant there were still eight HAHA seniors to place *some*where.

By commencement.

Jeff was not optimistic. He thought, even if it's not eight, even if Jose is not my responsibility, even if it's just seven, with so little time it's a reach.

It was ten a.m. Monday, May 2. Jeff had just gotten off the phone with Mr. Irving Knipel, who had promised to think about Jeff's offer and get back quickly.

Suddenly, as Jeff—with scant hope for the seven—resumed, on their behalf, working the phones in a spiritual desert . . .

. . . the heavens opened and manna fell.

Suddenly, ten a.m., five p.m. in Tel Aviv, he was able to park Ari Black for two years in an IDF cyber unit. "A real resume builder," Jeff told Ari's parents.

Then, twelve noon, he got a call from the Duke Admissions Office: "We've heard great things about your two outstanding social activists, Daniel Golub and Beth Katzendorf. Exactly the kind of students we love here. Why haven't they applied to Duke?" Daniel and Beth had become local media celebrities after their food desert petition garnered more than ten thousand signatures. Jeff explained: "They're not seniors, they're juniors." "Ah, well, next year, if you could point them here . . . ?" At which Jeff's deal-making reflex kicked in. He said, "Um, that's possible. But in return, I wonder if *this* year . . . "

He related the qualifications of his remaining six seniors. The Duke Admissions office quickly agreed to a trade: If you *guarantee* us Golub and Katzendorf next year, we'll take Guy Friedman and Lucy Greenberg now.

"Done," said Jeff. Of course, sorry, Duke, but for HAHA, there is no next year. In fact, Jeff had checked the bank account this morning and just four days from now, May 6, the school would be out of cash.

Hanging up, Jeff the flesh peddler congratulated himself on a productive day.

And discovered this productivity wasn't over. Starting early afternoon, he got Terri Fernandez, Drew Lazar, Evgeni Stamgazi, and Fanny Kolton into colleges that were *not* diploma mills. True, you would not frame those diplomas and place them on the wall that served as backdrop to your Zoom meetings . . .

. . . but they were colleges from which, if you did well enough in your freshman year, you might be able to transfer upward. "Every opportunity to do that," Jeff told their parents.

Then the Dean of the University of Oklahoma, Jeff's college roommate, called Jeff about a full scholarship for any Jewish undergraduate who committed to working weekends as a rodeo clown. "You might have a student who fits this, er, unusual profile," his old roommate said. Amazingly, Jeff did: Cooper Pressman let out a rodeo holler when Jeff told him the news.

This left only Ashley Friedlander.

And maybe Jose Rivera?

No, thought Jeff, I'm *not* responsible for Jose. Either Global Strategy's lavish video gets Jose off Harvard's wait list or he goes to Emory, which accepted him last week.

This left only Ashley.

Jeff was making a list of colleges to which, if he wrote a personal check, Ashley might be admitted.

He was at his desk, actually going through *US News & World Report's* annual college issue, looking for any such colleges, when his phone rang.

"No thanks to *you*," snarled Mrs. Friedlander, "but we got Ashley into the University of Texas, Austin. In its honors program."

"That's great," said Jeff.

"Yes," snarled Mrs. Friedlander. "Texas Austin is ranked forty-eighth and Buck-f**king-nell, which rejected Ashley, is thirty-fifth. But Buck-f**king-nell doesn't have an honors program—so *there*."

Whatever gives you inner peace, thought Jeff.

Ending the call and rising from his desk, Jeff thought: Mission Accomplished.

With my help, the Nervous Nine have been reduced to one, Jose— who is not my problem.

Now if only more manna will fall. Say, three million dollars. That will get us through May 6 all the way to June 21.

And now if only the esteemed Irving Knipel will agree to be our commencement speaker . . .

Jeff opened his desk drawer, took out his letter of resignation, and added a phrase—*it has been a truly unforgettable experience which I will cherish . . .*

"Jeff! How was your day?"

He looked up. Barbara was standing in the doorway. She said, "*I've* had a great one. *Strong East Wind* is cranking out a stream of air headed right towards Bailey's pigs."

"A good day here, too," said Jeff. He rose and went to his beloved, squeezed her hand. "Now, can you make *Strong East Wind* blow some money this way?"

SIXTY-FOUR

WHAT HAPPENS IN VEGAS

More manna!

The whale!

Seymour Gutfreund!

For the last twelve days, Clarice had been telling Jeff that the whale—or at least the whale's executive assistant—had been baiting Sammy.

A week ago Thursday Clarice had confided, "Jeff, Miss Kleinman just got a call. They said she should be in Vegas tomorrow morning, Mr. Gutfreund would see her. She had me get tickets for the two of you today—Bradleyville to Atlanta to Vegas. Now, ten minutes ago, they called again. 'Sorry, tomorrow's no good.'"

Four days later, Monday, Clarice had confided, "Jeff, it happened again. They said she should be out there the day after tomorrow. Ten minutes ago, they called again. 'Sorry, Wednesday's no good.'"

Jeff had not been surprised.

Soon after he had arrived at HAHA, Madison Angel had told him: "I've been here twelve years. For twelve years Sammy has been saying 'Next month, next week, I'm going to see Gutfreund.' It's like 'next year in Jerusalem.' The truth is, the Messiah is going to come sooner."

But eleven a.m. today, Tuesday, May 3, the call came again.

Poking her head into Jeff's office, Clarice said, "They're saying tomorrow ten a.m., in his office, Mr. Gutfreund will see Miss

Kleinman. This time, I believe it's for real."

By one p.m., the meeting hadn't been canceled.

Sammy—chanting "I've done it, I've done it!"—corralled Jeff. "Pack light, Jeffrey—just your silver tongue!" And Sammy hustled Jeff into an Uber to Bradleyville Airport where they flew to Atlanta, changed to a flight to Las Vegas, had a window and an aisle seat, no one in between. Mid-flight, Jeff typed arewebrokeyet615 onto his laptop. He showed the screen to Sammy.

"Don't be dreary, honey."

Jeff lowered his voice. "We're down to a hundred and eighty thousand dollars, three days' worth of cash. Come this Friday, HAHA's broke. We need a backup plan in case Gutfreund doesn't come across."

Sammy looked offended.

"Jeff, I've been on this for years, been rebuffed a hundred times. Finally break through, and what's top of mind for you? Failure." She tapped one of her diamond stud earrings. "Don't talk failure."

"Even if he says yes, it could take time to fund us. We are going to need—"

"Besides which," Sammy said, turning on her purr-growl, "we're not going to Vegas to fill the bank account for a month or two. We're going to Vegas for seventy-five million."

"That's great, but we need to be ready—"

"Be ready for the biggest meeting of your life," Sammy said. "That's all we both need to do."

Jeff closed his laptop and put it away. Okay, he thought. We can talk about it on the flight home.

They took rooms on The Strip in one of Gutfreund's three humongous casino hotels, the one in which the penthouse was Gutfreund's main office.

At nine a.m. Wednesday, May 4, when Jeff and Sammy were both in their business suits, another call came from Gutfreund's office: Mr. Gutfreund *will* see you today but *not* at ten. Please stay available.

Sammy told Jeff, "We'll stay available by staying here. An elevator ride away."

Jeff said, "If and when they call, call me. I can be back here in twenty minutes."

"*Stay* here." Sammy tapped her gold Cartier tank watch. "*Now.*"

Silently, Jeff congratulated Sammy for getting this close to the whale. But the mixture of self-congratulatory talk *and* self-doubt *and* rank fear pouring out of the usually brassy woman was too much. Twelve years of perseverance and scheming was either going to pay off . . . or not. Too Much Emotion. Jeff had to get away. He said, "No, I can't. But I'll have my harpoon ready."

Sammy said, "What?"

Jeff spent the afternoon walking around and watching the crowds. Observing the gamblers bet and lose, bet and lose, Jeff thought, And Sammy and I are here to try to get money out of the whale, the slyest fox of all? Ha! Seymour Gutfreund always wins. The house always wins. Sammy, watch out.

At 5:13 p.m., Jeff got a call from Sammy: "Seven o'clock. Harry Reid International."

Jeff took a cab to the airport, met Sammy on the tarmac at Gutfreund's Bombardier Global 8000—which, Sammy told him as they were ushered onboard, was the world's longest-range private jet. Sammy tried to act as if being here was better than being in Gutfreund's penthouse office. Jeff knew it wasn't. This was Gutfreund telling them, *I'm about to take off, state your case fast and get off.*

Seymour Gutfreund, age eighty-two, obese, thinning white hair, was sunk into one of the four even fatter armchairs in the plane's "club suite." He half-rose to meet Sammy, then collapsed and waved—with a small, pudgy hand—for them to sit across from him. He was swaddled in pajamas with the GG (Gutfreund Group) logo over his heart. If he has a heart, thought Jeff.

A brain, yes. Sharp baby-blue eyes connected to it. And within his jowls drooping like a bulldog's, a mobile mouth.

"Sit, sit. Thirteen hours here to Macau. You know the Giant Panda Pavilion, near my casino? Mei Shi and Zhu may be mating. My sports desk is offering odds. You're here because you want me to place a bet for you? No? Ha, my little joke. So, you're here to talk about your school. Excellent. Talk. But don't make it too exciting." He pointed to his pajamas. "I need to go to sleep. My beauty sleep, needed to deal with the Chinese. And people say *we* are cunning."

Jeff thought, No matter how cunning they are, the Chinese are no match for this Buddha-shaped Jew.

"So, talk," said Gutfreund. He turned to Sammy. "I knew your father. A great man. I had much respect for him. Talk."

"Thank you," said Sammy. "You know my father had a vision. A vision that has come true. We are a school that welcomes Jewish boys and girls from around the world. A school that trains Jewish leaders of tomorrow. A school that—"

"Won't make it until tomorrow," said Gutfreund.

"True," said Sammy.

Jeff was impressed with how swiftly Sammy changed gears.

Sammy said, "Yes, we need seventy-five million dollars to pay off the debt, get on sound footing. If you could help us there, we could do a lot. Here's my vision. You know I played hoops, right? Well, I have court vision and educational vision. So picture this. We become the Jewish Exeter. We name the school after you. You know the Duke of Wellington said, 'The battle of Waterloo was won on the playing fields of Eton'? In years to come, people will say the battle for the US Presidency was won on the playing fields of Gutfr—"

"Not interested."

"We could have you on the board."

"I don't go on boards."

"You could have us run the school as you want."

"I don't want. Casinos are more interesting. And a safer bet."

"Well," said Sammy, "You are also, here and in Israel, famed as a generous philanthropist. You could give out of—"

Sammy stopped. Jeff wondered if Sammy had been about to say "out of the goodness of your heart." Perhaps Sammy had realized how ridiculous that would have sounded.

"I give," said Gutfreund, "only to causes that are solid. I am not going to be your savior."

For the first time since Jeff had known her, Sammy looked flummoxed.

Gutfreund appeared to warm to his put-down. He told Sammy, "You have a Jewish boarding school in the middle of Georgia. It makes no sense. You are not in the Negev, you cannot make your desert bloom. Now, if you told me your property was a casino, maybe it would make sense."

Sammy looked even more flummoxed.

Having finished with Sammy, Gutfreund turned his cold but merrily-dancing eyes to Jeff. Okay, thought Jeff, Seymour, let me have it.

To Jeff's surprise, Gutfreund said, "Your former boss, Evan Rose. He put me in a one-off private equity deal. I gave him fifteen million, he gave me back a check for sixty-five million."

Encouraged—the man is well-disposed toward me?—Jeff accessed what he hoped was his silver tongue and said, "Yes. A good return on investment. Here's another one. Forget saving the school long-term. Short-term, here to June twenty-first, the last day of school, we need three million. Otherwise, we have to close down. One hundred forty-five hardworking Jewish kids lose their semester, have to start over again somewhere else. Three million. In return, they get their semester."

"Huh," said Gutfreund. He appeared to be considering it. He said, "Rabbi Perl tells me Tzipora is happy at your school. She likes feeding your one hundred and forty-five."

Further encouraged, Jeff said, "Yes, and—"

"But, no," said Gutfreund. "I'm not going to do it."

Jeff sat flummoxed.

In the sudden silence, an aide came in from upfront, leaned

deferentially to the magnate. "Mr. Gutfreund, you have two calls. The Korean prime minister is on line one, the Israeli defense minister on line two."

Jeff didn't know if this was true, or if Gutfreund had pre-arranged it to get rid of his petitioners.

Gutfreund said, "Well, Miss Kleinman, Mr. Taylor, I'm afraid—"

Jeff said, "Yes, we do have to leave. I have a special lady waiting for me back in Bradleyville." He rose. "I appreciate the time you've given us and—"

"Sit," said Gutfreund.

Jeff sat.

"Special lady, eh?" said Gutfreund.

Oh my God, thought Jeff. Gutfreund thinks I mean Tzipora Perl? Tzipora told her father about the dinner at the Baums? She and I sitting next to each other? She told her father this, and her father told Gutfreund?

"Yes," said Jeff.

"Three million, eh?" said Gutfreund.

Which is how, five minutes later, Jeff and Sammy walked out of the Bombardier Global 8000 with a pledge for that amount. Sammy told Jeff, "I am going to buy you a drink!" and Jeff thought, No, what I really need is a shower: I gotta get *clean*.

Jeff thought Sammy's joy might be premature. Even with a twenty-billion-dollar net worth, was a Gutfreund IOU any more bankable than one from HAHA?

Well, it should be and therefore, he reminded himself, I am one step closer to my goal.

SIXTY-FIVE
ON THE VERY VERGE . . .

Irving Knipel told Jeff, "I've been thinking about your kind offer. And, yes, I would be flattered to be your commencement speaker."

"Great!" said Jeff.

Exhausted from the redeye from Vegas to Atlanta, and then to Bradleyville, but exhilarated by Vegas, Jeff was back in his office, on his phone. And with this "Yes" from Irving Knipel, Jeff felt, Hey, maybe my luck is holding. I wonder if it's the same for Sammy. She told me she was going to spend another day in Vegas and see how big she could grow a grand playing blackjack.

"Great," Jeff repeated to Irving Knipel. "I'll get right back to you. Run this past some people."

Which, all afternoon, walking the campus and working the phones, Jeff did.

And got just about what he expected.

From faculty, staff, students, and parents Jeff got, "Meh." Either the word itself or the equivalent. Either way, a perfect response to a Jewish Mr. Bland as commencement speaker.

At five o'clock, ecstatic, back in his office, Jeff emailed, texted, and phoned Irving Knipel: *You're it.*

Ecstatic, Jeff pulled his letter of resignation out of his desk drawer.

He re-read it for the umpteenth time, added the words "and enlightening" between "educational" and "experience." Taking out a fresh sheet of his personal stationery, he rewrote the letter. He was rising from his desk, about to go down the hall and leave it on Sammy's desk . . . when Clarice poked her head in.

"Mr. Taylor, it's happened again."

"What has?"

"Just now. Another bomb threat. Rapping again. This time it was like he—I think it was a man—was talking at me from underwater. He said, 'Hey, understand / Get off that land / Hey, Jews, make room / Or things go boom! / Ah got a bomb.'"

"Those words?"

"Oh, yeah. And I hit the button and recorded him. We *got* him."

"Did he sound . . . serious?" Stupid question, Jeff told himself. The man could have been speaking basso profundo or giggling. Same result.

Here we go again.

The letter went back into the desk drawer.

PART THREE

"All of HAHA's problems stem from the fact that we are not a true Torah school. Having a pig farm for a neighbor doesn't help."

—Rabbi Benjamin Baum
Dean of Jewish Life, Hampton Acres Hebrew Academy

"What's happening?! What?! What are we going to do?! Somebody do something! Do anything!! Just do it now!"

—The Beast
(Jeff Taylor's metaphor for the HAHA community)

SIXTY-SIX

KA-BOOM!

"**A**lmost certainly a hoax," said Jerome, trying to assure his fellow deans. "We can sleep easy tonight." He moved his wooden match from one corner of his mouth to the other.

It was eight Thursday evening. Three hours ago, when Clarice took the bomb-threat call, recorded it, and played it back for Jeff, he knew that somehow The Beast would immediately find out. Which The Beast did. Jeff's phone had again been swamped. As he had right after the March seventh bomb threat, Jeff did a walking tour of campus, projecting Calm and Confidence.

He again texted Jordan: *Another hoax. Don't worry.*

And as he had right after the March seventh bomb threat, Jeff had called a meeting of the executive committee. Back in the early afternoon, when he was busy getting approval of Irving Knipel as commencement speaker, he had canceled the regular Thursday afternoon meeting. But with this new threat, he needed a meeting right away. Needed to stop the deans from adding to The Beast's craziness. Needed to reassure the deans.

There was a screaming text from Sammy: *Another bomb threat?! And you didn't tell me! Call me now!* Which Jeff did, and absorbed Sammy's self-important posturing.

This time Jeff got to the conference room before any of the deans. He didn't want them feeding each other's anxiety while waiting for him.

So now, facing the deans plus Noga, Jeff echoed Jerome. He said, "Almost certainly a hoax. As was the phone call on March seven. And I have a plan to make them stop."

Make them stop by finding the culprit, thought Jeff. Find the culprit so I can submit my letter of resignation.

"And your plan is . . . ?" asked Rabbi Baum. "Jeff, as I have said, the only workable plan is to make this a real Torah School."

Except for Jerome, all the deans—Benjamin Baum, Rachel Fish, Stevie Blau, Bill Davidoff, Clara Glatt, and Madison Angel—looked grumpy. On the one hand, they wanted to be consulted, *because we are important.* On the other hand, it's night, we're exhausted, *let us go home.* Except Rachel—she was grumpy and energized.

"My plan," said Jeff, "is based on the assumption that, like the March seventh threat, we will soon learn that only we have been threatened." He smiled. "Beyond that, I'd rather not say. In case it fails."

"A plan devised by the Head could *fail?*" demanded kibitzer Noga Weinstein.

"I am merely mortal," said Jeff.

Noga was not a member of the executive committee. But she, the head of Cherev, was pissed at how (Cherev felt) HAHA was failing to protect itself. So Jeff figured—in the immortal words of non-rabbinic wisdom—it was better to have her inside the tent pissing out than outside pissing in.

Before Noga could press for "a real security plan," Jeff said, "So unless there are any questions about this bomb threat, I thank you for coming here at this time and—"

"Not so fast," said Rachel Fish. "Not the bomb, Jeff. Something else."

Jeff braced himself. "Yes, Rachel . . . ?"

"As Dean of Academics, I speak on behalf of the faculty. As you know, we have not had a raise in six years. So we are united on this. Unless we get a *significant* raise *now* we will boycott commencement."

Jeff sighed. "I agree you deserve a raise. The school doesn't have an extra nickel."

Glaring at Coach Bill Davidoff, Rachel spat, "The school somehow has millions for a gilded lacrosse palace."

"Not gilded," snapped Coach Bill. "Aluminum."

Rachel amped up her glare. Glaring back, Bill stiffened his spine like a drill sergeant.

Jeff sighed. Yes, the faculty deserves a raise. And yes, it will look terrible if the faculty boycotts the ceremony.

Jeff said, "Rachel, we will form a committee. You will chair it. The committee—"

"Will recommend a significant raise," snapped Rachel. "And *then?*"

Standoff. Silence.

During which Jeff realized he had a solution to this problem. He said, "Then, to fund the raises, we will take money out of professional development. Strip *it* to zero."

"You wouldn't!" said Rachel.

"Yes, I would."

Ah, "professional development." This was money for courses and presentations to help the faculty burnish their academic credentials, so they might have some chance—some!—of ever getting hired at a better private school.

Faced with losing this . . . ?

Rachel Fish's face fell. Jeff saw that Rachel et al would cave.

"Anything else?" asked Jeff, cheerily.

"Sorry, Jeff," said Madison, "but I have, unfortunately, a message from the parents."

Jeff was surprised. Madison was the sanest dean. Madison did not like bringing up problems. But as Dean of Student Life, Madison was a conduit for complaints from parents.

"Yes?" said Jeff.

"Actually," said Madison, "two messages. Two different groups of parents. One group is concerned that handing out awards at commencement is damaging to the self-esteem of students who do *not* receive awards. Having heard of the efforts of this group, other parents have formed *their* group, to insist that we indeed hand out awards."

Jeff was surprised, and thankful, that these parents hadn't been deluging him with this. Before Jeff could say anything, Coach Bill did. "Excellence must be recognized." No surprise here—Bill's goal was to fill the athletic center's trophy case.

Rachel—no surprise—countered, "Awards are hierarchical and divisive."

Jeff sighed. Someone threatening a bomb, teachers threatening a boycott, parents divided among themselves . . . another day at HAHA.

God gives burdens, he heard Michelle say. *Also shoulders.*

Thanks, he said. Thanks for the Hallmark card.

He told Madison, "We'll expand the number of awards"—and Madison nodded her thanks.

He thought, I'll make sure all forty-one seniors get at least one. When I have a full list of awards, email it to all parents. The "awards are damaging" crowd will be placated.

Jeff caught sight, at the other end of the room, of the bronze bust of Manny Kleinman, Manny's fierce eyes on him. How'm I doin', Manny?

Jeff figured Manny would be awarding him *no* awards.

"Well," said Jeff, cheerily, "the end of the year is drawing near, which means so is summer break. Let's finish strong."

His eyes fell on the only member of the executive committee who hadn't participated. Stevie Blau. Stevie, I need something from you.

SIXTY-SEVEN
AN INSIDE JOB?

As everyone walked out of the Admin building, Jeff fell in step with Stevie. "We've got to find out who's calling in the threats."

"You bet."

"I've told no one this, and I'm telling you in strictest confidence." They were now alone just outside Admin. Jeff put an arm around Stevie's broad shoulders. "Because I have confidence in you. You as Dean of Information Technology."

"Uh . . . thank you."

"You heading home now?"

"Yeah."

Releasing Stevie's broad shoulders, Jeff nodded toward Beit Rashi. "Mind if I walk with you?"

"Uh, fine."

They walked that way, and Jeff said, "Today, thinking about the three bomb threats—January, March, and now—all three delivered as raps, they've rung a bell. They echo something somewhere in the emails that students have sent me since January first. On Parochet. Something in an email or two. The same . . . rhythm. Not some student *rapping* to me, and not writing anything about a bomb, but some student writing in the same *rhythm* as the bomb threat. Understand?"

"Uh . . . I think so."

"The problem is, which email is ringing this bell? Which email or two? Every day our students send me, anonymously, forty-five to fifty emails. Say fourteen hundred a month. Since January first, six thousand emails. The email that's rung a bell is in those six thousand somewhere. Tonight I will start going through all of them. As Head, I assume that responsibility. To find that one or two. You agree"—Jeff fixed Stevie with a firm gaze—"that it's *vital* we find it?"

"Uh . . . sure." The Dean of Information Technology was uncertain, nervous.

"But, Stevie, when I do find it—and no matter how long it takes, fifty hours, a hundred hours, I will find it—there is a problem, right? And you know what that problem is."

Jeff waited to make Stevie say what the problem was.

"You still won't know who sent it."

"No. *We* won't know who sent it. And because we won't know, that student— who, for his or her *own* sake, and for *our* sake, needs to be found—that student will be able to keep threatening us. Right?"

"Uh . . . right."

"We need to know who that student is."

"But . . . Parochet. It's the curtain that covers the Torah Ark. The whole purpose of our Parochet is to allow students . . . " Stevie trailed off.

"To continue to hurt themselves?" said Jeff. "To continue to hurt HAHA?"

"Uh . . . "

"Stevie, you and I—I as Head, you as Dean of IT—have the responsibility to save that student and save this school. It is our solemn duty. It's a commandment."

"It is?"

Now the two of them stood at the front door of Beit Rashi.

"Leviticus 19:16," said Jeff. "'Do not stand by as your neighbor bleeds.'" Jeff knew he had distorted the passage. It actually said, "Neither shall you stand against the blood of your neighbor." But

Jeff doubted Stevie would check. Jeff added, "That's God speaking. To you and me. I'm asking you to give me access to the names of the Parochet emailers."

Stevie gulped hard. He stood silent and sweaty. He turned, went inside. He returned with a thumb drive for Jeff to insert in a USB port of his computer.

SIXTY-EIGHT
READING, LISTENING, AND WORRYING

I n the Kingdom of Israel, in the house of the Head of School, at his kitchen table, with the thumb drive in a USB port on his laptop, Jeff was re-reading Parochet emails from early January. As he read, he played, on his smartphone, today's bomb threat—he had recorded it off the device at Clarice's desk.

"Hey, understand / Get off that land / Hey, Jews, make room / Or things go boom! / I got a bomb."

In the rhythm of words on his screen, Jeff tried to find any match to the rhythm of the threat. So far none. He didn't think he was going to be so lucky to find a match right away. And the prospect of maybe having to re-read all six thousand Parochet emails he'd received since January 2nd? Read all of them by commencement, May 30—assuming the school made it to commencement . . . What would that take? Twenty seconds to read each one? He did the math. About an hour and a half a night.

Not impossible. But not fun.

Playing the bomb threat over and over, Jeff kept reading. Missives of legitimate concern mixed with victimization and score-settling: *My roommate doesn't shower . . . my roommates make noise . . . my roommates leave stuff all over the place . . . there's a skunk who lives under the boathouse . . . I know a teacher and a student who are having sex . . . I know a kid who's selling drugs . . . I know a kid who's stealing from kids' backpacks.*

Most of these, when Jeff read them in early January, he had ignored. A few of these—accusations of teacher-student sex, cheating, drug-dealing or theft—he had tried to learn more about and sometimes had learned enough to take action.

And a few, when he first read them and now as he re-read them, just made him shake his head: *Rabbi Baum is sending coded messages in his sermons, every fifth word, I can prove it.*

Fueled by coffee, Jeff kept reading, looking for a rapper's rhythm, finding instead boarding school life and teenage craziness.

Jeff wondered: Would the complainers and conspiracy theorists be holding it together without Parochet? Perhaps he should ask Baum to lead the executive committee in a prayer of gratitude for their steady, silent partner, Parochet, who siphoned off just enough insanity to keep HAHA going?

SIXTY-NINE
THE WHALE DELIVERS

At ten a.m. Friday, Jeff was behind the wheel.

He was driving down Button Gwinnett Avenue with Madison Angel, fifteen miles to the very Jewish but WASP-sounding Partridge Ridge Country Club. He and Madison—she in her capacity as Dean of Student Life—were to meet with Ms. Brandy Blum, the club's Vice President of Event Planning. The event, fifteen days from now, Saturday, May 21, was the HAHA prom.

That is, it was scheduled for then.

But today, Friday, May 6, could be HAHA's last day. At sunset, the start of Shabbat, the sun could set on HAHA forever. Unless . . . Gutfreund came through. Unless, by end of day, the whale's three million dollars hit HAHA's bank account.

Jeff felt horrible.

Back when he was at the hedge fund negotiating a trade, he always assumed he knew something that the guy on the other side didn't. And he always assumed the other guy knew something that he didn't. A rough equality.

But to be driving to the country club with Madison, who was blithely unaware of what might be about to happen . . .

Madison, to whom this was just another ordinary day.

Plus all the other HAHA teachers, and staff, and students, and their parents . . . who also didn't know. All the people who, come sundown, Jeff might have to tell, "Uh, I'm afraid I've got some bad news . . . "

All the innocents.

No equality here.

Jeff told himself, Gotta believe the three million *will* hit today. Gotta deal with what may actually happen: in fifteen days, the prom.

Gotta reduce the number of things that could go wrong at the prom.

Last year's prom, at the same club, nothing had gone wrong. As far as he knew. But then, he reminded himself, he was often the last to know. So, heading to Partridge Ridge Country Club, Madison filled Jeff in on what he didn't know. Mainly, she told him what he had missed in the ten years preceding Jeff, years that she had been at HAHA.

"Drunken prom-goers: too many to count. Drugged-up prom-goers: fewer, but also plentiful. Cars smashed by drunken prom-goers: eleven, more than two dozen if we include fender-benders. Hospitalizations from drink, drug use, and car crashes: three. Injuries requiring only a Doc-in-the-Box: eight. Permanent injuries: one smashed pinkie finger. Fatalities: thank God, none. Pregnancies: one confirmed, two rumored."

Then he asked, "Any . . . ah . . . emotional damage?"

Madison gave Jeff a look that said *Now there's a dumb question.*

He pulled up to the very chic Partridge Ridge Country Club. Ms. Brandy Blum met them and showed them the ballroom. Jeff, Madison, and Ms. Blum discussed lighting (*no* dark corners), decorations, food (kosher), and drink (*non*-alcoholic). As scheduled, they were joined by the hippest Black DJ in all of Georgia. "Jamal," said Ms. Blum. "As of this year, Jamal is available." Jeff and Madison reviewed Jamal's suggested playlist. As far as Jeff could tell (and he couldn't tell much because he had stopped understanding song lyrics in the 1990s), there were no songs that urged listeners to have sex *right here and now, on the ballroom floor.* "Very cool," Jeff told Jamal. "The kids'll have a good time," said Jamal.

At noon, Jeff was back at HAHA.

He had intended to have lunch in the dining hall, but he was waylaid by Sammy.

"Jeff, lunch in my office."

Over smoked salmon sandwiches, Sammy said, "The Board is getting antsy. I told them we got the cash from Gutfreund to finish the year, but they're nervous about July 15. You talk Wall Street. You talk to Denenberg."

And say what? thought Jeff. That Gutfreund's cash hasn't shown up yet, and there's no way we are going to pay off the mortgage? Eric Denenberg—late fifties, tough, dignified, hedge fund honcho, very rich mainly through many well-timed shorts—was Chairman of the Board. A very hands-off Chairman of a very passive Board, a Board that had apparently bought Sammy's act all these years. Jeff thought, But I doubt Denenberg has bought it, he's too smart. And I'm supposed to pull the wool over his sharp eyes?

"Sure," said Jeff, "I'll call him."

Meaning, I'll call him, I'll get a reading on where he and the rest of the Board *are*, but I ain't gonna perform your smoke-and-mirrors act on him.

"And," said Sammy, leaning back in her chair, arms wide, expansive, "I've got some prospects beyond Gutfreund. Thread in more passes, rack up more points. Ten million here, ten million there, we can get to the fifty. Maybe even get the fifty in one fell swoop. There's a great prospect on Martha's Vineyard. Be prepared to fly there with me on a moment's notice, okay?"

"Sure," said Jeff, "I'm prepared."

Meaning: I'm prepared to come back from the Vineyard with zero millions, but maybe a Vineyard Vines fisherman's sweater for Barbara—that New England look, in case I can persuade her to come with me when, this summer, as HAHA implodes, I return to Connecticut.

And Jeff finished his sandwich and left.

At his desktop, he typed in the password, arewebrokeyet615, and got access to the school's bank balance.

There! Right there! Jeff stared, gaped. Yes—three million in cash!

Gutfreund had promised, and Gutfreund had delivered in the nick of time. The prom is on! Graduation is on! The school makes it to year end!

And you did it, said Michelle in his head. *Not Sammy. You.*

Yes! So now maybe anything is possible? Now that we've got the three million, could we somehow, somewhere, get the fifty million? More?

Yes!—and Jeff did a few dance steps.

Um . . . well . . .

Jeff stopped, came down to earth.

Um . . . well . . . no, the three million was a miracle. But another fifty? No, there would be no happy ending here. Yes, we're okay through June 21. After that, chaos.

Okay, no one can save the school. But what more can I fix? Jeff asked himself. How about the pork molecules?

Jeff went to his window, checked the gauge. Still a high level. He left his office and went to Leopold Hirszfeld Hall. Climbing up to the roof, he used his key to open the control panel to his beloved's *Strong East Wind.* Barbara had warned him to keep the fan speed at four, but he was running out of time. Ella might break the story if she realized he was stringing her along. Okay. He turned the twelve dials to five. The bicycle wheels rotated faster, and turned from quiet to obnoxious. The fast-moving air lifted his hair up. What a sight he was, standing on the roof with his fright wig, praying this contraption would kosher the school's air.

Strong East Wind. Jeff hadn't the heart to tell Barbara that the east wind comes up several times in the Bible, mostly to bring famine or plague.

SEVENTY

AT THE REAR END
OF AN EIGHTY-PERCENT-RED
HEIFER

A fter a week of inquiries throughout Georgia, Emmitt Bailey had found and, with Reverend Travis's funds, purchased the reddest heifer available. About eighty percent red. He had the heifer delivered to his CAFO, where he set her apart from his pigs.

Emmitt Bailey had also purchased a pedometer, Kamar patches, tail paint, a chin-ball marker, and a radio-telemetric system. Emmitt had applied these to his heifer. At 10:15 this Saturday morning, these told him that his heifer was in heat! Emmitt had an expert standing by: Sam the Inseminator.

Now, 5:30 Saturday afternoon, Sam arrived at the CAFO. He brought with him an AI (artificial insemination) gun and a flask containing a 0.5 milliliter straw full of frozen semen from the reddest bull available.

Reverend Travis arrived with a Bible.

Emmitt Bailey secured the heifer's head in a stanchion. To relax the heifer, Emmitt talked to her and petted her. To warm the AI gun, Sam rubbed it between his hands. With forceps, he removed the straw from the flask and, to thaw it out, submerged it in water. He wiped the straw dry and placed it in the AI gun. Holding the gun vertically, he gently pressed the plunger upward until the semen rose to the top. The gun was now primed.

Sam nodded to Reverend Travis. Okay, go ahead.

With his Bible open, Travis recited Deuteronomy 7:14: "You shall be blessed above all people. There shall not be a male or female barren among you or among your livestock."

With the AI gun in his right hand, Sam inserted the gun several inches into the vagina at a 30-degree upward angle.

"Ready," Sam said.

Reverend Travis recited Isaiah 66:9: "Shall I bring to the birth, and not cause to bring forth? Saith the Lord: shall I cause to bring forth, and shut the womb? Saith thy God."

Counting, "Five, four, three, two, one . . . " Sam slowly pushed the plunger.

Reverend Travis recited Job 5:25: "You shall know also that your offspring shall be many, and your descendants as the grass of the earth."

Emmitt said, "But Reverend, you'll settle for one offspring—'long as it's one hundred percent red."

Patting the heifer's head, Reverend Travis said, "I christen thee Mama Korban."

"Korban?" asked Emmitt.

"Korban means sacrifice," said Reverend Travis. "This heifer will be the mother of the great sacrifice unto the Lord."

Removing the AI gun, Sam the Inseminator said, "I wish you guys luck."

Hopefully impregnated, the eighty-percent-red heifer mooed.

SEVENTY-ONE
STRENGTHENING THE SOUL

Sunday morning. At his kitchen table, at breakfast, Jeff read the *New York Times Book Review*. A Yale professor of the humanities had an essay appraising—and mostly praising—Isak Dinesen's *Out of Africa*.

Skimming it, Jeff felt a pang.

Out of Africa had been one of Michelle's favorite movies. She told Jeff she saw it when it came out, when she was just starting puberty, just noticing boys. Then and there she fell in love with, up on the big screen, the blond and beautiful Robert Redford. "So romantic," she told Jeff. "I always wanted Robert Redford."

"The uber-WASP," said Jeff. "Instead, you got me."

"You'll do," Michelle always said, ruffling his very un-blond hair.

Jeff set the *Book Review* down. Today was May eight. Four days from now, May 12, was the day Michelle had been killed. It would be three years.

Each anniversary a tough day for me. And for Jordan.

A tough day for you guys, said Michelle in his head. *True enough. But how about for me?*

Got me there, agreed Jeff.

Look, big guy, don't sit there. Get together with Barbara. Get out of the house, get out of yourself.

So Jeff phoned his beloved. He told her, "You must know at least a

236

dozen dumps that are open today. Want to go scout them? I bet there's tons of rusted metal just crying to become a Barbara Travis sculpture."

"You're on."

Jeff jumped to the end of the essay, to a sketch of the professor's career. Her scholarship made the case that reading literature and philosophy was more than an intellectual exercise: it was good for the soul.

In his head, Michelle told him, *And today will be good for your soul.*

Four days from now, this anniversary.

Yes, my soul needs some reinforcing.

SEVENTY-TWO

FOR BREAKFAST, SWALLOW A LIVE FROG

Long ago, Jeff had been told, "You should always swallow a live frog for breakfast because that's the worst thing that can happen to you all day."

Acting on this advice, at nine a.m., the start of the business day—and this being Monday, the start of the business week—Jeff called Eric Denenberg. As Denenberg's assistant put Jeff on hold, Jeff reflected that this was indeed going to be by far the worst thing. I am calling a Wall Street titan, a man who has some respect for me, a man whose respect I want to keep. And while I am not about to lie to him, I *am* going to sugar-coat the truth. And Denenberg is going to tell me, "Don't waste my time."

Denenberg came on the line and skipped the small talk.

"Are you calling to tell me the school is going to avoid bankruptcy?"

Jeff said, "Look, you and I have been around. Optionality. It's always smart to own a few call options. There's always the chance of a big turnaround. I wouldn't give up hope."

"Do you have any new facts for me?"

"No."

"Then I know this better than you. This thing is going down. Don't waste my time."

Denenberg hung up.

Clarice poked her head in and announced, "Mr. Pettiver on the line."

Jeff nodded. He sympathized with Hugh. Now it was Hugh's turn to swallow the live frog.

While Jeff would not give false assurances to Eric Denenberg, Jeff—as usual—was ready to give them to Hugh Pettiver.

"Jeff . . . " said the loan officer at Bradleyville's M&F National Bank, his voice dripping worry. "Jeff, can you tell me what the June first numbers are going to be?"

Meaning, HAHA's financial statement for the preceding three months.

"They're going to be excellent," said Jeff. "We just got another three million."

"Well, that's fine, Jeff. But you need far more than that. Fifty million on July fifteen."

"Did you see the opinion from our accountants? Our financials are in order and our health is solid."

"Yes. Sammy sent it to me. From your accountants, Ritchie & Ravenel. But it's got all these . . . caveats. And on every page, it's stamped DRAFT. You could drive a Mack truck through it. Jeff, it's . . . flimsy."

"Hugh, you're a smart guy, you know how these things work. An educational institution isn't a factory. We're not turning out widgets here, our bottom line isn't profit, it's young people enriched with knowledge and confidence to go out into the world, to make something of themselves. So we depend on contributions from people who see the value in that. Getting those contributions is an art, not a science. And believe me, we're working our artistry here."

"I'd like to believe you, Jeff." A nervous laugh. "I *need* to believe you."

Meaning, Hugh Pettiver needed to believe he would not be fired. Because if—no, not if, *when*—HAHA declared bankruptcy on July 15, he probably would be. While Hugh hadn't made the fifty-million-dollar loan, he had inherited it. And M&F management would need a fall guy. The last four phases of any corporate debacle: 1. Panic. 2. Hunt for the guilty. 3. Punishment of the innocent. 4. Praise and honors for the uninvolved.

Knowing that the innocent Hugh Pettiver needed false assurances made it easier for Jeff to continue giving Hugh false assurances.

Jeff thought, Hugh, I lied to you. We *are* a factory and our assembly line is powered by smoke and mirrors.

SEVENTY-THREE
BLACK SWAN EVENT

Heat lightning. Like the skin of a kettledrum under impact, his kitchen windows shivered white, the sky shivered white. Whenever he saw lightning, Jeff thought of three words.

Black swan event.

A black swan event can destroy a hedge fund. When Jeff was number two to Evan Rose, this always nagged at him.

By definition, a black swan event is a highly improbable and impossible-to-predict event—in fact, it lies beyond computation by any scientific method—with severe consequences. Even worse, because forecasting tools offer false security against it, they increase vulnerability to it. Like black swans were, in ancient times, thought not to exist, a black swan event supposedly can't come into existence today. Until it does. Then, with the benefit of hindsight, people say, *Well, of course.* Financial people say this after hundreds of billions of dollars are, virtually overnight, wiped out.

The Russian government debt default of 1998, which destroyed the famed hedge fund Long-Term Capital Management, was a black swan event.

So was the dot-com bubble-burst in 2001.

So was the crash of the US housing market in 2008. (That one had taken down Manny's business, leaving HAHA in a precarious state ever since.)

At the hedge fund, Jeff was not happy living in the shadow of a black swan event. So he charged himself with trying to protect against one. Depending on where, at any moment, he thought a black swan might emerge, he bought credit default swaps on corporate debt . . . bought puts on the S&P . . . bought puts on the NASDAQ . . . shorted the Euro . . . shorted European banks . . .

At any moment, out of the ten billion dollars in the fund, Jeff had up to two hundred million dollars in investments like these. If a black swan hit, these investments might suddenly be worth a billion or two. In the meantime, as no black swan had hit, these investments lost value; they cost the fund about a hundred million a year. Jeff felt this was worthwhile insurance.

What did Evan Rose say?

"Jeff, I believe in you. I will never second-guess you."

This meant, "I will second-guess you."

Okay, Evan, thought Jeff. I'm going to do my thing.

Because Jeff had lived through the Russian government default, the dot-com bubble-burst, and the US housing market crash, he expected that eventually another black swan event would hit the financial world.

He never expected one to hit his personal world.

Therefore, he was not prepared for what the two young Greenwich policemen told him on the night of May twelve three years ago when the pair pulled up in their car and rang his bell and quietly asked if they could come in. It was calm out. An hour ago, there had been a swiftly-passing thunderstorm. Jeff had been reading. Michelle was at a PTA meeting at Jordan's school. Expecting the two cops to tell him . . . what? he had no idea what . . . he said, sure, come in, and they did, and sat on a couch in the living room and told Jeff what had just now happened to Michelle.

She had been driving on a nearby backcountry road, past a horse farm. A horse had suddenly plunged through the fence, into the road. Hitting her car, it had been propelled up into the air and through her windshield, into her.

Michelle had been crushed to death by a half-ton horse.

Michelle whom he loved, Michelle who was his wife, his life.

Why had the horse suddenly plunged through the fence?

As the police reconstructed it the next day, lightning had hit the steeple of the Congregational church next to the horse farm. The noise had made the horse bolt.

Jeff thought, My wife was killed by a black swan event.

When he came to HAHA and got to know Rabbi Baum, he knew what Baum thought, what Baum, drunk, might even say: "Jeff, it's because you and your wife were living in WASP-land. Surrounded by churches. A skyline of steeples. If the two of you had been living where you should have been, among your fellow Jews—say, in Brooklyn, surrounded by synagogues—this never would have happened."

Jeff would have replied, "There are more churches per square foot in Brooklyn than in Greenwich. Goddamn it, Brooklyn is called 'The Borough of Churches.'"

"Yes," Baum would have answered, "but it has fewer WASP horse farms per square foot. What were you doing living among WASPs?"

What would Michelle have said?

In the three years since that night of May twelve, as he imagined Michelle talking to him, Jeff heard her say, *A black swan disguised as a black horse. I was killed by what you guys call animal spirits.*

"Animal spirits" was the term coined by the economist John Maynard Keynes to explain what makes people buy and sell securities.

Jeff replied to his dead wife, Damn it, don't joke.

She replied, *Hey, at this point, all we can do—you and I—is joke.*

In the three years since that night of May twelve, Jeff had replayed the event a thousand times. The lightning doesn't hit the steeple. The horse doesn't bolt. Michelle lingers at the PTA meeting. He did this obsessively. He tried to stop. Gradually, as year one turned into year two and then year three, he did this less and less.

But Jeff Taylor remained a firm believer in black swan events.

Certainly *that* one made him leave the fund, leave Greenwich, take this job.

As Jeff was on his way out of the fund, he convinced a reluctant Evan Rose to let a young trader continue Jeff's practice of hedging against a black swan event. When two flash crashes disrupted markets, Evan phoned Jeff and said, "Hey, Mr. Black Swan. You saved us billions. So leave that school. Come on, genius, come back here."

Tonight, in the kitchen of the house that HAHA provided him as Head of School, seeing, through its windows, the sheet lightning continue, Jeff thought about the "black swan" metaphor and about real swans.

Real swans mate for life. He had wanted to stay with Michelle for life.

As the sheet lightning flashed, he heard Michelle say, *Yeah, well, swan, move on. There's Barbara. You two'll be fine. Lightning ain't gonna strike twice.*

SEVENTY-FOUR

NOURISHING THE BODY
AND THE SOUL

As heat lightning flashed around them, Jeff and Jordan lit the Yahrzeit candle and set it on Jeff's kitchen table. Together, they recited: "*Neir Adonai Nishmat Adam. Yehi Ratzon Mifanecha, Adonai Eloheinu Veilohei Avoteinu, Shetehi Nishmat* Michelle *bat Mordechai Tzerurah betzeror hachayim, im nishmot Avvraham Yitzchak ve'Ya'akov, Sarah, Rivkah, Rachel VeLeah, Tehi Menutchatah kavod, Selah.*"

The human soul is a light from God. May it be Your will that the soul of Michelle, daughter of Mordechai (Mitchell), enjoy eternal life, along with the souls of Abraham, Isaac, and Jacob, Sarah, Rebecca, Rachel, and Leah, and the rest of the righteous that are in Gan Eden. Amen.

Jeff hugged Jordan. She hugged him back, then reached into her backpack. "Dad, look what I brought."

She put two bottles of Michelle's favorite iced tea on the table. Honest Iced Tea, honey green.

"Mom always had two bottles waiting when she picked me up from soccer. 'Drink up, star.' That's what she'd say when I'd get in the car. You know, I'd talk the whole way home. About soccer, about school, about my friends . . . "

"That explains why you were too talked-out to say anything to me."

"Dad!"

"Sorry, kiddo."

Jordan said, "Mom was a great listener. I would tell her things and, weeks later, after I'd forgotten what I'd said, she bring them up. She paid attention."

"Yes," said Jeff, "she did."

Jordan sat down at the kitchen table and Jeff joined her. "Let's make our own custom to go along with lighting the candle," she said, nodding to the bottles of tea. "To Mom."

"To Michelle."

They clinked bottles and drank.

"Now drink up, star, and tell me about your day."

But Jordan sprang up from the table, saying, "I gotta go. Love you, Dad."

Jeff checked the sky, which was now clear and quiet. Satisfied, he hugged Jordan, and watched from his front door as she dashed towards her dorm.

Returning to Parochet, Jeff skimmed for an hour or so, saw nothing that sounded like the bomb threat. Having completed his daily quota, two hundred and fifty emails, he went to bed.

At seven a.m., Jeff went to the Beit Am for Shacharit, the morning service. As Jeff, Baum, Coach Bill Davidoff, Stevie Blau, Isaac Greene, Sacha Reznick and four other boys made a minyan, Jeff recited kaddish for Michelle. Starting with *"Yitgadal v'yitkadash sh'mei raba . . . "*

Glorified and sanctified be God's great name . . .

. . . and ending with *"shalom aleinu v'al kol-yisrael, v'imru: amen."*

. . . peace for us and for all Israel and say, Amen.

Then Jeff re-assumed the duties of Head of School.

That night, at his kitchen table, on his laptop, Jeff resumed going through Parochet emails.

Next to him, the Yahrzeit candle was guttering down.

Thank you for remembering me today, said Michelle.

Every day, said Jeff.

SEVENTY-FIVE
(NOT QUITE) BETWEEN
A ROCK AND A HARD PLACE

Whitewater!

At the northern border of Georgia, coming down through the gorgeous Blue Ridge, the Adako River was thirty-nine miles of mostly fast-moving water, including eleven miles with eight serious rapids. Four Class IIIs, three Class IVs, and one Class V. "These eleven miles will get your pulse pounding," Barbara had told Jeff.

Jeff had always wanted to run whitewater; today he was doing it.

This Sunday noontime, Jeff, Barbara, and Jordan were in a paddle boat owned by Adako Expeditions. They shared it with three other paying customers and, in the stern, their guide, Blake. All seven had just paddled hard through the first rapid, Lonnie's Regret, a Class III—which, Jeff had to agree, had set his pulse pounding. One mile ahead, about a half-hour ahead, was the next rapid, Nordhaus Creek, a Class IV. In total, there would be four hours of good, safe fun, maybe four minutes of it pulse-pounding.

Because it was a beautiful day, there were other boats on the river: Kayaks, paddle boats, and rafts. Except for the kayaks, which were mostly in small groups, there were three hundred, four hundred yards between each craft.

Everyone wore life vests and helmets.

As the six paying customers in Blake's boat had put on their life vests and helmets, Blake had said not to worry.

"If you fall out in a rapid, no big deal. Just sit in the river pointing downstream. The river pushes you toward any rocks, use your feet to push off against them. When the rapid ends—and it'll end fast—swim to shore. No big deal."

The woman sitting closest to Blake had asked how many people had ever drowned on this eleven-mile stretch. Blake professed not to know.

When parents of prospective students asked Jeff how many students had ever been kicked out of HAHA for drug or alcohol or disciplinary problems or even crimes, Jeff said, "I don't know."

Which was true. So he could honestly answer "I don't know," Jeff had made a point of not finding out.

And he was pleased that Blake professed not to know. Jeff wanted to, mindlessly, enjoy this afternoon. Sun on his body. Gorgeous land around him. The two people he loved most in the world within arm's reach. This morning, Sammy had phoned, told him that Martha's Vineyard was off and he should stand by instead to fly to Jackson Hole, Wyoming tomorrow morning, to romance another billionaire, but for now HAHA felt as far away as Wyoming. There was only the river. Let it go on and on . . .

Then, halfway between Lonnie's Regret and Nordhaus Creek, in water with riffles, small waves, which required hardly any paddling and no attention, Barbara fell out.

Jeff didn't see it happen. He was sitting in the front of the boat, starboard side. Barbara had been right behind him. He just heard her blurt "Hey!"—and jerked his head to see her hit the river.

Looking amused and annoyed at herself, she dogpaddled and grinned sheepishly at the boat which was already past her. Blake yelled, "All BACK!" Jeff dug his paddle in, and sensed everyone else did, too. But the boat was caught in a current. *We are not going to get back to reach her.*

So Jeff dove in.

Surfacing, he saw the boat receding downriver and Jordan standing up in it and heard her shout "DAD!" and she screamed it again, tottering, and then Blake pulled her down so *she* wouldn't fall out and Blake yelled back at Jeff, "No problem! Swim to shore!"

Jeff spun around, looking for Barbara. She was maybe fifteen yards back, the current and her swim strokes taking her toward him and he tried swimming toward her and made no progress—difficult to swim in a bulky life jacket—but his effort kept him from going further downriver. So Barbara swam into his arms.

"Dumb of me! Sorry!" She nodded her head toward the nearest bank, ten yards away. "We go there."

"Okay."

They tried to swim there, couldn't. The current drove them downriver at a flat rock, midriver, about the size of a cot, sticking up two feet above the surface. Jeff helped Barbara scramble up onto it, scrambled up after her. On the narrow space, they hugged, bulky life jackets between them. They watched, downriver, the paddle boat disappear around a bend. "No problem," said Barbara—which, Jeff realized, was exactly what Blake had said.

"No problem," she said. "The next raft that comes along . . . picks us up."

Made sense. Jeff figured there were plenty of rafts behind them on the river.

Except, just as Blake had been wrong about "No problem, swim to shore," Jeff realized Barbara was about to be proven wrong.

Because suddenly the sky darkened—they were in the Blue Ridge, mountain weather could change *fast*—and thunder slammed. Lightning flashed. The sky opened up; rain came down hard, a thick curtain. Jeff thought, Thank God there's no horse nearby to stampede into us. Sorry, Michelle.

Jeff realized that any guide running any raft or paddle boat behind them on the river was quickly getting his or her craft off the river, onto a bank. Not going to stay out on the water where lightning could strike.

No one coming anytime soon to pick up Barbara Travis and Jeff Taylor.

Of course many kayakers—mostly young guys who, being young guys, felt immortal—would be staying on the river. Three came by now, whooping and hollering. One guy whooped at Jeff and Barbara, "Hang on there! Storm'll be over in—" but his next words were drowned in a thunderclap, so Jeff didn't know whether the words were *a few minutes* or *a few hours.*

Thanks, thought Jeff. Appreciate it.

The kayakers disappeared around the bend.

"Could be worse," Jeff told Barbara. "We could be *between* this rock"—he pointed to the rain-smashed river—"and a hard place. Instead, at least we're *on* it."

"Rock of Ages," said Barbara, trying to laugh, hugging Jeff as he hugged her. She sang, "Cleft for me / Let me hide myself in thee."

"Excellent Christian hymn," said Jeff.

"But a Jewish source," said Barbara. "Exodus 33:22. 'I will put thee in a cleft of the rock, and will cover thee with my hand as I pass by.'"

Rain drilling his helmet, rain drilling his face, Jeff nodded upward. "But He ain't passing by. He's staying on us."

"A message," said Barbara. "He is telling you *you* are meant to stay."

"Here? On this rock on the Adako? Moses on a rock atop Mount Nebo? Never to come to the promised land? "

"No. Stay at Hampton Acres Hebrew Academy. You're meant to."

"Oh, c'mon. As some of the HAHA girls say, puh-*leeze.*"

"No, really. I have seen you there, seen you smile there. I have seen you when you talk about the place. You gripe and you gripe but then this misty look sometimes comes over your eyes and—"

"Seasonal allergy. Eyedrops."

"No," said Barbara.

"Or," said Jeff, "because I'm looking at you and I realize I love you."

"Thanks. But, no, you're talking about the school. You love the place."

"The place I love to hate."

"No, trust me," said Barbara. "I'm right about this. HAHA is your promised land."

Jeff said, "It doesn't matter that I love it. You know it won't exist much longer. It's going to be"—he pointed to the river—"swept away."

"Nonsense. You are a financial wizard. Big money, creative deals. You know how to save the school. God intends you to save the school."

"Ha."

Then, twenty minutes after it hit, as suddenly as it had hit, the storm ended. Again, the sun blazed in a blue sky. The world, rain-washed, renewed, glistened. The sun started to dry them off. Ten minutes more and a raft came alongside Jeff and Barbara and picked them up off the narrow, cot-sized rock.

They rode the raft down through the rest of the eleven miles, through Nordaus Creek and then the three remaining Class IIIs and the two remaining Class IVs and the one Class V, named Terminator. Six rapids that they whooped through. As they stepped off the raft at the take-out and as Jordan came running to join them and hug her father, Barbara told Jeff, "Remember what you admitted back on that rock."

"What?"

"You said you love the school."

"Said under the influence of a storm," said Jeff. "Doesn't count."

She's right, said Michelle in his head.

SEVENTY-SIX

TIME TO WORRY?

The day after the whitewater adventure, at noon, Jeff opened a pleasantly surprising email.

This email, from Irving Knipel, came with a rough draft of what Knipel said would be, eleven days hence, his commencement address. Jeff read it. It was not weird like some of the messages he had read last night on Parochet—good! Nor was it cliché-ridden like last year's commencement address from Bradleyville's drugstore king. Good!

Instead, Knipel had found some not-quite familiar quotes from familiar sources (Rabbi Jonathan Sacks, Golda Meir, and Hannah Senesh) that Jeff felt would please the audience. Knipel had done a pretty good job of weaving these pieces of wisdom into a short, coherent address. And Jeff could hear the man delivering it in his American TV announcer English: calm, confident, low-key, level.

Okay, Knipel!

Then, starting at four o'clock, the regular Thursday meeting of the executive committee proceeded much more benignly than usual. Rabbi Baum asked for no new fast days, Rachel Fish started no new arguments with Coach Bill or anyone else, and Celine Johnson did not invite herself in. Stevie Blau and Madison Angel stayed as cool as Jerome McKool. With some equanimity, Jeff and the seven deans discussed how, this Saturday night, they would keep the prom festive and safe for all students.

"It will go smoothly," said Madison. "This isn't our first rodeo."

A little after six p.m., when Jeff walked across the bridge to his house, he felt all was well in the Kingdoms of Judah and Israel.

And that worried him.

SEVENTY-SEVEN

PROM NIGHT

"**P**rom."

Jeff observed that it rhymes with "bomb."

Jeff was *not* worried about a real bomb. The threat was a hoax. But "bomb" in the sense that HAHA's prom could end in an explosion of drunk-kid-drives-rented-sports-car-into-tree? Oh, yes.

There were many well-dressed candidates for such an ending.

Of the one hundred and forty-five students at HAHA, about one hundred and twenty were going to the prom, most as boy-girl couples. There were also a few all-girl threesomes. All the boys were in rented tuxes. Almost all the girls were in gowns. Some girls were going classy, some provocatively.

Jeff felt keenly that The Beast was up and active. Sniffing the air, snorting, pacing, itchy, anxious to do *something*.

To *try* to keep an eye on these one hundred and twenty prom-go-ers, Jeff and thirty of HAHA's sixty teachers would be on hand at the Partridge Ridge Country Club. This was a teacher-student ratio of 1:4.

Twelve or thirteen of the sixty teachers would be back at the school to try to minister to the twenty-five HAHA students not going to the prom, to reassure them they were just as good—*you really are, really*—as the one hundred and twenty. This was a teacher-ratio of 1:2.

Jeff felt this was misplaced. The kids *at* the prom were more likely to get themselves into trouble—drinking, puking, screwing. And then, please no, getting behind a wheel. The kids back at the school—sick, shy, or in quiet trouble—were, at the most, likely to be sobbing.

Jeff sighed. What could a Head do? For that matter, what could a father do? He figured Jordan would, as soon as she could, leave the Partridge dance floor to be with Jose. And back at the school, Celine was in charge. Even though Celine was thrilled at having twelve teachers reporting to her, she had, predictably, argued against having the prom. "It will cause too much heartbreak, Jeff. Among those who are going and especially among those who aren't. We'll need a suicide watch."

You do that, Jeff had told her. Set one up.

Saturday night drama.

The prom would start at nine. But now, eight-thirty, as night fell, lots of prom-going kids piled into Ubers, Lyfts, and limos to go to Bradleyville to eat a celebratory, almost-grown-up dinner. As they left, an unhappy Baum was quick at Jeff's shoulder. "Jeff, Shabbat isn't over. I see only two stars."

The rule was, Shabbat isn't over until you see three stars. Jeff said, "Rabbi, it's overcast. If it weren't overcast, you could see a dozen stars."

Baum saw through this lie.

And Baum was not happy with the Partridge Ridge Country Club. "Jeff, they've hosted interfaith weddings."

Jeff wanted to say *As long as, tonight, they don't host any Jewish conceptions.*

Now, as the first HAHA school bus started to fill with kids who could not afford Ubers or limos, Jeff turned to Barbara. She looked like the very best prom date a man could have. He told her, "We gotta go. Gotta beat the kids there, act like I am in charge."

He drove them there, and walked with her into the ballroom.

His ears were hit by a tidal wave of noise-music.

His eyes took in an adolescent dreamscape.

Above, bathed in strobe lights, revolved a huge, glittering ball of mirrors, casting moving glitters on the floor. On three sides nestled huge, inflated mylar objects, including six-foot-tall high-heel shoes for a queen and a ten-foot-wide swollen baseball mitt for a jock. Against the fourth wall stretched a buffet table heavily laden with pizza, nachos, tacos, Buffalo wings, potato skins, and chilled cans of Red Bull.

Over it all, up on a dais, cloaked in shades and 'tude, presided Jamal, Georgia's hippest DJ.

At Jeff's shoulder, Rachel Fish was saying, "This place fought integration into the 1970s. Today they're tough on trans people. Is this really the best we could do?"

"Hmmm," said Jeff.

He moved away, leaving Ms. Fish to stew—Fish stew, he thought.

And now, as the school buses disgorged their passengers and, soon after, as the Ubers and limos disgorged theirs, the ballroom filled.

Asking for quiet, student-body president Isaac Greene took the mic, congratulated everyone, and wished everyone a great time. "A *safe* time," underlined Isaac, as he had at Project Ruach four days ago.

Would Isaac's injunction do any good? Jeff surveyed the prom-goers. The Mexicans probably weren't listening. The Russians were pretending they didn't understand. And the Israelis . . . ? The Israelis always did "what was right in their own eyes."

Then too-cool-for-school Jamal the DJ started another thrashing-pounding number that sounded to Jeff like an invitation to a sex-and-car-crash finale. Wincing, wishing he had brought earplugs, Jeff, with Barbara at his side, began circulating the room to check on the adults whom he sure hoped would stay in charge tonight.

Among others:

He checked on Bill Davidoff (looking like a capable bouncer), Preston Tom, Stevie and Meadow Blau, Madison Angel, and Noga Weinstein (looking like she wished she'd brought her Uzi).

He checked on Jerome McKool keeping a gimlet eye on the kids.

He checked on Tzipora Perl and, with Tzipora, Chava Baum.

He came upon Rabbi Baum, now standing with the Reverend Pat Travis.

"Barbara," said the Reverend to his favorite niece. "You look mighty fine. Doesn't she, Jeff?"

"You bet," replied Jeff.

"Jeff," said Baum, frowning at the Jamal the DJ, "some of these lyrics—they are very suggestive."

"You can *hear* the lyrics?" asked Jeff. All he heard was thunder.

And the evening unrolled.

As far as Jeff could see, in the ballroom, no problems.

But he knew any problems were probably outside.

Telling Barbara, "You can tell your uncle I've gone go protect *my* flock," he went alone out into the parking lot. Taking a flashlight from his own car, he began—flashlight off—to walk amid the limos. If I were having sex, he told himself, that's where I'd be. Not in the cramped back seat of a car. Instead, inside something very roomy. With a wet bar.

Damn. All the limos had tinted windows.

He started pulling on door handles.

SEVENTY-EIGHT

LIMOUSINE SCENES

In the country club parking lot, pulling on limo door handles, Jeff asked himself, Why am I doing this?

He remembered *his* eighteen-year-old self and *his* girlfriend at the end of *his* senior year in high school . . .

I am betraying them.

But I am Head of School. I am Responsible.

Yea, Head! said Michelle.

One pull of a door handle produced, from the dark interior, a girl's screams of "*You didn't lock the f**king door!*"

Jeff recognized the confident voice of Liz Rosenthal. Jeff knew that her boyfriend was . . . Dave Gilders. No reason to shine the flashlight on the couple. For one thing, if Liz is ah . . . *improvising* . . . with someone else, it's not my business.

Jeff said, "Look, guys, I don't want to write you up. So just stop it. I'm walking away. A minute from now, I'll be back and you'll be gone. And *not* into the bushes. Go back inside. All you have to lose is your eardrums."

"Thank you, Mr. Taylor," said Liz.

Jeff continued his tour of the parking lot—and then stopped for a moment.

He was struck by something in the air. A faint scent.

Not, from the edges of the parking lot, the sweet fragrance of honeysuckle. Something from a few miles off. From somewhere between here and HAHA. From exactly halfway between? Yes, from Emmitt Bailey's CAFO, Emmitt's pig farm, Emmitt's manure lagoon.

Pig shit.

If that's not enough to drive me back inside, nothing is.

But one last limo. This one a stretch limo. If there was any setting for a drunkfest-sexfest, this would be it. Jeff went to it, pulled on a passenger door handle.

From the richly alcohol-scented dark interior, a boy's drunken voice: "Hey! Aaron! Close the door!"

"It's not Aaron," said Jeff.

"Oh, shit! Mr. Taylor."

This time, Jeff did turn on his flashlight. The beam hit seven boys, no girls. Seven boys in disheveled tuxes, each holding a glass. As the beam hit Stan Pincus, Stan had dropped his full glass in his lap. Wiping his lap, Stan now got, from Jonathan Bloch, "Asshole, did you just piss in your pants?"

Stan protested, "Mr. Taylor, you scared me. But not *that* much."

"Too bad," said Jeff. "You should be scared that much. Scared I'll kick you out of school."

"Mr. Taylor," said Mike Tarnovsky, "you wouldn't do that."

"No. Just out of the prom. You're going back to campus."

"But it's the prom!" protested Aaron Fabrikant.

"The prom is special!" said David Chafetz.

"Apparently not special enough," said Jeff. "Or you'd *be* there."

Keeping the flashlight beam on the seven drunks, Jeff took out his smartphone, called Baum, asked Baum to come out here please.

Waiting, he observed all seven drunks sink into sullen acceptance of their fate.

Showing up with Reverend Travis, Baum took one look and muttered, "About what you'd expect at this place"—as if, thought Jeff, no boys had ever gotten drunk at a more *Jewish* Jewish country club.

"Yes," Jeff told Baum, "and would you now *remove* them from this place? Be the designated driver. And when you get them back to school, keep them at your place, keep an eye on them."

Baum nodded. With Reverend Travis riding shotgun, he got behind the wheel and drove off.

SEVENTY-NINE

FAR FROM THE PROM,
FAR FROM PRINCETON,
FAR FROM HAPPY

No, I will *not* be placated, thought Ashley Friedlander. This movie is *not* going to make me forget what has been done to me.

The movie was *Booksmart*. Ashley and most of the other two dozen HAHA students who were not at the prom were watching it on a huge screen in the Beit Am, watching it under the eyes of Celine Johnson and a dozen other HAHA teachers-staffers. Along with supplying the teen-friendly movie, the adults had supplied the room with tables of the same food—pizza, wings, etc.—being served at the prom. The adults' none-so-subtle message: You two dozen are *not* losers—you have the same menu as the prom-goers, see. And you can have just as good a time here on campus tonight. *Aren't* you having a *great* time?

No, I am *not*, thought Ashley. I am *pissed*.

First of all, she was pissed she wasn't at the prom.

Two months ago, mid-March, Gary Glassman had sort of invited her. But then it turned out that, just as the Princeton Admissions Office betrayed her, so did Gary; he invited Susan Zax. And while three other senior girls who hadn't been invited by guys (Sharon and Dafna and Ruth told Ashley *come with us*—"To hell with the guys, we are going as a trio, let's make it a quartet"—Ashley felt that would be *awful*.

Better to stay here on campus.

Second, of course, Ashley was pissed she wasn't going to Princeton.

She had tried to make herself okay with her fate: University of Texas at Austin. She had read about Austin, how it was such a hip city, artsy and everything, the home of SXSW, South by Southwest, the music and film festival, with the sort-of cool name South By. But f**k it, Austin isn't Princeton. I do not, for four years, want to be surrounded by idiots yelling "Hook 'em horns!" I deserve Princeton's orange, *pure* orange. U of T's *burnt* orange burns my buns.

And, speaking of film, I hate this movie.

It is so blatantly *transparent* why the HAHA teachers-staffers have chosen *Booksmart* for tonight. See, up on screen, these two high school seniors, Amy and Molly, friendless losers, deciding to go to a graduation party and have a good time *anyway*. More bullshit than one of Rabbi Baum's sermons.

It did not help Ashley's mood that Molly, up on screen, has gotten into Yale. It did not help Ashley's mood that Molly, up on screen, is, at graduation, delivering an improvised valedictorian speech that was getting her a standing ovation.

Booksmart was making Ashley's wounds smart.

Ashley thought, I'm getting a movie turning sentimental, and I'm getting pizza turning cold.

I am *not* placated.

Worse, I am here in the Beit Am with kids who—to be blunt—are losers. Kids like that prima donna of a loser, Hannah Newins. Kids like Shark Boy.

Worse, I am under the eyes of Celine Johnson, who is just hoping that one of us losers will break down in tears so she can clasp us to her sweaty boobs and give us counseling on the level of Dr. Phil. "You are worthy of self-love and inner peace."

F**k that. I deserve a hottie to take me to the prom and admission to Princeton.

No, movies and wings will not placate me.

Speaking of movies, there was that great movie *Carrie*, in which, on prom night, this bullied high school senior gets revenge and uses her superpower to kill nearly every student and teacher at her school and then burns her school down.

Not that I would *do* that, thought Ashley. But I sure would like to make a *movie* like that. Of HAHA being destroyed.

A recently-digested spicy Buffalo wing rose and burned in Ashley Friedlander's chest.

EIGHTY
FUELED BY FLASKS

n the second-floor common room of Beit Gibborim, one floor above the apartment of Rabbi Benjamin Baum and Rebbetzin Chava Baum, a pity party was in progress.

Stan Pincus, Aaron Fabrikant, Jonathan Bloch, Mike Tarnovsky, Peter Altman, David Chafetz, and Stu Gilford were saying it was unfair. Their grievance was fueled by the twelve-year-old scotch which Stan, Mike, and Stu had in flasks under their tuxes, flasks which neither Mr. Taylor nor Rabbi Baum nor Reverend Travis had inquired about.

"We're not going to take this," said a drunk Stan Pincus. "Not gonna be confined here."

"Freedom," slurred an even more drunk Peter Altman, "means being bold."

"F**king right," said Jonathan Bloch. "Who said that?"

"Martin Luther King," slurred Peter Altman, who wondered whether it was actually Barack Obama.

"Yes!" said Mike Tarnovsky. "Let's do something bold. Only the bold are free!"

"*Freedom!*" cried David Chafetz. "We should seize our freedom!"

"And free *others* who are confined!" cried Stan Pincus.

"Who?" asked Jonathan Bloch.

Stan Pincus explained what he meant. The other six immediately agreed this was an excellent idea. From the flasks, they drank a toast to this excellent idea. They called Uber and Lyft. Twenty minutes later, they piled into two cars and pointed the drivers to where they would execute this excellent idea.

EIGHTY-ONE
GIVE ME THAT OLD TIME SLOW TIME

Patience.

Emmitt Bailey had it.

It requires patience to raise pigs. Pigs do not like to be pushed; you must let them move of their own accord. Stressed pigs will, at harvest, have damaged muscle and yield poorer meat. To anyone who would say, "Science will find a way to accelerate putting good meat on pigs," Emmitt would say, "When pigs fly."

Take Big Bob.

While every one of Emmitt's other six thousand pigs was being raised to be slaughtered at six months and two hundred eighty pounds, Big Bob—Emmitt's Landrace boar, age eight and eight hundred twelve pounds—was still growing. Emmitt watched Big Bob's progress with great patience.

And Emmitt suspected it would require even more patience to raise a red heifer. He did not share the Reverend Travis's all-fired-up impatience to bring about The Rapture. Hey, I'm enjoying this life, I can wait for The Next. And if the Reverend thinks we are going to get a 100 percent red heifer from this first insemination of the mostly-red heifer now contentedly chewing her cud out in a warm (and away from pigs) corner of Building No. 3, well, the Reverend has another thing coming. She's Mama Korban? Mother of the Sacrifice? No, it's going to take generations.

Farmers and breeders have patience.

Similarly, it requires patience to enjoy baseball. Even with the introduction of the pitch clock, a sl-o-o-o-w sport. An echo of an earlier, cow-slowly-chewing-her-cud rural America. Emmitt liked it that way.

So, for background, Emmitt had a game on right now on his TV, the Atlanta Braves versus the Washington Nationals, a 1-1 pitchers' duel somewhere in the late innings (Emmitt had lost track) that was, no doubt, a disappointment for folks who wanted your juiced home run derby, but was deeply satisfying to Emmitt.

Don't push a pig, don't push a heifer, don't push a pitcher.

Also slow-moving: Emmitt's mouth, working on a BLT—the bacon, of course, from his own pigs.

Emmitt was patiently recaning a chair seat. The traditional six-way pattern, the work done in six stages. He was using strong, pliable, bright Borneo rattan, smooth and shiny on one side. And he was using pegs that he had whittled himself. Right now, nearly three hours in, he was completing stage two, carefully running the cane in place side-to-side through each hole. About five hours from now, when he had completed stage six, he still wouldn't be *finished*. There were sixteen specific steps in what was called *finishing*.

Rattan in hand, Emmitt Bailey was stopped cold by a thunderous roar from his CAFO.

Pigs do not like to be pushed, you must let them move of their own accord.

But when you open the pens that have confined them and then get behind them and wave your arms and scream at them . . .

EIGHTY-TWO

YIPPIE-KI-YAY!

With heedlessness born of twelve-year-old scotch and strength born of eighteen-year-olds' testosterone, the seven drunken boys snapped off the lock on Emmitt Bailey's CAFO Building Number 3, rushed inside, and threw open the pens of one hundred, two hundred . . . all one thousand two-hundred-fifty-pound pigs. Yippie-ki-yaying, they drove the pigs outside. Then, with equal heedlessness, they threw open the pen of Big Bob and drove all eight-hundred-twelve pounds of him outside.

Now *where* shall we drive them?

Pumped, whooping, the seven boys eyed each other and, without speaking a word, *knew.*

They whipped out their phones. Shooting video of the pigs they were driving ahead of them, they livestreamed this to HAHA kids back in the Partridge Ridge Country Club. They added the question: *Will the fence hold? It's eco-friendly but is it pig-friendly?*

Aaron Fabricant wrote: *Watch them come, fast. You'll say SWINE FLEW.* Stu finished with: *We're the guys making them fly, Stan, Jonathan, Mike, Peter, David, Aaron, and Stu!*

Then, running hard with the others, Aaron twisted his ankle and collapsed. Helpless, envious, he watched his six colleagues and the one thousand-plus pigs stampede into the night woods and vanish.

EIGHTY-THREE
THE HEAD LEARNS LAST

I n the Partridge Ridge Country Club ballroom, Jeff had been enjoying the students' exuberant, unrestrained dancing. Their endless energy was making him feel younger, lighter. But now something strange was happening: all around him, instead of thrashing the air with their arms and legs, kids—first ten kids, then twenty, then all of them—had whipped out their smartphones and were staring at them. They were gaping in a mixture of horror-delight. Fingers flying, they were texting, spreading the word. And they were grabbing each other on the dance floor and saying what looked like *Can you believe THIS?!*

What is "this"? The Head of School is always the last to know.

Jeff needed to know *now*. Kids, what the hell is happening?

Now, kids were shouting, screaming, *"PIGS! THEY LET LOOSE BAILEY'S PIGS! BAILEY'S PIGS ARE HEADING TO HAHA!"*

Thanks, thought Jeff. Now I know.

EIGHTY-FOUR
TWIST OF ANKLE, TWIST OF FATE

L eaving behind the partly-recaned chair seat and the Braves-Nationals game, Emmitt Bailey—annoyed at having to move fast—moved fast out of his house into the night and ran toward his CAFO to check out the roar.

At the pried-and-smashed-open doors of Building Number 3, he stared in dismay. The entire building was empty. One thousand market pigs, meat pigs . . . gone. Big Bob . . . gone. The pigs' roar could be heard receding in the distance, heading west, through the woods. Nearer, in the dark, only a few feet away, was the plaintive cry of a teenage boy. "Oooh, it hurts. Oooh, I can't move."

A large, meaty hand descended onto Aaron Fabrikant's neck and hauled him to his feet.

A slow, deep, rumbling voice demanded, "Son, what have you done?"

Tottering on one good left foot and one badly-sprained right ankle, face to face with a Georgia pig farmer with the visage of an unforgiving Torah prophet, a terrified Aaron Fabrikant explained.

"And your friends are driving my pigs toward your school?"

Aaron gulped and said this was so.

"Son, how do I reach the man who's the head of your school?"

Handing over his smartphone, Aaron explained how to text and call Mr. Taylor.

Emmitt's call went to voicemail. But he figured Jeff Taylor read his text because Jeff called right back. Emmitt explained what was happening.

"Thank you," said Jeff, "but I already know this. If we end up with your pigs, any suggestion on how to send them back to you?"

"Your men guarding the school—they have any BB guns?"

"No."

"Too bad. Because if you sting my pigs, they might run back here."

"Thank you," said Jeff, "but we don't have any BBs."

"A shame," said Emmitt. "Gonna have to charge your school a lot for my pigs."

"We don't have a lot. Don't have any."

Emmitt Bailey sighed. He considered calling the Bradleyville Police and the Bradleyville Fire Department—but what could they do? Nothing. So, what more to say? He told Jeff, "Well, sir, you were concerned your school was getting pig molecules. Now you get the pigs themselves."

"Aren't we lucky," said Jeff.

"Good luck," said Emmitt, and he handed the phone back to Aaron Fabrikant.

"Well, son, I can't do anything for my pigs tonight . . . but you? That's a sprained ankle? Let's get you inside."

Helping Aaron in, Emmitt sat the boy down in front of the Braves-Nationals game, put the boy's right foot up on a hassock, wrapped the ankle in an ice pack.

Then he noticed the boy eyeing what was left of the BLT.

"Son, you hungry?"

Aaron allowed as how he was.

"But Jews don't eat bacon," said Emmitt.

Aaron allowed as how some did. He explained that he did. But please don't tell my parents.

Soon Aaron was watching baseball and eating a freshly-made BLT.

EIGHTY-FIVE
THE PROM IMPLODES

Aren't we lucky. That's what Jeff had said to Emmitt.

Standing in the ballroom of the Partridge Ridge Country Club, standing amid HAHA students milling and shouting, Jeff stared at what Isaac Greene was showing him on Isaac's smartphone: hundreds of pigs stampeding through the woods, pigs with six HAHA boys whooping and hollering behind them, pigs illuminated by the flashlights in the boys' smartphones, boys driving the pigs toward the eastern fence of the HAHA campus.

A fence that, Jeff knew, could not, would not, withstand hundreds of pigs.

This was the thing he had always, back of his mind, most feared. Not emotional epidemics rising from the petri dish that was the school and infecting students and faculty. No. Real, concrete, physical harm. Harm to bodies. Harm to buildings.

A half-ton horse flying through a car windshield.

Hon, said Michelle, *the pigs are not going to crush the kids.*

We don't know that, replied Jeff.

He had to get back to the school.

But first he had to stop more kids here at the club from putting themselves at risk. Twenty boys—about one third of the boys here— had already ditched their dates and had run out the ballroom's main door, run for waiting limos. They had run yelling, "The lacrosse stadium! The best seats! Watch the pigs come!" Some of their dates had run after them.

Jeff went fast up onto the dais, grabbed the mic. "Nobody leave! You're safe here! Stay put!"

Sweeping the crowd, he eyeballed the forty teachers—and was pleased to see Coach Bill, Rachel Fish, Stevie Blau, Madison Angel, and Preston Tom go to the doors and, like Jerome McKool, block the doors, and try to reason with the kids who hadn't already escaped.

"Thank you," announced Jeff. "Stay here and have fun."

Dropping the mic, he went to Madison. "You're in charge here. Keep them here. Keep them . . . having fun."

"How? Jeff, they want to go *see*. Every school gets a prom, only we get a pig invasion."

"Drinks for all. Instead of swine—wine!"

"Really?"

"Better them falling down drunk *here* . . . better than . . . " Jeff imagined kids falling under thousands of hooves. "*Do* it, Madison."

Then Jeff grabbed Stevie Blau. "Stevie, send out a text. Level five alert. All students and faculty. Shelter in place. Got that?"

Stevie gulped. "Yes."

"Good, because . . . " Jeff imagined some of the girls in the Beit Am imagining the onrushing pigs as so many cute Wilburs of *Charlotte's Web* and rushing out to greet them.

Then Jeff grabbed Preston Tom. "Preston! I'm going to the school. Leaving in five minutes. But you leave now. I'm deputizing you. Until I get there, you're in charge."

"But isn't Celine already . . . ?"

Ha! The question answered itself. "Leaving now, Jeff," said Preston, and strode off.

Jeff yelled after him: "Anybody who's left the Beit Am, get them back inside! Anybody who shows up—any limo kids—get *them* inside!"

Then Jeff called Celine, got her voice mail. So he texted her: *Preston coming to take charge. Do a head count. Lock the doors.*

Then Jeff grabbed Jerome. "How many men do you have to stop the pigs?"

"There are two already on campus. And I just reached the guys off-duty tonight and asked them to come. They're . . . uh . . . reluctant. Nobody is eager to put themselves at the fence up against a thousand pigs."

"But with BB guns? Can you get any?"

"No BB guns at ten-thirty Saturday night."

"Tear gas?!" said Jeff, aware he sounded frantic. "Pepper spray?! Flashbang grenades?!"

"Get them at ten-thirty on a Saturday night?" said Jerome. "If there's a mass of pigs hitting the fence, it'll go down."

Jeff had already told himself this. In his mind, the fence was suddenly like half the surveillance cameras: fake. All the school's defenses were suddenly what Sammy always said HAHA was made of: smoke and mirrors.

Our Potemkin Village will fall.

Jeff sighed. "We'll do what we can. Come with me. Back to campus."

With Jerome—and with Barbara grabbing his hand—Jeff headed toward the ballroom's main door.

Only to be bushwhacked by Ella Bronstein. "Mr. Taylor, any comment on this pig attack?"

"Ella, not *now*."

He got rid of Ella only to be bushwhacked by a Noga Weinstein call: "Jeff, this pig attack is almost certainly a diversion for a terrorist attack. Cherev is mobilizing, will be at the school to . . . "

Jeff's blood froze. As dangerous as the pigs were, they weren't carrying. Cherev would be. Turning to Jerome, he said, "Find Cherev and make them stand down."

"You bet," said Jerome.

Jerome, Barbara, and Jeff got out into the parking lot. Here, a half dozen boys were piling into a limo and three girls were trying to stop them. Pounding both her high heels on a limo window, Liz Rosenthal was screaming, "Richard, you creep! I am more important than some pigs! Richard, *you* are a pig!"

The limo pulled away.

Jeff phoned Preston Tom: "More kids coming. Grab 'em as they come in. Don't let them get to the lacrosse stadium. Don't let them anywhere near the fence."

For a moment, Jeff stopped, looked up. The stars had been replaced by a big yellow moon that seemed to hang over only Bradleyville. He thought, Such a beautiful night for a disaster.

Barbara took his arm. "Every confidence in you," she said.

At which Jeff now noticed his screaming phone: texts from parents, more parents, more parents: *Mr. Taylor! These pigs?! You are failing to protect my child from these pigs!* First among these was the ever-outraged Mrs. Friedlander: *You schmuck. Who puts their school next to a pig farm?!*

The pigs had unleashed The Beast.

Jerome had headed to his car. With Barbara, Jeff headed to his. To get back to the school. He demanded of himself, And then do *what?*

EIGHTY-SIX

SLIVOVITZ AND
THE LAST DAYS

"**R**efill your glass?" asked Rabbi Benjamin Baum.

"Oh, yes," said Reverend Pat Travis.

The two men of God sat in armchairs in Baum's cozy living room. They were savoring an excellent kosher slivovitz: Bohemia Honey Liqueur, aged plum brandy blended with pure honey. After they had arrived here, after Baum had herded the seven drunken boys up to the boys' rooms, Reverend Travis had asked if Baum would like some company. Reverend Travis had said, "Another day, I'll reciprocate. Perhaps tonight have a l'chaim with you?"

Baum said that was an excellent idea.

Thus, confident that the seven drunken boys upstairs were upstairs, the two clergymen had been drinking and talking.

The subject?

Since Reverend Travis had the goal (which he was not yet ready to share with Baum) of causing a red heifer to be born in Jerusalem (hastening The Rapture), he wanted to better understand Judaism's take on The Last Days.

Thus, as the alcohol produced a warm, honeyed glow, the two scholars—two colleagues—were discussing eschatology: death, judgment, and the final destiny of humankind.

They were now an hour into the talk and the slivovitz.

Holding out his glass to Baum and saying, "Truly refill it," Reverend Travis asked about the Third Temple. "It's the subject of my sermon tomorrow. I'd like to know more. I understand in Jerusalem there are people who are ready?"

"Oh, yes," Baum said, filling the reverend's glass to the brim, "indeed we are—"

"*PIGS!*"

Just outside Beit Gibborim, two girls—the leading edge of the country club escapees—were shouting, "*PIGS! PIGS ARE ATTACKING THE SCHOOL!*"

Rising from his armchair, rising along with Rabbi Baum, Reverend Travis sensed that, for a while at least, The Last Days could wait.

EIGHTY-SEVEN
OUTNUMBERED

Jeff was driving fast down Button Gwinnett Avenue, two-lane blacktop, fifteen miles toward HAHA, dark woods all around them, the taillights of Jerome's car just ahead. Jeff had just said to Barbara, "One thousand pigs stampeding toward HAHA and how many human beings to try to stop them? Not enough."

So Barbara was offering some historical perspective.

"The Battle of Sandersville," she said. "Late November 1864, just over a few hills from here. Partway through Sherman's March to the Sea."

"What happened?"

"Sherman's army versus General Joe Wheeler's cavalry unit. Sherman had overwhelming strength."

"Ah," said Jeff, "but Wheeler somehow prevailed."

"Nope. Sherman whupped the Rebs real good."

"And you said you have every confidence in me."

"I do. Every confidence that you will do your best. I'm just saying, you may have to prepare yourself for the fact that the pigs *will* overrun the campus. So the question is—"

"*YEOW!*"

Jeff screamed because surging fast out of the woods to his left, pouring across the road immediately in front of him, was a huge dark mass of *some*thing and he stomped on the brakes and the mass filled his headlights—a bright mass of pigs.

He stopped. The pigs stopped. Thirty, forty pigs turned and stared, transfixed, at Jeff's SUV.

Jeff leaned on the horn. A long-lasting blast. C'mon, *move!*

The pigs didn't move.

Gently stepping on the gas, Jeff nudged his SUV up into the pigs. Who stood their ground.

Jeff backed up, to give him space to go around the pigs. The pigs quickly filled the space. Now two, three deep, the pigs surrounded the SUV.

Jeff said, "Gotta have a serious conversation with those guys driving the pigs toward the HAHA fence. *Not* doing a perfect job. They let *these* pigs get diverted."

Again, Jeff leaned on the horn. To no effect.

He turned to Barbara. "You ever herded pigs before?"

"No, and now's my chance?"

"Right."

Opening their doors—each door slowly pushing several pigs away—Jeff and Barbara managed to get out. Waving their arms and shouting, they tried to drive the pigs away. Slow going. Each two-hundred-and fifty-pound creature seemed to want to nuzzle into them.

"Hey!" said Jeff. "Your dress. You'll get it all—"

"I know a dry cleaner who badly needs the business."

"If you say so," said Jeff, as he and Barbara continued to work.

"Look at it this way," she said. "Now, headed toward HAHA, not a thousand pigs. Thirty, forty less. Improves the people-to-pig ratio. We get to HAHA, we're less outnumbered."

"*If* we can get to HAHA."

"Haven't you seen those TV commercials for SUVs? Show 'em running through everything. Rocks, rivers, sand dunes, snowfields, pigs. Certainly you've seen them."

Finally, Jeff and Barbara succeeded in shooing away most of the pigs. They got back in the SUV. Jeff slowly nudged it through the few remaining pigs.

Taking out his phone, he texted Preston Tom and Jerome McKool: *Been a bit delayed.*

EIGHTY-EIGHT

HUNKERING DOWN

Preston Tom had been on the HAHA campus about fifteen minutes.

In that time he had gone to the Beit Am and confirmed
that Celine Johnson, while prone to drama, had not gone hysterical.
She and the teachers still had *some* control over the kids in the Beit Am.
These kids seemed *some*what okay watching, on their smartphones, the
pigs stampeding through the woods toward the school. But these kids
sure did seem to envy the two dozen boys in the lacrosse bleachers.
Those boys had their cameras on, ready to capture the moment the
pigs breached the eastern fence. Their livestream carried their drunken
chant: "Three! Six! Nine! Give us swine! Kosher?! No, sir!"

Jerome McKool had been on the HAHA campus about twelve
minutes. He had texted Preston that as soon as he dealt with Cherev he
would get to the lacrosse stadium and send those boys to the Beit Am.

Visible on everyone's smartphones: The Stan Pincus posse—the
six sloshed swineherds—on the move, driving the pigs ever onward.

Meanwhile . . .

At the fence that ran along the *western* edge of HAHA, convinced
the pig attack on the *eastern* fence was a diversion, Cherev was on full
alert. Each armed with an Uzi and Israeli certainty, Noga Weinstein,
Ilana Weiss, Shulamit Mouchly, and Nadav Peretz patrolled the fence.
Through their Uzis' night-vision scopes, they peered west, into the

darkness. Checking their smartphones, they monitored—by tapping into Jerome's command center—video from the cameras on this fence. At the moment, nothing. Out of habit, Nadav Peretz also checked his three-pound watch. As a commando in Lebanon, he had used it to coordinate IDF air strikes. Tonight, no air support. Cherev would defend the school alone.

Taking a few seconds away from monitoring, Noga texted Jeff: *Ma shlomcha? Ha kol beseder?* (How are you? Everything okay?) *Everything okay here! Cherev will save the school!*

Jeff texted Noga: *Where are you?*

Noga told him. Jeff relayed this to Jerome, who texted back: *Headed there now.*

EIGHTY-NINE

INTO THE BREECH

Carrying their full glasses of excellent kosher slivovitz—Bohemia Honey Liqueur—Rabbi Benjamin Baum and Reverend Pat Travis walked out onto Baum's front stoop to investigate. There, consulting their smartphones, the two men saw what was happening. They began walking through the darkened campus toward Manny Kleinman Quad.

Meanwhile . . .

Looking out the Beit Am windows, Preston Tom was shocked. Pouring onto the campus were a dozen kids from the country club. Racing outside, he tried to herd them into the Beit Am. Laughing at him, they ran towards the lacrosse stadium. He followed them in determined but fruitless pursuit.

With Preston gone, Celine Johnson and the dozen other HAHA teachers and staffers immediately lost control of the situation. First, three girls bolted from the Beit Am, screaming *"LET'S GO TO THE PIGS!"*

Then, as Celine screamed, "Don't follow them!" and tried to summon the other teachers and staffers to block the doors, most of the two dozen other students (Hannah Newins among them) beat Celine to it. They made it through the doors and out onto the quad.

Then, with only two students left (Eli Margulies and Ashley Friedlander), all the other teachers and staffers (except Celine) had figured, What the hell, let Celine guard those two—we're also outta here. We're also gonna see the pigs! And they ran out the doors.

Twenty-three kids who had been trained from birth never to eat pig were now thrilled to realize that no commandment prevented them from watching said animal storm their school.

Now, as *Booksmart* continued to play on the screen behind her, Celine eyed Eli and Ashley. "Well, she said, "I'm glad to see that at least two students at this school have some maturity."

At which Ashley yelled, "Watch out, Dr. Johnson! Behind you! The pigs have broken in!" As Celine, stunned, turned, Ashley grabbed a handful of Buffalo wings and hurled them at the screen—hitting Molly, up there on screen, bound for f**king Yale. Ashley bolted, ran for the doors, made it out. Where to? she asked herself. Well, of course, to see the pigs. But not just *see* them—*video* them. Record the thousand pigs destroying this school! Video to edit, to make into a stunning documentary to send to Princeton!

Ashley sprinted toward the lacrosse stadium.

Leaving, alone in the Beit Am, a distraught Celine Johnson facing Eli Margulies, Shark Boy.

Eli cursed himself. Why didn't *I* run for it? Everyone else is gone. Even my three buddies. Even manipulative Hannah—probably to fake getting hit by a pig, so she can make another big production. But I'm sitting here. Not being a Shark. To keep oxygen-rich water flowing over their gills, sharks keep *moving*.

Eli's thoughts were interrupted by a deep, vast Celine Johnson sob.

"Dr. Johnson," said Eli, "is there anything I can do for you?"

"Eli, everyone has abandoned me. Even Hannah. Only you are left." She buried her head in her hands.

"I'll get you a Kleenex," said Eli to the psychotherapist, who, her tearful eyes covered, did not see him.

He ran out the doors.

Meanwhile . . .

Chased by the six sloshed swineherds, all one thousand pigs (minus the forty or so that Jeff and Barbara had encountered) hit a hundred-foot section of the eastern fence. The fence went down. The pigs poured onto the campus of Hampton Acres Hebrew Academy.

NINETY

A BATTLE PLAN IS BORN ON BUTTON GWINNETT AVENUE

As Jeff sped on Button Gwinnett Avenue, Jerome got through to his phone.

"Jeff, I've told the Israelis to stand down three times. They're not budging."

Jeff swore, but Jerome said, "It's for the best. They're dug in on the west, far from the action."

"You're right," Jeff said, feeling that he had gotten his first lucky break.

Meanwhile, Barbara, who had been fixed on her smartphone, shouted, "*THEY'RE ON THE CAMPUS!* They're just north and east of the stadium, heading for Judah."

"Damn, no way to stop them now," Jeff said.

"We *can* stop them!"

"What? How?!" Jeff said this as he sped to the front gate and the guard at the gate jumped aside.

"Leopold Hirszfeld Hall." She pointed. "Get us there."

Speeding through the gate, onto the campus, having no clue, but believing in Barbara, Jeff headed toward Hirszfeld Hall . . .

NINETY-ONE

RESCUE!

I ntent on getting into Princeton, intent on never having to say "Hook 'em horns," Ashley easily outran everyone else headed for the lacrosse stadium. Reaching it, Ashley sprinted out onto the field and faced the twenty boys in the bleachers. Most of them were stupid-drunk, all of them were stupid-shouting stuff. Gary Glassman shouted, "This little piggy went to HAHA!" Eyeing him, Ashley thought, So, Gary, you dumped me for Susan Zax, and now you've dumped Susan for the pigs. You're gonna get the pigs.

Spotting her, Gary yelled, "Ashley, c'mon up here! It's gonna be a great view!"

Aiming her smartphone, videoing Gary and the rest of the boys, Ashley figured two minutes before the pigs hit. One minute and thirty seconds to video the boys, then run for shelter behind the cinderblock concession stand. From there, video the disaster.

Now, behind her, she could hear thunder—the pigs fast approaching. The boys' shouts continued: "Kosher?! No, sir! Swine are fine!"

A fabulous documentary for the Princeton Admissions Office, thought Ashley Friedlander.

Then the thought hit her: But what if the boys get hurt? Not just bruises. Broken bones. Maybe . . . worse.

"Gary!" she yelled. "Guys! You could get *killed!* Guys, get *down!* Take cover!"

Gary yelled back, "You're a wimp!"

The boys took up the chant, "Wimp! Wimp! Wimp!"

Ashley didn't know what to do. Then she did.

She yelled, "Oh, so you guys have balls?! Let's see who can prove it. Anybody who wants to show what's he's got, get over here behind the concession stand with me."

Shakily, drunkenly, Gary Glassman stood up, took one step down toward Ashley. So did another boy. And another.

In her head, Ashley heard her mother, the domineering Rhoda Friedlander, screaming, "Ashley! What are you doing!? The pigs trampling the boys—get *that* video for your documentary and get into Princeton! Without it, you're stuck at the University of f**king Texas!"

Trying to ignore her mother's voice, Ashley kept on enticing the boys and videoing them—and now they were all down from the bleachers. Then, shaking the earth, the pigs poured onto the lacrosse field. Just ahead of them, Ashley quick-led the boys to safety behind the concession stand. From there, she videoed as the pigs hit the bleachers. The bleachers crashed. A mass of crunched metal, a mass of still-stampeding pigs. Behind the pigs came the six sloshed swineherds, yippy-ki-ay-ing the pigs on. Amid the drunk and dazed boys from the bleachers, Ashley kept videoing and her mother kept screaming, "Ashley! I raised you to look out for yourself! Ashley, you're giving up your body to save *theirs???!!!*"

Ashley mentally told her mother, Hey, I didn't say what they think I said and, on top of that, I had my fingers crossed behind my back. And on top of that, they're all falling down drunk. Three escape clauses.

Still videoing, Ashley watched the pigs stampede through the wrecked stadium. Behind them, driving them, came the sloshed swineherds. And now, fast behind the sloshed swineherds (and leaving the bleacher boys behind the concession stand), Ashley took off—to video more of tonight's drama. The drama unfolded westward, deeper into the campus of Hampton Acres Hebrew Academy.

On Manny Kleinman Quad . . .

While moving toward where their smartphones told them the pigs were heading, Rabbi Baum and Reverend Travis were struck stock-still. Now they could see it:

Stampeding toward them, thundering, with nearly two thousand red eyes glowing like fireflies, was the mass of pigs.

In awe, thinking of Matthew 9:28-32, Reverend Travis recited from memory, "And behold the whole herd of swine ran violently down a steep place into the sea, and perished in the waters." Which, Reverend Travis was convinced . . . Yes, it *is!* A sure sign of the approaching End of Days . . . Praise the Lord!

Except how, thought Reverend Travis, can we avoid be trampled to death?

Dropping their glasses of excellent slivovitz, Baum and Travis scrambled to shelter behind a nearby elm. The pigs were coming faster. Behind the pigs, the swineherds kept shouting, "Onward!"

Meanwhile . . . Barbara scampered up the narrow ladder to the roof of Leopold Hirszfeld Hall, and Jeff, with mounting understanding, followed her up through the hatch.

Once on the roof, Jeff texted a warning to Stevie, Jerome, Preston, and Cherev, typing faster than he ever had. Barbara, at *Strong East Wind's* control panel, turned up the dial through six and seven, and then all the way to ten. The twelve motors groaned, screamed, and finally smoked, producing a cacophony that kept growing to an eardrum-damaging, metal-on-metal shriek. Each fan was rotating faster than an airplane propeller, making the pillar on which it sat sway crazily. Each pillar's base began to give way. The roof beneath their feet rolled like a suspension bridge in heavy traffic. Barbara grabbed his wrist and pulled him toward the hatch and down into the building.

She hollered into his ear: "In about thirty seconds *Strong East Wind* will sound like the voice of God." Jeff remembered the midrash that said when God spoke at Sinai, His voice was so awesome it drove the souls of the Israelites out of their bodies—temporarily.

Meanwhile . . .

On Emmanuel Kleinman Quad, the two dozen students who had fled the Beit Am didn't need their smartphones. Now they could see the pigs with their own eyes. Here came the pigs. The two dozen scattered. Running for shelter behind an elm tree, Shark Boy was reassured to see that all three of his sort-of buddies had reached and now crouched behind similarly thick trees. Only Hannah Newins—confused?—stood out in the open. Stock-still. Looking around, wide-eyed.

Eli thought, Yeah, Hannah, we see you. Everybody sees you. We see you about to get yourself fake-hit by the pigs.

Then the thought hit him: No, she's not gonna get fake-hit. It's going to be for real.

Serves her right.

No, it doesn't.

Eli yelled, "Hannah! Move! Over here!"

Hearing Eli, Rabbi Baum stopped, turned, looked.

Hannah Newins remained rooted to the spot.

As the leading edge of the one thousand pigs poured onto the quad and as the distance between the leading edge and Hannah was twenty yards, now ten yards . . .

Seeing this, Baum thought of the Israelites frozen in fear as the waters of the Red Sea rose around them. Then Nahshon, a leader of the Judahites, broke ranks and walked in nose-deep until the sea parted. Who, here on Emmanuel Kleinman Quad, would unfreeze . . . ?

Eli Margulies unfroze.

Dashing out from behind the tree, Eli grabbed Hannah and, with her in his arms and pigs roaring at them so close he could feel their hot breath, hurled himself behind another tree.

And the pigs thundered past.

Shark Boy thought, That was worthy of a Great White.

Meanwhile . . .

In his living room, Emmitt continued re-caning the chair. But his mind was on his pigs. How am I going to retrieve my one thousand market pigs? And how am I going to retrieve Big Bob? How?

Nearby, Aaron stared at his ice-wrapped sprained ankle and turned his eyes from the Braves-National game. Taking out his smartphone, Aaron put in earbuds and closed his eyes. Faintly, urgent-pounding rap music leaked out of the earbuds. Emmitt sighed. Kids today—they don't appreciate baseball. Too slow for them. Instead they love everything fast, including their music.

And then . . .

On the HAHA campus . . .

The nearly one thousand boy-harried pigs had their ears assaulted by a sound so terrifying that the posse behind them seemed, by comparison, puny. As the swineherds scrambled to get out of the way, all but one of the nearly one thousand squealing pigs from Emmitt Bailey's Building Number 3 did a 180 and made a beeline back that way.

One pig did not turn back. That pig—a *big* pig, a big *angry* pig—kept barreling west. It shrugged off the sound waves that had scared off the rest of the herd. It headed for the Zelda Kleinman Center for Enlightenment. Smashing its way in, it burst into the dining hall. Careening amid the tables, snorting and sniffing the air, it sought the kitchen.

Just behind the swinging kitchen door, a trembling Tzipora Pearl cowered.

Tzipora knew that the kitchen in any Jewish school is sacrosanct. To get a "Hechsher"—a kosher certification for the kitchen—from her father the rabbi cost twenty-five thousand dollars. If the kitchen is defiled, the school will have to lay out thousands to clean it and then another twenty-five thousand for a new Hechsher.

Tzipora did not want that to happen. Saying the Shema, Judaism's most basic prayer, because that is what a Jew facing death does, she opened the kitchen door and pushed out a tray of pumpkin chocolate babka with candy corn. A tray large enough to feed thirty students.

Drawn by its delicious aroma, Big Bob trotted over to the babka and scarfed it down. As he did so, the anger and terror that had vied for control of his porcine mind faded and, by the time he had tucked into a second tray, had been entirely forgotten. Realizing that the monstrous chazer (pig) wouldn't know any better, Tzipora had soaked the second batch of babka with cooking wine. She did the same to the cinnamon rugelach-laden third tray. Feeling more contentment than he had ever before known, Big Bob finished off the rugelach, emitted an enormous burp, and fell into a deep sleep in which he dreamt of a farm with fields of rugelach and troughs of babka.

Meanwhile . . .

A vast roar coming from the school rattled the windows of Emmitt's farmhouse. "Good Lord, what now," Emmitt said. A pig stampede, a red heifer, the Reverend's Hebrew mumbo-jumbo, and now an ungodly clamor—was this the start of the End Times? Aaron, suspecting a connection between the din and the chaos he and his buddies had unleashed, checked his smartphone. His partners in porcine crime had changed direction and were now videoing the pigs' imminent return.

"Mr. Bailey, your pigs—looks like they're heading back here."

Emmitt sighed. Stampeding through the woods and into the school and now stampeding back, the pigs were burning off good muscle and fat. Less profit for him.

"Well, let's go outside and see if we can get them back in their pens. Need a hand?"

Emmitt helped Aaron up, and they went outside into the night, waited and watched.

Soon, the first pigs appeared. Walking now. The terrifying noise had stopped. Then more pigs. Soon, to Emmitt's eyes, pretty much all the one thousand. They milled around outside Building Number 3.

Pigs are smart, thought Emmitt, but not smart enough to go *inside*. And how do I herd in one thousand pigs?

At which, Aaron hit something on his smartphone and the phone started playing—*REALLY LOUD!*—what, a half hour ago, had leaked faintly from his earbuds. It was a rap song from Jamal the DJ's prom playlist.

As it played, nearly all one thousand pigs trotted toward Aaron.

"Son," said Emmitt Bailey, "seems they *like* that music. If you wouldn't mind keep playing it and coming with me inside this building—it's what the pigs call home—I think the pigs will follow."

Which Aaron did.

And a limping Aaron, holding up his blaring smartphone like a hi-tech Pied Piper, brought the pigs home.

NINETY-TWO

ALL CLEAR

E merging from behind the elm where he and Reverend Travis
had sheltered from the pig attack, Rabbi Baum went to check on
Hannah and Eli. Seeing that they were unharmed, he continued
on to his home in Beit Gibborim. Returning to Manny Kleinman Quad
with his shofar, he blew loud and comforting blasts. The peril is passed.
The children of Israel are saved. (Baum noticed that the shofar blasts
seemed strangely muted. Like most people who were on campus for the
pig invasion, it would take a few days for his hearing to return to normal.)

Emerging from behind or within other buildings, and from behind
trees and bushes and from everywhere else where they, sheltered or
not, had witnessed and experienced the pig attack, dozens of students,
teachers, and staff—most exhilarated, a few still frightened, a few
both—harkened to the shofar's blasts.

A cloud of acrid black smoke hung over Leopold Hirszfeld Hall.
Walking with Barbara away from it, Jeff found Preston Tom heading
back to the dining hall. Jerome, who had been patrolling the campus
in his golf cart after leaving stiff-necked Cherev by the western fence,
joined them. Jerome gave Jeff a preliminary damage report: A section
of the lacrosse stadium's bleachers knocked down. Also, a hundred feet
of fence. There's a ginormous pig sleeping in the dining hall. Three of
Strong East Wind's burned-out fans had come unbolted from the roof
and fallen to the ground, luckily without falling on anyone.

And Cherev? Jerome said, "Still dug in. If no one tells them it's over, they might stay till the Messiah comes."

The campus, blazing with light, seemed bathed in quiet. A delicious, mind-soothing quiet. Continuing to walk the campus with Barbara, coming upon dozens of students and teachers and staff, Jeff exuded the calm and confidence called for. He told everyone the peril is past. He told the students: go to your dorms, go to bed, go to sleep. He told the houseparents: head count now! And he prayed for a full count.

Returning from Partridge Ridge Country Club, all the students, teachers, and staff who had spent the attack there mingled with their counterparts who had experienced the attack on campus, and exchanged stories. Of course the people who had experienced it on campus had far better stories, but their hearing wasn't as good as their off-campus colleagues.

Continuing to walk the campus with Barbara, Jeff came upon Jordan and Jose. He didn't ask his daughter where she had been the last six hours—back in Partridge Ridge Country Club? Off somewhere with Jose? He just hugged her. And he told her, go to bed.

Receiving a phone call from Emmitt Bailey, Jeff was pleased to learn that all thousand pigs were back in Emmitt's CAFO. He told Emmitt that Big Bob was asleep in the school's dining hall, and Emmitt said he'd come right over with his tow truck. Jeff apologized for the trouble that Emmitt had suffered, and said, "I hope it didn't have you up and running after the pigs."

Emmitt said, "No, I've mostly been sitting here with one of your students."

Continuing to walk the campus with Barbara, Jeff was confronted by Ella Bronstein, who peppered him with questions. Jeff told Ella, tomorrow. And, go to bed. He was also confronted by Celine Johnson, who started telling him dozens of students were traumatized. Exuding calm and confidence, he told Celine: "Don't worry." (But he knew this time she was right.)

Emerging from the woods through which they had driven the thousand pigs, the six sloshed swineherds were greeted by some students as heroes and by all teachers as miscreants. Coming upon Stan Pincus and posse, Jeff told them: go to your dorms, go to bed, go to sleep. The Sanhedrin meets Monday afternoon; tomorrow, find yourself a defense counsel.

Aware that in many places there was fresh, moist pig shit underfoot, Jeff was not surprised to be confronted by Rabbi Baum, who held forth on why this had happened. Why? "Because HAHA has failed to be a true Torah school! The work of the seven Pig Platke-Machers—the pig troublemakers—is Hashem's message. The entire campus has become *tamé*, impure! It all must be purified! Must be! I will search the Talmud and the Commentaries for the proper means."

Jeff said, "Thank you, please make everything *taharah*, pure, again. ASAP." Jeff pondered—quite aside from what Baum would do—how to get the pig shit removed by commencement, which was only eight days away.

Coming upon Barbara and Jeff, Reverend Travis congratulated his niece. He said he understood that she had saved the school. "You are the heroine! Your giant fans! Your Twelve Tribes of Israel! I will make this the centerpiece of my sermon tomorrow morning."

But of course it was already Sunday morning. It was two a.m. Barbara told Jeff, "I'd better go home. I'm ready for bed and for sleep." Jeff promised to take her home as soon as he took care of the last and largest pig left on campus.

He met Emmitt Bailey and two of Jerome's men at the dining hall. Big Bob was still asleep, snoring mightily. Jerome, his men, and Emmitt shoved and dragged the eight-hundred-twelve-pound pig outside. There, Emmitt wrapped a harness around Big Bob, attached his tow truck's hook to the harness, and he and Jerome's men got Big Bob up into the truck. Emmitt drove away.

Only then did Tzipora emerge from the kitchen, her face tear-streamed, a small book of psalms in her hand, her lips moving in prayers of gratitude with more fervor than she had ever before felt.

Driving Barbara home, Jeff texted all houseparents: *Let all the kids sleep late.*

And Jeff sent an email to all students, teachers, staff and, especially, all students' parents—in other words, The Beast. He made the subject line: ALL PIGS GONE, ALL PEOPLE SAFE. In his email, he reassured everyone: "The only pig left on campus is in a book in the children's section of the school library: Winnie-the-Pooh's friend, Piglet."

NINETY-THREE

PURIFICATION

At eight a.m. Sunday, Jeff woke the seven swineherds. He told Stan Pincus, Aaron Fabrikant, Jonathan Bloch, Mike Tarnovsky, Peter Altman, David Chafetz, and Stu Gilford, "Here's how you're going to spend today. You dry out all the pig shit and shovel it all into garbage bags. Aaron, you've got a sprained ankle, you're still working. The other guys work the heaters, the rakes, and the shovels—you hobble around with the garbage bags."

When the seven boys winced and emitted a few moans, Jeff reminded them, "The Sanhedrin meets tomorrow. What you do today might buy you some mercy. Might."

Unspoken: For what the seven had done, the judgment should be expulsion. If expelled, they could petition to return in January, the start of the second semester of the next school year. But in January, the school would not exist. And six of the seven—all except Aaron Fabrikant—were seniors, bound for college this September. Notified they had been expelled, colleges would rescind their admissions.

Jeff was not going to let that happen. But the seven didn't know that; getting dressed fast, they went to work with the heaters, rakes, shovels, and garbage bags.

Then, on Manny Kleinman Quad, Jeff met up with Rabbi Baum.

Baum was in his mode of enforcer of ritual purity: "Jeff, the dining hall and the campus—everywhere the pigs trod—they have been infected by *tzaraat*, a spiritual malady, the inevitable consequence of our shortcomings. But Leviticus tells us how to cure it."

Jeff tried to remember Leviticus. It had so many ritual instructions.

Baum said, "Based on the verses, we may need to break down a small part of the dining hall wall."

Jeff said, "No. How about a creative solution? One that marks you as an up-and-coming Talmudist?"

Baum brightened. "Luckily, last night, in a dream, my Rebbe spoke to me. He told me of another way to clean the dining hall and the whole campus—a way that requires tearing down nothing."

"Great! What is it?"

"Certain prayers. Prayers found, my Rebbe said, only in a little-known medieval commentary. He spoke them to me and I have memorized them. Now I could speak them. In the dining hall and everywhere the pigs have trod."

"Please! Do it!"

"Um, Jeff. These are powerful prayers. The medieval commentary warns that speaking them puts the supplicant's life at risk. In good conscience—not for my sake, of course, but at the risk of leaving my dear Chava a widow—I cannot do this unless . . . "

"Unless?"

"There is something in return. Not for me, of course. But as a . . . um . . . insurance policy for Chava."

Jeff had enough to increase (again!) the rabbi's household budget. By an amount that Jeff and Baum worked out and shook on. As Baum headed toward the dining hall, Jeff watched him go with a kind of admiration. As when Preston Tom had negotiated the centrifuge out of Jeff in return for keeping quiet about the pork molecules, Jeff thought, *Rabbi, you played me like a pro.*

Now, to reassure The Beast. Jeff went to his office, but before he could email the community, Sammy stormed in.

Sammy told Jeff that he had mishandled the response to the pig attack, and that the Silicon Valley billionaire had just called, cancelling the meeting. "We won't be flying to San Francisco today, so you can stay here and clean up the mess the pigs made and the one you made."

Then Nurse Clara Glatt burst into his office.

She said, "Jeff, pig excrement all over! Some of it is also in the air. We are breathing it." Reaching into her hazmat-like outfit, she pulled out one of Preston's air monitors. And waved it in Jeff's face. "I found this on the ground, and, as Dean of Healthcare, it was my responsibility to have it analyzed. Every Jewish person here has been breathing pork molecules for months."

Jeff smiled. For months I've been worried about this getting out? Considering what we just dodged, I'm not going to sweat it.

Glatt's outburst was overheard by students and staff in the Admin lobby.

Five minutes later, Ella Bronstein was in Jeff's face:

"Mr. Taylor, I was supposed to have an exclusive on this!'

Jeff told Ella the pork molecules were a religious non-event. He offered to let her hear that directly from Rabbi Baum, whom Jeff had just summoned to his office by text.

But a distraught Ella walked out of the office without answering.

Moments after Ella left, Rabbi Baum sat down facing Jeff.

"Rabbi, those prayers cleaned up the air as well as the grounds and buildings, right?"

Jeff fixed his I-could-fire-you-face on Baum.

"Uh, right."

Thanking and dismissing the Rabbi, Jeff composed an email. He made its subject line: ENTIRE CAMPUS BEING RITUALLY PURIFIED. In the body of his email, he reassured everyone: "We can all breathe easy."

NINETY-FOUR
THE COURT IS NOT
IN SESSION

Monday morning.

To Jeff's relief, his clear-the-air email quieted The Beast. The Sanhedrin would be meeting today to consider the fate of the seven swineherds.

But since Jeff had final say over the Sanhedrin, and since the seven had thrown themselves into the clean-up with vigor and had removed all the pig shit, Jeff did something he had never done before: he threw out their case. But someone had to pay. And Jeff had, from Coach Bill and Jerome, the cost of restoring the smashed bleachers and fence. Coach Bill further demanded a penalty be added to cover the cost of having to cancel the HAHA invitational lacrosse tournament. Jeff thought that was reasonable. Finally, Barbara provided the cost of replacing *Strong East Wind's* burnt-out fans. Emailing and phoning each set of parents, the Head of School said, "You owe one-seventh of the following sum . . . due now."

Then he told the seven boys.

A moment ago, told they would not be facing the Sanhedrin, they had been hugely relieved. Now, knowing their parents were about to come down on them . . .

Jeff left them to their emotions.

NINETY-FIVE

TROUBLE COMES
IN THREES?

C runch time: commencement in six days, May 30. Could the more than two hundred attending relatives be accommodated without prom-like surprises?

The weather forecast looked good. As for the emotional weather on May 30 . . . impossible to forecast.

Where was Samantha Kleinman in all this? Sammy couldn't be bothered with details. "I handle the big picture." But of course if something went wrong on commencement, some "i" undotted, some "t" uncrossed, Sammy would blame Jeff.

The end of the day Sammy announced, "Big-picture trip," and, with her rolling suitcase, she disappeared into an Uber to the airport.

Fine, Sammy, enjoy your top-secret trip.

Jeff left his office and went back to his house to read the last of the Parochet emails.

Now he was up to April 29. At the rate he had been going, tonight he could read through May 4 and be done. Great! But not so great. Because now there were so few messages left. So few in which he might find the message he was sure he had read before, the message in the rhythm of the May fifth bomb threat.

Playing the May fifth recording, he started reading. The emails were mind-numbingly banal.

Jeff despaired. He had now re-read almost every single Parochet message between January second and May fifth, all six thousand of them. Such effort! And such futility! Yes, thanks to the thumb drive from Stevie, he had been able to attach a name to each of the nearly six thousand—but so what. He had learned who the real weirdos were, the kids who, everywhere they looked, saw conspiracies and paranormal activity.

But *so what?*

I've failed, thought Jeff. I thought that if I could identify the May fifth caller, I could, in good conscience, tell Sammy, *Come June 21, I'm outta here.*

I'm still stuck. All the way to bankruptcy on July 15?

He was now re-re-reading the May fourth messages.

The first one stopped him. It was from Eli Margulies, Shark Boy. Jeff read *Hey, Mr. Taylor, what's the deal? The kids keep making fun of me. Please tell them stop.*

Playing the May fifth bomb threat, Jeff read it again, then took a pen and notated it the way he had learned years ago in high school English class. Unstressed syllable, stressed syllable, unstressed syllable, stressed syllable . . .

Yes!

While Eli's message didn't rhyme, its iambic meter and its length exactly matched the May fifth bomb threat: "Hey, understand / Get off that land / Hey, Jews, make room / Or things go boom! / I got a bomb."

Eli Margulies was the culprit? He complained on the fourth, and the next day he lashed out?

And Eli had also called in the March seventh bomb threat? As Jeff recalled, it also was iambic.

Damn!

Jeff was angry at the kid. And Jeff felt sad for the kid. Because, these last few weeks, Eli had seemed a different kid from the one who had been so alienated. Prom night, Eli had been a hero; he saved Hannah Newins from the pigs. And as Shark Boy, Eli had just given a Project Ruach talk on tolerance for kids who seem strange. The talk had gone so well that, with Eli's permission, Stevie had sent the video to the HAHA community.

But how can we know for *sure* if Eli is the culprit? Well, the FBI has audio experts, right? Experts who can match voices. Match the recording of the May fifth bomb threat with the Project Ruach recording.

Jeff called Jerome and explained his suspicions. He asked, "I've emailed you Eli's Project Ruach speech. Can the FBI compare Eli's voice to the May fifth bomb threat? The bomb threat was made through a distorter but . . . "

"I bet they can," said Jerome. "You really think it's Eli?" He sighed. "My, that's sad."

Jeff said, "I'm pretty sure it's Eli."

That was how Tuesday ended for Jeff. On Wednesday morning he returned the thumb drive to Stevie. "Did you find it?" asked Stevie. Jeff gave a non-committal shrug. He said, "Thanks for letting me try. And, like I said when I started, we keep this between ourselves. It never happened."

Then, thinking about student heroics on prom night, Jeff had an idea.

Going to his office, he phoned a woman he knew in Princeton's Admissions Office. He said, "Ashley Friedlander. I know you guys rejected her and I'm sure, based on her application, you had good reasons. You probably know she's a talented cinematographer, and she will be sending you soon a dramatic video of something that happened here three days ago. But what her documentary doesn't show is that Ashley risked her life to save twenty of her classmates from one thousand marauding pigs. Yes, she kept her wits in a middle of a crisis and, disregarding her own safety, sprang into action . . . "

On Wall Street, at Rose & Company, Jeff had learned that to sell a prospect on a deal nothing beats a good story, especially if the story is true; especially if the truth can be gently enhanced.

His good feeling lasted the rest of the morning. Handing the six seniors in his Jewish Thought and Culture class a final exam (the three juniors would get theirs in three weeks), Jeff anticipated giving them marks that would gently enhance their transcripts. Nothing less than A-minuses.

Right after lunch, he gave himself an A for Acceptance as the crew that had installed Barbara's *Strong East Wind* atop Leopold Hirszfeld Hall came and installed her *I Saw Another Butterfly* right outside his office.

After dinner, walking back across the campus, heading home, Jeff's phone rang.

It was Jerome: "Jeff, I've just learned. In Atlantic City. At a casino. At the craps tables. Arrested for indecent exposure. Irving Knipel."

Jeff stood rooted, stunned. There goes my commencement speaker. Two troubles looming.

And this thought intruded: *Trouble comes in threes.*

Nonsense. Bubbe-meise—just nonsense.

Then Jeff heard, approaching, that telltale *squeak-squeak-squeak*. The wheels of Sammy Kleinman's rolling suitcase. And that telltale *click-click-click*. Sammy's Christian Louboutin heels. Sammy is back.

"Jeff!" said Sammy. She was Ms. Enthusiastic. "Jeff, I had a *great* trip. We've got a *great* commencement coming up. And right after the ceremonies and lunch, right here"—Sammy tossed her head of salon blow-dried-out blonde hair at the Admin building—"in the conference room, a meeting of the Board of Directors."

What? The Board had never met on campus. Never in the twenty-two months that Jeff had been here, never—as far as he knew—in all the years that Sammy had been CEO.

A Board meeting here for *what?*

NINETY-SIX

LEAKY HAHA

*T*he Head is Big Brother! The Head is an asshole!

Jeff knew everything leaked at HAHA; nothing stayed secret amid the campus's many spying eyes, listening ears, and telltale lips. Had someone been watching when he returned the thumb drive to Stevie in front of Beit Rashi? (But no one could have known what was on the thumb drive.) Had Stevie told Meadow their secret and been overheard? Perhaps Jeff would eventually learn how his unmasking the Parochet emailers had itself been unmasked. But it hardly mattered now.

Now, this Friday morning, he was stunned by the ferocity of the attack on him. It made the pig stampede seem orderly.

From parents, teachers, staff, and students came phone calls, emails, and texts blasting him for having violated the sanctity of parochet@ haha.org. Now that group, including some parents who lived close enough, were crowding into his office and blasting him in person.

In many languages and in many colorful phrases, their message was the same: *You went too far.*

The Beast was aroused as never before.

Jeff couldn't understand the virulence of his critics. Yes, he had violated a principle. But for a *greater* principle. In law school, he had learned the famous observation that the Constitution is not a suicide pact. Now he mentally added, Nor are the rules that govern Hampton

Acres Hebrew Academy. One of the attacks on him demanded *Did you get anything out of your violation?*—and Jeff wanted to snap back *F**king right I did! I found the culprit!*

But he couldn't say this. He had to wait for confirmation from the FBI.

Still, did no one see that he had done this to protect the school?!

Apparently not.

What everyone believed in was the sanctity of the parochet. For the parochet is not just the curtain in a synagogue that covers the Torah Ark. It was originally the curtain that covered the entrance to the Holy of Holies in the Jerusalem Temple, which only the high priest could enter once a year. No Jew dared to violate it.

Thus what The Beast *roared* for was that Jeff Taylor don sackcloth and ashes and grovel before The Beast.

Not going to do that, thought Jeff. And once everyone learns I found the culprit, they'll thank me. I'll be vindicated.

In phone calls, emails, and in texts, and in person to the crowd—no, the mob—pressing into his office, he stood clothed in jacket and tie and he stood tall. He explained, defended, even pushed back. Did everything except say "It's Eli!"

Hardly anyone was having it.

Rabbi Baum said, "God is telling you something. You need to shrink yourself. *Bitul*, Jeff. Negate the ego."

Sammy said, "If commencement weren't Monday, I'd cut you loose. Your approval rating is in the toilet."

Rachel said, "It's just what I expected. The privileged white male thinks rules are for others."

As for the students:

Waving her smartphone, showing Jeff the editorial she had just written for *The Lamp*, Ella Bronstein quoted, "This is a betrayal of trust that goes beyond—" She broke off. She said, "Mr. Taylor, we had a deal. I've been holding off on running stories in return for you keeping me in the loop. I *trusted* you."

At noon, *The Lamp* came out with a one-page special edition. Across the top:

HEAD OF SCHOOL BETRAYS SCHOOL

Further down the page were headlines that, any other Friday, would be across the top:

COMMENCEMENT SPEAKER ARRESTED

And . . .

BOARD MEETS HERE MONDAY
WHY?

At noon Jeff got in his car, drove off campus, found a quiet spot, and started writing notes for what he would say at Shabbat dinner.

Normally, Shabbat dinner brought together HAHA's one hundred and forty-five students and twenty or so of its teachers and staff. But because this was commencement weekend, this Shabbat dinner would also include the more than two hundred relatives. And because everyone would want to see what the accused Head would do here, Jeff knew that almost all one hundred teachers and staff would be here.

In all, more than four hundred people would come for dinner.

Come for my blood, thought Jeff.

Early that afternoon, Jeff returned to campus and found it bustling with the first wave of the seniors' relatives. Ignoring some cold looks, he continued attending to the details of commencement. About which he felt pretty good except—big exception—he had no commencement speaker.

Then . . . it was dusk. Time to bring in Shabbat.

Inside the Beit Am: more than four hundred people stood in a circle around Jeff. Hors d'oeuvres had been eaten. Now the main course would be served: Rack of Head of School.

Standing next to Jeff, acting as emcee, was Ella Bronstein. Almost everyone here had read Ella's editorial in the special edition of *The Lamp*, her editorial stretching and breaking Jeff Taylor on a Procrustean bed of righteousness.

"And now," said Ella coldly, "a few words from Mr. Taylor."

Handing him the mic, she left the inner ring of people who encircled Jeff. Jeff was now alone.

He met the cold eyes of the people in the inner ring and chose not to look beyond them. Well, he thought, here goes . . .

He said, "As you know, it is a principle of Jewish law that saving a human life overrides virtually every other religious rule. When life is at stake, almost any command to not do an action becomes inapplicable. And while I didn't believe that the bomb threats to this school—and to the lives of everyone here at this school—were real, I could not, as Head, shirk the responsibility of doing all I could to identify the person making those threats. If my actions have offended anyone here—"

"Damn right they have!" A man's voice from an outer ring.

Jeff kept going with his classic non-apology apology. One learned the formula watching public figures answer accusations of everything from unwanted sexual advances to non-Woke slips of the tongue. Reading the faces of the parents, he felt he was gaining. Parents lived in the real world, and knew that sometimes some principles had to be sacrificed to other principles. But reading the faces of the students, he was still losing. Especially with the seniors. They had finished school. They didn't have to be as respectful to him as, just one week ago, they had had to be. But Jeff kept going . . .

" . . . Rabbi Baum would tell you that in judging another, that person's *kavanah*—the sincere direction of his or her heart—must be considered. Rabbi Baum would tell you that because my sincere intention was to . . . "

As Jeff said this, he eyed Baum, dared Baum to contradict him . . .

" . . . save lives . . . "

"MIERDA!" This from deep in the crowd, from a Mexican student, probably a senior, thought Jeff. Spanish for bullshit.

" . . . and because I sincerely believed that, in the emails to parochet@haha.org, I had read language similar to the language of the bomb threats . . . "

"CHUSH'SOBACH'YA!" This also from deep in the crowd. From whom? Jeff had no idea. And he had never before heard the phrase. But it had to be Russian for bullshit.

Peering deep into the crowd, unable to link the insult with any Russian student, Jeff's eyes lit on someone else. Someone wearing a plastic shark on his head. Jeff wanted to yell, *It's not bullshit! It led me to the culprit. There! It's Eli Margulies! He's the one who's betrayed our school!*

But the plaster *Tzadik* had to bite his tongue. What Jeff actually said was . . .

" . . . I felt I had no alternative but to search . . . "

Jeff kept going. Finally, after about another minute, trying to find some ringing language that would sway the undecideds, he stopped.

He handed the mic back to Ella.

Who gave him a cold, "Thank you."

To Jeff's surprise, Ella let it go at that. He thought, She's saving her rebuttal for the next special edition of *The Lamp.*

Then students lit the Shabbat candles and said the blessing, initiating a time of rest, peace, and harmony.

Amen!

NINETY-SEVEN
SECRETS

Saturday night, Barbara had Jeff over to dinner. As they were drinking wine with their appetizers, Emmitt Bailey phoned Jeff. "Jeff, my new gas-fired heaters. I'm getting readings saying they've brought the CO_2 concentrations way down. Check your gauges. I think any molecules from my pigs—they're below detection."

"Thank you, Emmitt. You've been a kind and patient neighbor." Jeff paused. He thought, What the hell. "Say, Emmitt, day after tomorrow, Monday around noon, you doing anything in particular . . . ?"

Sunday, back on campus, Jeff was pleased there were fewer seniors' relatives to deal with. Many were taking in the local sights. In the absence of many relatives, Jeff more easily concentrated on rehearsing the ceremony. The six marshals (six responsible-looking juniors) and six teachers are stationed *here* . . . the marshals and the teachers will escort our guests in *like so* . . . then the forty-one graduates will march in *like so* . . .

And so on.

He was interrupted by Sammy demanding, "*Who*, Jeff? No Irving Knipel, so who did you invite?"

"A friend of the school," said Jeff, smiling.

Jeff thought, You have your secret for tomorrow—why a Board meeting here?—and I have mine. "Now, Sammy, would you let me please continue with the rehearsal?"

Resuming the rehearsal managed to keep Jeff's mind off the mystery of Sammy's trip. Where had she been? And did Sammy's trip have anything to do with the Board meeting?

NINETY-EIGHT
A CHAIR RESERVED
FOR . . . WHOM?

Memorial Day. Monday morning.

So here we are, thought Jeff, commencement. On Emmanuel Kleinman Quad, five hundred folding chairs had been set up facing a stage. On stage: the American and Israeli flags on flagpoles, a lectern, and six chairs, at the moment, 10:30 a.m., a half-hour before the ceremonies would begin, all six empty. Why six? One was for Jeff as Head of School, one for Rabbi Baum as Dean of Jewish Life, one for Rachel Fish as Dean of the Faculty, one for Sammy as CEO, one for the commencement speaker . . .

But there were *six* chairs on the stage. Who was the *sixth* chair for? An hour ago, when Jeff saw the chairs for the first time, he asked Isaac Greene—who was in charge of this—why six? Isaac had said, "Ms. Kleinman told me set up six." So Jeff had immediately found and cornered the lady. "Who, Sammy? Who's the sixth chair for?"

Jeff got what he had half-expected. From Sammy a smug grin and, "Honey, I'll tell you what you told me: a friend of the school."

From many of the parents, though, Jeff was getting no grins. Rather quite a few cold stares from some of the relatives still upset about Parochet.

Sammy! thought Jeff. *I* shouldn't be greeting the parents; *you* should be.

This is Sammy's element. This is the place for Sammy the glad-hander, to try wheedling a few more dollars (or pesos or rubles) out of the parents.

Sammy should be doing this, especially after the Parochet fallout. Where the hell is she?

Taking a break from yet another cold handshake, Jeff turned and looked back at the stage.

And got his answer about the sixth chair.

A large man and a svelte woman were walking up the three steps onto the stage. On the first step, resplendent in an academic gown that resembled Joseph's coat of many colors, was Sammy. Just ahead of Sammy (with Sammy the sycophant gesturing *Of course, your Greatness, you go first*), waddling, hefting his great bulk from the top step onto the stage, was . . .

Seymour Gutfreund.

NINETY-NINE
WITH THE WHALE AMONG US, WE CAN COMMENCE

The white whale! The gaming emperor!

Gutfreund's presence explained Sammy's mysterious trip middle of last week: Sammy had gone to Vegas to secure the whale. But it raised a bigger question:

Why is Gutfreund here?

To part with maybe twenty-five million? And Sammy has someone else for the other twenty-five million. And thus save the school?

Now Jeff understood why Sammy was not down here gladhanding relatives. Sammy had a more vital mission: cling to the side of the billionaire like a leech. Or, since real whales have barnacles, cling like a barnacle.

Turning back to the relatives, Jeff noted that a few of them seemed to have also recognized Sammy's guest. Excellent, thought Jeff. Now, you can be distracted from asking *What is Jeffrey Taylor doing here?* Instead, you can ask, *What is Seymour Gutfreund doing here?*

Soon, whatever they were asking, all the families were seated.

Taking his own seat on the stage, Jeff said hello to Gutfreund and shook the man's damp, fleshy hand. Thanking him again for the three million, Jeff said, "It's made today possible." As Rachel and Baum were now also seated, Jeff exchanged pleasantries with them.

While Baum was in his standard plain black suit, broad-brimmed black hat and dark tie, Rachel was preening in her NYU gown, purple with—for her PhD—gold piping. And now, as the rest of the faculty filed in, Jeff saw it as a grand procession of pride. Evaluating each other's academic gowns, the teachers cast envious and scornful looks. What colors, what stripes, signifying what heritage, what achievement? Greater than mine? Less than mine?

They sat. Now, except for the graduates, everyone was here.

Time to be the Head.

Jeff rose, went to the lectern, tapped the mic, got a reassuring noise, and announced, "We will sing the American National Anthem." He nodded to a junior girl. "Deborah Ehrenreich will lead us."

Everyone rose. Deborah sang. The Americans joined in. The families of foreign students looked respectful.

"And now," said Jeff, "Hatikvah, the National Anthem of Israel."

Deborah sang. The previously quiet foreigners sang loudly.

"And now," said Jeff, "Hampton Acres Hebrew Academy proudly welcomes this year's graduates."

Over huge speakers, "Pomp and Circumstance" blared and, to enthusiastic applause, HAHA's forty-one cap-and-gowned graduates marched in. Their relatives went way beyond enthusiastic; they broke out in wild, our-team-won-the-Super-Bowl cheering. Most of the graduates tried to look solemn, a few grinned goofily. The Hammerin' Hebe ran alongside them, theatrically swinging his mallet and shouting "Make way!" Drawing laughs, the foam-armored mascot kept the relatives at bay, allowing the seniors to take their reserved seats up front.

"And now," said Jeff, "Rabbi Benjamin Baum . . . "

Baum rose and intoned the shehecheyanu prayer, first in Hebrew, then in English. Then Baum read a short letter from his Rebbe praising the value of a Jewish education.

As Baum read, Jeff pondered Gutfreund's presence. *Is he in for the whole fifty million?*

Baum sat and Jeff rose again, to deliver a brief "Welcome, every-one" talk. As he uttered his very first words—"We gather on this glorious spring day to celebrate . . . "—first three, then four more, then five more graduates rose. A dozen protesters. Half of them turned their backs on him. The other half silently held up signs. DROP THE EAVESDROPPER . . . SEND THE HEAD TO THE SANHEDRIN . . . A TAYLOR-MADE BETRAYAL.

Lucky me, thought Jeff, only twelve out of the forty-one. The real Sanhedrin required a majority to impose the death sentence.

All Jeff could do was soldier on. Such a contrast between now and a year ago: the previous commencement, his first at HAHA. Then, although he was already frustrated with the school, he had still been hopeful. And the faces in the crowd at that commencement had said, We believe in you.

Following Baum's praise of Jewish education with a plug of his own, Jeff finished with, "And so our graduates will pursue worldly success while, we hope, devoting their lives to the Jewish values they have learned here."

On that, he proceeded to the awards.

Welcoming each recipient onto the stage, Jeff announced each award and handed it out. He mixed the serious awards (The Richard Feynman Medal for Science . . . The Greta Thunberg Award for Environmental Activism) with the awards he had created, just so everyone would have one (The Jerry Seinfeld Award for Humor . . . The Faculty Award for Knowing Everything). Handing out the new awards, Jeff feared someone in the audience would snigger.

No one did. Everyone applauded all the honored recipients.

Since several awards went to some of the dozen graduates who had stood and rebuked him, Jeff handed them out with qualms. Would one or more graduates refuse to come up? Refuse to shake his hand?

No one did.

Then Sammy rose to give the last two awards. Of course, thought Jeff, everyone has to be a warm-up act for Samantha Kleinman.

First, The Manny Kleinman Award for Visionary Leadership. It was a small-scale duplicate of the bronze bust of Manny in the conference room. "My father's vision," intoned Sammy, "is today embodied in . . . " and she presented it to Daniel Garelick, who had earned it by most conspicuously, for the last four years, sucking up to Sammy.

Then, The Manny and Malka Kleinman Award for Lifetime Achievement Supporting Jewish Education. Carried onstage by two of HAHA's biggest junior boys, it was a plaque the size of a Ford F-150 tailgate. Of course, as far as Jeff knew, the winner, Seymour Gutfreund, had never done anything for any Jewish school until three weeks ago when he gave HAHA three million dollars. But Sammy praised Gutfreund with words as substantial as the magnate's gut. Gutfreund then hauled that gut out of his chair. Accepting the plaque (but letting the two boys hold it), the sweating casino tycoon kept his thanks short—"I had to see for myself whether your campus is as beautiful as the pictures—it is!"—and sat back down. His three hundred pounds didn't like to have to stand.

Why is Gutfreund here? Jeff toggled back and forth between "to give maybe twenty-five million" and "to give the whole fifty million." And it struck Jeff that the answer might even be "to give seventy million"—and thus not only save the school, but also enrich Sammy.

Jeff marveled. Sammy! I underestimated you! I'm the goat here today (the scapegoat,) and you're the GOAT (Greatest Of All Time). You didn't use smoke and mirrors on the whale; you used a rocket-propelled harpoon.

I am in awe.

Two big junior boys carried off the giant plaque.

Then Rachel rose and, as Dean of the Faculty, saying "on behalf of the faculty," more or less—Jeff thought—subtly took credit for everything. Credit for everything that all the graduates and all the other HAHA students had done and ever would do. Rachel Fish's brand was "I despise hierarchy." Jeff noted that when it suited her, Rachel Fish, PhD. NYU, gloried in being a big Fish in a small pond.

Done praising herself, Rachel sat.

Now Sammy took the lectern and delivered a serious talk quoting Maimonides, Jefferson, Heschel, and Ben-Gurion. It reminded everyone that, while she might be a ferocious fundraiser, Samantha Kleinman had gravitas. It received proper applause. Sammy sat down.

Jeff observed that Sammy, having bagged Gutfreund, having delivered a serious talk, and having correctly pronounced "Maimonides," was now as happy as a pre-teen Jewish girl who, on a single day, has enjoyed Hanukkah *and* a mani-pedi, *and* (shooting guard on her middle school team) has hit the game-winning shot.

But glowing Sammy was not glowing at Jeff. Turning to him, she said, "Okay, you see who I brought. So who's the mysterious commencement speaker?"

Jeff smiled, went to the lectern.

He told the assembly, "They say good fences make good neighbors. Well, as you all know, on a recent night, we learned our fences weren't so good. But that same night, we learned our neighbor is terrific. With a heart full of compassion, he has forgiven our school for the thoughtless prank played on him, a prank that could have seriously damaged his business. For this man, our neighbor, is a shepherd and a spiritual descendant of Abel. In his long life he has learned much and today he will impart some of that wisdom to us. Therefore, Hampton Acres Hebrew Academy is proud to grant him an honorary diploma, and to welcome him here, to this lectern, to deliver the commencement address . . . "

Jeff paused. He saw, through the assembly, a buzz had been growing. *Can't be? Not the pig farmer!*

And behind him, from Samantha Kleinman, a screech: "Jeff! You can't *do* this!"

Ignoring the buzz, and ignoring the gapes from Baum and Rachel, Jeff waved a Come-on-up-here to the last row. And Emmitt Bailey, in his best Sunday-go-to-church suit, walked up the aisle past disbelieving parents, faculty, and graduates, and stepped onto the stage.

ONE HUNDRED
WISDOM SLOWLY GAINED AND SLOWLY DISPENSED

Jeff shook Emmitt's hand and read from a diploma. "Whereby Emmitt Charles Bailey has been and is a good neighbor to us, Hampton Acres Hebrew Academy hereby confers upon him an honorary diploma with all rights and benefits thereunto."

Saying "Congratulations," Jeff handed him the diploma.

Emmitt managed a shy and barely audible, "Thank you."

Stepping aside and sitting down, Jeff gestured *All yours* at the lectern. Emmitt nodded, went to it. From inside his suit jacket, he took a many-times-folded piece of lined paper, unfolded it, set it on the lectern and . . .

. . . froze.

Come on! From his seat, Jeff silently, intently, urgently urged. *You can do this.*

Jeff had zero idea what *this* was. Four days ago, agreeing to this, Emmitt had said, "Um, yes, I'll say a few things, lemme work on it . . ."

Into Jeff's right ear Sammy was already saying more than a few things. In Russian and what Jeff guessed might be Tajiki, a stream of curses that Sammy had acquired hondling with cab drivers and bazaar merchants on her countless recruiting trips.

On the faces of many graduates were smirks.

Finally, Emmitt seemed to gather himself.

He cleared his throat. He spoke into the mic.

"Ladies and gentlemen . . . "

If Sacha Reznick was a *bullettrainspeaker*, Emmitt was his polar opposite. "La . . . dies . . . and . . . gen . . . tle . . . men" took forever to come out. And what followed—"I'm very honored that . . . "—came out no faster.

Jeff wondered if the audience would have the patience for this. But *I invited the guy. For good or bad—and if it's really bad, I'm in the shit that Sammy is promising me in seven different tongues—I'm listening.*

Emmitt began:

"I'm very honored that you asked me to be here to today and share my thoughts with you. I don't know much about this school or—now I mean you seniors, you graduates—or about you. But I'm guessing you are in a hurry. A hurry to get somewhere, to succeed. And I'm guessing your parents are in a hurry for you to do that. Maybe so they can stop supporting you?"

From many parents in the audience, gentle laughter. Jeff smiled.

Emmitt continued:

"And I agree that speed *can* be good.

"Like it says in the Bible, before the Pharaoh could stop them, the Israelites got away. Because 'thou camest forth out of the land in Egypt in haste,' that's why on Passover you eat no leavened bread, why you have matzahs.

"But the Bible also says it can be good to slow down. At Jericho, the Lord made the sun stand still and the moon stand still—hey, that's *really* slowing things down—so Joshua and the rest of the Israelites had time to win.

"And today, in this busy world, I think slowing down can be a good thing. I raise livestock. And I know you can't rush raising animals. Like right now, I've got a heifer who may or may not be with calf. If she is, that calf is going to develop inside in its own good time. I can't rush its life along.

"And I don't rush my life along. I'm seventy-two. I want to savor what time I have left. I urge the same on you.

"Slow down. Savor things. Yes, right now, probably you're in a hurry. But take it from me, in ten, twenty years, you'll blink and you'll say where did the time go? Twenty years, thirty years, forty years. In a blink.

"Ask your parents and your grandparents—they'll tell you I'm right."

Eyeing his audience, Emmitt asked, "Am I right?"

From parents and grandparents, murmurs of agreement. Jeff smiled. Emmitt continued:

"And they'll tell you they wish they had some of that time back. So take it now. Slow down to savor things. And slow down to do things right.

"It's like baseball. A pitcher shakes off one sign from the catcher, he shakes off another. If he agrees too fast, if he throws a pitch he really doesn't believe—*wham!*—the batter hits it out of the park. But if the pitcher takes his time, more likely he gets the batter out.

"And it's like caning a chair, weaving a seat. You don't run your cane just back and forth, left to right and right to left—like so."

To show "like so," Emmitt held up his left hand, fingers together, pointing horizontally.

"That won't make a strong seat. You also take the time to weave cane across that cane—like so—up and down and down and up."

To show "like so," Emmitt held up his right hand, fingers together, pointing up, across the fingers of his left hand.

"And then take more time to weave diagonally. Like so." Emmitt indicated. "A six-way pattern. Takes longer, makes it stronger. Same way you should weave your life.

"Job says, 'My days are swifter than a weaver's shuttle, and are spent without hope.' I say don't use a shuttle. Weave by hand. Your hands will take their own good time.

"Mainly, I urge you to take your time in getting to know people.

Before you decide to go to work for someone. Or before you decide to go into business with someone. Before you decide to trust someone. Like Job should never have trusted his three comforters—they led him astray. Especially take your time before you decide to marry someone. Getting to really know someone takes time.

"And if you ever lose someone—and you will—getting over that loss takes time. Time heals all wounds. But only time does—nothing else. And take it from someone who's seventy-two, you will be wounded."

Jeff heard Michelle say, *Jeff, give yourself time.*

Emmitt continued:

"As Ecclesiastes says, 'To every thing there is a season.' And that includes 'a time to plant and a time to pluck up that which is planted.' Maybe you think that after your time here—where your teachers have planted learning in you—that you can rush and start plucking up. Okay, you can pluck up *some.* But you still need more time to plant more learning. Take that time. Learn more. And when you do pluck up, don't jam all that plucking down in your mouth all at once. Take *time* to savor it.

"Act in haste, repent at leisure. I urge you, act slow. Or, as we say around here, don't always be as busy as a moth in a mitten. Sometimes, take things as long as a month of Sundays."

Emmitt added, "Thank you."

From the assembly: a stunned silence. Then mounting applause.

Turning around, Emmitt smiled shyly at Jeff and, as Jeff pointed to the chair reserved for him, took it. With obvious relief.

Reclaiming the lectern, Jeff thanked Emmitt and announced, "And now the moment you've been waiting for . . . " and turned the lectern over to Rachel.

Alphabetically calling on the forty-one graduates, calling each one's name in English and in Hebrew, Rachel welcomed each to the stage. Here, Jeff shook hands and handed each an impressive nine-by-twelve-inch envelope. Each graduate was so pleased and proud that nobody remembered to glare at him. And the relatives went wild, crazy, and rushed to embrace the graduates and jostled for angles to snap photo after photo.

From many relatives Jeff heard, "Open the envelope . . . Let's see your diploma!"

As he knew they would, the graduates pretended not to hear. For they knew that inside was a "diploma" with their name but otherwise blank: no official seal of the school, no date, and no signatures by Sammy and Jeff. Also a letter saying, "You will receive an authentic diploma once you have satisfied all outstanding obligations"—meaning, once your parents have paid every penny they owe HAHA.

Sammy had found this was the only way to get some parents to pay. Sammy, who operated on smoke and mirrors, knew how to out-maneuver people when they tried to do the same.

Then, as "Pomp and Circumstance" again thundered, the forty-one graduates, gripping their envelopes, marched out, and threw their caps in the air.

And Jeff noted, amid the joyous pandemonium, in the very last row of chairs, Barbara giving him a nod and thumbs-up.

The only person here today who still likes me.

I like you, said Michelle.

ONE HUNDRED-ONE
TWO METAPHORICAL BOMBSHELLS

After the commencement ceremony, lunch.

In the dining hall, Jeff sat at a table amid a clutch of graduates' relatives from Mexico, Israel, and various central Asian "Stans." These parents and grandparents hung on his every word. Had they not fully absorbed, from their young progeny, the news of Jeff's betrayal? Or, regardless of his betrayal, since this was their first time in the States, did they so much want to be close to the Head of School? In either case, they paid him rapt attention. Jeff was telling them, "While standardized tests are still important, we try not to teach to the tests . . . "

. . . when Jerome appeared at Jeff's side and leaned down and softly said, "Jeff, a word with you?"

Excusing himself, Jeff rose, and walked with Jerome a few feet away from any table.

"Yes?" said Jeff.

Jeff was eager. He thought, This is it! The report from the FBI audio experts! Yes, they've confirmed it *is* Eli Margulies!

Jerome said, "We've learned who called in the last bomb threat."

"Right! Right!"

"I got a call from an old FBI buddy in the Las Vegas office. There's a place on Fremont Street that the office has under surveillance. Called The Spy Store. Lots of stuff to make you think you're James Bond."

"So . . . ?"

"Gadgets like burner phones. Mobile phones with a temporary, disposable phone number. You make a couple of calls, you throw the phone away, nobody can trace it to you."

Right! thought Jeff. So Eli used a burner phone. But wait! Eli bought a burner phone in Las Vegas? Well, okay, so he bought it online and the Spy Store mailed it to him.

Jerome continued: "They also sell voice distorters. Apps."

Right! thought Jeff. We know the caller used one. Changed the amplitude, pitch, and tone. Jerome, get to *it*. Tell me Eli made both purchases. And tell me the FBI has matched Eli's voice.

Jerome continued: "You load the app into your burner phone, nobody knows the caller is you. All perfectly legal—but favored by drug dealers, terrorists, other bad guys. So Friday, the Las Vegas office is going back through surveillance video from late April, early May. To see if there was anything they missed first time around. And they see this one particular woman buying a burner phone and a voice distorter app."

Woman? thought Jeff. *Not* Eli?

Jerome continued: "It's a woman who's pretty well known, a woman who's said stuff—public stuff—that there are some recordings of. So the Bureau made a match with the May fifth recording."

A well-known woman? thought Jeff. Okay, Eli, I apologize for even thinking it was you. Shark Boy is innocent. So *who is it really?*

Jerome concluded: "The woman is Samantha Kleinman."

Jeff needed to sit down. "Sammy?" Was it possible? Yes, Sammy's natural voice was low. But to stoop *this* low? Jeff said, "Jerome, her father founded this place. She's been traveling the world for this place. Why?!" Jeff sat down. He asked, "So what happens now?"

"The police and the FBI are putting the case together. There is the pesky question of motive. Do you have any idea why?"

"Clueless," said Jeff. "Brain-freeze clueless."

"Okay. Well, think about it and let me know if you get any ideas."

Shaking his head sadly, Jerome walked away.

Heading back to his table, Jeff scanned the crowd eating lunch. But before he could reach his table . . .

"Mr. Taylor!"

. . . he was intercepted by Ella Bronstein.

Jeff was shocked. He had always seen the enterprising investigative reporter and diligent editor of *The Lamp* with a face full of confidence, drive, spunk. Now she was fighting back tears.

"What is it, Ella?"

"Mr. Taylor, could we . . . ?" She motioned to the side. Another person with bad news afraid to be overheard?

"Sure," said, Jeff. With Ella, he walked far from any table.

Here, Ella gathered herself. She said, "My boyfriend, Joey Singer."

"Yes . . . ?"

"You know who his father is?"

"Yes."

Joey Singer, who just graduated, was one of a handful of non-boarding students. Joey's father, Marty, was Georgia's top bankruptcy lawyer.

"So, yesterday I was over at their house. We were all by the pool and I went in looking for the bathroom. I started to walk past his father's office. From the doorway, I saw his father's desktop was on. I . . . I know I shouldn't have, but . . . " Ella was closer to tears.

"You went in. That's okay, Ella. No law broken. That's what good reporters do. They seize opportunities."

Jeff felt it wasn't okay. Ella had betrayed the trust the Singers had put in her. But she was about to break down . . .

"Anyway . . . " Ella again gathered herself. "I went to the desk. On his computer, there was . . . " Ella whipped out her smartphone. "I took a screenshot." She thrust the phone at Jeff. "This," pronounced Ella.

Jeff looked, squinted. On it was the first page of a legal document titled "A Plan of Dissolution." In legalese, it listed the steps for shutting down Hampton Acres Hebrew Academy and turning the school from a non-profit to a for-profit institution.

Sammy! Jeff wanted to shove the burner phone with voice distorter app down the woman's throat. Sammy, you rat! Almost everyone here today thinks I'm the traitor, but Sammy, your betrayal of this place makes me look like a *Tzadik*.

"Do you *know* about this?" Ella wailed, softly.

"No!"

"I want to believe you."

"Ella, it's the truth. I had no—"

"Can they *do* this?" Ella's soft wail grew. She was on the verge of tears. "Can they destroy our school?"

"Um . . ."

"Mr. Taylor, I just graduated. I'm going to Brown. But, I *care* about this place. We *all* care about this place. All the students, the teachers, the parents, *everyone!* Can whoever is behind this"—she waved the phone at Jeff—"*can they really destroy it?*"

Jeff knew the answer: Even without this, the school is a goner. Come July, the school will have to file for bankruptcy. Gutfreund will buy it and make it a casino. Sammy has cooked up a deceitful scheme to take care of herself.

So now, of course, it all fit together. Sammy called in the bomb threat to decrease the value of the school's debt—*that* was her motive. And Sammy has Marty Singer working to make the school a *for-profit* institution so when Seymour Gutfreund buys the debt—which Gutfreund can now do for a lot less than before—Gutfreund can turn the school into a casino.

This is why Gutfreund is here!

Jeff said, "Um . . . Ella, I can't talk about this now. But, if you sit on this story for now, if you drop in on me after the board meeting this afternoon, I'll have the *full* story for you."

"You're not *answering* me. Can they really destroy this school? Can you *stop* them?"

Jeff knew the answer: no. But the answer is, I can make Sammy Kleinman and Seymour Gutfreund pay up.

"Ella, drop in on me later. Right now I have to make a phone call."

Ella gritted her teeth, turned, walked away.

Ella! thought Jeff. Every other time this semester that she had come to him with a scoop, it was a scoop that was bad news for him, news he couldn't *do* anything with. Now, for the first time, he could.

Poor Hugh Pettiver, Jeff thought. The bank officer had been stressing all year about the mortgage, and now it was money good. If he told Hugh, the bank officer would finally get a good night's sleep. And that was the problem. After riding the bank debt rollercoaster for months, Hugh would sell too cheaply. No, Jeff couldn't count on Hugh to hold out for ninety cents on the dollar—or better—in order to make Gutfreund pay through the nose. Who could Jeff count on to make Gutfreund pay up?

From a corner of the dining room, Jeff called Evan Rose.

Evan's new assistant didn't recognize his name. She balked at connecting him. If she knew how close the tip he had was to insider trading, she would never let him through. Not that Jeff was worried about breaking securities law. There were no victims here, just big boys throwing elbows. Jeff said, "Tell Evan that I have the trade of the year wrapped in a ribbon for him. But it goes away in one minute."

ONE HUNDRED-TWO
THE BOARD OF DIRECTORS MEETS

A t two o'clock, Jeff walked into the conference room for the meeting of the Board of Directors of Hampton Acres Hebrew Academy.

Jeff's chief source of strength was his letter of resignation, which had, with constant revisions, ballooned to six pages.

In his left hand: eleven copies of the letter. One for each member of the Board: Sammy plus the ten people whom Sammy had conned into serving.

Jeff's chief emotion was sympathy.

Shaking hands with the ten—eight men, two women—he felt, *You poor schmucks. Five minutes from now, as soon as Sammy walks in, I resign and I'm outta here. But you'll be stuck here fighting a losing battle with Sammy over her and Gutfreund turning* HAHA *into a casino. As you lose, you'll be thinking,* Back when Jeff Taylor resigned and walked out of here, why didn't I do the same? *And a month or so from now, when it comes out that the third bomb threat was called in by Sammy—to make the deal cheaper for Gutfreund!—and when Sammy is maybe arrested, you're going to feel fingers pointing at you. Me—Head of School—I'm just a hired gun. You have responsibility for the actions of the* CEO. *You'll be thinking,* Why didn't I resign years ago?

"Hi, Eric."

Shaking hands with Eric Denenberg, Jeff mentally apologized for having phoned the hedge fund honcho and having told him, *There's always the chance of a turnaround.* Denenberg's icy glare told Jeff he remembered that call.

Jeff exchanged small talk with the nine others: people with academic credentials, with expertise in education, and in adolescent development. The Board was HAHA's impressive face. But, as had HAHA's fence, they will—Jeff knew—collapse.

Sammy Kleinman, now in a Michael Kors pantsuit and Louboutin heels, strode in.

Bustling with energy and confidence, Sammy greeted Eric and the nine others with smooth bonhomie. Then, turning to Jeff, her face registering consternation that Jeff was standing here, she announced:

"First order of business. Jeff Taylor, you're fired."

"You can't fire me, I quit." Jeff took out the sheaf of eleven letters, brandished them at Sammy.

Officiously tapping one diamond stud earring, Samantha Kleinman announced, "You aren't listening. You can't quit. You're fired. You let a pig farmer deliver the commencement address. And then you gave him an honorary diploma! His pigs defiling the school wasn't enough?!"

Jeff ignored Sammy. His eyes went to Denenberg and the nine others. He wanted to tell them: *This woman exhibiting moral outrage has threatened to bomb the school.* He contented himself with telling them, "Ladies and gentlemen. You have lost more than a Head of School. You have lost this school. Samantha here has made a deal with Seymour Gutfreund . . . "

Sammy yelled, "Out! Out!" but she was faced by Eric Denenberg's icy glare conveying, *No, Sammy, we want to hear this . . .* and she shut up.

Walking around the table and handing a letter to each board member, Jeff briefly explained how, behind their backs, Sammy was changing the legal status of HAHA to a for-profit institution and how, on this spot, where Jewish youths from around the world had gone forth from classrooms with a Jewish education, local Georgians would go forth from slot machines and craps tables with their pockets picked.

Concluding his circuit of the table, Jeff handed the last remaining letter to Sammy.

As he did, he leaned into Sammy and whispered, "Las Vegas, Fremont Street, The Spy Store, one burner phone."

And had the pleasure of seeing Sammy's lovely face go ashen.

Then Jeff left, to go down the hall to his office, to pack.

ONE HUNDRED-THREE
BUBBLE WRAP

"**C**ome the end of this school year, I resign."

For the last two-and-a-half months, he had so wanted to be able to say that. He had worked so hard to be able to say that.

Now that he had said it . . . now that, in a few hours, he *would* be out of here . . . naturally . . .

I'm sad, thought Jeff.

I came here so wanting to make this place work. *Tikkun olam*. Well, not the whole world. Repair just this one small part.

And even through the mounting frustrations of not being able to do that, I fell in love with this place. In the middle of Georgia, adjacent to a pig farm: the Kingdoms of Judah and of Israel.

Okay, start packing.

As he walked the short hallway from the conference room to his office, Clarice looked up at him, troubled. Clarice had good radar. She said, "Jeff . . . ?"

He held up an index finger meaning, *One moment*. He went to his desk and retrieved the box of chocolates he had bought for her. He gave it to her and told her that he had resigned.

As he did, she teared up. They hugged.

Jeff said, "But this news, Clarice, it's just between us, okay? Otherwise, there is going to be a crowd here, in your face, demanding to know what's going on, demanding to see me—and we don't want that, right? Everyone's going to know soon enough."

He let Clarice think "this news" was his resignation. But far, far bigger news was about to leak from the conference room: *This school is becoming a casino?!*

Jeff told Clarice, "Let's buy ourselves some calm before the storm, okay?"

"Okay, Jeff." She managed to stop her tears.

"Thank you. Now, if you could please get me some boxes and bubble wrap?"

Clarice nodded, picked up the phone.

Jeff went back into his office, sat at his desk. His eyes went to the framed photographs on his desk.

Jordan, in her HAHA soccer uniform, grinning, pretending to spin a soccer ball on her right index finger. Ah, Jordan, he thought, no senior year for you here at HAHA close to Jose at Emory. Because no HAHA. Instead, you'll come back with me. Back where? Go to school where?

Michelle, photographed squatting with a trowel in the garden of their house in Greenwich. Michelle, what's best for our daughter?

He heard Michelle say in his mind, *What's best for her?—right. But also, what's best for you? Wherever you go, I hope you get Barbara to go with you. Jeff, you should marry her.*

Well, he thought, wherever I'm going, I'm not going now. Yes, I've got to be out of the Head's house by tomorrow morning. But the next three weeks, the last three weeks of school, I've got to live nearby.

All the HAHA juniors, sophomores, and freshmen, all angry and confused—*Come September, where am I going to be?*—I owe it to them to be around. Right now they see me as a traitor. But with the school gone . . . I think they'll want my shoulder. And not just that. Got to give them tangible support. Help them and their parents. Write recommendation letters to whatever schools they choose. And work the phones, just like the college scramble for the Traumatized Ten, except now for a hundred.

And the HAHA teachers and staff, also angry and confused. Got to do what I can for them.

And after that? Leave for Connecticut? No. Instead, rent a house in Bradleyville for the summer. Give Barbara and me time to figure things out: Do we have a future together? And give Jordan and me time to figure things out: Jordan, come September, where do you want to go to school?

And give me time to figure out what I'm going to do.

But, at the edge of Jeff's brain another question hovered: Did Evan buy the bank debt? And thinking of finance . . . right there, outside Jeff's window, was Gutfreund's stretch limo with Gutfreund inside, on the phone, wheeling and dealing.

Now Jeff saw one of Jerome's men approaching in a golf cart heaped with flat boxes to be assembled. The golf cart passed Gutfreund's limo and Barbara's I SAW ANOTHER BUTTERFLY, and stopped.

Then the man came in with the boxes and bubble wrap, and Jeff started packing.

He looked outside again. Now, in the back of the stretch limo, Seymour Gutfreund, on the phone, did not appear to be wheeling and dealing. Instead, he was now gesticulating wildly.

Jeff smiled. It could mean this: Evan bought the debt. Gutfreund has learned Evan has bought the debt, and is going batshit.

At which, Jeff's phone rang. It was Bobby C.

ONE HUNDRED-FOUR

BIDDING WAR

"Hey Jeff!" said Bobby C. "What the f**k? After all I've done for you with this freakin' credit, you coulda told me it was gonna start a bidding war."

"Bobby, I can't tell you what I don't know. What's the story?"

"Story is, an old friend of both of ours comes to me an hour ago and takes the whole credit over the wire, as is, for twenty-eight cents. No sooner do I hang up the phone, another whale comes into me with a thirty-five cent bid for the exact same paper. 'Sorry,' I tell him, 'you're too late.' 'Forty cents,' he says. 'Look,' I say, 'you're too late—I ain't about to break a trade.' 'Fifty.' It's like he speaks just numbers—no words. Jeff, he doesn't give up. He's on my other line, still bidding."

Jeff looked again at the limo, at the wildly-gesticulating Seymour Gutfreund. Jeff smiled.

"Is that right?" Jeff said.

"Whackadoo," said Bobby C.

Thinking how happy Evan was going to be, Jeff's smile broadened. Maybe Evan'll carve out something at Rose & Company for me: boarding school debt trader. Jeff told Bobby, "Tell our friend about the other whale. It will make his day and your month. You'll get all the firm's trades for a week."

"He ain't picking up his phone. Too busy to shout-out a four million profit in under a minute? Jesus." Normally, having told Jeff the gossip, Bobby C. would have jumped to another line where another trade was shaping up. But he stayed on. "Hey, look, I've been a good friend to you, isn't that right?"

"You have."

"Tell me then how it came to be that a piece of shit debt of a school out in Nowheresville, Kentucky suddenly becomes the street's hottest credit? What's next? Jim Cramer gonna tout it on *Mad Money*? Holy shit . . . wait a second."

Bobby C. put Jeff on hold and then returned, breathless.

"He's at sixty-three plus all my legal expenses for breaking the trade."

"What did you say?"

"I said, let me show your bid to the owner of the credit."

"Make him sweat, Bobby," said Jeff.

He let Bobby C. go. And returned to packing.

In the quiet of his office—an office now ready for the casino executive who would occupy it—Jeff sat and marveled: It *is* quiet. I would have thought, by now, three hours after the start of the Board meeting, the news would be out that this place is going to be a casino! I would have thought The Beast would be up and roaring.

But, nothing.

But, out the window, in the back of the stretch limo: a whirlwind. Seymour Gutfreund, on the phone, mouth open, was still waving his arms.

Thank you, Evan, thought Jeff. You have inflicted suitable pain upon—

At which Evan Rose walked into Jeff's office.

What?

Evan, chipper and casually elegant in dark blue slacks, collarless black T-shirt, sports jacket, and hand-made Italian loafers with no socks. He grinned, and waved a *C'mon.*

"Jeff, good buddy, to the conference room."

ONE HUNDRED-FIVE
THE NEW OWNER OF WHAT? THE NEW EMPLOYER OF WHOM?

Having zero idea what Evan Rose was doing, Jeff followed him toward the conference room. From it came Sammy's voice. With a would-be persuasive flattery that was tinged with fatigue, Sammy was saying, "No group could have done a more conscientious job than this Board—and me—to realize my father's dream. But now we need to turn this school over to . . . "

Sammy was trying to get the Board to vote for the school's dissolution. Jeff knew Sammy would succeed—it just might take another hour.

" . . . someone who can make it more successful as . . . " Sammy was saying.

Then Evan and Jeff walked in—Evan like he owns the place, thought Jeff, which of course he does. Caught mid-sentence, Sammy whirled on Jeff and snapped, "You don't belong here"—and then, to Evan, "This is a private meeting. Who are you?"

"I belong here," said Evan. "I own this place. I own the bank debt."

Jeff noted that the other ten Board members—who had, a split second ago, looked worn and irritated—immediately perked up, amazed. Unscripted moments at board meetings were rarer than ten-million-dollar bequests. Good or bad, their faces said, this is going to be entertaining.

Before Sammy could say anything, Seymour Gutfreund waddled in. Ignoring Jeff and Evan, the casino billionaire addressed Sammy: "You fool. Somebody bought the bank debt. I've been trying to buy it back. They won't sell. Who—"

"That would be me, Seymour," said Evan. "I bought the debt."

Now Gutfreund recognized him. "Evan Rose. How much do you want?"

Evan: "It's not for sale."

Gutfreund: "Let's not screw around. It's not worth more than seventy-five cents, period."

Evan: "That means it *is* worth more."

Gutfreund: "Okay, eighty-five cents. There was an expensive general manager in the budget, but I just cut her out."

The blood drained from Sammy's face.

Evan: "Seymour, if you offered me a hundred, I wouldn't sell it." He softened a bit: "Look, your business is casinos, mine is trading securities. We shouldn't be competing."

"So?" demanded Gutfreund. "So what the hell are you doing here?"

Yeah, thought Jeff, what?

Evan told the Board, "To tell you my plans. I don't want a casino here."

At which, Jeff went *What?*

The ten Board members gaped.

Sammy yelled at Jeff: "You did this! You shafted me! Why?!"

Yes, thought Jeff. All I meant was to make this smelly deal cost Gutfreund a lot more, and have Gutfreund take it out on you, Sammy. But am I pleased this has turned out to cost you your general manager sinecure? Yeah, since you threatened to bomb this place.

But what *is* this outcome? Evan doesn't want a casino here? What *does* Evan want? Evan hopped in his private plane and flew down here to do *what?*

As Evan, eyeing Sammy and Jeff, held back explaining to the Board, Jeff got in a word to Sammy. Jeff said, "You screwed yourself. And I don't answer to you anymore. But you'll always answer"—Jeff pointed to the stern bust of Manny Kleinman—"to him."

Jeff had the pleasure of watching Sammy glance at the bust and grimace.

Gutfreund whipped out his phone and barked an order: "Bring in that goddamned plaque."

Sammy grimaced again.

Now Evan explained. He told the Board: "On my flight down, I was on the phone with the mayor of Bradleyville. He doesn't want a casino here. And I was on the phone with Reverend Pat Travis, Bradleyville's spiritual leader. He doesn't want a casino either. I assured both men there would be no casino here. Instead, this school—Hampton Acres Hebrew Academy—will continue as is."

Jeff went *What?*

Around the conference table, ten faces grinned with relief.

"Therefore," said Evan, "our first order of business is to vote down the proposal of dissolution. All in favor . . . "

Around the conference table, ten hands went up.

At which, Gutfreund barked, "My brand—luxury casino-hotels from Vegas to Macao—and my bottom line do *not* require a casino in Nowheresville, Georgia."

"Our second order of business," said Evan, "is to dismiss the school's CEO. All in favor . . . "

Again, ten hands went up.

"Traitors!" yelled Sammy—and started to stalk, *click-click-click*, out of the conference room. But at the doorway, she ran into Gutfreund's chauffeur walking in with the award.

The chauffeur handed the humungous plaque to Gutfreund and helped Gutfreund hold it. The casino king thundered at Sammy, "*Your* award? Champion deal-killer and school-closer!" Putting all of his three hundred pounds into it, Gutfreund hurled the plaque at Sammy's feet. Showing the quickness that had made her an all-Ivy point guard, Sammy sidestepped the airborne plaque.

Trailed by his chauffeur, Gutfreund waddled out.

Pleading, "Seymour, Seymour . . . " Sammy pursued him.

"Our third order of business," said Evan, "is to approve a new Chairman of the Board. That would be me. All in favor . . . "

Again, ten hands went up.

"Our fourth and final order of business," said Evan, "is to approve a new Head of School. That would be"—he nodded at Jeff—"Jeffrey Taylor."

What? Jeff tried to find something to hold onto. He wanted to say, But I've spent the last three months trying to announce that I'm leaving.

Evan put an arm around Jeff. He said, "The first rule of investing I taught you, Jeff. Back the guy who's doing what he's meant to do."

Dazed, Jeff felt an old reflex kick in: I've got to warn Evan. This is a terrible trade. The school is a money pit. Get the fat guy back now . . .

Evan, who had sat next to Jeff on a trading floor for fifteen years, gave a Jeff a smile that said *I know what you're thinking*. "Jeff," he said, sotto voce, so the Board couldn't hear, "relax. You'll make it work. And if you don't? My downside's capped. I'll sell it to Seymour or another casino macher."

Jeff stood there absorbing the beaming smiles of relief from the Board members. Their smiles said *My reputation is saved*.

Now The Beast was up.

But not up in anger. Instead, The Beast had somehow learned *The school is saved!* What's more, The Beast had somehow learned *The school is saved by a friend of Jeff Taylor!* So now, from outside the conference room came cheers and whoops and now, defying all order, pressing into the conference room, came cheering students, teachers, and staff—and even many parents of graduating seniors, parents thrilled they hadn't yet left campus. Everyone wanted to shake Jeff's hand, shake Evan's hand. Embarrassed, Jeff made his way out through the mob, out of the building, onto Manny Kleinman Quad. The celebrating students, teachers, staff, and parents followed him. A chant went up: "Jeff Tay-lor! Jeff Tay-lor!" All last week, the chant would have been "Jeff *Trai-tor!*" But now . . . ? Here, where five hours ago the commencement had been held, there was a celebration of—if one wanted to be unbearably corny, thought Jeff—a new beginning. As the chant continued—"Jeff Tay-lor! Jeff Tay-lor!"—Jeff was embraced by Barbara, Jordan, and Clarice.

Then the chant changed to "Rab-bi Baum! Rab-bi Baum!" Ascending the podium for the second time today, Baum raised both arms, pointed his palms toward the crowd and, just as he had at commencement, recited the schechiyanu prayer.

And then, seemingly bringing the extraordinary day to a close, Baum lifted his shofar and blasted a prolonged blast.

Bringing the extraordinary day to a close?

Not quite.

Mobbed by people congratulating and thanking him—But *I* didn't do anything, thought Jeff—and with one arm around Barbara and the other around Jordan, Jeff saw, fifty yards away, a clutch of students yelling and chasing what could only be Emmitt Bailey's one still-at-large pig. Not a large pig. It was an ordinary-size porker, but it had extraordinary broken-field running ability as, dodging and weaving, it led the ebullient students on a merry chase. And one more sight: Jeff saw, a few feet away, Rachel Fish very intent on Evan Rose. At first Jeff thought she was arguing; Rachel always wanted a fight. Then Jeff heard what she was saying: "I am so thrilled that you've committed to this being a totally green school. It's an honor to continue teaching here—you're making it possible." Evan looked very puzzled as Rachel then hugged him.

With a diplomatic nod to Rachel—as happy to escape her as the pig was to escape its pursuing students—Evan Rose made it to Jeff.

Evan pointed to Barbara's I SAW A BUTTERFLY statue in front of the windows of Jeff's office.

"Who's the artist? For my Hamptons house, I want a piece exactly like that, but larger."

ONE HUNDRED-SIX
THE FOUNDER PRONOUNCES HIS VERDICT

Late Monday night, alone in the Admin building, Jeff was in his office, unpacking some of the things he had packed earlier. Needing a break, he walked down the hall . . .

. . . and found himself standing in the conference room. He was drawn to the bronze bust of Manny Kleinman, which sat contentedly on its plinth.

Jeff met Manny's sharp eyes.

He thought, Ah, Manny, what your eyes saw today. Your daughter dismissed. Your school saved. A new whale backing it.

What are you thinking?

Jeff knew what Manny would think.

"My daughter—she never quite got it. In my time, hey, I also used smoke and mirrors—but not *just* smoke and mirrors. Now this Evan Rose—first guy to step on this campus who's in my league. A macher. Bone of my bone, flesh of my flesh."

Jeff imagined the bust's sharp eyes demanding of him: "And now you're gonna run my school for him. You run it *right*, understand."

"Yes, sir," Jeff promised.

ONE HUNDRED-SEVEN
WEDDING DAY

It was the first day of summer, a gloriously green and golden day in Georgia. It was the last day of school, the day Jeff *had* intended to be when his resignation took effect. And now, for him and Barbara, it would the first day of their lives together in marriage.

And much to Jeff's relief, Michelle fully approved—*Hey, Big Fella, the only issue between the two of you was where the two of you might live. And since you are staying put, why not marry her now?*

Why not—never a simple question when Rabbi Baum claimed authority to decide.

"There will be no interfaith marriage on this campus," he said. "I will not permit it. Have we learned nothing from this year? Hashem will not permit it."

But Baum's objections were overcome by Barbara's big surprise.

"Hon," she told Jeff, "I have a confession: I've been working with Rabbi Micah from the Reform Temple on converting ever since our whitewater adventure. The Head of HAHA should have a Jewish wife. And that's what you shall have under the chuppah tomorrow."

Before a flabbergasted Jeff could respond, Barbara added, "How could I tell you to save HAHA without going all in myself?"

This news did not placate Rabbi Baum, who spluttered about "so-called conversions." But the Rabbi's grumbling did not move The Beast, which was all in for the happy couple.

Public opinion rules, Michelle exulted. *Tell the rabbi, case closed!*

And so: on the lawn of the Head's House, all the chairs from commencement had been set up, aimed at the chuppah, the wedding canopy. Seated in all the rows except the first three were HAHA students, teachers, and staff. The first three rows were for the relatives of the bride and groom.

Jordan, Jeff's only relative here, beamed. Standing beside her was a grinning Jose, who had traded his crimson blazer for a Navy blue one—Go Emory! Despite Moises' mad campaign, Jose never got off the Harvard wait list. He was headed to Emory, to enroll in its honors humanities program, and be only two hours away from a deliriously happy Jordan.

Barbara's many relatives looked even happier. And her uncle, the Reverend Pat Travis, who was certain HAHA's narrow escape from casino purgatory had been divinely arranged, looked as close to heaven as an ecclesiastic can get while still here on earth.

Rabbi Micah first welcomed Barbara to the Jewish people, giving her the Hebrew name Batya. Then, after a brief ceremony, he proclaimed Barbara and Jeff married "in the eyes of God and humankind."

With the vows complete, the Rabbi placed a shot glass wrapped in a cloth napkin beneath the newlyweds' feet. "Crushing the glass signifies that our joy can never be complete until the Temple is rebuilt," he explained, hastily pulling his hand away.

But damn it, thought Jeff as he and Barbara stomped the glass to smithereens, my joy *is* complete.

EPILOGUE

THIS YEAR IN JERUSALEM

"**B**reakthrough in sonography! New technique can show skin and hair color at five weeks!"

So read the press release from a med-tech company in North Carolina's Research Triangle.

Six days ago, this advanced sonography, applied to the womb of Emmitt Bailey's five-week pregnant heifer, showed that the fetus—a female calf, a heifer—was one hundred percent red, not a single hair of a different color. If this red heifer were born in Israel and then ritually slaughtered in Israel . . .

. . . the Third Temple could be built and the Messiah would come!

Thus, seven days after their wedding, Jeff and Barbara were at the Bradleyville airport, in Evan Rose's Airbus A220 configured for luxurious private travel, set to take off to Israel on their honeymoon with, in the cargo compartment, Emmitt Bailey's pregnant heifer, Mama Korban.

With them—the only other human passengers—were Rabbi Benjamin Baum, Reverend Pat Travis, and Emmitt Bailey.

All courtesy of Evan Rose's wallet.

Evan certainly didn't believe the red heifer ritual would lead to the Messiah's coming. But he *did* believe in the value of PR. Six days ago he had overseen a PR blitz announcing the red heifer, a blitz which made the heifer sound like a project of Hampton Acres

Hebrew Academy. Two hours ago, as Jeff and Barbara were packing, Evan called with an update. "HAHA just got another contribution. A million from Zev Wolfsheim. He even offered me his jet for the heifer. I told him he was too late. But Zev's eager to give again. And he will. And Jeff, as you know . . . "

And Evan went on to enthuse how the PR was working. Twenty-two million dollars in contributions had poured into HAHA, and student applications to HAHA for the next academic year were up eighty-three percent over last year and, all over America, dozens of Jewish scholars were applying to teach at HAHA.

"Home run!" said Evan.

Which indeed it was. And when Hugh Pettiver of M&F Bank had called Jeff to discuss this turn of events, Jeff sympathized with him: "I'm sorry you guys sold out. I told you we'd pay."

Hugh said, "Well, I told my bosses *not* to sell. So I came out looking smart."

A lot better than being fired, thought Jeff.

As for Jeff . . . he felt great. Yesterday, his fiftieth birthday, he had seen no gray hairs in the mirror. With energy and optimism, he looked forward to showing Barbara Jerusalem.

About which, Evan had asked, "Jeff, how long do you plan to stay over there?"

"Just a week."

"Make it five days. I need you back at the helm."

"Will do." Ah, Jeff thought, to be working for Evan again.

Just as Jeff had clicked off, his phone had rung again. Seeing the caller, his heart sank. "Yes, Mrs. Friedlander, how are you?"

"Mr. Taylor! Fantastic news! Princeton called! They've accepted Ashley! Come September, Ashley will not be a Texas longhorn! She will be a Princeton tiger! They love her documentary of the pig attack! Love it! Well, she is a genius. And, Mr. Taylor, a little birdie told me that a call from you may have had something to do with this."

"Well, I . . . "

"Yes. Now, Mr. Taylor, our son, Thayer, come September, will be a junior at the Academy. Naturally, it would be devastating if he were not able to follow in Ashley's footsteps. So we expect the Academy to do everything in its power to . . . "

As Jeff continued packing, the indefatigable Mrs. Friedlander laid out the game plan to get Thayer into Princeton early action.

Unable to zip Rhoda Friedlander's lip, all Jeff could do was zip his luggage.

Now, ten minutes to take-off, Jeff and Barbara were in Evan's jet, sitting with Rabbi Baum, Reverend Travis, and Emmitt Bailey.

They were munching mini-bagels covered with fifty-dollar-per-pound lox, served by a gorgeous flight attendant in—for Baum's benefit—a very demure skirt. Jeff observed that Emmitt seemed to be adapting quite well to the high life.

"This delicious bagel," Emmitt said between bites, "reminds me—what did y'all feed Big Bob that night? He had his best weekly weight gain in two years after visiting your dining hall."

Jeff mused about the very odd company he was in. Yes, wonderful to be with Barbara. But he never imagined himself about to take off to Israel with a rabbi, a preacher, a pig farmer, and a pregnant red heifer. Sounds like the set-up to a Jackie Mason joke . . .

. . . whose punchline was cut short immediately. A too-familiar *squeak-squeak-squeak* made Jeff's stomach clench. Bustling onto the Airbus A220 at this very last minute, full of luggage and energy, dressed in her traveling clothes—black trousers and dressy white shirt—and broadcasting her expensive perfume, was Samantha Kleinman. Tapping her gold Cartier tank watch, she announced, "On time."

Jeff gaped at HAHA's deposed CEO.

Out of loyalty, Jerome had deep-sixed the evidence of Sammy's bomb threat. (The identity of the person or persons who had made the other two threats was still a mystery, but Sammy had been ruled out.) So the woman would never be indicted, never go to prison. But what was she doing *here?*

And the brassy Boss Lady was definitely here. With her usual flamboyance, Sammy explained: "Going to Tel Aviv to scout locations for a Gutfreund casino." Turning to Jeff: "Seymour and Evan have patched things up. An hour ago, Evan said I could catch this flight." As Jeff felt his eyes roll and his jaw drop farther, Sammy added, "He didn't tell you? Well, he's a busy man." Then, spotting the attendant replenishing the tray of lox and bagels: "Ah, miss, I'll have some of those."

Settling into the luxurious seat kitty-corner from Jeff, Sammy grew expansive: "I'm back, and you should rejoice. We were always a great team. Let's keep this winning backcourt together."

"Aren't you working for Seymour now?"

"Jeff honey, getting Evan Rose was a coup—kudos to you. But Evan could lose his money. Or his mind. Or both. Think of my poor father. To be ready for anything, you need to put me on the executive committee."

Gripping Barbara's hand for support, Jeff repeated dully, "The executive committee."

"Yes, Dean Samantha Kleinman. Dean of Smoke and Mirrors."

THE END

ACKNOWLEDGEMENTS

Writing *The Academy of Smoke and Mirrors: A Boarding School on the Brink* proved to be much more demanding than I had imagined. The process from start to finish reminds me of a hike I did years ago. Under the guidance of a close friend we scaled one of the Tetons. Tired when we reached the top, and taken by surprise to learn that going down was as hard as ascending, I began to tell myself after each downward circuit that we had finally reached the end – only to see that there was further to go. So it was with *Smoke and Mirrors*, but today, after too many announcements that "this time we're done," the novel is indeed finished.

I want to thank the many people who helped us along the journey, which started with nebulous hunches and inchoate ideas until gradually becoming the book you hold in your hands. Thanks must always begin with my wife Dale, who supported and encouraged not only the writing, but also the adventures that inspired it. How blessed we were to have crossed paths on the Yale campus that warm September night in 1979.

My friend David Lane deserves a special shout-out for introducing me to my writing partner, Jim Parry. When I complained to David that I had an idea for a novel but was making no progress writing it, he said, "You have to meet Jim." David brought Jim and me together for a lunch at which we instantly connected.

Without Jim, *Smoke and Mirrors* would have remained as insubstantial as, well, smoke and mirrors. Jim is a member of a talented writing group, and each of them was generous with their time, insights, and advice. Thank you Susan Shapiro, Jon Stone, and Sarah McElwain, and good luck to each of you in your writing.

Jon Stone in turn introduced me to Jeff Matthews, an accomplished author and Sherlock Holmes chronicler, who was always generous with his time and wisdom.

My college classmate and friend Jennifer Weis, who knows the publishing industry, gave me excellent advice. I also appreciate the encouragement of friends Carll Tucker and Dr. Joanna Bronfman, each of whom encouraged me to write long before Jeff Taylor and Hampton Acres Hebrew Academy were glimmers in the imagination. The same is true of lifelong friend Robert Pante. Bob loved literature and music and was always generous with his suggestions and encouragement when I started writing fiction. Bobby, you left too soon, and I miss you.

West Orange, the town where Bob and I grew up, offered fertile soil for cultivating long, durable friendships. It was there that Glenn Tongue, David Sable, Barry Rosenstein, Mitchell Milstein, Eric Freiser, and I befriended one another for life. Each of my West Orange friends has patiently helped me with my writing and encouraged me at every step. Guys, if *Smoke and Mirrors* makes you laugh and smile then consider it a gesture of reciprocity for all the happy moments you had a hand in making.

My friend Professor Rick Schneid is, among many other distinctions, the dedicated leader of one of the great book clubs of the South. Rick and his clubmates read *Smoke and Mirrors* with care and thoughtfulness and made many useful suggestions. Ted Winokur and his wife JeanMarie were careful and sensitive early readers, who among many other things, made sure all animals in the novel were treated humanely. Talented poetess Joan Winokur was another early reader who provided many useful insights.

My cousin Robert Troy invented the "streetcar named Galut" quote that precedes the opening words of *Smoke and Mirrors*. It fit so well that I borrowed it and here acknowledge its talented creator.

Our editor Leslie Wells did an exceptional job of reducing the massive manuscript we presented to her with a much more compact and entertaining story. Leslie's red pen deleted superfluous characters and repetitive dialogue, while teaching me about story-telling along the way. And, while praising Leslie, it is appropriate to state the obvious, namely that responsibility for any shortcomings, flaws, or offensive material in *Smoke and Mirrors* rests my shoulders and on Jim's alone.

I also want to thank my daughters Ariel, Abigayle, and Rachel, each of whom gave me expert advice on subjects important to the plot, including fashion, boarding school life, and gender dynamics. Dear daughters, I know you'd rather I'd be stock-trading than story-scribbling, so double thanks for supporting me nonetheless.

When I wanted to learn to write fiction I took many courses and programs. Of the many strong teachers I had, one stands out for her excellence and her drive to make her students, and herself, better writers. Kerri Maher was that teacher and remains a friend.

Finally, I would not be myself if I didn't acknowledge one other source of inspiration, one that must—for reasons that will shortly be clear—remain anonymous. A big thanks to those literary agents who treated my query letters, synopses, and writing excerpts with the silence of the tomb. The feeling that those materials went not into cyberspace but rather deep space fired my determination to see the novel published. Thanks to a rapidly changing industry, there are alternatives to the traditional route.

Jim and I have now spent more than five years getting to know Jeff Taylor and his school. We have become so fond of Jeff and HAHA, and of each other, that we are now hard at work on a sequel. I look forward to writing an acknowledgement like this for that book, but experience has taught me that we have just started our climb up a new mountain, and the hike has many steps ahead.

Until then dear reader please stay in touch. We'd love to hear from you.

Alex Troy
Jim Parry

May 23, 2023

Printed in Great Britain
by Amazon